THE FALLING RAIN

Steve Worthington

First published in 2025 by Blossom Spring Publishing
The Falling Rain© 2025 Steve Worthington
ISBN 978-1-917938-29-7
E: admin@blossomspringpublishing.com
W: www.blossomspringpublishing.com

For my long-suffering, football-widow wife, Jane, and for my two fabulous daughters, Katy and Molly.

"Hate is poison and ultimately, those who hate, poison themselves."

Anita Lasker Wallfisch – Writer and surviving member of the Auschwitz Women's Orchestra.

The Falling Rain

The stage is set, the die is cast,
A calmness that can never last.
No hands to help, no eyes that see,
A penance dealt, without pity.

One step forward, two steps back,
A bottle drained to fill the crack.
No safety net for moods that swing.
His fall from grace, from everything,

Upon the precipice once more,
When fortune crashes to the floor.
A torment burns, his hell insane,
Ablaze beneath … the falling rain.

Herbert Gaggs – 1956.

Chapter 1.
Troubled Waters

His ringing office telephone signalled the end of a long and taxing day. The sort of day on which he should have gone straight home, fixed himself a mug of hot cocoa, slumped down in his favourite chair, kicked off his shoes, and let his eyelids drop like the final curtain of a deep and draining performance. He should have let his worries drift up the stack above the warm glow of his crackling log fire. He should have expected that company could arrive at any moment — letting down his guard only in the knowledge that his trusty revolver was stashed and loaded within easy reach in the middle drawer next to the cast iron hearth. He should have done all those things ... but he hadn't.

The day had begun like every other day. A customary routine that slipped into effortless action, like the casual flow of a drowsy river. He parked the car in his reserved space behind the tired old headquarters. He checked out his reflection in a glimmering shop window and stretched out a smile of newfound confidence. He strolled past the newspaper stand and, with a wink, dropped a daily thruppence into the palm of the hardy old flower lady. She handed him a spray of radiant lavender and — with accustomed Mancunian monotony — groaned, 'Looks like rain again, love.'

A nod of respect to the doughty doorman, and he trotted up the stairs to the fourth-floor Press Office, where he buried his head in the task at hand.

Still a young pup with a lot to learn. Ambitious, a grafter with an excellent nose for a story ... and what a story this one could turn out to be. Not the greatest writer, but certainly good enough to get him where he wanted to go. The owner would see to that, but only *if* the pieces of his jigsaw fall into place. Trussed up in a Press Room straitjacket from eight 'til late on a Saturday was a small price to pay.

The office was busy and distracted with sports — a good day to push forward the covert case that was beginning to crack. The incoming call from a public phone booth made him lift his gaze from the battered Imperial typewriter. He looked up at the clock. He gathered the files with frantic eyes, plucked flowers from the vase, and rushed out of the office, leaving a trail of droplets in his wake.

Going home was out of the question: he couldn't wait to hold her in his arms once more. Luckily, he'd remembered to bring a change of jacket — a quick switch from work to play. He'd never been a snappy dresser. It would suffice.

He jumped into the car without a comb of his hair or a bite to eat: neglectfully oblivious to the imminent peril that lay in wait …

David Adams' veteran, 1940s green Morris Minor, ploughed through the torrent flowing along the dimly lit asphalt road. The small green convertible was no match for the storm. Lightning forked down from the charcoal sky, challenging Adams' limited driving skills. He gazed through the glass, but the beat of the wipers was too slow to handle the onslaught of stair-rod rain. A wipe with his best Saturday night blazer sleeve smudged the misted windscreen. He shook his head in exasperation.

Battling the bullying wind with the slack steering of

his "Moggy" Minor was not yet beyond Adams' capabilities, but it was close. Determined not to pay a penalty, but well behind schedule, left no choice but a rodeo ride in such dicey conditions. Forging ahead with dissipating headlights, Adams sucked another deep breath. A glance at his treasured gold watch: a gleaming Rolex, the only inheritance by which to remember his beloved father.

Late again.

Too late to find shelter and let the storm subside. It was already halfway through the supporting B movie as he fought his way towards the distant provincial picture house rendezvous with Joan Baker: his stunning damsel, patiently sheltering in the foyer of The Hippodrome cinema in Altrincham — ten miles south of his Manchester office.

Adams had been trying to get to the main feature for weeks. The evening show was his last chance to see the latest Hitchcock thriller. *The Man Who Knew Too Much* would close that night. He saw the irony in the title. He also saw the danger of putting his foot down too hard and aquaplaning off the road, crashing into the colonnade of horse chestnut trees, hissing under the menacing, gunmetal grey clouds hanging above the vast footprint of Wythenshawe Park.

Another flash revealed the approaching silhouette of an unlit, black automobile in Adams' rear mirror. A second glance, as a surge of wind shunted the Moggy towards the kerb, prompting a desperate turn of the steering wheel to correct the line.

The imposing Humber Hawk saloon swooped forward, pinning itself to the Moggy's tail as rippling waves obliterated shallow kerbs on either side of the flooded road. Late triggering of full-beamed headlights behind him and repeated blares of the angry car horn confirmed Adams' worst fears. Stomach churned. Two shady figures. Double trouble. Kids on a Saturday night joy ride? Adams knew better.

The files… The files! Dammit! Should have hidden them in a secure place. Should have found the time. Why do you always do things at the last minute? You bloody fool, thought Adams.

Caution to the howling wind as he pressed down on the accelerator, but the Moggy was built for sedate Sunday afternoon picnics in the country, not Saturday night car chases on the fringe of the shady metropolis. His dream sports car had been forsaken. Saving up for marriage had taken priority. He was exposed, and he knew it. Danger doesn't clock off. No going back.

Should have brought the gun. Joanie doesn't like the gun.

He glanced down at the aromatic lavender trembling on the passenger seat. Fear was now the dominant scent. A rasping shunt of his rear bumper rattled the nerves as the Moggy leapt forward.

They're after my blood …

His heart pounded like a gavel in an unruly court — another manic glance in the mirror. Adams braced himself as he searched for a way out: a second thrust and another lurch towards his steering wheel as bumpers collided. Teeth clenched. Adams fought frantically to swerve the besieged car back on course.

Eying his target for a final attack, once again the black Hawk drew close, flew past, and cut in hard.

Adams slammed on the brakes. The Moggy veered out of control and slashed through the wash with a guttural roar.

Hurtling off the road, the car crashed into the kerb and careered over the cinder track, scything through a thicket of bushes to an abrupt stop: just short of the rising trunk of a giant oak tree, its limbs rioting in all directions.

The hawk slipped into reverse, wailing like the siren of a Stuka dive bomber preparing to strike.

Adams was hemmed against the driver's door — in turn, trapped against a stubborn stump. He grabbed the passenger door handle, but his jacket pocket was caught on the raised gear stick.

Get out. Get out! Come on ... Get out, damn you!

Two heavyweight, balaclava-wearing attackers — Lofty and Stocky — jumped out of their ride and sprinted towards the Moggy. Adams tore his jacket as he broke free and forced open the passenger door, but his lightweight frame was grabbed and dragged from the car — then dumped face-down onto the ground. The glowing headlights formed a private amphitheatre for the mismatched gladiators.

The dull thud from Adams' sudden drop was echoed by a swift steel-capped boot to his chest. The attackers dragged their victim to his feet, but before a windmill punch could land, Adams broke free.

'Come on then, you pair o' bastards,' roared Adams, who in the blink of an eye delivered a head butt hard and true into Stocky's woollen-clad nose, followed quickly by an uppercut that rammed against his chin. Stocky slumped to his knees, barely conscious as his partner waded in — but Lofty's head recoiled from a fast piston combination.

Lofty shook his head to clear his mind as Stocky grabbed Adams' right leg and clung on like a mountaineer dangling from a rope. Off-balance, Adams struggled to break free once more as Lofty charged forward, wielding his heavy truncheon with the wind behind him. The crack against Adams' left temple cried louder than the bawling thunder. Adams was out for the count before he hit the deck.

Spattered with mud and mashed leaves, Stocky pulled himself up and swung his right boot hard into the ribs of the motionless Adams. After another hefty kick to the side of his head, Lofty lunged forward. He grabbed hold of his irate partner in the nick of time and ordered, 'Leave him alone. He's 'ad enough. D'ya wanna kill 'im or what?'

With boiling eyes, Stocky tore off his mask and grunted through crimson teeth, 'The little bastard's broke me nose.' He fired blood and snot down his swollen chin and wiped it clear with a slash of his sleeve, then slammed the Moggy door in anger.

Both men grabbed Adams by the feet and dragged him face down through the mordant undergrowth as sideways rain continued its assault. With vindictive force, Adams' left shoulder was wrenched from its socket as his limp body was bundled into the boot. His hands were cuffed to the point of strangulation before the boot lid slammed shut.

The fuming attackers lunged into the belly of the Hawk — then set off back into the howling night.

The trail had changed from smooth to rugged. The black bird's beady eyes stared behind the glass headlight casings while waddling down a secluded country lane in search of the gap in the fence that hemmed the Bridgewater Canal.

Ripping wind plastered waves onto the brooding water

as the restless suspension jarred Adams into consciousness from his cosh-induced sleep. His eyes opened within his rolling prison. Pitch black incarceration left him oblivious to the double vision that had merged slowly into one.

Initial panic through instant memory. The parameters of his cramped cell contracted against his tightly coiled body. He could feel the sharp metal rings cutting deep fissures into his wrists, swelling his fists like his familiar red boxing gloves. An incessant high-pitched ringing tormented his pulsating head. No saliva but a taste of warm, coppery blood from the split that had left the flesh of his upper lip dangling like an empty udder.

The excruciating pain prevented clear thought. His nose was pinned against a punctured tyre. Cold stale air mixed with an industrial whiff of oil and rubber. Every bump in the road another kick in the gut.

Stay quiet. Suppress the groans. Think, man, think!

A check of each limb. Movement in every finger and toe. All wiggled, just a tad, but just enough. Aware of the need to quell the shock, a deeper breath whistled through his blood-crusted nasal passages, inducing an agonising, all-consuming pain that restricted inhalation. His body was clamped in a vice. Short, rapid breaths that wheezed like a ruptured bellows.

A broken rib cage or a punctured lung? Not now. Not now when I'm finally ...

The car skidded to an abrupt halt.

A heavy lurch against the back of the boot cracked his dislocated shoulder back into its socket. He suppressed his scream but couldn't stop the salty tears that stung his facial wounds. Behind the rapid beat of his heart, Adams heard the muffled ratchet of the cranked-back handbrake.

His foetal position was far from the safety of the womb. His passionate love for his girl fuelled his desperate determination to stay alive and scramble for crumbs of comfort.

They haven't removed their masks. This isn't a kill. There's a chance. A chance to see her again ... but box clever. Channel your determination. Wait for the moment. Stay focused. Seize the opportunity when it arrives. If it wasn't for these blasted bracelets ...

The attackers pulled their balaclavas back on as the heavy doors slammed shut. Chins tucked in, they pushed through the howling wind towards the boot of the car: its lid shooting up upon release. Stocky caught it just in time to stop the crosswind from ripping it from its hinges.

Adams cowered as the attackers dragged him out of the boot and dropped him face-down onto the muddy pathway that bordered the secluded country road. His left eye was swollen like a giant walnut.

'Get up. Get to yer feet, you scum,' shouted Lofty.

Adams struggled to his feet and was shoved towards the edge of the deep embankment that cradled the sunken canal.

Lofty led the way as Stocky held onto Adams' locked cuffs. A strong sideways gust and all three plummeted down the slide of the glistening bank, cascading into an entangled pile at the bottom of the waterlogged towpath.

Now!

First to his feet, Adams saw his chance and made a break toward the inviting gateway of an arching, stone footbridge, but was quickly hauled back by the collar. His head dropped backwards, thumping against the stony ground. A frenzy of kicks hammered into Adams' exposed torso.

Left to struggle back to his feet once more, Adams staggered around in despair like a drunk at the end of a wake. His attackers mocked and teased as he tried in vain to fight his corner, swinging his clamped arms and kicking out wildly with no chance to connect.

'Take the cuffs off and see what you get … Yer bastard cowards … Come on … I'll show yer … You're nothin' but a pair of gutless chickens … You're nothin' without your clubs … You yellow bastards. You're nothin' … The pair of you,' cried Adams with diminishing strength and volume.

Drained to exhaustion, he dropped to his knees and slumped backwards onto the ground. The rain bounced off his twitching face.

Stocky rolled Adams over onto his chest, then straddled his back. 'I'll show yer who's nuffin',' he said as he grabbed a fistful of hair and forced Adams' head face-down into a puddle.

Adams coughed and spluttered as the muddy water flooded into his single inflated lung. A fleeting image of Joanie's porcelain beauty flashed through his mind a split second before his battered body finally surrendered.

Stocky hauled himself up and backpedalled a few blind steps toward the open canal bank. 'Get back 'ere and help me get 'im up,' he rasped.

'Ow about you get 'im up?' shouted Lofty.

Stocky moved forward and arched over Adams' limp frame. 'Come on, sunshine, get up.' He glared at Lofty. 'Come on. Get over 'ere, will yer?'

Lofty stepped closer for a better look. 'He's not getting up. He's dead.'

The miraculously unscathed gold watch clamped to Adams' wrist was removed and pocketed by Stocky —

who cleaned out the wallet plucked from Adams' inside jacket pocket — then slipped it back.

A glimmer of light from a distant car shimmered in the distance. Without delay, the killers dragged their victim towards the canal bank, where David Alexander Adams' corpse was dropped into the shallow depths of the cold and restless water.

The dishevelled duo slunk away into the night.

The Hitchcock thriller had ended. Darts of rain strafed down from the erupting heavens as Joan Baker crouched into a taxi outside the popular cinema and settled into her solitary journey home. She would speak to David in the morning. He was caught up in the story of another Saturday night murder, no doubt.

Chapter 2.
A Room for Optimism

His rapid eye movement flickered like a failing light bulb. His Garden of Eden bathed in a hypnotic haze of beguiling sunshine. A vibrant flutter of restless butterflies tangoed with gay abandon as they hovered above the vivid rainbow of fragrant flowers that swayed in God's gentle breath. Joyful Kathy came to the fore as she played on the lush green grass with her precious twin daughters. A mother radiant in the sensuous white of silken attire. Children's laughter. Beaming smiles. Happy hearts ... a recurring dream with subconscious significance.

The alarm clock woke Avi Falco from his sleep. Rubbing his eyes sparked a slight panic as he failed to recognise his surroundings. A fog of unfamiliarity still lingered. He rolled out of bed and took a short stroll, eventually reaching a chequered flag bathroom. He took a prolonged look in the mirror. His pencil moustache complemented his Boston-style mop of greying hair, congruent with rugged good looks that were older than his thirty-nine years had suggested.

Today's the day. A good day for a change of image, thought Avi.

He looked down at the scythed facial hair and drips of blood clinging to the sides of the sink. He smeared toothpaste along the bristles and scrubbed his teeth vigorously. He had never liked smokers' breath and wished he didn't smoke, but nicotine was calming and gave his hands something to do. Before re-adopting the habit, kissing had been more intimate, prolonged, and frequent. A solid reason to quit ... but not today. Today, all props would be needed.

Back in the bedroom, his worn double-breasted plaid grey suit drew a self-deprecating tut. The whistle of a boiling kettle nearby signalled the start of breakfast. After checking for his Zippo lighter and the packet of Woodbine ciggies tucked in his jacket pocket, he clumped down the hollow staircase: its wood exposed where the carpet had been 'liberated' by previous tenants. His nostrils flared at the scent of succulent rashers.

Avi pushed open the door to the small kitchen. His wife, Kathy — six years younger and charmingly brunette — was at the stove, casually aware of his presence. He sat at the tea-ringed table, hooked his horn-rimmed glasses over his ears, and lowered the volume on Tony Bennett's *Blue Velvet* playing on the tinny wireless.

Moving with unconscious grace, Kathy sidestepped the mangle and greeted him with a fond peck on one cheek. She handed him a cup of tea and a yellow pill, smiling as she lightly stroked the back of his shorn neckline.

He looked both vulnerable and cute without his glasses, although the latter trait was in the eye of the beholder. Soft daylight revealed his furrowed features, accentuated by the deep and distinctive Y-shaped scar carved into his prominent cheekbone. The blood-soaked, stiff piece of Izal toilet roll stuck to his upper lip drew her attention to the change in his appearance. Raising her eyebrows, she said, 'You've shaved off your pencil 'tache … that's a pity.'

'That's a pity? I thought you said it made me look "spivvy",' he replied in his light, Austrian accent.

'No. That must have been someone else. I said it made you look like Errol Flynn. Not to worry. The most important thing you have in common with Errol Flynn is his extremely large sword … but yours is not limited to reputation.' She smiled mischievously. 'If you're a good boy, we might even get it out later and give it some practice. Perhaps it's time to get things moving in the right direction?'

With misguided masculinity, the hint of her desire to explore the possibilities of future procreation was mistaken for an invitation to indulge his recently neglected lascivious urges. His eyes dipped as a sudden animal urge stirred in his loins.

Did I bring that packet of three? Pretty sure I did, although it's been so long, they've probably perished. He glanced at his watch. *Not nearly enough time. Today she shows an interest — today of all days.*

The sight of her slender, curvaceous rear retreating towards the cooker summoned a mischievous grin. Kathy's tightly clad derrière was his favourite view on the planet; one he never took for granted.

With girl-next-door good looks and an enticing glow, she kept turning heads, especially when dressed in uniform. However, her physical assets weren't the main attraction. His heart was won by her intelligence, compassion, and a puzzling ability to see the good in everyone … well, almost everyone. There were a couple of exceptions in her past she'd never dared to mention.

Kathy scooped bacon from the frying pan and planted it on a door wedge of crusty bread, which she then placed on a warm plate. She smiled as she handed it to her eager husband.

'So, what have I done to deserve this?'

'I can't control much, but I can make sure you won't go hungry on your first day. Besides, it's a glorious new day, a day for new beginnings. A day for fresh starts. Is that why you shaved off your moustache … I like your thinking, Avi.'

I like yours too. Excellent attitude. I must adopt the same. If she is happy, then I am happy and vice versa. If one takes care of the other, we'll soon be back on track.

He smiled, took a huge bite, and nodded in approval as his cheeks bloated with satisfaction. As he chewed, he reached down among sealed tins of paint and fished out a calendar from the cluttered tea chest, nudging his feet.

A tatty, sepia photograph — of a smiling family outside a restaurant — fell to the floor. Kathy's back was turned as he picked it up and slipped it into his jacket pocket. Avi had promised to be more open, but some things were better left untouched. Least said, soonest mended. Some scars *hadn't* healed with time.

He studied the calendar. Friday, 22nd March 1957 was circled. 'Today's the day,' he said, while glancing at his cheap yet trusty watch. 'I should be home for dinner later.'

'By 'eck, they call it "Tea" up north, eh, lad,' said Kathy, with an exaggerated Northern accent. She looked up at the clock. 'It's nearly quarter past. You need to get a move on. Don't want to be late. Your tea will be waiting for you at six. Let me know in good time if you can't make it, sweetie, and don't forget to bring me back an evening paper. I want to start looking for an opening.'

'They'd be lucky to have you.'

Glancing out of the kitchen window, he noticed the grey sky rolling like an incoming tide.

'Better take your new Mac,' said Kathy, one step ahead. 'You don't want to catch a cold.' She handed him his well-worn black trilby and a pack of cheese sandwiches wrapped in greaseproof paper. 'Here's your butties.'

Still chewing, Avi shook his head as she stooped to straighten his tie.

' "Best foot forward, sunshine," as my mother would say,' said Kathy, now drawing on her natural southern accent. Staring at him with bonnie blue eyes, she cupped the back of his head, pulled him closer, and planted a gentle kiss on his forehead. 'I do love you, Avraham, I love you very much.'

Mumbling an unintelligible reply, he slipped on his hat, hugged his wife, and swallowed. He left the house with a spring in his step, as chipper as a spring nightingale.

Returning to the kitchen, Kathy picked up a paint scraper in readiness for her day's solitary toil. Her mood was lower than her outward appearance suggested. She had been contemplating her future for some time.

Kathy knew what she wanted from life. Her best friends had children. She had Avi. When he was in good form, he was all she needed. But good form was temporary — like Avi's powers of abstinence.

Most of Kathy's belongings had remained at her mother's house in Croydon. It wasn't often that she travelled light. This was an issue that had evaded debate between them. They were still tied together, but the thread had frayed. For the first time, Kathy had hedged her bets, and Avi knew it.

In joining her husband in acceptance of his new promotion, she had sacrificed three out of the four things that she loved most in life: her mother, her job, and her friends — although some friends had already fallen by the wayside through their marriage of inconvenience: an unlikely liaison that had sorted the wheat of forbearance from the chaff of intolerance.

Avi was Kathy's second true romance. He remained at the top of her ladder, but the rungs had worn loose. Her patience was running out, and her body clock was ticking. He had persuaded Kathy to give their ailing marriage one last try, and she had vowed to give it her all. 'Last chance saloon' was an ironic phrase. Avi needed to avoid every saloon to have a last chance at their survival.

With a heavy sigh, Kathy looked at the nicotine-yellow paint on the walls and ceiling. She gazed at the weathered wallpaper, frayed at the edges. She pictured Avi in his tatty suit with nicotine-stained fingers and then shook her head. If she planned to succeed, there would be a lot of hard work in more ways than one. Perhaps they had already stumbled into a blind alley?

Time will tell soon enough.

Chapter 3.
Welcome to Manchester

Whistling a wonky version of *Blue Velvet*, Avi left the 1930s semi-detached house carrying a large black umbrella, his rustling lunch package, and a toothy grin. A blaze of optimism filled his mind. A positivity that sparked a rare romantic glow.

It is indeed a day for new beginnings. Spring awaits behind the nearest trees. Bulbs have awakened in their beds in anticipation of their annual thrust to the surface. Kathy is cheerful, and all is well with the world...

A bus with Avi's number sailed past without stopping. The dull grey pavement mirrored the thick blanket of clouds looming above. His neglected overcoat remained on the peg. His manic mind remained as capricious as ever.

What if I am met with disdain and suspicion? What if I can't find an early lead and it all goes belly-up?

Brief euphoria hadn't subdued ingrained anxiety. Nevertheless, a smile continued to lift his cheeks.

I hope I'm still smiling when my head hits the pillow at the end of the day.

Avi's leather-soled shoes clicked against the dry flagstones as the neighbour — the retired Mr Wilkins — approached with a noticeable limp while puffing on a briarwood pipe. His *Manchester Chronicle* was tucked neatly under his arm. Avi had tried to break the ice when he and Kathy moved into their rented house two days earlier, but Wilkins had proved to be aloof and unfriendly. Avi understood that first impressions were not set in stone. Most people carry a burden that shapes their post-war expressions. He also believed that persistence was a good trait in his line of work. A limp for a man of a certain age hinted at its own story. Both World Wars had taken their toll. Giving the benefit of the doubt was a wise approach.

As Wilkins drew nearer, Avi's courteous nod and a hearty 'Good morning, sir,' met with no response. The slightest raise of his pipe would have sufficed— just a flicker of an eyebrow or a twitch of a lip in recognition.

Perhaps he doesn't like the cut of my jib? Perhaps he's just having a bad morning? Perhaps he knows I'm Jewish? Perhaps he's just an ignoramus. Perhaps you think too much.

Avi joined the queue of two little old ladies chatting with each other at the unsheltered bus stop. A rumbling of thunder announced the imminent downpour. The storm began as both women cowered under their bulky handbags in a vain effort to keep their recent blue rinses dry.

With a polite smile, Avi said, 'Quickly, ladies, you can use this.' He handed over his umbrella and was immediately drenched for his trouble.

Stolidly unconcerned, he tried to light a cig with his Zippo lighter beneath his cupped hand and the brim of his hat — but the rain slipped off the narrow brim, preventing any chance of ignition.

He should have known better, but his mind remained fixed on the day ahead. With good timing, another red double-decker bus — bound for Piccadilly — soon arrived. Its tyres churned up a shallow wave that splashed over Avi's polished leather brogues. But it was a minor inconvenience.

Carefully protecting his lunch package, he helped the ladies onto the open-back bus and then jumped aboard.

The bus conductor dinged the bell as the taller of the two ladies tried to return his umbrella. Avi pushed out a flat palm and smiled. 'It's all right. You keep it. The rain looks set for today.'

'Oooh, ta very much, young man. A true gent.'

As the bus chugged away, the bus conductor nodded at Avi in approval.

Climbing up to the top deck to join the scattered chorus of coughing commuters, he cut through the suspended haze of blue smoke, making it swirl and dissipate.

He settled into a vacant front seat and finally lit his first cigarette of the day. Outside, the rain stopped as quickly as it had started. He relaxed, settled down, and slipped into a daydream. He imagined himself as Humphrey Bogart playing the hard-boiled detective Sam Spade. A long white cigarette dangled from his lips. A wide-brimmed trilby was tilted on his head. He looked casual but strategic. Cool and confident. Entirely in control with a loaded gun in his coat pocket. Then it struck him…

Bogey wouldn't have left his overcoat on the peg back in his semi-detached house. He would have deduced the weather conditions and figured out for himself that he needed a coat. Besides, I don't have a gun in my pocket, just a pencil … and the great Sam Spade wouldn't be riding upstairs on a double-decker bus soaked to the skin … and he wouldn't have had a wife nor ignored her sound advice. And yes. It was sound advice.

They say that behind every great man is a great woman. Kathy is undoubtedly a great woman, but I am far from a great man. Perhaps you should take a little more notice of what she has to say in future, then maybe you could be a great man, or at least a man worthy of such a great wife?

As the bus lurched from side to side, Avi dampened his jacket sleeve still further as he wiped a broad, clear swathe through the misted, wet windows. Travelling the indirect route north from the 13th-century leafy hamlet of middle-class Didsbury, the bus stuttered towards the bellowing queue of chimneys, stacked on the outskirts of the inner city. The panoramic view of achromatic cloud was stained by a plume of black smoke that stretched from a distant blazing building.

The scar provided a sinister backdrop to legions of inhabited or vacated back-to-back slums. He didn't remember any of this when they had arrived at the dead of night. There was certainly diverse 'splendour' on offer within Manchester's boundaries.

These must have been the "Smoke-dim, labyrinthine slums of Manchester" that George Orwell had described ... Oh well, I was warned. It certainly is "Grim up North".

Regimented rows of derelict dwellings suffered the ignominy of the wrecking ball, tearing down walls that had once stood proudly to attention during the six years of the War. The next in line seemed to quake in their foundations at the impending prospect of capitulation. Urban renewal provided tangible evidence that Britain was getting back on its feet. Regeneration delivered opportunity, and opportunity attracted opportunists like hyenas to the kill.

Passengers boarded and alighted as the bus ventured into the depths of low-calibre Victorian 'Homes *un*fit for Heroes'. The row-end boozers and corner shops cast shadows across squalid, cobbled alleys. Puddle-pocked streets were crammed with rag-arsed kids and packs of skinny dogs. Camaraderie and Mancunian warmth of spirit in another 'dirty old town' where the common people were put in their place.

He spotted random open gaps forced between many terraced rows, where exposed gable ends were propped up by sturdy timber buttresses. De trop legacies of the German Luftwaffe's Christmas Blitz in 1940.

'Tickets, please!' shouted the conductor as the bus plodded towards the inner city.

An unscheduled stop in the traffic allowed Avi a glimpse of the colourful flock of Moss Side fledglings, plucked from their tropical paradise and now trapped in a cold, wet cage. Avi had recognised early signs of racial divide in London. Descendants of the West Indian slaves started to arrive in 1950s Britain to relieve the chronic labour shortage, help rebuild the war-torn country and then suffer the consequences. Most people welcomed the immigrants, while others greeted them with resentment and distrust.

Perhaps people will be different up here. Maybe they will look beyond labels.

Avi pondered the apparent loss of a nation's wealth that had once held the largest and most mighty empire in the world's history. But the world had changed. Britain had sustained its Second World War efforts through the debilitating 'Lend-Lease' scheme from the Americans, who had used its enormous profits to finance their new empire.

Avi's new world is Manchester: the neglected heart of the coal-driven, steam-powered Industrial Revolution. The former 'Cottonopolis,' where everyday Northern folk failed to reap the bountiful dividends to be gained at the centre of the global textile industry. An industry of untold riches fuelled by cheap cotton from Empire colonies such as India, but also through the labour of black slaves in the tropical paradise of the West Indies and the sun-drenched cotton plantations of the American Deep South. An industry driven by the advent of machines within the white Lancastrian slave mills of the 19th-century, lining the pockets of merchants, manufacturers, and the ruling classes.

But Avi also knew that Mancunian workers had rioted in support of Abraham Lincoln and the American slaves while refusing to conform to Confederate pressures. They had risked their livelihoods and very existence to oppose slavery, struggling through a cotton famine to bring about change for the better on the other side of the Atlantic.

Perhaps people are indeed different up here. After two draining World Wars, is the Mancunian spirit still intact? It could make for an interesting column or three.

Lighting his third cig of the journey, Avi took out his pocket pad and jotted down his thoughts as the bus crossed the city centre boundary.

To his surprise, his appreciation for fine architecture was stirred. He looked past droplets of rain chasing each other down the windowpane. He gazed beyond ingrained soot stains to admire a magnificent selection of neo-Gothic Victorian buildings and the Italianate Palazzo façades of the old cotton warehouses, ostentatious legacies of the Capitalist Revolution.

Avi stepped off the back of the moving bus as it reached the terminus at Piccadilly Gardens: a splash of colour amid the dark, grim facades of frowning buildings and a statue of the equally grim Queen Victoria, both speckled with pigeon droppings.

Still in good time, he checked his watch. Another sudden downpour lashed the hat-and-Mac-clad commuters as they hurried towards their workplaces, all the while avoiding the overwhelmed drains, which caused rainwater to swell from puddles into small ponds.

Heading briskly towards the Withy Grove area, he was accosted by an agitated tramp with his trolley full of nonsense, shouting at the world. Avi had first-hand experience with a deranged mind. He had witnessed the pain and torment of shell-shocked soldiers. He had been up close with bearded sailors lost at sea in the dead of the night. Bewildered by the blast of the striking torpedo. Marooned in the clinging oil-slick. A guilty survivor reliving his helpless plight over and over again, his time-locked mind irreparably damaged. Medals don't pay the bills. No peace for the brave. No help for fallen heroes. Dark burdens laid bare for all to see … and to ignore.

Avi slipped a shilling into the tramp's pocket unnoticed. Soaked to the bone, he clutched his lunch parcel and took a quick step beyond the newspaper stand. He swerved past the flower lady and entered the vestibule of the five-storey Kemsley House building, home to his new employer: The Manchester Chronicle.

Refuge at last.

Avi was greeted at the military-style wooden entry hut by 'Bandy Bob', the braided and bow-legged concierge, drowning in an oversized, brass-buttoned uniform. While offering a polite greeting, Avi checked his watch as he made his way to the lift labelled with a handwritten OUT OF ORDER sign dangling from the shutters. A building plan on the wall advised PRESS OFFICE FLOOR 4.

Great, thought Avi as he squelched up the draughty

staircase, ascending to the fourth floor two steps at a time.

Dripping and bedraggled, he collected himself, took a deep breath … then stepped into the threshold through the stippled-glass windowed door marked PRESS ROOM.

The office was functional and cluttered. A hive of activity wrapped in nicotine-stained walls. A newspaper headline cutting was clipped to the cork noticeboard: TRAGIC ACCIDENT KILLS YOUNG REPORTER.

And there it is in a nutshell.

He turned his attention to the young peroxide-blonde secretary sitting at her desk as her red-painted fingernails danced on the typewriter like Tiller Girls on stage at the Palace Theatre.

She looked up with a welcoming smile.

'Ooh hiya, love. You must be the new boy?'

'Must be. I'm Avi Falco.'

'You a German?'

'No. I'm Austrian.'

'Oh, right. I'm Doreen … Doreen Colman. Colman, like in the mustard — not like in the 'coalman' who lugs bags of coal about for a livin'. Yer might want to think about buying a brolly and a Mac sometime soon, love. It rains a lot around 'ere.'

Avi offered a wry smile as he commandeered the empty desk next to a red-hot iron radiator. He took out his package of sandwiches and placed them onto a fraying blotter tattooed with inky doodles by its departed artist. He flipped the nameplate marked DAVID ADAMS. Acknowledging his presumption, he asked, 'Doreen, is this my desk?'

She nodded. 'I see you kept your butties dry.'

Avi raised an eyebrow as he realised what 'butties' were. He looked down at his wet clothes and asked, 'Where is the restroom?'

'Yer mean the loo? No time for that, love. You've got a nine o'clock meeting with Mr Lewis. Have yer met Mr Lewis before?

'No. Not yet.'

'Well, yer don't want to keep him waiting. Not on your first morning. Not on any morning really, and I'd do me tie up if I were you.'

The clock on the wall showed one minute to spare.

Let the show begin ...

Chapter 4.
Down to Business

The gold leaf lettering of BERNARD LEWIS, CHIEF EDITOR, etched on the frosted door window stood between Avi and his new boss. Avi tightened and raised his Half Windsor, took a deep breath and tapped lightly on the pane. Without invitation, and with a somewhat different knot lodged in his stomach, Avi nudged into the expansive but cluttered goldfish-bowl office.

At first glance, the ageing Chief Editor in his thronal leather chair projected an aloof, regal image: resplendent in a well-tailored three-piece pinstripe suit, snug at the waistcoat. A bow tie added an extra touch of elegance to his look. The strands of raked-back grey hair failed to conceal the balding pate of the skittle-shaped Bernard Lewis.

With no reaction to his entrance, Avi let out a subtle grunt.

Finally, Lewis lowered his half-moon glasses and lifted his gaze. He gave Avi a quick once-over and then stirred into life with a voice intoned with a spoonful of gravel. 'Ah, Mr Falco, there you are. Didn't hear you enter. A small piece of advice, young man: an umbrella would be a wise investment in this city.'

Avi nodded.

Lewis continued, 'It's a pity you weren't here earlier. It's been all hands to the pump since the Ringway Airport aeroplane crash last Friday. We've been rushed off our feet ever since. There hasn't been a minute to spare.'

Avi looked down at the failed crossword puzzle on Lewis's desk, fresh from the morning edition. Lewis turned it away with a grunt of discomfort and continued,

'Nevertheless, I'm glad to see you made the effort to keep good time despite your obvious discomfort. Punctuality is the politeness of kings, Mr Falco, the politeness of kings.'

Lewis rose from his throne and gave a hearty shake of the hand. The Chief Editor was much shorter than his highchair had suggested. 'May I welcome you to Manchester. I do hope your new home suits you. A telephone wired into the kitchen, no less. Such opulence. Mustn't let Mrs Lewis hear of it. She might get ideas beyond her station.'

'Thank you for the indulgence, Mr Lewis. It was my wife's idea. The kitchen is her hub.'

'I understand. Good thinking. Keep the little lady happy in the kitchen and she'll keep you happy in the bedroom!'

Lewis's laugh added to Avi's discomfort.

'Uh, well, not quite, Mr Lewis. I thought a few creature comforts might help with the transition. It's tough to move a Londoner up from The Smoke, away from her widowed mother.'

Embarrassed by his *faux pas*, Lewis cleared his throat, but then moved the conversation onto his main agenda.

'Speaking of which, we both know why you were sent up here, and I will support you as much as I can. David was one of our own.'

He handed Avi a buff file marked DAVID ADAMS, with a portrait picture of the late subject paperclipped to the cover. 'The poor lad was only twenty-five years old. The conclusions of my investigation are contained within. Keep me informed of any new developments. The case retains my interest. However, I can assure you that I have left no stone unturned. I must confess that I am disappointed that Mr Gaggs failed to apply his normal sagacity in sending you up here to make sure I have done my job properly.'

'I wouldn't take it too personally, Mr Lewis. "Scepticism is the first step towards the truth".'

Lewis lowered his eyebrows.

Avi continued, 'Surely you must have heard Mr Gaggs use that quotation – from the French philosopher Denis Diderot? It's one of his favourites.'

'Yes, well, the enigmatic Herbert Gaggs possesses a unique philosophy on life I often fail to comprehend.' Lewis shook his head. 'I saw from your résumé that you were also a student of philosophy. That doesn't give you licence to bombard me with ancient quotations from flighty theoreticians whose tenuous relevance has withered with age. Mr Gaggs' array of exacting traits is more than enough for one man to bear.'

Avi held his tongue.

Lewis glanced at the ceiling and continued, 'Take the morning to settle in. I haven't informed your new colleague, Mr Spencer, that you have taken over as our new Chief Reporter. He's out covering the blaze at Paulden's department store over on Cavendish Street. Not a word until I've dealt with it.' Lewis raised his right index finger to his lips.

Avi dipped his head in acknowledgement.

Lewis passed over a set of car keys and a crumpled street map of Manchester. 'I apologise for the poor quality of the only automobile available. I will procure an upgrade for you once things return to normal. Besides, I didn't want to arouse Spencer's sense of fatalism by providing a new car and then not assigning it to him his way. This afternoon, I require you to drive over to Maine Road and gather some quotations about tomorrow's match.

Manchester City are at home to the Arsenal. As a surrogate Londoner, I suppose you'd be rooting for The Gunners?'

'No,' replied Avi. 'I'm more of a Spurs man.'

The dampness in his suit had long since faded, and Avi became occupied at Adams' old desk, reassuring Kathy over the telephone. 'Yes, they are all very nice ... Yes, it is going well ... Yes, I'm fine, I should be home around six ... I must go ... You too.' He hung up and avoided Doreen's smile.

Avi resumed his study of the Adams case file before glancing up at the clock hanging above Doreen's perfectly coiffed hair.

As lunchtime approached, Peter Spencer entered the office. His gaunt face was smudged with black soot ... much to Doreen's amusement. 'Bloody Hell, it's Al Jolson! Boss wants to see yer right away.'

Spencer hung up his coat and then entered Lewis's office without replying. Avi unwrapped his butties as muffled shouting between Spencer and Lewis echoed next door...

'*What!* After all the late nights and shitty jobs, and for what? You said the job would be mine if ...'

'... I said the job might be yours *if* you showed me that you've got your act together, and this type of behaviour shows me that you have not! Coming in here and shouting the odds! I'll speak to you later if you still want to work for the Chronicle. Now get out of my office!'

Spencer's slam of Lewis's door was thwarted by the door restrictor. The soot smudges that shaded his twisted face had transformed into stripes of war paint. He marched across the office and cast a disdainful look at Avi before grabbing his coat and leaving, this time successfully slamming the Press Room door behind him.

Doreen shook her head. 'Well, that went well. Give him an hour to calm down and drown his sorrows.' She rose from her desk and wrestled with her coat. 'He's got a job down on the new Wythenshawe Housing Estate this afternoon. It's not going out until tomorrow afternoon's edition, so tell him he can write it up in the morning. Five thousandth house opening or summat. Snapper is booked. He'll meet him in the car park at two-thirty. You'll have to drag Spence out o' The Green Man across the road or he'll be too pissed to bother. Right, I'm off for me Friday 'air do. Back in bit. See ya later, Avi love.'

Avi savoured the last bite of his 'butty' and from an impressive distance tossed his wrapper into the small wastepaper basket … before setting off for the pub.

The cramped vault of the Victorian watering hole was brimming with ruddy-nosed, yellow-fingered journos: all disappointed by the lack of fatalities to beef up their reports on the Paulden's fire. The greater the tragedy, the better the story. No sign of Pete Spencer as Avi nudged a careful path towards the snug through the strident din of the pie-eyed herd in full swing of their free-flowing Friday lunchtime session.

At a cluttered table, a growing tower of empties clustered beside Spencer's right elbow, which propped up his sullen face. The irate reporter sat up straight, sucked a long drag of his cig, and gulped down half of his fresh pint of mild in one visit.

Back in the office, Avi's first impression of Spencer had been one of accurate presumption. He'd met Pete

Spencer's type before. He was indeed the owner of the silver-spooned, smarmy face which Avi would never tire of slapping, especially when coupled with a tendency to rub people up the wrong way. Avi noticed the twinkle in Doreen's eye when Spencer entered the office. Despite his apparent lack of good looks, which often drew incredulity and annoyance among his male peers, many attractive young women found Pete Spencer's distant manner appealing.

Avi eased his way into the snug. His outstretched hand was ignored by Spencer with disdain. Unperturbed, he introduced himself. 'Hello, Mr Spencer. I am Avi Falco, the new Chief Reporter.'

'I know who you are. Another Jew who jumped the queue,' said Spencer loudly enough to be heard over the Friday crowd. 'You're from Head Office in Fleet Street. Not the first time the owner has stepped on my toes. I've got a contact down there. Tried to top yourself a few years ago, didn't yer? Well, don't worry, your secret's safe with me, pal. Are yer having a pint?'

'No, thank you, *pal.*'

'Oh yeah, forgot. Your lot can't handle your drink without fear of drowning in it.'

Avi could feel rage searing through his body. For a moment, he clenched his fists, but instead, he relaxed, grabbed a chair, and dropped it next to Spencer with calm precision.

Dragging the chair closer, he sat and whispered into Spencer's ear, 'I take it you want to keep your job, or you would have told Lewis where to shove it. I understand your disappointment, but it was Mr Lewis's choice to appoint me, not mine.'

'Do me a favour,' said Spencer with a sneer. 'Lewis

would never have brought in an outsider from down south to fill this position. Especially one of *your* religious persuasions.'

'Does Mr Lewis have anything against Jewish people?'

'Not that I am aware of, but we all know that Lewis plays the puppet for our Jewish owner, Herbert Gaggs. It is a role he doesn't like. David Adams was also Jewish. You lot are as thick as thieves.'

'An unfortunate expression. I am neither thick nor am I a thief. You should be more careful about what you say and to whom you say it, but I won't take it personally. In this regard, you presume too much and know too little. Perhaps it is simply that I am the best man for the job?'

Spencer shook his head. '*I'm* the best man for the job, and you're too late to cover the plane crash. It doesn't take much of a leap to understand why you are really here, but you're wasting your time. Lewis tried his damnedest to uncover the truth about David Adams' death. He succeeded. It was no great mystery. I will enjoy watching you make a fool of yourself as you struggle to find useless answers to irrelevant questions. Adams was in the wrong place at the wrong time. Simple as that. He was the victim of a robbery gone wrong. Never overlook the obvious, Mr Falco. You can have that advice for free, seeing as Herbert Gaggs isn't here to hold your hand.'

Avi smiled. 'You certainly like to stick your neck out, Mr Spencer. Whether you like it or not, and for whatever reason, I am the new Chief Reporter. No hard feelings?'

Avi offered his hand once more. This time Spencer took it. Avi gripped tightly and continued to squeeze. 'If you retain aspirations for career progression and a long and healthy life, we shouldn't get off on the wrong foot.'

Avi's grip tightened even more.

Spencer winced as the resistance in his hand began to weaken. His eyes bulged. The bones in his hands were almost at the point of collapse.

Avi's voice remained impassive. 'So far, you're right about one thing. I am an outsider looking in, and believe me, I will be taking a long, hard look at everything and everybody ... you understand?'

'Yes. *Yes*. I understand.'

'Good. I'm glad.' Avi released his vice-like grip.

Spencer sighed with relief and shook blood back into his crumpled hand.

Avi smiled again. 'Oh, I'm sorry. My father always said, "Never trust a man with a weak handshake". Besides, it's my understanding that pain can be extremely useful in focusing the mind. Is your mind focused, Mr Spencer?'

Spencer dipped his head.

'Good. Now we understand each other. Make that pint your last. Go back to the office. Clean yourself up. Drink some coffee, and then head over to Maine Road for the pre-match piece. A reporter is booked to meet Manchester City's Manager, Mr McDowell, at three. Do not be late. Phone it through to Doreen, and the rest of the day is yours to enjoy. I will cover the "Shitty" estate job for you.'

Breaking eye contact, Spencer gritted his teeth and then nodded in reluctant acceptance of his subordination. His face still reddened, Spencer got to his feet and headed for the door.

That's right, off you go. We'll have another little chat once your feathers are unruffled, Mr Spencer.

Chapter 5.
The Big Bad Wolff

Pre-war *Sicherheitsdienst* agent, pseudonym *Jens Wolff,* spent his first hour of the new spring day lost in dark contemplation. The former Nazi SD intelligence officer stared at the water-stained ceiling. A half-smoked roll-up was trapped between his thin, grey lips. The interlocked fingers of his cupped, weathered hands were clasped tightly behind the back of his shaven head. Sunken lines furrowed his face like the contours of a topographic map. Wolff's bald, corrugated cranium was a stark legacy of his wretched post-war existence, where a decent crop of hair was a superfluous burden, serving only as a haven for typhus-spreading lice.

A sudden cough dislodged the ash from his burnt-out dimp. Tumbling gently, it tickled his stubbled chin. From the corner of his eye, he noticed a brazen cockroach scuttle past the matted rug, which partially covered pitted floorboards.

Wolff's open arms revealed the crude scar inside his left arm from his hastily erased ᛋᛋ blood group tattoo. An extravagant yawn stretched his gaping mouth, exposing the remaining grotesque teeth that resembled moss-covered gravestones rotting slowly in a decrepit churchyard. Even as an enthusiastic young Nazi, smiling was never an attractive option.

This was Wolff's first visit to England. He was supposed to land with the planned German invasion force in 1940, but the *Führer* was forced to abandon 'Operation Sealion' after failing to defeat the Royal Air Force and the British Navy. Wolff finally arrived in Britain seventeen years later via the cross-Channel ferry. A slightly less conspicuous entry, but more suitable for the low-profile operation he had in mind.

Disturbed by the approaching procession of clopping hooves and rumbling cartwheels descending the narrow, cobbled street, Wolff cast another nervous glance through the window. The cries of "Raaaaay bow" sung with harmony by an inveterate rag-and-bone man reassured him.

A solitary lightbulb illuminated the small bedroom, casting light on the exposed parts of the Commercial Imperial German Luger P08 Pistole Parabellum, which he had smuggled past customs with ease. Wolff liked to keep his pre-World War I weapon in pristine condition, polishing it regularly with obsessive care.

His paranoia rising, Wolff reacted to the latest threat of heavy footsteps ascending the stairs. The blue vein protruding from his right temple began to throb. Reassembling the gun with the breakneck slickness of an expert gunsmith, he clipped the magazine into the grip, checked the safety switch, and moved swiftly toward the locked door.

After a triple rap, the nosey landlady, Mrs Sproston, called out, 'Hello, Mr Fox, love. It's only Brenda, the landlady. Breakfast will be over in ten minutes. I've got a nice bit o' gammon leftover from Mr Wallace's plate if you fancy it. It'd be a shame to waste it, love.'

'No, not today, thank you, Mrs Landlady,' said Wolff in pidgin English.

'Are ya sure? A good bit o' gammon's still 'ard t' get ' old o', yer know?'

Silence.

'So, you're not comin' down for brekkie at all then Mr Fox?'

'No, no thank you … and my name is Mr Wolff!'

'Yeah, and I'm Little Red Ridin' Hood,' said Mrs Sproston, with typical sarcasm.

Wolff took a deep breath. He moved to the end of his bed and eased into his single clean shirt. Although just over a year into his newfound freedom, Wolff still looked scrawny. He had gained some weight since returning to the West, but his exposed ribs still resembled a birdcage wrapped in tracing paper. His fading jaundice blended with nicotine-stained lace curtains hanging from the exposed window rail: a pallid complexion that matched his dull personality.

Wolff was yet another worn soldier of the War who looked a dozen years older than he was. It was the very least that this veteran killer had earned.

Starting his 48th birthday in such squalor was of no consequence. After years of degradation, Wolff remained arrogant that he deserved a better life. A better life that would not be handed to him wrapped in a bow. A better life he would have to seize with all his cunning and guile. He knew that he must be even more selfish, canny, and ruthless than his target. No more sacrifice of the individual for the common interest.

Now was the time for self-interest. His appetite for food had diminished, but his hunger for money was undying. Today was the day his life would be reborn, but only if he played his cards right. A visit to an ironmonger for a brush and a tin of red paint, and everything would be in place.

Thanks to greasing palms and a chance article in the local press, his plan had gone well so far. Wolff had managed to hunt down his target far quicker than anticipated.

The damp wallpaper, sullied with creeping mould, was irrelevant. An ironic smile cracked Wolff's wizened face as he gauged the relative luxury of a rundown North of England lodging house against Joseph Stalin's wretched hospitality in Soviet Russia. As a 'Political Nazi,' Wolff spent most of his fourteen post-war years fighting to survive during his captivity in the Siberian GUPVI POW camps.

Yet, he had managed to keep the secrets of his brief membership in the murderous ᛋᛋ *Einsatzgruppen* death squads and the personal atrocities he had committed against the *Untermenschen*: the Jews and the Russians — Sub-humans unfit to breathe the same air as the German Master Race. Atrocities such as the liquidation of the Jews in the Ukrainian village of Bila Tserkva. A merciless massacre of 800 Jewish men and women: parents of the subsequently ninety orphaned children below the age of twelve. *Kinder* who were themselves slaughtered a few days later, aided by regular Wehrmacht 6th Army soldiers and the Ukrainian Auxiliary Police. Guiltless work for men without conscience.

While serving in Russia, Wolff recognised the dangers of his role in relentless point-blank executions. Deep into the campaign, a written order from Heinrich Himmler, the supreme *Reichsführer* ᛋᛋ, had permitted traumatised individuals to transfer out of the cold-blooded Nazi killing units.

Wolff noticed his opportunity. By feigning a nervous breakdown, he would enforce his release, but his plan had backfired. Rather than being sent back to Germany and admission to the sanctuary of the ᛋᛋ Hohenlychen Sanatorium in Lychen, he was instead rested, and then ordered to fight with the 'honourable' *Wehrmacht* on the frontline. Eighteen months later, he was among the estimated 91,000 rabble of defeated German 6th Army taken on the final day of the battle of Stalingrad.

During prolonged captivation, Wolff was tramped from one hellhole to another, incarcerated in numerous abject work camps within the Russian Motherland. An ironic turn of events. The Wolff became the sheep, the master now the slave.

Against overwhelming odds as a former SD & ᛋᛋ, he survived the beatings, the bitter cold conditions, and near-starvation rations served within pestilent camp compounds riddled with vermin and swimming in faeces: managing stoically to rebuff Communist indoctrination and better treatment it ensured from the Russians.

Wolff was a consummate survivor. He took great pride in being among the last of the remaining 6,000 Stalingrad *Kriegsverurteilte* to be returned to the Fatherland in 1956.

The vivid image of his family waiting for their father's return in Southern Bavaria motivated Wolff to return to Germany. However, upon arriving at Augsburg, he quickly discovered that his house had been destroyed during the American bombing raid on the Messerschmitt plant in February 1944. One of the few remaining neighbours told him that his wife and daughter had been killed. His surviving son, Dietmar, was last known to be in an orphanage in nearby Munich.

Angered and embittered, Wolff's quest to find his boy led him to the home of the proprietor of the eponymously named 'Spangell Orphanage' on the edge of Munich. There, Felix Spangell informed him that Dietmar had died during a Scarlet Fever epidemic five years earlier. He was buried in a marked grave in Nordfriedhof

Cemetery in Munich.

Wolff's family was now gone, and so was his sanity. He flew into a rage and pistol-whipped Spangell to within an inch of his life, punishing him for not saving his son. It was better for Spangell that Wolff was unaware that the orphanage master had actually murdered young Dietmar by suffocation during an orgy of sexual child abuse.

With the loaded gun pressed against the back of his neck, Spangell had saved himself with frantic lies about Wolff's son's plight and the gift of an impressive diamond. This was accompanied by a garbled tale of "The lost treasure of Auschwitz". Spangell, a former resident of the nearby Bavarian town of Dittenberg, thought he recognised the donor of the diamond: a donor whose credentials the clever Wolff had thoroughly checked himself. These were the credentials of a notorious Auschwitz guard known as *Der Folterknechte*.

With nothing else to do and nowhere to go, the glittering prize became the catalyst for the trail that eventually led Wolff to the Northern English city of Manchester, where he had been hiding and waiting, patient as a hungry sniper.

Wolff slumped back onto his bed. His manic eyes fixed upon the large V-shaped crack embedded in the ceiling plaster. Each winding fracture plotted alternative pathways to the day's outcome. One crack wound its way to the open window and the financial freedom he would inherit if his plan came to fruition. The other terminated at the top of the wall in an uncompromising dead end.

Certain that he was soon to be a rich man, with the means to start anew, Wolff was ready to reap his rewards. Today's rare public appearance of his target would create the opening that he had been seeking. He was the monster who would kill the monster.

Wolff got out of bed, picked up his leather satchel from the floor, and tucked his gleaming gun inside. Finally, he was ready to face his day of destiny.

Chapter 6.
Arbeit Macht Frei

Way beyond the rooftop of Kemsley House, the sun hid behind livid clouds. Avi tucked his folded copy of the *Manchester Chronicle* under his arm. He lit up a cig while cheerfully humming 'Blue Velvet'. Trying to locate the registration of his 'new' car, he scanned the row of motors parked up in the potholed car park. The location of David Adams' dented 1940s green Morris Minor Convertible was not hard to find.

There it is. A tired old pensioner conspicuous within a line of glamorous young models. Thanks a million, Mr Lewis.

From the corner of his eye, Avi caught the slender, middle-aged photographer slinking into view.

'You Falco?'

'You the snapper?'.

With a glance at the camera around his neck, he smirked. 'Derek Grimshaw, at your service.'

'Staff or freelance?'

'Freelance. Adams' old Moggy, eh? Not exactly a Roller. The suspension's got less bounce than a knocking shop mattress.'

'You could always walk … Smoke?'

Grimshaw nodded. Avi lit him a cig from his smouldering dimp and they clambered aboard the old jalopy. Avi handed Grimshaw his newspaper as he turned the key in the ignition. The car didn't start, but the wipers smeared across the windscreen like a slow radar. He turned the key back. The wipers stopped.

No, it's certainly not a Rolls-Royce.

Grimshaw cast a smug grin as he unfolded the

newspaper.

Observing Grimshaw's distraction, Avi looked under the steering wheel at the unfamiliar pedals. He moved back his foot and felt a small but distinctive lump under the well-worn mat. He ducked, pulled back the mat and pocketed a grubby, gold cufflink. He turned the key once more. The wipers resumed.

Grimshaw pointed to the dashboard, 'I think you have to pull on that starter knob to get it goin'.'

Avi obliged. This time, the car spluttered to a start. The double-declutch gears crashed and grated like the sound of a tramp clearing his throat as the bereaved Moggy pulled away.

The newly built corporation houses were decorated with patriotic red, white, and blue bunting, centred around a sign attached to a new show home that declared the 5,000th NEW HOME FOR THE COMMUNITY.

A crunch of the reverse gear announced Avi's car as he reversed into a vacant space at the side of the road. On the neighbouring grass verge, a tin-ribbed whippet trembled timidly. The car doors snapped shut after Avi and Grimshaw got out and strolled from the back of a new house towards a small crowd gathered in a cul-de-sac. Avi was impressed.

This is more like it—a long-overdue upgrade to the city's dilapidated housing stock.

Formalities were about to commence as Avi and Grimshaw sauntered over to the edge of the crowd and took a vantage point behind several chain-smoking locals.

Bumptious family butcher, Councillor Norman Simpson, was standing high up on a podium next to enigmatic Building Contractor, Helmut Lehmann. Their appearances were in stark contrast. Dressed in a sharp bespoke suit, the tall, athletic Lehmann boasted a full head of slicked-back, greying blonde hair. His gold-rimmed glasses magnified intense, steel-blue eyes. With impressive pearly white teeth tucked away behind a thick, tawny, handlebar moustache, Lehmann cut a debonair figure, particularly when compared to the short, fat, bald, sweaty and shabbily dressed Simpson, whose flaking, bulbous head resembled one of his stale pork pies. The deep scar above Lehmann's right eye was his only unnatural blemish.

Comfortable in smokers' corner, Avi split open a new packet of cigarettes with a jagged fingernail and then sparked one as the microphone called the audience to attention. Always eager to hear his own voice, Simpson began the proceedings. 'Afternoon, ladies and gentlemen. You all know me. Councillor Norman Simpson, Chairman of the Corporation Housing Committee.'

'Yeah, we all know what a swindling little bugger you are!' shouted a wag at the back, prompting chuckles in the ranks.

Avi covered his smile.

Simpson coughed into his clenched fist, pulled up his collapsed chin and continued. 'Before we begin, I'd like you all to observe a moment's silence for the twenty-two victims of the Ringway Airport plane crash on Shadowmoss Road last Friday.

Instant silence fell as all hats were removed, and all heads bowed in unison. Avi looked around and observed the genuine show of respect from all concerned.

Simpson tapped the microphone once more. 'Thank you, ladies and gentlemen. On a more positive note, I also thank you for coming out today to celebrate all the hard work that has gone into building this great new Garden City, with its spacious new dwellings, blessed with indoor toilets and front and back gardens for all. Proper Homes for Heroes! I'm sure you'll agree that they are a vast improvement on the slum dwellings of the inner-city areas from which you've migrated.'

'*Oy, less of the slum — fatty!*' yelled a heckler.

The crowd sniggered once more as the thick-skinned Simpson ignored the insult and carried on. 'These wonderful new dwellings are provided, thanks to your great Corporation and F&G Construction.'

A ripple of apathetic applause.

'Without further ado, I'd like to introduce you to the head of that company and thank him for his efficient work in achieving all of our targets on time and on budget. A fine bloke indeed. Good people of Wythenshawe, I give you Mr Helmut Lehmann!'

As he took hold of the microphone, Lehmann was met with a more enthusiastic round of applause. In his scratchy, staccato voice, he addressed the crowd with a steady manner.

'Gut afternoon. It is my pleasure to serve the gut people of Manchester in providing the skilled men who have worked hard to construct this fine housing estate.'

Avi was shocked to his core. The half-smoked cig dropped from his open mouth. His eyes narrowed and squinted as the hairs on the nape of his neck stood on end. He took off his glasses and stared hard towards Lehmann.

Surely not. That's impossible...

Further polite applause followed as Lehmann moved away from the microphone. Avi hooked his glasses back

44

on. He grabbed Grimshaw's arm, pulled him close and asked flatly, 'Who is he? Where does he come from?'

'Helmut Lehmann? He's a former German soldier who built up his business from the lowly beginnings as a POW. His scratchy voice makes me think of Hitler calling out the bingo.' Grimshaw chuckled at his own failed attempt at humour.

Avi remained sullen. He turned up his suit collar to ward off the cold, then looked at his trembling hands. He took a deep breath, exhaled, and relaxed his shoulders, all while following the well-practised advice of his former psychiatrist.

With his hands tucked into the deep pockets of his gabardine overcoat, Jens Wolff's billiard ball bonce joined the audience. His leather satchel was stashed away.

Thunder clouds brewed and tarried as Grimshaw snapped the smiling Simpson as, to a ripple of applause, he cut the red ribbon at the 5,000th new house on the new Wythenshawe Housing Estate. Wild-eyed Wolff was also caught in the shot.

Simpson took up the microphone once more. 'Before we all get drenched, it is my pleasure to invite you all to the new Trades and Labour Club. Tea and biccies for the ladies and perhaps something a little stronger for the men?'

'Tea and biccies? I'll give 'im tea and bloody biccies,' shouted an earthy woman standing behind Avi. Not happy at such a tame prospect, she added, 'Sod that for a game of soldiers. Come on Mildred, let's go and get pissed!'

As Avi and Grimshaw strolled back to the car, they

couldn't fail to see *ARBEIT MACHT FREI* freshly daubed in dripping blood-red paint on the back wall of the ceremonial house. The brush and tin were carelessly discarded underneath. Blood drained from Avi's face.

Grimshaw was puzzled. 'Arbeit Macht Frei'?'

'Work Makes Free.'

'That doesn't make sense.'

'It wasn't meant to.'

Grimshaw nodded and aimed his camera for a snap of the glistening aphorism.

Avi slumped into the car and sank into a listless state. There was never any warning. Over the years, the triggers of his flashbacks had changed. They chilled him to the bone and brought him back to the bloodstained death mask of the boy on the train. Once more, 'The Devil's Genie' had escaped from the bottle.

A slam of the passenger door jolted Avi back to reality, but he remained outwardly dazed. He tried to act normally, but his right knee jittered as if it had a mind of its own. He took off his glasses. In a vain attempt to clear his eyes of his haunting vision, he suppressed a loose tear by rubbing his bloodshot eyes with clenched fists.

'You all right?' asked Grimshaw.

'Yes, yes,' said Avi, defensively. 'Why do you ask?'

'You look like you've had a seizure. My wife has epilepsy. I know the signs.'

'Uh, yes … no. Uh, I'm fine, thank you. Come on, let's go to the club for some tea and uh, biccies.'

Several minutes later, Simpson and Lehmann approached the red graffiti.

'That spells more bloody trouble!' said Simpson with folded arms.

'Don't fret. I will deal with this here and now,' replied Lehmann, his voice cold and calculated.

'No, Helmut, this *will* wait. It's good for you to spread some cash and

drink with the locals. Show you are one of them.'

'Anything for a free pint, Councillor Simpson?'

In the background, the sound of Avi's persistent abuse of the Moggy's starter motor grated out loud, reverberating all around the block.

Chapter 7.
A Swift Fall from Grace

The throng of locals poured into the recently christened, single-storey working men's social club.

The spacious games room reeked of a pungent concoction, reminiscent of a barmaid's apron dipped in cheap disinfectant. Neat rows of stark, Formica-topped tables and metal-framed plywood stacking chairs lined the room. A damp, black log-end Manchester dartboard waited in a far corner. Two strobe-lit snooker tables dominated the centre of the well-ventilated room. The liberal scattering of ashtrays and cardboard beer mats gave a clear indication of the forthcoming indulgencies waiting to be abused.

The tight-fisted, but rapacious, Councillor Simpson deliberately hung back while Helmut Lehmann marched towards the busy bar with his confident gait.

Avi pondered on his choice of beverage as the first order was confirmed.

Right then, remember. Stay off the booze ... Stay off the booze. You're on a promise, tonight.

Avi was second in line behind an already half-cut local who led the queue of beer-thirsty working men as they shuffled slowly towards the pumps of ale.

'The usual, Tommy?' asked the barman.

'Yeah, bitter, please, Ray.'

Ray moved to pull the pint, but Lehmann cut in at Tommy's expense.

Don't stare. Let it play.

The tall German outsider was greeted like an old friend by Ray, the Head Steward. Lehmann reached into his wallet, pulled out a £10 note, and placed it by the tilted hand pump, which was pouring out a pint of brown bitter.

'Put this in the till and look after everyone properly,' said Lehmann.

'Thank you, Mr Lehmann.' Ray smiled and nodded.

'I've told you before, please, call me Helmut.'

'Never mind 'im, I'm next,' said Tommy Green. 'He thinks he can buy anyone with his big-money ... the big shot German Helmet.' Tommy grabbed his crotch. 'I've got a German Helmet and it's far more useful than 'im. You can stick your free pint up yer ...'

'*You* could do with a free pint. *You* already owe me enough money, Tommy Green,' said Whittaker.

'I can pay; I can pay. I'll 'ave a pint and a double whisky chaser.'

'Please, let me get these,' offered Avi, taking the opportunity to get in on the action.

'No! I pay me own way.' Tommy smiled. 'Nice little accumulator on the dogs.' He picked up a pint and wandered back to his usual seat.

Avi followed the angry little chap with the top half of his right ear missing. Carrying a glass of lemonade and a pint of bitter, he dodged through the thirsty queue and cut an indirect route to Tommy's table to get a line on Lehmann.

Tommy was sharing his company with a tall, thick-set bruiser and a wounded old veteran, the latter sporting an eye patch. The old campaigner skilfully rolled up a cigarette with one hand as an old black Labrador slept by his feet. Avi moved to sit with the party.

Still flustered by Lehmann's presence, Tommy took a proper look at the stranger and barked, 'Just 'cos you offered me a pint doesn't make you me your best pal, particularly another bastard German.'

'But I am Austrian.'

'So was bleedin' 'itler.'

Tommy revealed the ceremonial ᛋᛋ dagger he had concealed in his pants. It wasn't the first time Avi had been threatened with an *Ehrendolch*.

'You'd better sod off now if you know what's best for yer,' said Tommy.

You little ... Avi's face reddened with rage. His fists tightened. Retreat was anathema to him.

Hold back. Hold back. Leave it. Don't draw attention. Avi backed away with a feigned smile and moved to sit with Grimshaw. Failing to disguise his disdain, Avi motioned to hand Grimshaw the pint.

The photographer raised his hand with an open palm and offered, 'I'll have the lemonade. You take the pint. You look like you need it more than I do.'

No. No. No ... Well, maybe. Perhaps a quick drink to calm the nerves. A drink wasn't my idea, Kathy. Just the one should be fine. She'll never know if it's just the one. Just one pint to steady the nerves. What about the tablets? Take a tablet instead, that'll do it.

Feebly trying to soothe his conscience, Avi reached into his inside pocket for the bottle of yellow pills. But Grimshaw was watching, and for Avi, pills were a sign of weakness. Instead, he took a sip from the top of the pint.

Ooh, that's a nice pint of Northern nectar. Perhaps just a couple will be okay. 'Can you drive, Derek?'

Grimshaw nodded. Avi slid his car keys onto the table and gulped down the pint, stumbling at the first hurdle. He wiped his lips with the back of his hand, then looked over to Simpson and Lehmann, the magnets for sycophantic locals.

Avi's eyes shifted to one of the occupants at Tommy's table. 'Do you know any of the blokes sitting with that scruffy fella, Tommy Green?

Grimshaw took a look. 'Yeah. I think the big chappie is called Hyland. Can't remember his first name. I did his daughter's wedding not long ago. Big do. Paid well. Don't know the bloke with the eye, though.'

Avi pulled up his chin.

'Ronnie! That's it, Ronnie Hyland,' said Grimshaw.

Kathy looked at her watch in the half-stripped kitchen. It was ten past six. Avi was already late, with no word on what time he would be home. Kathy consoled herself with hopeful thoughts.

He'll be okay. He said the people were nice.

Ray the steward and the solitary barmaid continued their effort to keep up with the avalanche of orders. Lehmann turned away from the busy bar with a whole tray of ale. He ambled over to Green's table. Hyland took a pint and exchanged a furtive glance with the bearer of the drinks.

Bill Haley and His Comets' *Rock Around the Clock* blared from the jukebox as the club became fuller, smokier, and livelier.

Amid the din, Avi struggled to take notes while questioning Councillor Simpson for a line on the new housing scheme. Predictable public relations patter persisted as Simpson lubricated his tonsils on the free drinks passing his way, an obvious source of the greedy Councillor's gin-blossom, purple conk.

All the while, Avi's eyes wandered. He was preoccupied with Lehmann's side profile and his hoarse rasp, which, without the microphone's embellishment, sounded less convincing than he had first imagined. However, Avi's thoughts remained consumed ...

But it was seventeen years ago. His voice would have changed, matured with age, and he's not speaking German. The inflexion would be different in English. No identifying physical features except for that scar on his face. Was there a scar on his face? Surely, I would have remembered that? Dammit! I wouldn't have registered much without my glasses. Besides, anything could have happened to him during the five years left of the War.

At the end of Simpson's interview, Avi pocketed his pen. 'I thank you for your time. Now perhaps you could introduce me to Mr Lehmann? I want to hear his thoughts on your ambitious housing regeneration schemes.'

'I'm sorry, but Mr Lehmann doesn't have much time for the press, what with him being a Jerry,' said Simpson. 'He doesn't do interviews. He's been misinterpreted so many times. Helmut is a shy, modest man. It took all my powers of persuasion to get him here today. Best leave him. I've given you all you need.'

Shy and modest? He wasn't shy or modest at the bar.

Avi shook Simpson's hand, stood up, and moved towards Lehmann's table. His pathway was blocked by man-mountain Ronnie Hyland, who pushed out his shovel-sized right hand.

'Not today, little man,' he said in his threatening voice.

'Perhaps some other time then, Mr Hyland?' said Avi with a wry smile.

'I doubt that very much.'

We'll see about that, thought Avi, who smiled, took his leave, and wandered back to the table where Grimshaw was waiting amidst the thick cloud of blue tobacco smoke that had filled the room.

Time and beers flowed into the evening's drinking shift. Tommy Green finished another pint and slammed it onto his cluttered table. A rowdy gang of crêpe-soled, high-quiffed Teddy Boys, dressed in drape jackets, laughed scornfully as Ray the steward lectured them for leaving their pints on the snooker table.

Unbothered, they continued dancing in the aisles, spilling beer on the new parquet floor — much to the steward's further annoyance. Noticing the tension, the barmaid hurried from behind the bar and unplugged the jukebox.

Whittaker was at his wits' end. 'Right, that's it. Yer can piss off out, the lot of yer!'

The gang paid no attention.

With an untouched half-pint in front of him, Lehmann watched impassively, but before things got out of hand, he caught Hyland's eye and nodded from across the room. Hyland rose from his pew and strode over to the Teddy Boys. Aware of the approaching bruiser, the gang backed down and scarpered.

Avi returned from the toilets, having missed the drama. He picked up his glass and necked a double brandy chaser with ease.

Kathy was on the kitchen phone, chatting with her mother, long-distance. She glanced at her watch once more. It was now eight o'clock. She decided to wrap up her conversation. 'Best get off the line now, mum. Avi might be trying to get through. Speak to you tomorrow, sweetie. Love you.'

It was darker outside and smokier inside. Avi kept glancing in Lehmann's direction. His descent into paranoia was complete. The more he drank, the more obsessed he became. He wore his glasses, but his vision was blurred — blurred like his vision in the past — blurred like his view of the past. Peering through the cigarette smoke, Avi saw Jens Wolff skulk into the room and pick his way towards Lehmann and Simpson. Both remained seated.

Stern-faced, Wolff bent down for a word in Lehmann's ear. After a brief exchange, Wolff straightened up and then turned to leave. Lehmann resumed his conversation with Simpson while glancing at his watch.

His handwriting deteriorating into illegible gibberish, Avi noted their interaction on his pad. On his way out, Wolff bumped into the careless Green as he staggered from the crowded bar with yet another pint.

The spillage slapped down onto Green's shoes.

Avi had a grandstand view as yet another fracas was in its infancy.

'*You clumsy bastard*!' shrieked Green.

'I am so sorry, my gut man.'

'*Gut* man? Not another bloody sour Kraut? It's gettin' like the Nuremberg rallies in 'ere. Why don't you all just piss off back to Nazi-land and slaughter a few more helpless Jews? *If* you can find any left to slaughter. You murderin' Kraut bastard.'

Wolff shoved Green with all his might. Green rocked backwards, slipped on the wet floor and crashed into the beer-drenched tables.

Empty pint pots and schooners lay shattered on the floor, with Green on his backside covered in ale and broken glass. He staggered to his feet. He threw off his jacket and pulled out his ⚡⚡ dagger. The horseshoe of baying patrons encouraged him to take it further, but Green dropped the dagger of his own accord.

Just as he was about to launch himself at Wolff, Whittaker grabbed Green from behind by his collar and wrestled him onto a seat.

'Sit down and shut up! That's the last time I ever see that dagger in here. Tell me you understand?' said Whittaker.

With raging eyes and gritted teeth, Green panted as he continued his stare out the German, whose movement was held at bay by Hyland's vice-like grip. The two combatants were restrained like baiting cockerels.

Whittaker kept a firm hold on Green by the scruff of his neck as he repeated, 'Tell me you understand, Tommy. Tell me you got it or yer barred for life?'

'I got it, *I got it*!' said Green, finally relenting.

Avi noticed Hyland picking up the dagger.

'Forget that pint, Tommy, you're goin' 'ome,' said Hyland as he yanked Green away from Whittaker's grip.

Back in the kitchen, Kathy had taken Avi's parched supper out of the warm oven and scraped it into the bin. She dialled the Press Office number but didn't wait long for someone to answer before deciding against her call and putting down the receiver. She didn't want to be a nuisance on what remained of Avi's protracted first day at his new job. Once more, Kathy comforted herself with positive thoughts.

He'll be all right. Perhaps they've taken him for a quiet pint of 'shandy' after work? No need for the lingerie, tonight, that's for sure.

Grimshaw had left the club, but the car keys still sat on the table. Avi checked his watch. It was 8:30 pm.

Plenty of time for another double.

When Simpson's driver entered the room, Simpson and Lehmann got up to leave. That was the signal for Hyland to help Green to his feet and escort him out through the front door. Wolff noticed the move and quickly retreated out of a rear exit.

The resulting draught invading the room caught Avi's attention. He grabbed the car keys and followed Wolff as he staggered outside into a murky backyard cluttered with stacked wooden bottle crates.

Avi arrived at the back door. He wasn't as sober as he thought, and the force of the fresh air struck his face with a slap. He swayed like seaweed on a rock, then missed the small back step. His legs buckled as he stumbled to the stony ground, dropping his car keys in the fall.

On his knees as if in prayer, Avi looked around. The grid by his foot yawned.

Oh dammit.

Wolff pushed his way through the remaining trio of the banished Teddy Boy gang, who had loitered in the car park with mischievous intent.

Abandoning Wolff's tail for a more urgent matter, Avi struggled to his feet.

The gormless gang chuckled as Avi grappled with the heavy iron grille in a feeble attempt to retrieve his keys from the drain. He was unaware of his vulnerability, which was amplified once he opened his mouth. 'Perhaps you could help me, please?' called Avi, in his friendly Austro-Bavarian tone.

Avi's request sent the trio into a confused discussion.

'Bugger me! A pissed-up Nazi!'

'Them bastards killed me Uncle Brian!'

'Pissed-up Nazis killed your Uncle Brian?'

'That's bang out of order. Let's do 'im!'

Without hesitation, the three Teddy Boys charged into the attack with all arms flailing. Avi's drunken state made him unable to defend himself against the rowdy youths. He shielded his face, protecting his glasses as a flurry of windmill punches and free kicks hammered into his arms and torso.

Avi staggered backwards, accidentally knocking over an empty dustbin with a loud clatter, but miraculously stayed on his feet.

The commotion had alerted Ray the steward, who stepped out from the back door, wielding a sturdy cricket bat. He delivered a graceful hook shot that cracked against the nearest Teddy Boy's right ear.

The Teddy Boy teetered, then collapsed to the ground like a shot game bird. 'You've had it when me dad gets hold of you, Whittaker!' called the young victim, his ear ringing from the blow.

Ray mimicked another swing.

The Teddy Boy cowered, got up quickly, and ran off into the night, followed by the rest of the stray cat gang of ruffled quiffs.

Avi straightened himself up and brushed himself down. 'Do you think you could help me lift this, please, uh, Ray?' asked Avi, in slurred English.

With an exasperated shake of his head, Ray took a quick scout around, then picked up Avi's keys from the floor beside the door. 'Oy, Max Schmeling, you lookin' for these?' Ray moved to toss the keys to Avi, but realised his parlous state, and handed them over securely. 'Best be on your way, lad. I might not be around if they come back.'

'Thanks for looking after me, but I really can look after myself.'

Ray shook his head, smiled, and relented. 'Okay. Come on back in, lad. It's been a long night for both of us. You look like you could do with a bucket full of coffee.'

'I would rather have a bucket full of brandy.'

'You look like you've already had one!'

Avi followed the smiling Whittaker back inside the bar.

Chapter 8.
The Set-Up

It was 9:30 pm when Kathy switched off the kitchen light and went upstairs to bed, alone. She was concerned and frustrated, but her thoughts remained upbeat.

Perhaps he's forgotten the new phone number. That's it. I should have written it down for him.

It was 9:30 pm when Avi slumped into the Moggy and struggled to start the car. In his drunken state, the short journey home from the club would be a challenge. It was also complicated by the fact that he was unfamiliar with the route. At least he was still able to hold Lewis's map, although initially upside down. Avi was well acquainted with the foolish perils of drunk driving.

Nice and steady does it. One easy little drive home ...

It was 9:30 pm as drizzle flowed down a grey downspout on the dimly lit Port Street. The water gushed along a pavement gully straight into a gurgling grid set into the smooth cobblestones. The weather kept rats at bay while shooing away occasional brass in search of a five-minute knee trembler for a ten-bob profit.

Screwed into a high wall, a rotting wooden sign announced the location of F&G CONSTRUCTION. A boundary wall capped with a regiment of shards of broken beer bottles offered a formidable barrier to would-be intruders. Shadowing the sheen of this secluded street, a white Mercedes-Benz W180 pulled up outside the builders' depot.

Helmut Lehmann stepped out of his car and looked at his elegant gold Swiss watch, which shimmered in the glow of a solitary lamp post. He was right on time. He unlocked the smaller door set into the two metal doors. Stepping inside the depot, he was startled to see Jens Wolff standing with a large leather satchel gripped in his left hand. Initially surprised, Lehmann regained his composure. 'How can I help you, Herr Wolff?'

Wolff smiled. 'I know you will be interested in what I have to offer.'

'Not here. Come into my office.'

Pointing to a well-worn wooden door marked FOREMAN, Lehmann took out a key and unlocked the padlock. He flicked on the strip lights, which blinked slowly into life. They revealed a tight, modest room containing several battered filing cabinets. Like a sumo wrestler anticipating a battle ahead, an antique safe squatted defiantly in one corner, drawing Wolff's attention.

Lehmann sat down in the seat in front of his cluttered desk. Wolff tentatively followed and took the opposite pew. Both of them reverted to their native German as Lehmann began.

'What is it that you want Herr Wolff?'

'I have evidence that you are not who you say you are.'

'Evidence? Evidence of what?'

'I have something of yours that is worth a lot of money to you and therefore worth a lot of money to me.'

Lehmann shook his head, offering a patronising smile. 'You have nothing. I am sorry to disappoint you, my friend, but I am just a simple builder.'

Wolff pulled out his Pistole Parabellum and pointed it at Lehmann, who raised his hands.

'Enough of this nonsense, *enough*! I know you! Herr

Spangell is my ...' Wolff paused to avoid revealing all his cards. Taking a deep breath, he continued. 'I have been finding the people whom Herr Spangell accommodated.'

'Who is this Spangell?'

Wolff flipped the safety catch, ready to shoot. 'I am losing patience, my friend! As you well know, Herr Spangell from the orphanage in Munich. This is your last chance.'

'Ah, yes, yes, Spangell, of course. Herr Spangell has nothing on me.'

'Then why did you not wait for official clearance to bring your daughter over to England?'

'I wanted to get her over here as quickly as possible.'

'You gave Spangell a diamond just to save time? You are ᛋᛋ. Your tattoo will prove it. Take off your jacket ... *now!*'

Wolff trained the gun on Lehmann's face as he slowly removed his coat. 'Now roll up your sleeve!'

Lehmann motioned to roll up his right sleeve.

'Don't play games with me. Your left sleeve, *as you know damned well!*'

Lehmann rolled his left sleeve upwards to the elbow. Impatient, Wolff came in closer.

Lehmann grabbed for the gun but was too slow.

A shot rang out.

The bullet blasted through Lehmann's lower left arm. Off-balance, he crashed to the floor, clutching the wound in agony.

Wolff dropped and rammed the gun against Lehmann's right temple. He ordered, 'Open the safe... right *now!*'

Lehmann let go of his wound and crawled through his

spattered blood towards the safe in the corner of the room. With his good arm, he turned the combination lock and yanked open the heavy door.

Wolff grasped Lehmann by his blood-soaked left arm and dragged him out of the way of the safe. Wolff grabbed the cash, but was disappointed.

'Fifty pounds is nowhere near enough.'

'I can get more.'

'You *will* get more. Ten thousand pounds will make me disappear, or the same in diamonds or Deutsche Marks. I don't care which.' Wolff stuffed the money into his satchel. 'This will do for now. I will be in touch very soon.'

Lehmann remained grovelling on the floor. Retaining his grip on the Parabellum, Wolff backed out of the office.

A swift blast of cold wind chaffed Wolff's face as he stepped back into the rattling depot yard. He looked down at the satchel and smirked contentedly. His ball was rolling. As Wolff's gaze returned, he was oblivious to the devastating granite punch to his chin, unleashed by Ronnie Hyland from out of the shadows.

Wolff plummeted backwards. His feet were still airborne as a sharp crack announced the back of his head smashing against the cobblestones. Hyland reached down and took the Parabellum from Wolff's grip as a stream of claret oozed from a fatal head wound. It was Wolff's uncompromising dead end.

With a long, robotic stride, Hyland burst into the office, aiming the pistol. He saw Lehmann on the floor, grimacing as he clutched his bloody arm.

'You got him?' asked Lehmann with a grunt.

'He's in the yard.'

Lehmann grabbed Hyland's arm and staggered to his feet. They moved swiftly outside.

Still holding the firearm, Hyland frisked Wolff's clothing. He pulled out a leather wallet, a half-empty pack of cigarettes, and a key with the number 35 stamped on the brass tag. He picked up the keyring and dangled it in Lehmann's view.

Lehmann studied it and said, 'Take him somewhere remote. Shoot him with his gun. Make it look like suicide.'

Hyland smiled as he produced Tommy Green's ᛋᛋ *Ehrendolch*. 'I also have this. It's a pity to waste such a fine Luger.'

Lehmann stared in awe as Hyland displayed the Parabellum in one hand and the ornate Nazi dagger in the other. Coveting both, he took his time to make a choice. 'Perhaps I might have a better idea than merely shooting him?'

Avi's car was parked uncomfortably close to his neighbour's car as he staggered toward his new home. Dishevelled, battered, and bruised, he fumbled for his key. With squinted eyes, he struggled to insert the key into the wobbly door lock.

Carrying Wolff's body over his shoulder, Hyland stepped out from behind a protective horse chestnut tree into a clearing in Wythenshawe Park. He slammed the corpse into a supine position and then knelt over Wolff's face. He took out Green's ᛋᛋ dagger and, from above, plunged it deep into Wolff's abdomen. He wiped the handle clean and retreated into the trees.

Lehmann grimaced at his depot desk as he struggled to rotary-dial the phone with his blood-soaked shirt tightly wrapped around his wound.

Chief Inspector Collins was working late in his office at the Bootle Street Police Station in central Manchester. Although the late shift switchboard operator was slow to connect his call, Lehmann managed to keep his short temper under control.

'Collins?'

'Yes, it's the Chief Inspector.'

'Good. It is Lehmann. I've been shot. The shooter is dead in Wythenshawe Park. I will be in Baguley Hospital. Meet me there in the morning. I will explain everything.' Lehmann hung up.

Chapter 9.
Let the Nightmares Begin

Avi had made it up the stairs and into the bedroom without incident. Kathy was sound asleep. He kicked off his damp shoes and struggled to stay upright. His trousers were stained with the day's trials and tribulations. He had managed to remove his shirt, but undoing the Windsor knot of his tie was beyond him. He abandoned the task, leaving his beer-soaked tie dangling over his vest.

With an uncertain balance, he flopped into bed in his underpants, vest, and socks. Despite his clumsy lack of grace, coupled with the foul odour of stale fags and alcohol polluting his breath, Kathy had failed to stir.

Staring up at the ceiling, Avi's head was swirling—not with the velocity of a fairground Waltzer, the prelude to the vomit of many a beleaguered drunk, but it was close. His eyes were heavy and drooping slowly.

He didn't fall asleep immediately and was briefly aware of dancing phosphines on the back of his eyelids. The strange red shapes soon cleared as he slipped into a deep and vivid dream. His heavy breathing provided a fitting accompaniment to his dreaded nightmare ...

... Young Avi was surrounded by terrified prisoners, crammed into a seatless omnibus. He looked around for his lost student friend, Günter Kraft. The bus swerved violently from side to side as it ploughed along the pot-holed road. Avi was pressed against a young Hasidic Jew who muttered Sh'ma Yisrael in relentless prayer.

The charabanc broke to a sharp halt on the 'Avenue of the ϞϞ'. The prisoners crashed forward. The driver looked behind, grinning at the tangled carnage he had caused. He hawked up a green phlegm ball and spat it into the face of a fallen prisoner floundering face-up in the aisle. With sadistic pleasure, he announced, 'Welcome to Dachau, jew pigs!'

The doors were busted open to a cacophony of abuse, barking dogs, snarling thunder amid an intermittent sush of rain. The prisoners spilled onto the wet cobblestones, glistening in the raking searchlights from a gun tower set into the roof of the Jourhaus. Along a corridor of ruthless guards, the prisoners were beaten relentlessly with rifle butts, cudgels, and bullwhips. Leashed but un-muzzled German Shepherd dogs snapped white razor teeth while straining from either side of the rasping 'welcome party' who ordered their captives to 'keep moving, you schweinhund — now!'

Avi and the frenzied rabble stumbled toward the archway of the Jourhaus with Arbeit Macht Frei welded into rod-iron gates. Clinging to each other, confused and consumed in disbelief, they bumbled through the camp entrance. Avi tried to hide in the group, but to no avail. An ᛋᛋ guard cracked him in the face with a rifle butt, which devastated his left cheekbone. His glasses lay shattered on the floor. Blind terror as blood streamed from his swollen eye.

The prisoners dragged themselves into the vast Appellplatz roll-call square and onto the 'Protective' Custody Compound. They stumbled past the mocking guards screaming at them to: 'Get in line, get in line!'

From Avi's compromised view, the band of prisoners searched for order, colliding frantically in loosely serried lines. Bolts of blue lightning illuminated the sweeping rain. A large, wounded prisoner collapsed to the floor as blood leaked from his head and his slashed clothing.

A young ⁴⁴ Unterscharführer strolled across to the malaise. He grabbed the prisoner by his neck and dragged him up to his feet. The prisoner pushed him off with a foolish thrust of defiance. Knocking the Unterscharführer off his balance would be a costly mistake.

Avi turned to see the Unterscharführer recover his poise, take out his Walther automatic service pistol, and shoot Günter Kraft straight through the forehead. The bang made Avi jump. He shivered both in the dream of the gravelled compound and in the reality of his sweat-soaked bed.

Noticing Avi as a witness, the Unterscharführer strode to the front of the group. He addressed the remaining prisoners with a well-rehearsed soliloquy: 'You've all been wondering whether Dachau truly is the absolute hell of your worst nightmares. Have no illusions. This hell is not a nightmare. This hell is your reality!'

In the blinding shaft of white light spearing from the roof of 'The bunker', the Unterscharführer strolled down the line. He studied the young Hasidic Jew shaking next to Avi. 'Any more of you dogs unable to stay on your feet?'

The Unterscharführer's face was a blur. An apparition like every face Avi had ever seen: an apparition like no face he had ever seen. He was standing with his legs apart, desperately holding his balance while straining to retain composure.

The Unterscharführer smirked and then kneed Avi hard in the groin. He doubled over but managed to remain on his feet. The Unterscharführer slowly crouched to Avi's level. 'You are determined to live. That is good. I will ensure you will stay alive for as long as it amuses me.'

A senior ᛋᛋ *Obersturmführer approached, shouting, 'Unterscharführer! Stop playing games with the prisoners. Get them stripped and clear up that mess. We haven't got all night!'*

Curled up in the foetal position, Avi awoke with a start in the dimly lit room. Restless beads trickled down his sweat-soaked face.

Kathy was also awake. Her eyes were wide open and already used to the gloom. With an affectionate reflex, she moved one arm toward Avi and took his hand. She turned her body around and spooned her restless husband. Her cuddle provided mutual comfort.

She had experienced nightmares of her own ...

Chapter 10.
Little Girl Lost

Circumstances had been very different the first time Kathy migrated from London. A devout Catholic, God-fearing girl with a cheerful, easy-going personality, Kathy Falco — née Kathleen Cranighan — was born in the East End at no. 21 Lydia Street, next door to her nan and Grandad on her mother's side. Fish on Fridays. Mass on Sundays. Saturday confession of sins, which were never severe enough to warrant penance.

Mother, Eileen, and her father, Derek, were a well-known and respected family within the close-knit, working-class community on the doorstep of the docklands in Stepney.

Kathy cherished her happy and carefree childhood. She enjoyed a comfortable life thanks to her father's steady job. Derek Cranighan was a hardworking labourer at the local brewery in nearby Limehouse, close to the River Thames. His muscular six-foot frame and tough, no-nonsense attitude earned him respect in the neighbourhood. He was not a person to cross, and no one had ever taken such a risk.

As the dark clouds of World War 2 gathered, Kathy was fourteen years old when evacuated among the mass exodus of children two days before Britain declared war on Germany on 3rd September 1939. In the first four days of that month, over 6,000 evacuees left London. More than 3,000,000 people were eventually transported from British towns and cities. They evaded the threat of enemy bombers to occupy havens of safety in the countryside as part of *Operation Pied Piper*. Most of the children were looked after and cared for ... but not all these innocent angels were delivered from evil.

Her father championed Kathy's evacuation. He remembered stories of his parents and their memories of civilian helplessness during the Germans' first strategic bombing campaign. During 'The Great War,' Londoners were attacked from above by Zeppelin and Schütte-Lanz airships. The Ministry of Health's evacuation scheme was promoted by the Government to prevent a repeat. Modern aircraft posed a much greater threat.

Widespread scaremongering predicted that up to four million civilians would be killed during the mass bombing of large industrial cities in England. The docklands in the East End of London would be one of the *Luftwaffe's* primary targets. Escaping bombs and the psychological scars of war was essential for the preservation of future generations. Kathy's father could understand the reasoning and was adamant that she must leave. Kathy's mother had a feeling of foreboding.

The tidal wave of evacuation struck suddenly. Kathy was one of the 'Cheerful little Cockney urchins' who could hardly believe the good luck of being sent to the countryside on what seemed to be a long and adventurous holiday. Clinging to their tiny suitcases and awkward gas masks — some bewildered, some excited — the youngsters boarded the snaking chuffer trains that would take them to unknown destinations. Derek was working hard at the brewery on the day his only child was sent away. Eileen chose not to see her off from Myrdle Street School to avoid causing further trauma.

Kathy saw her evacuation as an opportunity to embrace the countryside and escape the dark city, but her parents were overwhelmed with worry. This was Kathy's first time venturing into the wider world alone. They doubted her confidence and wondered where or if their beloved daughter would be safe. Strangers can be strange, and none were stranger than those she was soon to meet.

The evacuation operation was intended to be as smooth as possible, but ended up chaotic. With insufficient rations supplied, many children were sent to the wrong places and arrived at incorrect destinations. Unlucky siblings were divided and separated against their will. The children of the East End were billeted all over southern England. Some were welcomed, while others faced resentful receptions and were often looked down upon as rough lower classes within the class-structured society.

Eventually, Kathy arrived at the sleepy Suffolk village of Littleby, located just outside the rural town of Ipswich. Although Suffolk was a safe refuge from the Blitz, it had proved susceptible to stray bombs and planes shot down en route to and from London. However, her main dangers were more concealed.

Following a humiliating but necessary examination for head lice, she endured a cruel selection process. This involved already homesick children being paraded and then lined up against a wall on the village green. They were chosen for billeting, often by reluctant and cynical adults.

Kathy was the first pick of a gruff, middle-aged dairy farmer named John Winnot and his compliant wife, Winnie. As the oldest of her group, Kathy was selected under the Winnots' guise because they needed a strong, mature girl to help with milking and other laborious chores. None of the locals were confused by her selection.

Even though nine-tenths of the people in Stepney had no baths in their homes, Winnot Farm did not live up to any idealistic vision of rural bliss. It was isolated and lacked basic amenities, such as gas, electricity, and running water. Kathy's new environment was challenging for an innocent young teenage girl going through puberty. She was the only child on the farm.

Despite the abundance of food available, she was underfed, overworked, and treated with contempt by the owners. Kathy was housed in a cramped attic bedroom in the main cottage, confined to a dingy room with a single bed.

Isolated from other young evacuees in the village, her dark and lonely nights soon became more terrifying than those endured under the hail of blitz bombs. Kathy's recurring nightmare remained one of deep distress ...

A long, malnourished day on the farm was followed by another harrowing night in the attic. Kathy was alert and awake, restless amid the shifting shadows of the night. Her arms ached. Her legs hurt. Her ripped fingernails were a painful distraction. Her mind was on edge. It was cold, and she was hungry.

The wind howled through the rafters and gaps in the eaves, creating a nerve-jangling atmosphere for one so young. She shook — shaking from the chill, shaking from fear. The fear of nightly visits from her tormentor, John Winnot.

A dim orange light flickered along the bottom of the attic door. She heard his familiar shuffle down the corridor. The squeaks of his swinging lantern only heightened her trauma. The wooden staircase to the attic groaned for the fifth night in a row as John Winnot climbed up. Kathy held her breath as she counted the twelve slow steps towards the door.

One ... two ... three ... four ... then stop.

Each night, the torment climbed one step higher. Winnot was toying with his prey. But tonight, he couldn't wait any longer. He salivated as if he was about to devour a fresh and succulent meal.

Terror took its grip. Upright and rigid, Kathy clutched the bedding with clenched fists, her nails digging through the sheets and into her palms. She could smell the stench of his sour breath.

As the black lust in his brain drove him upwards, she cupped her jaw to stop her teeth from meshing. Her heart pounded, as if trying to burst from her chest and flee to safety.

Five ... six ... seven ... eight ... then stop.

Kathy dropped to her knees and prayed harder than ever before. Hail Mary, full of grace, the Lord is with thee. Blessed art thou amongst women. Fists clenched tighter. Getting closer. Getting louder. Four steps to go.

Nine ... ten ... eleven ... twelve.

The lantern rattled as he dropped it on the top step. Kathy looked around the room, but she was helpless. Hopeless. No place to go. No place to hide.

Winnot scratched on the door with dirty nails, his manner fiendishly menacing. She slipped underneath the bug-ridden bed as the door handle turned. The door opened. His silhouette was suddenly framed.

Pools of tears welled in Kathy's eyes. Her sunken face painted with dread.

Winnot put down the lantern and approached the foot of the bed. She saw his filthy grey trousers to the top of his bald white shins. He was inches from her face.

A clink of the belt buckle and Winnot's trousers dropped around his ankles. She bit hard on her index finger. The taste of her blood didn't register.

Kathy Cranighan screamed for her life as 41-year-old paedophile John Winnot dragged her out from under.

In the front room below, Winnie Winnot heard the commotion. She put on her earmuffs and smirked as Kathy's frantic pleas faded from awareness. Nobody listened. God had turned a blind eye.

Kathy jolted out of an atavistic nightmare, but a new one was about to begin …

Chapter 11.
Reasonable Doubt

It was the morning after the night before. Daylight peeked through the brocade curtains, casting a sliver of light on Avi's eyelids. The alarm clock pounded against his temples. He jolted into consciousness, stretched out, and knocked it off with a firm slap, sending it crashing to the floor.

Avi let out a huge groan. His head felt like it was wedged between two boulders. His mouth tasted as if he'd been licking a used nappy. His breath was a waft from a steaming sewer.

My hangovers never get any easier.

Returning to his senses, he eased himself up and yanked off his beer-stained vest and tie. Slitted eyes crusted with sleep; he fumbled for his glasses and then hooked them on with trepidation.

A quick scan around the room.

His notepad was open on top of the bedside drawer. His wild handwriting was the illegible scrawl of an infant's Christmas wish list.

With a slow blink of the eyes and a resentful grunt, Avi got to his feet. He teetered backwards, regained his balance, and then lurched toward the window with an unwitting imitation of Frankenstein's first steps. His first thoughts were of the German, Helmut Lehmann.

At least there was no confrontation with him... What on earth was I thinking? It's impossible. What are the odds? Last night could only have been worse if I'd crashed the car and killed someone on the way home.

With a yank of the curtain, he looked out of the window just in case. Squinting through the harsh daylight, there were no signs of an accident.

The car's not straight, but straight enough... a bit too close to the kerb, but not too bad.

The view had also allowed a sneak preview of the hostile weather — *another new day ahead, another grey day ahead.*

An unwelcome reflection in the glass was revealing. He poked a finger into one of the bruises and shook his head — *a beating from a gang of stupid kinder. Time was, you'd have taken them all with one hand tied behind your back, drink or no drink. You are slowing down like a lazy old soak. At least Grimshaw left early. He did not see my embarrassment.'*

Back in the early days in London, Avi started his journalism career as a promising junior crime reporter, but an unexpected opportunity diverted his path to becoming a political correspondent. This led to questions that puzzled him.

Why was I hand-picked for this story by the great man? I haven't worked crime for years, and my sickness record hasn't been the best. Surely there were better candidates he could have chosen with better track records than mine?

Avi lowered his arms and eased himself backward onto the edge of the bed. His head slumped into his hands, weighted like a medicine ball. His negative thoughts signalled an early depression. Yesterday's exuberance had vanished into the toxic fumes of last night's brandy. His smile was gone by the end of the day.

I need to get my act together, but it's been a long time since I was assigned to a murder story. The Adams case is a major responsibility. I must stay focused. This is a high-profile assignment. I was instructed to keep a low profile. Gaggs expects you to bring new energy to a case that had died long before you arrived.

He ran his clawed fingers through his ruffled hair and then rubbed his palms hard against his forehead.

Gaggs chose you because he knows you can still cut the mustard. He said it is like riding a bike: you never forget. Come on, you must shape yourself. There is a lot at stake ... it is all at stake.

From the corner of his eye, he noticed a new pair of folded paisley pyjamas, patiently awaiting his attention at the foot of the bed. They'd been thoughtfully left there by Kathy.

Oh, Kathy. I didn't get in touch all evening. She is already up and at 'em ... and I was on a promise. It's the doghouse for me.

He looked down at his matted socks in shame and then trudged into the bathroom. A long yawn followed by a stretch of the arms. A twist of the tap and a brief wait for the hot water to fill the sink. As rising steam began to heat the room, he immersed his hands in the warmth of the flow.

Warm water, warm hands in the morning. Pure luxury.

He enjoyed a moment of bliss until, as if a parasite had crawled into his ear during the night, Helmut Lehmann returned from the remnants of his nightmare ...

That unique timbre of his voice. I've heard nothing like it before or since. He was around the same height as me at the camp, give or take a couple of inches with the heel of his jackboots — and about an inch or so on the ridge of the top of his visor cap. Slightly taller than my eye level. He could be the right height. Maybe. Maybe not.

What are the chances of me bumping into him in

England, in Manchester? The odds are overwhelming that he must be dead. A man that vicious would have been hunted down and dispatched by now... but plenty have survived and fled to all corners of the globe. Would he be brazen enough to live here in plain view? Of course he would! He was a confident, arrogant bastard — a typical German.

The glance into Lehmann's eyes at the social club was unsettling but not revealing. Still, Avi's imagination started to race.

Those sullen eyes, calm and blue like a bottomless lagoon that tempts an innocent victim to swim in freezing water. Those sullen eyes, piqued like the shadows of a dormant volcano hiding its pent-up fury... No, stop it. You must halt it before it begins. If you let this gather momentum, it will be impossible to stop.

It is not him, so forget it... But what about the writing on the wall? What is the real meaning? Stop it now! You are here to solve the Adams murder.

He grabbed his shaving brush from the windowsill, dipped it into the hot water, and began rubbing it vigorously against the bar of soap, working up a thin lather to cover his jaw from ear to ear — a careless scrape against the cheek and an instant nick with the tired blade. The blood spilt down into the water, briefly holding its form and then dispersing to colour the pool pink. The wound began to sting.

He quickly finished his shave and gazed into the mirror of the medicine cabinet as blood rolled down his face from the plethora of cuts that had taken time to reveal. He pinched open the door and pulled out a small, brown bottle, unscrewed the lid, and swallowed two yellow pills. Thin parallel scars stretched along his left forearm. As he turned, the mirror showed numerous thicker horizontal scars crisscrossing his lean, muscular torso. These older scars had their own stories that were separate from the fresh bruises he had received the night before. He shook his head again.

This was not the start Avi had hoped for.

Today's performance must be of Oscar-winning standards, both at home and at work. Break a leg, Avi.

He took a deep breath and then eased his way into the kitchen, dressed smartly for work. The half-stripped walls looked as if they'd been mauled by a pride of angry lions. Kathy was indeed annoyed but had chosen to temper her response. She handed him a cup of tea and a dry piece of toast. Avi regretted the lack of foresight in his opening gambit.

'What happened to the bacon?'

'What happened to the bacon?! What happened to the *promises*? Your first day, and you come home steaming drunk!'

He widened the cheeky smile he knew she loved so dearly. 'I wasn't *steaming* ... although I was perhaps a little bit worse for wear.'

'A little worse for wear?! You wore your tie in bed last night. You were lucky you didn't strangle yourself ... or that I didn't strangle you.'

'First day introductions, I presume?' Kathy smiled as she added, '*And* you forgot my evening paper.'

'I was just being sociable. Besides, Thursday night has the classifieds, not Friday.'

Avi got to his feet and stepped across with arms extended. She backed away slightly, but he persisted and wrapped his arms around her waist. A mild hint of his favourite perfume lingered from the night before, a seductive aroma she usually saved for intimate occasions.

I missed out there, thought Avi, as a trouser tremor hinted at the way forward. Some things had a mind of their own, especially for Avi after a night on the tiles.

With a sudden shake of her head, Kathy plucked one of the bloodied shreds of Izal from his shaven face, which he'd used to stem bleeding again. 'You need some new blades and some shaving cream. I'll nip out and get you some today. You really need to take more care of yourself, Avi.'

'You really do look after me.'

'Yes, but it's all a bit one-way, isn't it?'

'I'm sorry, my sweetheart. I will make it up to you.'

'You're all talk, Avraham Falco.'

'You think so?'

As the kettle started to boil, Avi showered Kathy with gentle kisses. She relented, smiled, and gradually reciprocated his affection. It had been a while. The kissing quickly became more sensual, more intense. Their breathing merged into synchronised lust. He lifted her pleated skirt to reveal her suspenders and stocking tops as she fumbled to open his trousers. Their bodies convulsed as passion took its grip. The phone began to ring. Kathy unsheathed his large penis, which stretched to rigid attention. He simultaneously ripped down her slipover and bra shoulder straps. Her pert breasts responded to his feverish caress. Avi yanked her hard towards him, thrusting down her arching body into an accessible position on the sturdy kitchen table.

The phone continued its ringing as the boiling kettle's whistle neared its screeching peak. The phone, the kettle, and Kathy all screamed for his undivided attention. He took a swift glance at the phone as breathless Kathy implored,

'Leave it, Avi … *for god's sake leave it!*'

But Avi pulled back, fumbled for the phone, and picked up the receiver.

Kathy let out a long sigh of frustration. She composed herself, stood up, and grabbed the kettle from the stove, which instantly killed the whistle.

Avi tried to control his heavy breathing as he responded to Doreen on the line. 'Yes … yes, I understand … Wythenshawe Park? Don't worry, I'll find it … yes, yes. I will come as soon as possible.' He hung up and quickly tried to resume, but Kathy motioned him away, shaking her head.

'No, Avi. You won't be coming any time soon.' Kathy turned away to hide her distress. She feared that Avi had just made a significant choice. Her head dipped with despair.

This was not the start Kathy had hoped for.

Chapter 12.
A Puzzle in the Park

Avi stepped away from the tired-looking Moggy and headed towards photographer Derek Grimshaw. He loitered beside eight wooden-top coppers, including PCs Brookes and Taylor. Radiating authority in his full-dress uniform, Chief Inspector Collins was also present. His passive expression gave nothing away.

Tall and slim, Collins' impressive figure complied with his elevated status. He removed his braided visor cap to reveal a full head of black hair, tinged with grey. Three other seasoned journos were also sniffing around, along with a couple of dog walkers enjoying a gawp at the scene of last night's crime.

Wolff's body lay next to a sturdy Wythenshawe Park horse chestnut tree, which Hyland had used for cover the night before. The corpse was covered with the coroner's clean white nylon sheet. It wasn't lost on Avi that the outline of the dagger sticking out of the abdomen looked darkly comical, as if the victim had perversely enjoyed his last moment on Earth.

While familiarising himself with the terrain, Avi took copious notes. He went to shake Grimshaw's hand, but instead, he pulled him close. Without looking towards the Chief Inspector, he whispered, 'Is it usual for a top-ranking policeman to be present at a murder scene?'

Grimshaw was taken aback. 'Uh, no … not that I'm aware of.'

'Is he who I think he is?'

'*He* is Chief Inspector Collins.'

Avi stepped back, once again skirting the restricted crime scene. He paid special attention to the muddy footprint trail that led deep into the ground from behind the tree, pointing to the body. When the moment was right, he made his approach. 'Excuse me Chief Inspector Collins, have you any details for the Manchester Chronicle?'

With an imperious grin, Collins seized Avi's upper arm and steered him aside, out of Grimshaw's sight, then said, 'You must be Lewis's new Chief Reporter.'

'Yes, my name is Avi Falco.'

'A word of advice, Avi Falco. There are two ways of getting things done in this fine city. The easy way ... or the hard way. Are you an intelligent man, Avi Falco?'

'I should like to think so.'

'Good. Then I believe we can have a mutually beneficial relationship — both professionally and financially — as long as you don't become a burden to me. Do you understand?

'With crystal clarity,' said Avi with a restricted reply.

Financially? What are you insinuating, Chief Inspector? Don't ask. This is neither the time nor the place.

Away from Avi's view, Wolff's body was wrestled onto a stretcher. A sudden breeze disturbed the sheet, briefly revealing Wolff's bald pate. Grimshaw quickly took a photo. Brookes immediately slapped the camera from Grimshaw's hand. The camera clattered loudly onto the concrete path. Grimshaw reached to pick up the pieces, but Brookes gripped his arm firmly and whispered something in his ear.

His lower arm bandaged, Helmut Lehmann had decided that he'd languished in a Manchester Royal Infirmary recovery room long enough. His upcoming premature discharge was a decision he made despite his doctor's advice.

It was a struggle to put on the change of clothing provided by his high-maintenance blonde wife, Glenda. She hadn't offered any help but had successfully disguised her amusement at her husband's discomfort.

Since arriving at the hospital, she had spent most of her time complaining about the cleaner's inability to "Actually clean anything properly in this disgusting place". Helmut had shaken his head numerous times during her tirade, at the end of which he debriefed her on the previous night's events.

Glenda already very well knew what she must do, but she liked to goad him at every opportunity … and this was indeed a one to savour. 'So, let me get this straight — we stick with the false story that there was a break-in at *home*, although the break-in was actually at the *depot?*'

'Yes. That is right,' said Lehmann, beginning to lose his patience. 'For the last time, and as I quite clearly told you last night and again a few minutes ago, I went back to the depot for some building plans and disturbed a man trying to break into the safe. He shot me and ran off without the money.'

'But I still don't understand why you didn't just phone the police from the depot at the time? The depot has a phone. If you'd have done that, I wouldn't have to lie?'

'That is not your concern, Glenda. You will follow my orders without question. I don't need to remind you that I now hold all our money.'

'Of that, I'm well aware, Helmut. Thank you so much for the reminder,' she said, getting to her feet in a huff and collecting her handbag and coat. 'Get a taxi home on your own. You can obviously afford it!'

As she left the room, she saw CI Collins waiting at the door. She ignored his nod of acknowledgment before stomping down the corridor in expensive, high-heeled leopard skin shoes. In her haste, she slipped and fell flat on her backside on the freshly mopped floor. The onlooking cleaner struggled to hide her amusement as Collins entered Lehmann's room.

Back in Kemsley House, Avi was sitting at his desk, surrounded by buff files. Behind him, the pinned-up newspaper headline: TRAGIC ACCIDENT KILLS YOUNG REPORTER served as a reminder of the task at hand. Doreen bum-barged her way into the smoke-filled room, carrying two enamel mugs of steaming tea. The handles overheated, so she was relieved to put them down and pass one to Avi. He smiled and asked, 'Are you sure these are the last of Adams' case files?'

'Sorry, but that's yer lot, love.'

Shaking his head in disappointment, Avi reached into his pocket and pulled out his Zippo lighter and, unwittingly, the gold cufflink he'd retrieved from the floor of the Moggy. The small trinket caught his attention.

'Mrs Falco has rung twice now,' said Doreen.

'I'll ring her back later.'

'You should do, she's lovely to talk to.'

Avi took a large gulp of his tea while covertly dispatching a yellow pill. Doreen sat back down at her desk, thinking wistfully of Kendal's shop window and the cheeky blue dress that tantalised her vivid imagination.

'Doreen, were you in the office the day that David Adams died?' asked Avi.

She stirred from her daydream. 'Er, yes. It was a

Saturday, like today. I remember it well.'

'Who else was in?'

'Mr Lewis was in that mornin'. City were at home, so he covered the game at Maine Road in the afternoon. He came back by taxi to compile his match report as usual. I stayed late that day. I had to type up the Man United copy that came in on the teleprinter from the southern correspondent.'

'Was Spence in?'

'Yeah, he was in for the afternoon and then the graveyard shift, but he wasn't in the office when David's fiancée rang to tell him to get a move on. That was just before seven. I don't miss much and I remember it well because I were meeting me boyfriend in The Green Man across the road straight from work at seven, just so that I could finish with 'im. The two-timing tosspot broke me heart. I don't half pick 'em.'

Her head tilted. 'Anyway, David ran out of the office just before me. Spence had gone out on a job. Why d' ya ask?'

'Oh, nothing really. Just verifying what it says in the file. You and Mr Lewis were the last people to see him alive... You two and the man on the door downstairs.'

'Bandy Bob?'

'That is such a cruel name. Rickets is not a laughing matter.'

'Uh, yeah, I know, but that's what they all call him. At least he didn't have to go to war.'

'Perhaps he would have liked to have fought for King and Country? Perhaps he would have found it an honour to serve?'

'Perhaps he would 'ave. I never really thought of it like that, Avi.'

Avi raised his eyebrows, took another slurp of tea. 'Do you have any idea if David was a heavy drinker?'

'Blimey, where did *that* come from?'

'Sorry, but I'm curious.'

'Uh, no. Not really. Although …'

'Although what?'

'Well, I wasn't there, but I heard David made a right show of himself at Douggie Fowler's wake a few weeks earlier.'

'Douggie Fowler, the old chief reporter?'

'Yeah. It wasn't like him at all, but I heard David was really drunk that night. It was a free bar, you know. Owt for nowt take two, especially if you're a Jew.'

'That is a gross misconception. I am also a Jew.'

'Well, then I hope you can hold your booze a lot better than David Adams did!'

Silence. Discomfort. Avi took another gulp of his tea.

Doreen acknowledged her insulting remarks. She looked in embarrassment at her tightly clad thighs. 'Sorry, Avi love, I didn't mean anything by that. A great bloke was our David — a really great bloke. I've got nowt against Jewish people, and I do miss him … really, I do. Everybody does. It was such a shame.'

Avi smiled and nodded.

Doreen returned his generous smile and recovered her poise. She wiped the palms of her hands on the sides of her skirt and then continued philosophically. 'I'm not much into religion. Me parents were very religious though. Me dad worked the night shift at the Vimto factory and me mam worked days as a dinner lady at our school. Never the twain shall meet. They used to send me and our Jimmy to Sunday school every week. I only realised years later that they only sent us there cos

Sunday mornings were the only opportunity they had to 'ave a right good shag!'

Avi smiled politely and then asked, 'What is a shag?'

Doreen smiled, but then shook her head. 'You *are* joking?'

'*No*. Not at all.'

'Oh, right, uh, a shag: A bit of how's yer father, 'avin' it off, uh, rumpy pumpy … yer know, the 'orizontal tango.'

Clueless, Avi shook his head.

'Bloody hell, Avi, sexual intercourse!' cried Doreen as Avi just about managed to refrain from spraying his desk with tea. Deadpan, Doreen followed with unintentional irony. 'Some bloody detective you'd make!'

Avi nodded with a wry smile. 'So why weren't you at Douggie Fowler's wake?'

'I wouldn't cross the road for him, never mind go to his death do. Normally, I love a man with power and money, but Douggie Fowler was the exception. Slimy old tosser. He was a tightwad, and he had a right gob on him, even though he used to talk like his teeth were glued together. It's a pity they weren't, or perhaps he wouldn't 'ave looked like the Michelin Man after a four-week banquet. He was so big he'd o' made Henry the Eighth look like a clothes horse. He was a sweaty old sod with big bushy eyebrows and so much protruding nasal hair you could have plaited it. And he was a right bloody lech. He never used to look me in the eye cos he was always starin' at me bosom!'

Doreen adjusted her bra, inadvertently pushing up her exposed cleavage.

Avi averted his eyes as he replied, 'I take it that you didn't like him, then.'

Doreen rolled her eyes. 'Yeah, you could say that.'

'What did he die of?'

'It was quite ironic, really. He dropped dead in the baker's while queuing for a meat 'n' tater pie.'

'He must have really needed that pie?'

'No. He was just a greedy fat bastard. I don't miss him or his ways. He drove Mr Lewis to distraction. He wasn't a nice man at all.'

'Yes. I think I've got that, Doreen.'

'Anyway, if you want to find out what happened at Douggie Fowler's wake, you should have a word with Joan Baker.'

'David's fiancée?'

'Yeah. She works up in the staff canteen. Spence was head over heels on 'er. Good-looking lass. All the boys fancy Joan.'

'Blonde or brunette?'

'There's only one good-looking lass that works in the staff canteen.'

Avi reached for a cig. 'Have you any idea where Fowler's old case files might be?'

'You'd have to ask Spence. He cleared out the filing cabinets just after Fowler curled up.' From her handbag, Doreen took out a mirror and a stick of red lipstick. 'Oh, I almost forgot. The snapper was in earlier. Mr Grimshaw. He dropped off this envelope and a bill. Said he was going to stick to weddings. Summat about keeping his camera and his teeth in proper working order.'

Avi pulled out the developed pictures from the 5000th House ceremony. He flicked through and found one with *Arbeit Macht Frei* daubed on the Council house wall. Another print was framed from behind the podium. Jens Wolff's bald, egg-shaped pate was prominent in the crowd.

With a red ballpoint pen, Avi circled Wolff's stony face and then peered into Lewis's goldfish-bowl office. No Lewis. 'Any idea where Mr Lewis is?'

Doreen looked up at the clock. It was 3:40 pm. 'Of course. He'll be in the press box at Maine Road, swearin' his head off at City. Yer can give him a lift back. Mrs Lewis has his car on a Saturday.'

Avi slipped the pictures into a large buff envelope, plucked his overcoat from the bamboo coat stand, and exited the office.

Chapter 13.
A Careless Match?

Located on the inner-city boundary, the Manchester City football ground at Maine Road was the oasis for the discerning Mancunian working class. The Saturday rituals, cheering on the footballing greats of the day and lampooning the usual whipping boys, were almost at their conclusion as Avi chugged forward in the hapless Moggy.

Outside the Main Stand, a reversing Ford Consul offered Avi a parking space reserved for the press. As two mounted police horses clopped by, he was immersed in the atmosphere outside a massive football stadium where the game was still underway.

Disgruntled City supporters streamed out of the exits, accompanied by a chorus of muffled groans. Avi caught the eye of a frustrated-looking fan sporting a sky-blue rosette and asked, 'What's the score, mate?'

'3-1 to Arsenal. We're lucky it's not ten.'

Picking his way through the throng of gabardine coats, flat caps, and trilbies, Avi eased into the emptying theatre. Under the atmospheric dark canvas of the late evening sky, the muddy pitch was bathed in beams of floodlight from towering grey pylons at each corner of the stadium.

A constellation of stars remained visible on the pitch as Avi ascended the concrete stairwell and dodged into the paradoxically named 'seated stand'. The air was filled with a variety of aromas, including the expensive scent of pipe tobacco and the resignation of impending defeat.

Edging into the press box, Avi sat down on a pew beside his annoyed-looking boss.

Lewis's impartiality was instantly compromised as he applauded City's blonde German goalkeeper, Bert Trautmann, after yet another athletic save at the open Scoreboard End of the ground. His appreciation was accompanied by adulation from the crowd of die-hard admirers.

The referee blew the final whistle. City had lost. The result was met with howls of derision. A line of disgruntled City supporters filed past, offering unsavoury advice to the referee about where he should lodge his whistle.

Lewis grabbed his notepad and pen and muttered, 'For God's sake.' Finally noticing Avi's presence, he shook his head in despair at the result.

Just around the corner from the ground, Avi tapped impatiently on the wheel of the Moggy while stuck in match traffic on Claremont Road. Numerous home fans trudged past, while others clambered onto the open-back double-decker bus that coughed out blue exhaust smoke on the Moggy's rusted front bumper.

Lewis vented his anger at City's defeat. 'They might as bloody well have had Bandy bloody Bob in net today the way they played ... and he couldn't stop a pig in a ginnel! They were bleedin' useless except for Bert.'

'I take it you won't be putting that in your match report, Mr Lewis?'

Lewis frowned as Avi wound down the window to let out the hot air. This inadvertently allowed noxious carbon monoxide to seep into the car from the crawling bus ahead. Avi fished out an open packet of Woodbines.

He tapped one out and pointed it towards Lewis, who shook his head, and then let out a protesting cough as Avi lit up.

The smoke emitted from the open window was a minor contribution to local pollution. It added to the contamination from belching chimney pots on tidy rows of neatly arranged Victorian terraced houses, all within the newly established West Indian ghetto in Moss Side.

Despite Lewis's depressed mood, Avi got down to business. 'I need to speak to you about the murder last night. After the housing ceremony yesterday, there was a fight in the social club.'

'Hmm. An altercation with a local drunk and the dead German in the park?'

'Yes, but I also saw "The dead German" approach Helmut Lehmann. I didn't hear what was said, but Lehmann didn't look at all pleased.' Avi reached into the backseat and handed Lewis the large brown envelope.

Lewis pulled out the picture with Jens Wolff's face encircled. He studied the second print with *Arbeit Macht Frei* daubed on the corporation house wall.

Avi pointed to the message. 'It must have been done during the opening ceremony because it wasn't on there when we parked. The other is the dead German. If he painted Arbeit Macht Frei on the wall, it could have been some sort of message to Lehmann?'

'What sort of a message is "Work sets you free"?' asked Lewis as the car continued to inch forward.

'There are plenty of Nazis still on the run. Perhaps Lehmann has a hidden past. Perhaps he was being blackmailed?'

'You possess a fertile imagination, Mr Falco. I've rigorously checked Helmut Lehmann's War record. As you've just seen, Germans can be heroes in this city. Bert Trautmann, City's goalkeeper, was a former German paratrooper. They have worked hard to be accepted. Lehmann has built a solid reputation based on trust, respect, and loyalty. He employed local War veterans down on their luck. He trained them with building skills and paid them well. He has provided lads' clubs and children's playgrounds. He has contributed money for orphaned children. The working men's club whose hospitality you were enjoying to the full yesterday was built on Helmut Lehmann's money and hard work.'

And I wonder who spilled those beans? thought Avi.

'Lehman sees his duty is to serve the public interest, even if it involves personal sacrifice.'

'This does not surprise me. It is pragmatic old Nazi idealism.'

'That is harsh, Mr Falco. In your eyes, he is damned if he helps and damned if he doesn't. Generous acts of benevolence should be praised, not scorned, especially in this city, where poverty prevails.'

'Fair enough, Mr Lewis. Then perhaps his generosity explains an ulterior motive? Maybe it suits a purpose for Lehmann to curry favour to garner popularity.'

'I'm not sure why you have a bee in your bonnet about Helmut Lehmann, other than understandable Jewish prejudice. However, I also heard the drunk was brandishing the same ⚡⚡ dagger that killed the German.'

'Yes but …'

'Listen carefully, Mr Falco. In 1949, when Bert Trautmann signed for City, there was hatred and outrage, particularly within the large Jewish community. People took to the streets in mass protest. Matters became ugly until a communal Manchester Rabbi wrote an open letter in the Chronicle. He told his people that the atrocities of the War were not due to a solitary soldier. It will take time, but the Jews might learn to forgive, if not forget.

No need to set things back. Take my word, Mr Falco, it was the drunk who perpetrated this crime.'

I will not forgive, and I will not forget.

Avi switched on the *hrump-hrump* beat of his windscreen wipers as the rain began to patter. He dropped his cig dimp out of the driver's window and then wound it shut. The car continued its kerb-crawl along with the matchday traffic.

Lewis glanced out of his passenger window at the rows of terraced houses where several black immigrants headed for cover. He shook his head. 'Look at them. Everywhere you look, wogs are invading the country. It's just like during the War, only this lot are here to stay. It's only a matter of time before they take advantage of our morally loose young women and pollute our society for good. It makes you wonder what on earth we fought for?'

'To wipe out bigotry.'

Despite the rain, Avi rolled down his window and saw a young black man sharing an umbrella and chatting happily with an elderly white pensioner as they sheltered from the rain at a bus stop. Avi gave a wry smile.

Chapter 14.
Hidden Treasure

A gleaming Magnette ZB Saloon was parked outside London Road railway station. Ronnie Hyland was behind the wheel. He gnawed at his left thumbnail and fidgeted as he waited for his next instructions. The engine was still warm from his previous fruitless trip to Victoria Station, on the other side of Manchester's city centre.

Helmut Lehmann struggled into the car. His injured arm was wrapped in an off-white sling.

'Any good?' asked Hyland.

Lehmann looked down at the key Hyland had taken from Wolff. 'No. We shall try Central Station.'

Lehmann entered the busy Victorian train station, the northern terminus of the LMS mainline route from Manchester to London. A steam train billowed in, exhaling a thick breath of opaque vapour that further fogged the platforms. Clattering carriage doors, departure announcements, and shrill whistles accompanied the lively throng of commuters crossing paths around the terminal — a vibrant scene of monochrome beauty.

Surveying the station, Lehmann focused on the row of royal blue storage lockers. He fished in his pocket and retrieved Wolff's key. With trepidation, he inserted the key into locker 35 and turned. To his relief, it opened.

The locker contained a large manila envelope. He peered into the envelope, smiled, and slammed the locker shut.

The engine was still ticking over as Lehmann got back

into the car.

Hyland had noticed the envelope and asked, 'We happy?'

'Yes. It is wise for you to be out of town for a few days. Take another trip to Antwerp; we need more cash. Use the safe house on your way.'

Lehmann handed over a blue velvet pouch.

Chapter 15.
Taking the Lead

Bernard Lewis was sitting at his desk with the hot-off-the-press Sunday edition, admiring the predictable prose in his match report. The phone rang. Looking for a taker, his eyes peered through the dust-dulled glass and into the press office. Avi was playing his typewriter with the casual grace of a concert pianist. Doreen wasn't there to take the call.

Lewis shook his head and grabbed the phone. He immediately regretted his action. On the line was Herbert Gaggs, the owner of the chain of Chronicle newspapers, calling from his plush office on London's Fleet Street Press Parade.

Doreen entered Lewis's office mid-conversation and overheard Lewis's riposte.

'Yes, Mr Gaggs, but with all due respect, I believe I should take the lead on this. He doesn't know Manchester as I do. I thought you wanted him to focus on the Adams investigation … Yes, sir, you're right, it should be an open-and-shut case … I will tell him immediately.' Lewis hung up, shook his head, and then shouted at Doreen to 'Get Falco in here … this minute!'

Doreen scurried out. Avi had already overheard the blunt request. He aborted his literary concerto, stubbed out his cig, and strode purposefully into the Chief Editor's office.

Lewis had regained his composure. 'I have decided to let *you* head up the Wolff story. A Thomas Stanley Green has been arrested on suspicion of murder — presumably the drunk. Start with a brief holding article stating that the body of a man was found in Wythenshawe Park and that the police are following several leads. Mention Green, but no mention of Lehmann at this stage. Sometimes a good journalist prints less than he knows.

Lewis broke off eye contact and stood up to leave. Using a crumpled handkerchief, he dabbed a bead of sweat from his upper lip. 'By the way, I received a tip-off late yesterday that Helmut Lehmann was shot at his home in the early hours of Saturday morning. He discharged himself from the hospital earlier today.'

'And you didn't think this was worth investigating, given the murder in the park of a man he spoke to just a few hours earlier? We should be all over this.'

Lewis's cheeks reddened with embarrassment as he bit both bullets. 'Yes, well, uh, I didn't find out until late last night, and I thought it would keep until now.'

You thought that it would keep until now? Really?

Avi returned to his desk. He asked Doreen, 'Can you do me a favour, please, and find Helmut Lehmann's home address?'

Doreen smiled and nodded. 'No call from the lovely Mrs Falco today?'

'No … I think I might have upset her somehow.'

'Perhaps you should make time to call her more often. Give her some reassurance and support. You should never neglect a good woman, Avi. Especially one that's irreplaceable.'

'Blimey. I never had you down as a member of the Women's Union, Doreen.'

'Not just women. I try to look out for everyone I like. In my experience, most men are thick. They never realise what they've lost until it's gone. Maybe you need to pull your socks up, Avi.'

He looked down at his feet. Doreen shook her head.

Avi parked the Moggy outside Lehmann's large mock Tudor house, bathed in a welcome snap of bright Cheshire sunshine. He strolled up the gravelled pathway and rattled the fleur-de-lys iron door knocker.

No reply.

He wandered towards Lehmann's white Mercedes-Benz W180 parked on the front driveway. Peering through the driver's window, he noticed flecks of dried blood on the tanned leather steering wheel. He took out his pad and noted the car's registration.

A two-seater Austin Healey sports car skidded to an abrupt halt in the driveway, making the loose chippings crunch. Glenda Lehmann shot out of the driver's seat. In her typically brusque manner, she shouted at Julia Lehmann, 'Hurry up and get out of the car, child. I haven't got all day!' Julia clambered out without protest.

Glenda's scorn turned to the shifty-looking pressman lurking by the Mercedes. 'And who in God's name are *you*? Get away from that car this minute!'

'I am Avraham Falco, a reporter from the Chronicle.'

Julia was unable to contain her excitement. With a subtle hint of a German accent, she said, 'Wow, a real live reporter.'

Avi smiled. 'I just want to clarify a few details with Mr Lehmann about the burglary at this residence last Friday night. It is all right, madam.'

'No, it is not all right!' said Glenda. 'Mr Lehmann is out on his building site. Now, get off my property this instant or I will call the police!'

Avi shook his head. 'He's gone out on site? My information is that he was shot on Friday night. He spent yesterday in hospital and discharged himself this morning.'

'Well, your information is incorrect. He left that dreadful place yesterday! Manchester Chronicle, you say?' Glenda shoved Avi out of the way, grabbed the child's arm, and led her to the front door.

She jammed her key into the lock, ushered Julia inside, and then slammed the door shut with a loud bang. Picking up the telephone in the hallway, she dialled immediately.

As he sidled back towards the Moggy, Avi noticed a rustling in the bushes. His attention was caught by an elderly neighbour pruning her hedge with well-oiled secateurs.

He walked over to a gap in the privets and immediately saw her hearing aid. He was about to give a polite yet loud greeting, but was overtaken by someone else.

'You'll get nothing from that one. The only time she looks happy is when she's picked up by one of her fellas. Different fancy man every weekend. I can't understand why. Mr Lehmann is a lovely-looking man with such charming manners. He's a lovely man, is Mr Lehmann.'

'Is he really?'

'Oh yes. A lovely man. Good afternoon. I'm Mrs Timmins, and your name, young man?'

'Please. Call me Avi.'

'Avi. Ooh, that's a nice, simple name. Is it foreign? Mr Lehmann's a foreigner. Please call me Elsie.'

Avi smiled politely. 'Did you hear any commotion on Friday night, Elsie?'

'Good gracious me, no. I wouldn't hear anything on any night. My hearing aid is always on the side of the bed next to my teeth. Noise doesn't stir me. I used to sleep through the blitz before I got my hearing aid, and that was donkey's years ago!'

Avi smiled.

'Friday night, you say? Hmm. Come to think of it, I didn't hear anything, but I did see flashing lights through the curtains when I got up to use the loo. You have to go a lot when you get to my age. I'm 84, you know.'

'What time was that?'

'My first tinkle is usually around midnight. There was a big white ambulance, and the police were there. They took Mr Lehmann away on a stretcher. I do hope he's all right.'

'Oh, I'm sure he's fine at the moment, Elsie.'

Whether he remains so after I've had a little chat with him is an entirely different matter.

Chapter 16.
Divine Intervention?

Kathy was in the kitchen amongst shards of freshly stripped and shredded wallpaper. She stepped back to stare at the bare walls and then placed her scraper beside a copy of the News of the World, and realised ...

Blimey, it's Sunday already. I've hardly seen him over the weekend, so what will weekdays be like? So far, he's hardly lived up to his sales pitch: "Come on, Kathy, we can move to Manchester. I will give up drinking once and for all. It will be a fresh start for the two of us, a chance to find a new life together away from the pressures of London. We can have so much more time. It might be a promotion, but how much work can there be on the regionals? Come on, sweetheart, we should do this."

He didn't last a single day without a drink.

She pursed her lips, grabbed the telephone receiver, and dialled. She was met with a swift reply.

'Hello, Manchester Chronicle?'

'Hello, Doreen. Don't you ever go home?'

'Ooh, hello, Mrs Falco. Just doin' a bit o' catching-up. Filing, that sort o' thing, yer know. A bit of a slavedriver is your 'usband.'

'Please call me Kathy. Can I speak to him, please?'

'I'm afraid not. He's out. He buggered off this morning and he 'asn't come back. I'll let him know you rang. Tara, Kathy love.'

Kathy put down the receiver and picked up a screwdriver. She gripped it threateningly ... but then opened a tin of white gloss paint.

After leaving the Lehmann residence, Avi took a detour

on his way to the office. He parked near a vacant building site marked with a weathered F&G CONSTRUCTION sign.

He slipped on his overcoat and left a lit ciggy hanging from the corner of his mouth. His hands were casually tucked into his trouser pockets as he headed towards the sign. He stopped a few yards from the entrance and noticed a clear warning: NO TRESPASSERS. He took a deep breath and entered through the unlocked gate of the building site.

Acutely aware of his intrusion, he crossed the threshold of the churned-up yard, enclosed by a makeshift boundary fence composed of a rainbow of discarded wooden doors.

As he made his way towards the site hut, he sidled past a partially built block of three-storey flats. A loose tarpaulin fluttered gently in the breeze, revealing a large stack of bricks.

Avi scanned the yard. The place looked deserted.

As he took a final drag on his ciggy, the eerie silence was broken by the swish of a spinning slate falling from high scaffolding. It sliced into the ground, missing Avi's left foot by the width of his discarded fag dimp.

What the ... His eyes darted skywards.

Sharp reflexes threw him to the ground as a crashing cascade of roof tiles plummeted with deadly speed, detonating all around him like a Luftwaffe carpet-bombing.

Avi lay motionless on the muddy earth, his hands clasped over his head ...

Finally, the clattering subsided. The thick cloud of tile dust began to clear, revealing a groaning heap of a man in a state of shock. Shattered tiles surrounded Avi's curled-up body, some of which were embedded in dirt just inches away from his head.

Bloody hell... Am I okay? Can't feel any pain.

Coughing repeatedly, he gathered his senses and looked upwards. Through translucent dust, he saw the burly Site Foreman clutching a claw hammer while striding towards him with anger etched on his face.

Get up, get up!

He tried to rise, but couldn't.

A rusty old Bedford van skidded into the yard.

Avi and the approaching foreman looked at the van with eager eyes.

A cheery brickie jumped out of the van and shouted, 'Ey up, boss, won't be a mo'. Just getting me tools. Left 'em in the fuckin' site office last night. Went straight on the ale after work. Didn't want to leave 'em in the fuckin' boozer, pissed up! Had a bit of an accident, have we?'

The foreman looked down at Avi shuffling in the debris like an upturned tortoise. He lowered the hammer and extended a hand to pull Avi up while continuing to grip the would-be weapon in the other.

Avi shook his head. He struggled to his feet and dusted himself down.

The astonished foreman puffed out his cheeks and stared at Avi. 'Some fucker up there must *really* like you, son.'

'Maybe ...'

They both looked up at the top of the high scaffolding where a tall, dust-covered roofer appeared on a broken plank high above. His face was blackened beyond recognition.

'... Maybe not,' said Avi.

The roofer shouted down, 'Sorry Boss. Must 'ave piled

'em up too fuckin' high!'

The foreman shouted back, 'Yer will be sorry when I dock them breakages out of yer fuckin' wages. If yer brains were any thicker, you'd be grazin' in a field, yer fuckin' bonehead!'

The foreman turned his attention to Avi. 'This is a dangerous fuckin' building site. Accidents can happen. Serious fuckin' accidents. This is private property. What are yer doing snooping around here without a fuckin' invite?'

'I'm from the press. I'm looking for Helmut Lehmann.'

'Helmut Lehmann? He's in the fuckin' 'ospital, as far as I know. Copped for a fuckin' bullet fighting off a fuckin' burglar. He's not been in, so fuck off out of 'ere and don't come back without a fuckin' invite. You got that?'

'Uh, yes. Yes, I fuckin' 'ave,' said Avi, who scurried off towards the open site entrance.

Looking over his shoulder, he took a glance around the site. A telephone wire stretched from the roof of the site office. The apologetic roofer had disappeared.

Avi returned to the Moggy. Sitting at the wheel, his grubby hands trembled from both the cold and the shock of his near-death experience. It was time to take stock.

That's right, deep breaths. Relax, relax. You are still in one piece.

He looked down at his mucky trousers and stone-splintered palms. He flipped them over and noticed the withered veins burrowed in his wrists like decaying roots at the base of a rotting birch. Avi had never thought of the future, always of the past.

When did that happen? I don't even know the backs of my own hands. The signs of ageing are undeniable. Am I still the man I once was? Go back and follow the roofer. No. He is gone. He was covered in dirt. Didn't see his or Lehmann's face. What am I doing? Get out and find him? No, don't be a fool. You entered a dangerous building site without warning. Come on, come on, Avi, for God's sake, make a decision!

During the War, he wouldn't have hesitated about what to do. He would have dived straight into troubled waters and asked questions later. He ached to be younger again, fitter and more confident.

I'll soon turn 40! Where has the time gone? Where has my life gone? From now on, it feels like a downhill slalom. Perhaps the slide started years ago.

He took out his comforting bottle, put it to his mouth, gulped a couple of yellow pills and pondered further ...

If that was deliberate, how did they know I was coming? Either the foreman or Lehmann's wife is lying. Maybe neither ... Maybe both. If Lehmann was already in the house, he could have phoned the foreman to set up the fall once he'd questioned his wife? Or she could have called the site office to warn Lehmann that I was on my way. The journey took twenty minutes. It is possible if the tiles were already up there.

But why try to kill me? He can't kill every reporter who takes an interest in his business. Does he recognise me? He sounds like that bastard ... They said paranoia might be a side-effect of the tablets. Get a grip. The foreman seemed genuinely upset with the roofer, but maybe it was because he missed me? No, come on. Don't be stupid. It was just an accident, a coincidence. Wrong place, wrong time. Don't be naïve. Remember the basics:

there are no coincidences in this game. Gaggs chose you because you can still cut the mustard? Can you still cut the mustard ... Can you really, Avi?

A shrunken old man shuffled past the car with a small Yorkshire Terrier in tow. The dog stopped to cock his leg against a willing tree. The old man turned to wait and noticed Avi sitting in the Moggy. He cast his second glance into an intrusive stare. Aware of the company, Avi looked up and met his elderly observer's gaze.

The man tipped his cap and offered a respectful smile as he and his canine companion continued their walk. Avi's thoughts were suddenly filled with pessimism.

Time used to drag slowly when I was a boy, but as a man, the years have flown by. It doesn't seem like 40 years have passed. Is that bloke me in another 40 years? A lonely old man walking a dog with nothing else to do. Is that what I want to become?

The car rumbled to life with a prolonged splutter as Avi turned the key and pulled on the starter knob. He drove back to the office. The better part of valour. Was he weaker or wiser? He consoled himself by assuming the latter. Retreat was no longer anathema to his current state of mind.

With his grubby new overcoat taken off and placed in the boot of his car, Avi stepped into the Manchester Chronicle building. He nodded in acknowledgement of Bandy Bob's diligent security and headed towards the lift. The OUT OF ORDER sign had been removed.

The lift's arrival was announced by the dart of the counterweight racing upwards. Avi's mind remained fixed on the image of falling roof tiles as Lewis joined him, belatedly.

The lift shuddered gradually until it gave a jarring jolt. Avi grabbed the handle and yanked the shutters open forcefully, producing a clattering metallic sound. He stepped inside and gestured for Lewis to follow him.

Lewis shook his head. 'Not for me, thank you. I'd rather use the stairs. I abhor cramped spaces. A touch of claustrophobia, I'm afraid.'

Avi stepped out of the lift. He slammed the gates shut and joined Lewis on a steady climb up the spiral staircase.

By the time they reached the fourth floor, Lewis was puffing like a punctured blimp. He gasped a series of short observations: 'I'm glad you're back. I'm not impressed. Glenda Lehmann has made a complaint. She is furious. So am I. She demanded an apology and an explanation as to why one of my reporters was found lurking outside her house. I gave you specific instructions. *You* are on the case, but *I* am the Chief Editor. You have abused my clear orders. What didn't you understand about the words, *Leave Helmut Lehmann well alone?*'

As they reached the top of the stairs, Avi casually lit up a cig and replied, belatedly, 'A liar depends on not being questioned. Herr Lehmann appears anxious to avoid me.'

'No, he appears very annoyed.'

'Do not worry, Mr Lewis. As you said, *I* am on the case now.'

'Yes, indeed you are, but please tread more carefully and clean yourself up. I can't imagine how you have got yourself into such a state… and quite frankly, I don't want to know.'

Thank goodness for small mercies.

Chapter 17.
A Turn of the Screw

Sitting at his desk in his spacious office at Bootle Street Police Station, CI Collins grinned while trawling through the monthly crime statistics. The vintage Head Pathologist, Edward Wallace, knocked twice before entering. His off-white lab coat was slightly less crumpled than his forehead. Puffing on the lit pipe clasped between caramel teeth, he removed the pince-nez spectacles from his arching beak.

With a raised eyebrow, he dropped a file marked JENS WOLFF onto Collins' desk. He removed the pipe from his mouth and, in his smooth but deliberate voice, advised, 'I have concluded my interim report, Sir. The victim wasn't killed in the park, and the stabbing was post-mortem.'

'Go on.'

Wallace stroked his chin and smiled. 'He was killed by catastrophic intracranial pressure caused by a subdural haematoma. The neurocranium was severely damaged, causing instantaneous, terminal injury.'

'Yes, yes, yes, but what does that mean in plain English?'

'As you wish, Sir. The victim was killed by a heavy blow to the head. There was bruising beneath the mouth caused by a blunt object, likely a fierce punch that pushed him backwards. Traces of grit were present in his fatal wound. These have been examined. The back of his head struck a hard surface during the fall, the same Belgian block from which cobblestones are made. That's what killed him. His jaw was broken, and there were several cracked teeth in the hard palate. Uh, sorry, the roof of his mouth. The bruise on his chin tells the story. That was the initial point of impact. The perpetrator was a strong man — a very strong man who knew how to throw a punch. The victim was already dead when he was taken to the park and dumped. It's all in my report.'

Collins rubbed his chin. 'Are you sure of all this, Wallace?'

'Well, I could be wrong with my supposition, but I would doubt that very much. As you are aware, Sir, I am very good at my job.'

Wallace turned to leave. With a bite on his pipe stem and his hand on the door handle, he turned back. A knowing smirk overcame his dour expression.

'Oh, I am sorry, Sir, but I almost forgot. The victim had old, external parallel scars on the upper left arm … they resembled a through-and-through gunshot wound.'

'So, he was an ex-soldier.'

'I X-rayed his arm. I found no muscle or bone trauma. I saw this several times on POWs while working for the Ministry. Self-mutilation to hide an ϟϟ blood group tattoo. How strange that an ϟϟ man is murdered in one place, then taken to a feigned location, the very same night, the German, Helmut Lehmann, is shot at home while scaring away an intruder?'

Collins fished into his drawer and handed Wallace a manila envelope stuffed with cash. Wallace smiled and raised his pipe in appreciation as he paraded out the door.

Two floors beneath Collins' office, situated in the secluded, soundproofed basement, an unofficial interview room hosted a highly private interrogation. Black-eyed Tommy Green was leaning against the butterfly back of an industrial chair beside a solitary metal table that dominated the small room. PCs

Taylor and Brookes breathed into his face while crouching like expectant tigers, ready to pounce. Green was a rough, unshaven, sleep-deprived wreck of a man. Several buttons were missing from his shirt. His hands were trembling with the combined effects of fear, exhaustion, and an obsessive craving for a stiff drink. The former trooper was barely holding on with what little strength he had left. The interview was dragging on. Taylor used a tried and trusted tactic …

'Come on, Greenie lad. At least fifty witnesses saw you pull a knife on that Kraut. No one's gonna hang you for killin' a square 'ead. Sign the confession, then you can get some kip. We might even give you a bite to eat.'

'How many times do I 'ave to tell yer? Ronnie Hyland carried me 'ome. I was legless. I wasn't even there. On my left bollock, I didn't kill the Jerry.'

Brookes got in on the act. 'You'll have no bollocks in a minute if you don't come clean, you stupid little gett! Hyland took you home all right, but you went out again for more ale … didn't you? You walked back through Wythenshawe Park and came across the Jerry on his way home … didn't you? Then you stabbed him to death … didn't you! Your ᛋᛋ dagger was found in his belly. How did it get there, you murdering pig? *You will sign this confession right now!*' Brookes stood up, clenched his right fist, and punched Green squarely in the mouth.

Green recoiled but remained on the chair. Despite blood spilling from his punctured lip, the tough little soldier remained defiant. 'It'll take more than your cheap double-act to scare me. I was facing up to Panzer units when you two clowns were in short pants!'

Brookes hurled Green to the floor. The irate coppers kicked Green repeatedly as he curled up into a ball.

Chapter 18.
Herbert Gaggs

With its secluded ground-floor entrance and solitary exit to his 12th-floor penthouse office, Herbert Gaggs' exclusive lift had always contributed to his aloof persona. For privacy, he remained mysterious to the well-paid staff in his Fleet Street fortress.

A strong supporter of the noble concept of *Tzedakah*, his distant image concealed his philanthropy towards struggling Jewish individuals in need of his help. Sometimes he went further afield. The owner of the Chronicle Group of newspapers was both a trusted friend and a potential enemy. His straightforward outlook and simple pragmatism were shaped during extraordinary times of danger and despair.

In June of 1926, Herbert Gaggs was a middle-aged, trenchant Jewish political journalist. He worked in the haven of the socialist *Arbeiter Zeitung*, a workers' newspaper based in Austria. It was a bold decision to decant from the tranquillity of the Leopoldstadt area of Vienna to the melting pot of German politics that was Munich.

A rising writer, Gaggs gained notoriety for his forthright articles about the anti-Semitism fermenting beneath the veneer of respectability in Austro-German society. A brave idealist determined to make a positive difference, Gaggs was invited by his close friend and fellow journalist, Edmund Goldschagg, to voice his informed and compelling condemnations against the Far Right in the *Münchner Post*: the primary 'Marxist' publication of the Social Democrat Party. Their main aim was to promote non-revolutionary, peaceful democracy.

Herbert Gaggs and his wife, Marie, moved into the upscale Bohemian district of *Maxvorstadt* in central Munich. For good reason, they kept a quiet and watchful way of life. Since 1921, the Münchner Post had led a vigorous fight against violence, oppression, and anti-Semitism from the Far Right. Specifically, from Adolf Hitler. His National Socialist Party faced numerous critical articles revealing the Nazi's murderous actions. Hitler was so furious with the paper's criticisms that he dubbed the journalists working on the Münchner Post *'Giftküche'*, the Poison Kitchen.

In 1931, Herbert Gaggs was the first to uncover a Nazi document that outlined the final solution for the Munich Jews. The document was published. Provoking the Nazis was not a safe activity, and the Giftküche was soon to pay a heavy price. Once Hitler was sworn in as Chancellor of Germany in January 1933, the twelve-year opposition waged in the Münchner Post came to an abrupt end. All German newspapers were compelled to submit to the strict control of Dr. Joseph Goebbels, the appointed head of the newly formed Reich Ministry for Public Enlightenment and Propaganda. The era of freedom of speech in Germany had truly passed.

On March 9th, the newspaper's offices were ransacked by the Nazi SA *Sturmabteilung,* and its journalists were arrested. It wasn't their only port of call. Herbert Gaggs had experienced a narrow escape. He returned to the office from a late assignment, just as his colleagues were being hauled off to the Dachau Concentration Camp without trial or ceremony.

Upon seeing the arrests, he grabbed a taxi and rushed to his apartment, where he found his wife, Maria, strangled to death in the ransacked sitting room.

Gaggs was crushed. He was trying to revive Maria's limp body when a Jewish neighbour from the adjoining apartment stormed in and snapped Gaggs out of his daze. The SA would soon return. Aware of the risk of being framed for her murder — or meeting the same fate — the heartbroken reporter grabbed some essentials and hurriedly left the city.

Having safely travelled through Liechtenstein and on to Zurich, Gaggs accumulated a substantial inheritance from his wealthy industrialist father, Irwin. He stayed discreetly in Switzerland, mourning his murdered wife — instead of joining the growing number of Jews fleeing fascist Germany to start a new life in Palestine in 1934, he chose to migrate to Britain.

Gaggs quickly found work in London within The Chronicle group of newspapers — a group he would later own before the outbreak of World War 2.

If Gaggs believed Britain was an island of Jewish tolerance, he was greatly mistaken. Political and social unrest increased due to the Great Depression. The notorious right-wing politician Oswald Mosley formed the British Union of Fascists in 1932, a sinister-looking organisation. His 'New Party' sought to capitalise on the chaos.

Upon arrival in Britain, Gaggs was drawn to the radically politicised working-class East End community of London. It was an area that often sported graffiti exclaiming, NO JEWS ON OUR STREETS. He hoped that his wretched experiences in Nazi Germany would galvanise an active resistance to the Far Right. His new residence of Stepney held a population of 60,000 Jews, the majority of whom were settled refugees from the pogroms of Tsarist Russia, Latvia, the Baltic States, and Poland as far back as 1890.

Gaggs soon set to work on a series of passionate and compelling articles against the dangers of fascism and the rising threat of anti-Semitism in Britain. His swift rise through the ranks of the socialist *London Chronicle* also bolstered his reputation as a defender of the oppressed working classes. However, in doing so, he made many dangerous enemies.

As part of his campaign of intimidation, Oswald Mosley had given notice of intention for his Blackshirts to march into the "Jew ridden and communistic" East End dockside streets on Sunday, 4th October 1936.

On the Sabbath Day before the rally, Gaggs attended a late-evening extraordinary meeting of the Jewish Guardian Defence Committee, held in the Congregation of Jacob Synagogue on Commercial Road. The discussion had centred on passive tactics for thwarting the impending invasion by Blackshirts.

Despite numerous warnings, Gaggs was dismissive of the dangers of the night. At the end of the meeting, he started the short walk home alone along the eerily lit West Arbour Street.

Within sight of his house on Alward Street, Gaggs' thick clothes kept out the cold but offered little protection against any upcoming attack. A vicious gang of Black Shirted thugs suddenly emerged from the shadows. Gaggs was beaten unconscious with clubs and coshes, but it was a young local psychopath called Walter Dowd and his cut-throat razor that caused the most damage.

Approaching from the other side of the street, Derek Cranighan was on his way home after his evening shift at the local brewery. Without hesitation, he rushed to help the injured stranger.

Cranighan fought off Gaggs' attackers single-handedly as the Jewish reporter lay unconscious in a pool of blood. Fortunately, a local Beat Bobby had heard the commotion and ran to the scene, furiously blowing his whistle. The attackers fled. Cranighan was covered in blood as he pressed his hand against the open wound on Gaggs' neck. The startled policeman ran to the nearby police box to call for help.

It seemed like an age before an ambulance arrived, although the pair were soon on their way to the nearby London Hospital. Gaggs' severed neck injury was stemmed, and a hasty blood transfusion saved his life.

The following day, as Herbert Gaggs lay gravely injured in his hospital bed, the 5,000 men and women of Mosely's Blackshirts set off from Royal Mint Street beside the Tower of London. Their advance was accompanied by a proud singing of an Anglicised version of the Horst Wessel Song: *Die Fahne Hoch* — The Flag on High, the feared anthem of the Nazi Party.

Protected by an equal number of police officers armed with the authority of the State, the fascist marchers proudly flew their Union Flags as they ignored messages of: THEY SHALL NOT PASS, whitewashed onto the pavements.

When the Blackshirts arrived at Gardiner's Corner from Tower Hill, a stand-off ensued, mainly due to the overwhelming numbers on both sides.

The opposition comprised about 200,000 people, a vast working-class "Human Wall" including Jews, Communists, Socialists, Labourites, Christians, and Muslims. A large group of Irish immigrants also supported the cause, many of whom worked at the docks and took the chance to repay the Jewish community, which had cared for hundreds of their starving children during the Dockers' Strike of 1912.

After several hours, the fascist march resumed. They reached the hastily erected barriers at Cable Street but did not advance any further. Cranighan bravely participated in three hours of intense, three-way fighting that broke out as baton-wielding mounted police ran amok amid a barrage of fists, bricks, and bottles.

Mosely had expected to occupy the streets of the East End triumphantly. Instead, the Police Commissioner, Sir Philip Game, ordered the parade to stop. Mosely and his marchers were instructed to turn back, and they retreated in ignoble disarray to the Thames Embankment.

Herbert Gaggs was soon joined in hospital by eighty rioters as eighty-four others were arrested and carted off to Lemen Street Police Station and crammed a dozen to a cell. The working-class people of the East End had triumphed over fascism. The Jewish people had stood firm and fought their corner with pride.

Three days after the riot, Derek Cranighan visited the recovering Herbert Gaggs, where he provided his firsthand account of the 'Battle of Cable Street'. Cranighan also identified Walter Dowd as the local hoodlum who had slashed Gaggs with a cutthroat razor. The police failed to act on Cranighan's tip-off on the night of the attack.

The events surrounding the Battle of Cable Street served as a lesson to Herbert Gaggs. Nobody would take liberties with him in the future. Just five months later, Derek Cranighan noticed a small article in the London

Chronicle describing the apparent suicide of notorious fascist sympathiser Walter Dowd. The local thug was found hanging from a tree in the old Jewish Bancroft Road Cemetery off the Mile End Road. Nobody shed a tear… although Derek Cranighan wore a wry smile while raising an eyebrow of suspicion.

Chapter 19.
Meaningful Engagements

Halfway through smoking a tab as he fidgeted in the connecting corridor on the fifth floor of Kemsley House, Avi looked down at the gold cufflink resting on his right hand. His beige overcoat pressed tightly against the plain cream wall as he loitered for the purportedly stunning female subject of his surveillance.

Joan Baker exited the twin doors of the staff canteen, releasing a salivating whiff of bangers 'n' mash from the lunchtime rush. She removed her red gingham headscarf, freeing her sumptuous, shining brunette hair. Her high heels and balanced posture carried her into a light trot across the stone floor.

Doreen was right about this girl. What a beauty.

Kitchen staff, only brutal in appearance, plodded past Avi, with Joan behind them. Wearing a stiff smile, Avi approached her from behind. 'Excuse me, Miss.'

Joan ignored the request without breaking stride.

'I wanted to ask you ...'

She turned around. 'Ask me what? You've got David's job and David's car. Now you think you can get his girl as well, do yer?' Joan continued onwards.

Avi dropped his cig to the floor. His leather sole obliterated the glowing dimp as he exhaled a grey plume and took up pursuit. With the gold cufflink at the ready, he nipped past and stopped Joan. 'I just wanted to know if this was David's.'

Joan looked down in amazement. 'Where on earth did you find that?'

'It was in the Morris Minor.'

'You found it in his car? The police said it was

searched.'

'Then not very thoroughly.'

'It was his engagement present. We looked all over for that.'

Avi passed it over. 'I am so sorry about David.'

'I very much doubt it, mister, but thanks for the cufflink, it was nice of you. I must be on my way.'

Joan motioned to leave, but Avi blocked her path once more. 'My name is Avi Falco. I am the new Chief Reporter. You must listen to me, please.' He softened his voice. 'I am re-investigating David's death. I wanted to hear your side, nothing else. Please come for a drink and a chat. No strings.' He held up his left hand, showing her his golden wedding band.

Joan hesitated. For the first time, she looked properly at him as another canteen lady sauntered past and asked, 'You all right there, Joanie?'

'Yes. Thanks, Milly, love, I'm fine.'

The city centre's neon lights shone as Avi and Joan approached the terracotta block exterior of Mr. Thomas's Chop House. Its distinctive display of Art Nouveau motifs highlighted the vibrance of the ornate Victorian venue.

With expert stealth, Private Investigator Joe McClay trailed the disparate couple inside.

Clad in a rich glaze of jade green and teapot-brown tilework, the walls matched the similarly extravagant imitation Renaissance artwork ceiling. A regular haunt of the young and the fashionable, the cavernous establishment was chock-full to the brim. The neckties were loud, the music louder.

Through force of habit, and encouraged by a persistent

recollection of his near-fatal stapling by falling roof tiles, Avi scanned the electric blue haze of the smoke-choked bar. He looked for the exits and checked out young faces with their relaxed range of expressions. None of those from previous acquaintance or suspicion aroused his concern.

A young couple signalled they were leaving. Avi took the empty table and guided Joan to a free seat while accepting her best winter coat for temporary custody. He took off his overcoat and stingy-brimmed trilby. He caught the waiter's attention with a friendly smile and handed over the garments for storage.

Joe McClay kept an eye on the unlikely twosome, adopting a casual pose as he blended in against the busy bar. He pulled down on his wide battleship-grey Fedora brim, shading his attractive yet pockmarked, middle-aged face.

A pillar of the magnificent archway provided ample cover for plain-clothed PC Brookes, who also observed proceedings in nonchalant yet privately serious guise.

The couple were sitting face-to-face. It was the first time Avi had truly looked at her. It wasn't challenging to admire her perfect skin and striking film star appearance … looks that made him feel self-conscious in such youthful surroundings.

My word. I'm sitting with the most naturally beautiful young woman, not only in the room but further afield. At twenty-one, she's too young for my taste, but what a doll. I wonder what people are thinking with me sitting with her, old enough to be her father. My, I'll bet he is proud of his daughter's looks. I know I would be. Never mind that, you have a job to do, so get on with it.

The prolific background chatter was amplified by the

echoing, cavernous ceiling as the waiter increased his volume. 'Drinks, sir?'

'Joan?' asked Avi politely.

'Thank you. A lemonade for me, please.'

Avi pondered whether he should have the same? His deliberation was brief.

Sod it. 'And a large brandy, please.'

'Coming up, sir.'

The waiter headed for the bar as *Singing the Blues* by Guy Mitchell blared out of the jazzy Jukebox. Joan's exuberant personality remained stifled by the loss of her fiancé, but she was impressed with Avi's confident manner. Eager to hear his take on things, she made an effort to loosen up. 'How did you know about this place, Mr Falco? I've heard about it, but I've never been in it before.'

'I walk past it on my way to work. I liked the look. The building's exterior reminds me of a restaurant in Vienna I used to adore... although that one was somewhat quieter.'

'Ooh, Vienna, how romantic. Is that where you're from, Austria? David had relatives there. He promised to take me one day.'

'I was born there. Vienna wasn't so romantic by the time the Nazis arrived.'

The waiter quickly attended with the drinks. Avi handed him some money and an invitation to, 'Keep the change.' The waiter smiled.

Joan nodded in thanks for the drink. 'This is the first time I've been out since the night that David ... You know?'

'You were with him?'

'No. He were meant to meet me outside The

Hippodrome in Altrincham. He were desperate to see the latest Hitchcock film. It were closin' that night and it were his last chance to see it. I phoned him at the office just before he left, just to check he were leavin'.'

'Can you remember what David said on the phone when you called?'

'Word for word. I asked him if he was ready to leave, and he said, "Yes, sorry sweetie. I'll be on my way soon. Love you". They were the last words he ever said to me. When he didn't arrive, I thought he might have been sent out on another job at the last minute, so I went 'ome. He were usually late and it 'appened once or twice before, so I were a bit worried, but not frantic.'

Avi nodded.

'The next morning Mr Lewis arrived at me front door. I didn't know what to think. He told me that David was dead. They found his press card in the same pocket as his empty wallet. Mr Lewis went to the scene and then to the morgue to identify him. He noticed his dad's gold watch was missing. David loved his dad, and he loved that watch. At first, I thought it might have been a robbery that went wrong, but Mr Lewis investigated it. He found no witnesses, no suspects, no nowt.'

Joan's eyes welled up. She took out the cotton handkerchief that was tucked in the sleeve of her cardigan-clad blouse and dabbed away a tear.

Joe McClay stared over from the bar with a look of concern.

'I'm sorry, Joan,' said Avi. 'I'm just trying to …'

'No, it's fine. You need to know.'

Avi nodded. 'The pathologist's report backed the police theory that he was drunk when he fell into the canal and drowned. The police said his car was found parked on a nearby lane. The alcohol levels in his blood were those of severe intoxication.'

'Yeah, I know, but that's a joke. David never drank to excess, and Mr Lewis said he wasn't out on a job. Besides, he was scared of water. He wouldn't go near it. He couldn't swim. What was he even doing there? I can't believe it. I won't believe it. I loved him so much. We were made for each other. Everybody said so. He were always so positive … always the optimist.'

'Anyone who drives a convertible in this city must be an optimist.' *Bugger. This is not the time to be flippant.* 'I'm really sorry, Joan. I shouldn't have said that.'

Joan smiled. 'You're right, don't worry. It does rain here a lot.'

She's nice on the outside and nice on the inside.

They both grinned and sipped their drinks. Avi continued, 'Joan, I don't mean anything by this, but if David didn't drink to excess, why was he so drunk at Douggie Fowler's wake?'

'Blimey, you *have* been asking around. David swore blind that his drinks were spiked that night.'

'By Pete Spencer?'

'Peter is an old flame and I know that he wasn't too chuffed when David got Douggie Fowler's job, but if it was him, it was a mistake. I saw David back in a taxi. His house was on my way home. David was a shy lad, but once he was out of his shell, he was quite charming. It certainly broke the ice between us. Besides, Mr Lewis questioned Peter about that night. You could hear the row all the way up to the staff canteen.' Joan finished off her lemonade.

Avi halved his drink and said, 'Just a few more things, please, Joan.'

Joan looked at her watch. She smiled and nodded.

'Do you think David's religion may have had anything to do with his murder?'

'Oh, I doubt that very much. He wasn't one of them orthodox Jews. He didn't look typically Jewish. Not many people knew that he was. I had no idea until he told me once we started courtin'. It wasn't an issue for me, and he never said it was a problem in Manchester. I think most people feel sorry for them ... you know, for what happened in the War. That's why David's got no relatives left. He was brought over here from Poland. I think that the owner of the Chronicle had something to do with it.'

Avi smiled.

Joan took another sip. 'David's original surname was Adamski, but he dropped the last bit so he could fit in more. He did night school for years, learning the English language. He even took elocution lessons so he could lose his accent. It all helped with his writing. He was determined to be successful in England.'

'Was he working on anything big at the time of his ...'

'If he were, he wouldn't have told me. Nobody can keep a secret in that canteen.'

'Do you think that he ever kept any files or records of what he was working on at home?'

'Perhaps. He were always on his typewriter and he did keep files, but I never saw where he put 'em. D'ya really think that David was murdered?'

'I am convinced, but you mustn't tell anybody, particularly in the canteen.'

Joan delved into her handbag. She smiled and pulled out a set of keys. 'These are for David's bungalow at thirteen Dukes Street, Withington. You're welcome to have a look around. I can't bring myself to go in there ...

you know?'

Avi finished his drink. 'Would you like another?'

'No, thanks, best be off. Me mum will only worry if I'm out late.'

Avi looked over to the waiter. Joan blocked his view.

'D'ya mind if I mention one last thing, Mr Falco?'

'Not at all. Please do.'

'I spoke to Helen about David.'

'Helen?'

'Mrs Turner. You know, the nice lady who sells flowers outside our building. On the day David died, he bought me a bunch of lavender, just like he always did. Why would he buy me flowers and then go drinking somewhere on his own without telling me ... and then fall into a canal drunk in the middle of nowhere several miles from the nearest pub? And there was no bottle found in the car ... or near to the car, for that matter.'

'Did he ever keep liquor at his house?'

'No, not at all. You can see for yourself. I mentioned it to Mr Lewis. So, he went and checked all the off-licences near David's home and those in town near Kemsley House. He also checked all the pubs within a five-mile radius of the canal. He was extremely thorough. It took him ages, bless him. Not one person recognised David's photograph. It just doesn't make any sense. None of it makes the slightest bit of sense to me.'

'Yes, Joan, I think you are right. It is in Mr Lewis's case file. He did ask a lot of people and he visited a lot of pubs.'

Perhaps not the best move for me to double-check his findings.

Joan rose to her feet. The waiter was in brisk attendance. He helped Joan into her coat and then handed

Avi his overcoat, which he slipped on without fuss as they headed for the door.

McClay loitered and then followed. Brookes and McClay failed to notice each other as Brookes headed for the phone booth, hidden in a dark corner by the bar.

Outside on the bustling Cross Street, Avi flagged down a black cab that pulled up quickly. He opened the door, helped Joan into the cab, and paid the driver to take her home.

As frost started to cling to the shop windows, Avi's hands slipped into his overcoat pockets as he turned and headed down the street and around an empty corner.

He reached the secluded back alley where his car was waiting. Unbeknownst to him, he was being followed.

McClay dropped back and lurked in the cover of shadows.

In the flickering reach of a failing streetlamp, Avi wrestled off his dry-cleaned overcoat and dropped it into the boot. He nipped around to the driver's door and got in. A twist of the ignition and a pull on the starter knob … the car didn't start. He pulled out the choke all the way out.

The passenger door opened. McClay jumped into the passenger seat, startling the driver.

'What the …'

'It's all right, keep yer 'air on, I'm not gonna hurt yer lad,' said McClay in his eloquent North Manchester accent.

'I know you're not, lad!'

'I just want a polite word, son. I know what you're up to.'

'Up to? Up to what? What am I up to? Tell me who

you are.'

'I'm Joe McClay, Private Eye. You're chasin' the David Adams story, aren't yer?'

'You worked the case?'

'You'll keep well away from Joan Baker. You don't want to end up in the canal like David Adams, do you?'

'Is that a threat?'

'No lad, it's a fact.'

'What do you know about Adams?'

'Why should I tell you anything?'

'Why should I keep away from Joan Baker? I'm not afraid of the canal. I can swim pretty well when I have to.'

'Okay, I get it, Johnny Weissmuller.'

'No. My name is Avi Falco.'

'Yeah?'

'Yes.'

'I suppose they call you "The Falcon".'

Avi shook his head. 'No. Why should they?'

'You know, Falco the Falcon.'

'What does that have to do with anything?'

'Nothin'. Just wonderin'.'

'Well, no. No, they do not.'

'Why not?'

'I don't know why not. I wouldn't mind if they did … but they don't.'

'Perhaps they should.'

'Perhaps one has to earn such a nickname.'

'Perhaps one does.'

'Perhaps one will.'

McClay smiled and lightened his hostile tone. 'Did Joan tell you that David Adams was murdered?'

'Yes, she did.'

'Well, she's right. Fell into the canal, my arse.'

Avi dug into his pocket and pulled out a five-pound note.

McClay whistled and took the money. 'Swell.'

'Did you consider that it could have been suicide?'

'David and Joan were head over heels wi' each other. Would you top yourself if you had a real doozy on th' arm like Joan Baker?'

'She is a bit young for my taste. Besides, you never know the true expression obscured behind a mask. How about Pete Spencer? Revenge is a strong motivation, and I don't think he likes Jewish people too much.'

'Spencer was the first person I looked at. On the night of the murder, he was sent to Belle Vue to cover the evenin' speedway meetin'. The hat-check girl in the Press Lounge confirmed he was there. It was lucky she fancied him, or she'd never 'ave remembered. He then went on to the Greyhound Racecourse on the other side o' the park. He lost a fair-sized wedge. He always bet with the same bookie, Joe Palomo, and Joe remembered it clearly. He showed me Spencer's bets against the times of the races.'

'A conveniently high-profile alibi. Could he have paid someone to do the deed?'

'With wide-boy Douggie Fowler as his partner, he would've certainly known where to find the right bloke. But I seriously doubt it. That lad would be out of his depth in a bird bath. Besides, he wouldn't have had the money. Joan said he was always on his arse when they were dating. Never had two ha'pennies to rub together. After Adams were murdered, Spencer became a bit of a pest. Following Joan around, mithering for another chance, that sort o' thing. She had enough on her plate without him pestering her. She was frightened and vulnerable.'

Producing two cigs from the cigarette case from his right-hand pocket, McClay continued, 'So I found a quiet opportunity to put me gun to his 'ead.' McClay smiled. 'His stomach dropped like a fat kid on a seesaw.' He put both cigs in his mouth and then took out a Browning automatic pistol from his left-hand pocket. 'Spencer's not got the arse for murder,' added McClay, who put the gun side-on and in line with both the cigarettes ... and Avi's head.

Avi's eyes widened. McClay pulled the trigger. A small flame popped out of the barrel with which he lit both cigs. He handed one to Avi and continued, 'He shit his kecks. Literally. All puff 'n' wind, that one. He's got no bollocks.'

Avi had no idea of the meaning of *bollocks*. He let out a sigh of relief at the fake gun and asked, 'Did the police check him out?'

'He were taken in for questioning, but nothing came of it. He made a complaint against me, and the rozzers warned me off.'

'The police?'

'Yeah, and now I'm warning you off Joan. You're putting her in danger.'

'Why do you care?'

'I'm her uncle. They told me if I didn't keep out of it, Joan will be with David Adams once again ... sharin' the same tombstone on their foreheads. You understand, Tarzan?'

'The *police* threatened you directly?'

'Yeah. It's the way they operate in this town.' McClay smiled mischievously. 'A little dickie bird told me that Adams' car was found five miles away, stuck in a bush just outside Wythenshawe Park. It was moved in the early hours of the next morning by an unmarked tow truck. But the cops reported it was found by the canal near to where he drowned. Why would they lie about that?'

'So, you think the police are involved?'

'I wouldn't put it past 'em. They're either protecting someone, or they've got summat to do with the murder themselves.'

'This is the British Police we are talking about, not the *Schutzstaffel*. What about the robbery aspect? A vintage Rolex is worth a lot of money.'

'Yeah, it was. I saw it with me own eyes. A Rolex Cellini Prince with a distinctive oblong white gold case. Nice ticker. Worth a few quid.'

'Joan Baker told me it had sentimental value. Adams wouldn't have let that go lightly.'

'No, not at all. A bit of a pugilist, was David. He might have been a paperweight, but he sure packed a punch. Amateur boxer. A hell of a scrapper with the heart of a lion. I saw him in an amateur bout not so long ago. He knocked ten bells out of his opponent. A tough little nut to crack, that lad. It wouldn't have been easy to take that off him. Most likely one of the coppers pocketed it at the scene.'

'But wouldn't it have been water-damaged beyond repair?'

'Maybe … maybe not. I wouldn't put anything past those bent bastards.'

Both men drew another puff of smoke into their lungs. Avi wound down the driver's window. 'I have also had a brief chat with Spencer. He thinks the whole thing was a robbery that went wrong, or at least that's the conclusion that Lewis has reached.'

McClay flicked a speck of tobacco from his tongue. 'I don't think this is about a fancy timepiece that got nicked. I have no proof, but Collins is somehow involved in this. Mark my words, lad, Collins is a dirty rascal.'

'The Chief Inspector?'

'He thinks I've dropped it.'

'So as far as the police are concerned, you are out of the game?'

McClay nodded and glanced down at his watch. 'Well, that's me. Must be off. Got to go 'ome and let the dog in. It's non-stop glamour being a private detective. Tara, Tarzan.'

McClay got out of the car and sauntered off on foot towards the bright lights.

Avi tried to start the Moggy, but to no avail.

Hearing the cries of the spluttering engine, McClay stopped in his tracks. He wandered back to the driver's side, his breath steaming in the cold night air.

Avi reached over and wound down the window.

'It's turned bitter. Pull the choke out halfway, then pull the starter knob,' said McClay.

Avi reacted. The engine spluttered and then groaned into action. Pulling out more cash, Avi said, 'Here's the deal. I'll keep well away from Joan, but you must do something for me. Can you take a decent photograph?'

'I can do a bit more than that, lad. I were a top Commando during the War!'

Avi smiled. 'Well then … I suppose they call you "The Commando"?'

A wide grin spread across McClay's face.

Avi's car pulled up 100 yards beyond Adams' bungalow on Kinnaird Road in Withington, South Manchester. The half-moon peeked through a light curtain of grey cloud, offering extra light to the sparse illumination from the ornate wrought-iron lampposts on either side of the deserted street.

A lonely male alley-cat wailed for female attention as Avi took a deep breath and a yellow pill, then got out of the Moggy and back into the cold. He was careful not to slam the door, avoiding attention from prying neighbours. He realised he still clutched his street map and placed it back in the car. Then he headed for the empty detached bungalow. Upon arriving at the front door, he slipped the key into the lock.

Pushing aside a pile of mail that remained untouched on the mat, he stepped into the abandoned bachelor pad. The electrical power was cut off without a trace. Avi felt along the wall for a light switch but failed to find it. He sparked his Zippo lighter. Its pungent odour of paraffin briefly masked the musky miasma that filled his nostrils.

He crept cautiously towards the door at the end of the small hallway. The lounge, already ransacked, was in disarray. Avi examined the clumsy disturbances inside the littered room and then took a seat at Adams' desk. He casually lit a cig, still scanning the devastated scene.

Noticing that the patterned carpet had been disturbed in one upturned corner, he jumped from his seat as the headlights from an approaching car lit the lounge ceiling through the top of the maroon velvet curtains, casting a shadow: a flag of imminent danger.

Avi moved toward the corner. He pulled the carpet backwards to reveal a heavy sunken safe set into the floor. The lock was smashed. He pulled hard on the handle, and it opened. The box was empty.

The Black Hawk had arrived at the abandoned nest. The car's lights were killed. Its doors slammed shut.

Avi was quick to notice. He flipped down the top to extinguish his lighter, and then pinched out his cig.

Either side of the Black Humber Hawk, Stocky and Lofty yanked tight, fawn stockings over their heads. One stayed at the front of the house, the other shifted around the back.

Avi's eyes darted around the room. He lifted a vase from the top of the fireplace, but realised it wasn't heavy enough and carefully replaced it. Increasingly desperate, he strode over to the hearth and grabbed an iron poker, then crouched down behind a cabinet. His heart raced like a grand prix engine as he struggled to control his heavy breathing. Avi was in a fix, and he knew it.

The front door creaked open, followed by cautiously light footsteps. A tall silhouette entered the lounge.

Avi's grip tightened on the iron poker. He jumped out and struck the Lofty intruder hard on the back of the neck. Lofty swayed but remained on his feet. Avi hit him again – this time harder. Lofty went down with a thud.

Frantic banging came from the back door. Empty-handed, Avi rushed to the open front door but slipped on discarded envelopes and crashed into the door frame, landing heavily on his left arm. He groaned, pulled himself to his feet, and staggered onto the driveway.

Avi turned just in time to see a stocky, bull-like man charging straight at him. He sidestepped and kicked his attacker hard in the groin from the side.

Winded and wounded, Stocky collapsed to the floor.

His car keys spilled onto the path.

Avi yelped. The kick sprained his ankle. He picked up the keys and limped quickly to his car, clutching his left arm. Wincing with pain, he struggled into the Moggy and pulled out the starter knob. The car was dead. Seeing the black outlines approaching from the house, he put the starter knob back in, then pulled it out again.

The Moggy refused to start.

He looked in the mirror and saw Lofty homing in while gripping the iron poker. Realising his error, Avi pulled the choke halfway out and yanked once more on the starter knob. The car woke with the yowl of a wounded animal.

Avi winced again as he pressed down hard on the accelerator and hurtled forward from nought to thirty in ten seconds flat.

With another glance in the mirror, he saw a poker ricocheting on the tarmac just short of the Moggy.

Come on, Fangio, let's get out of here, thought Avi as he pulled away amid a bustling cloud of exhaust fumes.

The resigned silhouettes in his wake gave up the chase. One black outline dropped to his knees while clutching his neck. The other hugged his stomach.

'That bastard is for the high jump,' said Stocky.

'Yer not kiddin',' added Lofty.

Taking an immediate turn to ensure he was out of sight, Avi rested his left arm on his lap as he drove away from the built-up borough. He tossed the attackers' car keys out of the window with disdain. A cold chill passed through his body. His hands were shaking. Another yellow pill would mask his latest tremors.

Having plotted a quiet route home with the aid of his trusty map, Avi's car pulled up a few yards behind his neighbour's car. He got out, shook his sprained right foot, and took a couple of tentative steps toward his house, which was partially illuminated by the street lamp.

Sprinkled spats on the pavement confirmed the onset of the latest shower.

Avi stopped and turned.

He went back and opened the car boot. He lifted his overcoat and noticed it had been resting on a cutting of the same patterned carpet in Adams' lounge. One corner was slightly raised. He gave the crudely tailored cutting a second glance and then pulled it back. Hidden beneath were two buff files. One was marked SIMPSON, the other LEHMANN. Despite his pain, Avi was unable to contain a smile at this serendipitous discovery.

Now things will start moving ... Falco, The Falcon!

He tucked the files under his overcoat and checked his watch. It was past midnight. His limp disappeared, and he hurried toward the front door with unstoppable excitement.

Avi dropped the files onto the coffee table in the lounge. Dying embers in the hearth collapsed into wispy ashes as he cleared neatly folded washing from the table. He set out the files and began to read.

After a while, he moved to the kitchen to make a brew, noticing the newly glossed woodwork and, more importantly, that the time had advanced to 1:05 am. He returned to the lounge with a lit cig, his shirt removed to reveal his skin-tight vest and badly bruised left arm. The files were arranged haphazardly as smoke drifted up from the full ashtray next to an empty mug.

The clock on the mantelpiece soon said three in the

morning. He took one last look at a note relating to a Jewish organisation called the 'Nakam' signed 'G'. He studied a newspaper clipping with a picture of Helmut Lehmann and Councillor Norman Simpson shaking hands above an article with the headline: FORMER GERMAN POW WINS MAJOR BUILDING CONTRACT —

Crime and politics, both my specialities. Perhaps that's why Mr Gaggs hand-picked me for the job?

He put the files away, got up, and headed to the door.

With one eye open, Kathy had her back turned as Avi crept into bed. With a frowning face, she asked, 'Have you been drinking again until this time? Aren't we supposed to be taking it easier up here?'

Wide awake, Avi sat upright. 'I think I have stumbled on a *big* story, Kathy.'

'Is it big enough to finish *us* for good? Have you been taking your medication?'

'Yes. Yes, I'm fine, darling.'

Avi tried to spoon her, but Kathy straightened up. 'I mean it, Avraham. This is not how you promised it would be. Perhaps you can spare me some of your precious time in the morning?'

'Yes, yes, of course.'

Avi wasn't paying attention to Kathy's distress. He was still preoccupied with the contents of the Simpson and Lehmann files. Kathy kept talking with fake enthusiasm about her day, but he didn't listen. Despite the pain in his throbbing foot, his thoughts focused on Joan Baker, Joe McClay, and the complicated events at Adams' house ...

Why didn't I lift the mask of the attacker I floored? Why didn't I notice the make and number plate of the big black car the attackers were in?

They must have a connection to Adams. They would

have had time to note my registration. I was too busy trying to run away. I would have taken them both with my bare hands ten years ago. No. I would have killed the pair of them. Some Falcon you are. Falco the Feckless Failure.

Avi looked at Kathy and nodded. While pretending to be interested in the banalities of her day, his negative thoughts persisted. *Even my sex drive has reduced.*

Finally, Avi focused on his wife. He plumped up the pillow, but his eyes remained fixed on the ceiling. His mind was still on overdrive.

There are far more layers to this than I imagined, and there are far more questions than answers. Come on. Keep at it. At least now I appear to have an ally.

Kathy curled back into her original position. Staying at home alone all day had made her mind wander. Unlike her husband, she had never dwelt on the past, especially the most significant chapter of her life, which had been so cruel. This was long since banished to the dark attic of her mind, but old questions had crept back into the light — questions to which she had never dared seek answers. Unlike Avi's predicament, however, her answers were all available. All she had to do was ask.

Her mother knew everything, but she had intentionally kept some of the finer details to herself — details Kathy was never privy to.

Chapter 20
The Good Samaritan

The first year of the War wasn't going well for the Allies or for fifteen-year-old Kathy Cranighan. By May 1940, the Battle of Britain was about to begin, and the threat of a German invasion of Britain's southern shores was a real possibility. Despite the absence of air raids on London and the hundreds of children who had been evacuated to East Anglia, Kathy was sent further inland to another 'safe haven' in the north.

Her quick removal abruptly ended her time at Winnot Farm. However, she remained worried about the Winnots' death threats if she ever revealed their sordid story. Kathy was terrified, while the arrogant Winnots remained unconcerned.

Kathy, determined never to be sent away at the mercy of strangers again, managed to lose her adult guardians on the busy platform at Ipswich station. She sneaked onto the first train back to London, avoiding the train guard's ticket check by hiding in the toilet with one foot pressed against the door.

Arriving unannounced at her doorstep in Stepney on May 13th, 1940, Kathy collapsed into her mother's arms in a state of distress. Thankfully, her headstrong father, Derek Cranighan, had volunteered with the army to 'fight the fascists'. He was away at basic training when his only daughter returned home.

Kathy had planned to keep the abuse she'd suffered to herself, imagining that it was somehow her fault, but the physical pain and fear were too tough to bear alone. Her ordeal was compounded by additional distress. With no previous parental guidance on the 'birds and the bees' to draw upon, Kathy was convinced that her rape would lead to pregnancy and stigma. Now that she was clear of the Winnots, she poured out her heart to her mother, reciting within ten minutes of her arrival details of her horrific ordeal.

Despite her protestations, and after a thorough scrub in the cramped tin bath, her mother escorted her reluctant daughter to Bishopsgate Police Station the following day. Kathy lodged a complaint of rape against farmer John Winnot. She also accused Winnot's wife of aiding and abetting her husband's cruelty.

Regardless of Kathy's emotional sincerity, the young male sergeant leading the interview failed to take her complaint seriously. He made an official note of the accusations but neglected to follow up. Kathy's account was dismissed as another homesick young girl making up a story just so that she could 'go home back to mummy'.

It was clear that Kathy was not pregnant when her father arrived home on leave toward the end of June. Fearful of his quick temper and potential reprisals against the Winnots, Kathy made her mother promise not to tell her father about her ordeal. Instead, Eileen confided in Kathy's grandparents, who discreetly brought Derek Cranighan into the loop. Kathy was never the wiser.

Enraged and heartbroken over the abuse of his precious little girl, Kathy's father was consumed by vengeance. Guilt from insisting on Kathy's evacuation would haunt him until his dying day. As a member of the 18th Infantry Division, Derek realised that his first posting in July 1940 was to East Anglia on anti-invasion duties along the 'Coastal Crust', duties which took place in an army camp not far from Littleby … and the Winnots' Farm.

With no response from the indifferent police regarding his daughter's complaint, Derek Cranighan bided his time. He waited for the right moment to seek his natural justice, when one stormy night in August, his army training as a killer was put to good use. The police found John Winnot's body lying face down on a blood-soaked rug in his ransacked farmhouse sitting room. His neck had been slashed from ear to ear. His penis was cut off and stuffed into his bloody, toothless mouth.

Winnie Winnot was found barely alive, a witness to her husband's gruesome execution while trussed to a chair and gagged. She'd been beaten to within an inch of her life. But ultimately, Derek Cranighan didn't have the heart to kill a defenceless woman in cold blood. His second mistake was to leave behind the bayonet he had used to murder John Winnot. On the handle was a clear print from Cranighan's right index finger.

Once she had recovered enough to be interviewed by police, Winnie Winnot described a tall, dark soldier as the attacker. She then picked out Derek Cranighan from a parade line at Littleby Army Camp. The army informed Eileen of her husband's arrest via telegram.

Adhering to Derek's instructions, Eileen produced the weathered calling card of a Jewish acquaintance her husband had made on that raw night back in 1936. Since that time, Herbert Gaggs had become a senior consultant for the Ministry of Economic Warfare in the creation of the British Special Operations Executive.

Upon receipt of Eileen's call, Herbert Gaggs made his way over without delay from London to Littleby Army Camp. He immediately interviewed Derek Cranighan, who, in the strictest confidence, told him the sorry tale of Kathy's rape and abuse by both Winnots. Derek detailed his murderous attack and how he'd carelessly left behind the finger-printed murder weapon. It would only be a matter of time before the police connected all the facts and interviewed Kathy about her previous complaint against the Winnots.

The next day, Eileen Cranighan opened the front door after a rattle of the brass knocker. Herbert Gaggs introduced himself politely. Once inside the parlour, he warned about her husband's dangerous situation. 'I can assure you that it won't be long before the police arrive here to speak to your daughter about her stay at Winnot Farm. Please impress upon Kathy that when questioned, she must deny her accusations of rape and cruelty against the Winnots. You can leave the rest to me, but please do not tell your daughter about my involvement while she is still a child.'

Eileen agreed. Gaggs raised his black homburg hat, smiled, and left.

Sure enough, later that day, two detectives — one from the Metropolitan Police and one from the Suffolk Constabulary — arrived at the Cranighan's doorstep, questioning Kathy about her previous allegations. In her second interview at Bishopsgate Police Station, Kathy followed Gaggs' instructions as conveyed by her mother. She supported the police's original belief: that she had fabricated her story, was desperately homesick, and wanted to return home as soon as possible.

There had been torrential rain on the night of the murder, and any tracks Derek had made were soon lost, more by luck than judgment. Additionally, the soldiers in Derek's barracks had also supported his spurious alibi, but the local police still possessed the bayonet with the incriminating fingerprint.

Since they held Kathy's original signed accusation, the Suffolk Constabulary colluded with the Met, who dismissed their doubts from her first police interview. With a cast-iron witness, the murder weapon, and his child's original complaint against the victims, Derek Cranighan was formally charged with murder and attempted murder with an identifiable motive.

Two days later, with Cranighan in police custody, the Suffolk police found Winnie Winnot dangling by the neck from the rafters of her bedroom. She had been given the choice of a swift hanging or being burned alive while tied up in her cottage. Winnie Winnot had chosen the noose. Herbert Gaggs' 'Law of natural justice' had prevailed once more.

With Winnie's apparent suicide and Kathy's denial, the police case was leaking considerable water. It finally burst when the Suffolk Constabulary was instructed by the Secretary to the Minister of Economic Warfare, Sir Ross Whitfield, to "lose the incriminating bayonet and release Derek Cranighan back into the army".

The debt to the Good Samaritan had been settled. Herbert Gaggs and Sir Ross Whitfield continued working together to identify talented Jewish recruits for the newly established British Special Operations Executive, including young Avraham Falco, who had recently been smuggled into Britain after a brief exile in Switzerland.

In 1941, the bombing of London temporarily abated, as the Germans' focus diverted to the alternative theatres of Russia and North Africa. Following months of domestic army duties, Derek Cranighan's Foreign Service began when, as part of the 53rd Infantry Brigade of the British 18th Division, he was shipped to Canada in October. After a circuitous route toward South Africa, his unit was diverted to India to join the task force sent to confront the marauding Japanese Imperial army in Southeast Asia.

Chapter 21.
Going to the Dogs

In his corner of the press room, Peter Spencer hammered on his typewriter as Avi entered the door and said, 'Ah, Mr Spencer, just the man. I've been reading up on some of your work.'

'More like *checking* up.'

Avi smiled and shook his head. 'You're a good writer. I like to assess the calibre of my colleagues. What are you working on at the moment?'

Spencer had no choice but to engage. 'I'm doing some research for a social commentary piece on the new prosperity in Britain.'

'New prosperity?'

'With the upturn in the economy, the rise in export earnings, wage rises, and the end of petrol rationing, people will have more money in their pockets.'

'People like Douggie Fowler?'

Spencer shook his head.

'I have been looking for Fowler's old files. A little birdy told me that you cleared them out when Fowler died. At the risk of making obvious assumptions, that would appear to be the action of a man who has something to hide.'

'There was nothing in there relating to the Adams mystery investigation, if that's what you're after. Fowler didn't keep many detailed records for obvious reasons.'

'Obvious reasons? Nothing seems obvious to me right now. I am completely alone in this big, bad northern city. I need all the help I can get. I know you are ambitious and talented. I also have contacts in Fleet Street. Contacts who have helped me before. Contacts who could help you and your career ... if I can put in a good word for you.'

'I've heard plenty of promises before.'

'Not from me. If you are straight, you have everything to gain.'

Spencer glanced at the Adams headline on the wall, and then fiddled with the pencil lying on his blotter. He cleared his throat. 'Fowler was in the Chief Inspector's back pocket.'

'Collins?'

'Yeah, they were at it for donkey's years. During the War, Douggie Fowler was printing forged petrol and clothing coupons, as well as false identity cards, with the paper's typesetter, Sammy Duggan. Sammy was a true artist. They were coinin' it in.'

'What happened to Duggan?'

'He got run over. He was killed by a black cab during the blackout on his way home one night. He never saw it coming.'

Hmm. Yes of course ... Such tragedies were commonplace in the deadly nights of the manic ARP warden.

'Collins was just a sergeant back then. He helped protect Fowler while he sold forgeries to his network of spivs on the black market. The pair of 'em were creaming off protection money from the bookies at Belle Vue and White City. Fowler wrote a good word for the cops at every opportunity. They were more crooked than Bandy Bob's legs. Fowler showed me the ropes, but I wasn't on the take. I'm a hack, not a villain.'

'Fair doos, but why didn't Lewis react?'

'He did. He turned a blind eye to everything. Collins is strong. Lewis is a coward. Rumour has it that during the Great War, Lewis was given enough white feathers to fill a pillowcase. At least Bandy Bob had a proper excuse for not joining the army. Lewis hasn't changed.'

'It is easy to shit your kecks when you are scared.'

Spencer pressed his hands against his flushing red cheeks. 'You've been speaking with Joan Baker's uncle, Joe McClay, the Private Dick. He's not very private, but he's certainly a dick. He thinks he's Humphrey bleedin' Bogart.'

Avi suppressed a smile. 'What can you remember about the day of the murder?'

'It was a Saturday. United won and City lost. That's always a great day to remember for me.'

Avi clenched his fist. 'It was also a *great* day when a good man lost his life! That is the kind of ignorant remark that draws you to my attention, just like your stupid comment in the pub.'

'Uh, yes, you're right. I'm sorry. We sometimes make light of dark things in here. It helps to get us through the day.'

'Go on.'

'Yes. I was working. Got in mid-afternoon. You can check my clock card, and Mr Lewis will confirm it.'

'I have and he has.'

It was a long day. I was due to work through the graveyard shift until the early hours. Since there wasn't much happening on the news front in the evening, Lewis sent me out to The Aces to do a special report on the speedway at Belle Vue. We don't usually cover them in depth, but it was the last meeting of the season— a top-of-the-table clash with the Swindon Robins, so I went off.

'Anything else?'

Yeah. After that, I crossed over to the greyhound racecourse in the park to see the dogs. Lewis was a bit annoyed, but at least I got all the greyhound results firsthand and added them to the sports section the next day, so he was okay with it. Besides, after the dogs, I went straight back to the office to type up the speedway report and the night's national roundup. He got his pound of flesh. Bandy Bob would have logged the times in his register when he came in and out of the office.'

'Yes, I know. I've checked that as well. Your alibi appears to be strong, but you still had motive enough to get rid of Adams.'

'I admit I was jealous of David Adams, and I was in love with Joan. She thinks I spiked his drinks to make him look stupid.'

'Or to show him capable of getting into a drunken stupor for further down the line?'

'I'm not a murderer. Besides, what Collins says goes. If he says that Adams' death was an accident, then it was an accident. If Collins says it was a robbery that went wrong, then it was a robbery that went wrong. Lewis concluded the latter, and I have no reason to doubt him. Perhaps it was a combination of the two? Maybe it has something to do with Adams' mystery investigation?'

'And what do you know about that?'

'Absolutely nothing. That's why it was a mystery.'

Avi shook his head and smiled. 'Of course.'

'He was definitely up to something in his spare time, but … perhaps he stepped on the wrong toes? I don't know, and I didn't want to know. He didn't tell me, and I didn't ask. I haven't looked into David's death, nor was I requested to because of my previous involvement with Joan. Lewis cleared me, and that's good enough. Nevertheless, I've had to put up with the gossip ever since. Believe me, I would be very happy if the real culprit were caught, charged, and then hung, drawn, and quartered. The finger of suspicion has often pointed in my direction, but I swear, I had nothing to do with it.'

'And Douggie Fowler's old case files. You know where they are?'

'Down in the basement, bundled up behind the knackered old generator. I could have destroyed them, but I hid them away for a rainy day. He was as bent as a docker's hook, but it didn't rub off on me. I have nothing to hide. Having said that, I doubt there's anything in the files that can reflect badly on Fowler.'

'Why not?'

'Because he wasn't stupid. He wouldn't have kept anything incriminating. Besides, it doesn't matter. Nobody can touch him while he's rotting six feet under in a big, fat wooden box.'

'True indeed. I think that you are sincere, and I thank you for your candour. I am glad that we cleared the air,' Avi smiled and stretched out his hand. 'No hard feelings?'

Spencer moved to shake, but still unsure of another crushing, he quickly withdrew his hand as Doreen elbowed her way into the room with a steaming brew.

'I didn't play my cards right with Joan,' said Spencer. 'We live and learn. There are plenty more tropical fish in the sea.' Unconsciously parting his lips, Spencer glanced at Doreen.

Avi winked. 'Leave that piece with me when it's finished. I'll see what I can do.'

With a respectful nod, Spencer nipped out of the office to answer a call of nature. Doreen sat down at her desk and sipped her tea as Avi wandered over to the coat stand. Spurred by a rekindling of his recent conversation with Joe McClay, he focused on a point of clarification.

'Doreen.'

'Yes, Avi?'

'What are bollocks?'

Doreen almost spat out her tea. 'Uh, the crown jewels, your love clackers, your man sprouts, you know?'

Avi shook his head.

'Your *testicles*. Why do you ask?'

'Oh, nothing really. Someone told me that Spencer doesn't have a pair. Has he been castrated?'

'Not that I know of love. Ooh, but I wouldn't mind finding out someday,' said Doreen with a cheeky wink.

Avi shook his head and then smiled. He plucked his coat off the hook.

'Where you goin' this time?' asked Doreen. 'Off to see a man about a dog?'

'Uh, no,' said Avi, 'I'm off to see a dog about a man.'

It was Doreen's turn to be bemused. Avi left the office, closing the door behind him.

The phone rang. Doreen picked up. 'Oh, hello Mrs Falco … no, he's just left … yes, lovey … I'll tell him you rang.'

Chapter 22.
Keeping up Appearances?

Mulling over a suitable approach to his forthcoming encounter, Avi sat in his parked car a few houses away from the Lehmann residence.

Lehmann's story was suspicious, and questioning him was justified, but there could be consequences of an aggressive confrontation on the night of the Wolff murder. Avi needed to find a way to get inside Lehmann's mind — a way to provoke him into lowering his guard — a way to tease out the truth.

Dressed in grey shorts and colourful blazers, a group of schoolboys strolled past the Moggy. A school cap was playfully thrown onto Lehmann's driveway. The young victim vaulted over the front gate to retrieve it.

Retrieving another chilling memory from the dark depths, Avi's face dropped into his hands. He closed his eyes and took a deep breath. He relaxed his shoulders. His head twitched as he summoned a mental vision, a vision more vivid than his witness at the time, of the Dachau KZ in the bleak mid-winter of 1940…

… Avi and four bedraggled prisoners were huddled together, shivering violently in the shadow of a snow-covered hut, trying to find warmth under the clear, night sky. Their room was under inspection by the ᛋᛋ guards. The steam of the prisoners' shallow breath created an illusion of illicit cigarettes.

A roving searchlight revealed the ᛋᛋ Unterscharführer in a menacing pose. His legs were spread. His knees were taut. He tapped his bullwhip casually against the shining black leather of his jackboots.

Seeing him, the prisoners removed their caps in a feigned show of respect. Their close-cropped hair plotted a shorter path in the middle of their mottled scalps.

'You are smoking without my permission? All of you, step into the light. Now!' cried the Unterscharführer, summoning the emaciated group towards both him and the barbarous perimeter fence.

The security tower guard observed the movement and trained his searchlight upon the scene.

'Show me your hands,' said the Unterscharführer.

The prisoners opened their palms. There was no cigarette. He remained undeterred. 'Hand me your caps. Come on, get moving, I haven't got all night!' He held Avi's arm to prevent him from handing over his cap, but grabbed the other four caps.

Walking into the neutral zone towards the perimeter wire, the Unterscharführer grinned as he threw the caps over the moat. They landed on the taut grid of barbed wire fastened to the electrified perimeter fence, temporarily denied its lethal voltage of electricity. He stepped back. 'You know the penalty for losing your caps. Retrieve them ... now!'

Without hesitation, the prisoners jumped into the moat and helped each other onto the ascending barbed wire. The tower guard shouted down, 'Unterscharführer?'

The prisoners struggled to retrieve their caps.

The Tower Guard cocked his machine gun as the Unterscharführer backed away, dragging Avi with him.

The Guard repeated, 'UNTERSCHARFÜHRER!'

The Unterscharführer shouted back, 'Guard, they are trying to escape!'

The tower guard opened a short burst of screaming machine gunfire. All four prisoners were mowed down in *a bloody heap.*

Away from the others, one prisoner was still breathing. His arms were caught in the barbed wire. The Unterscharführer took his Walther service pistol from his leather hip holster. 'Hands in the air ... now!'

Unable to move his twisted body, the prisoner raised his head towards the star-strewn sky. The Unterscharführer shot him through the heart. He smirked and then moved towards Avi. He pulled him close. 'Don't worry, your time will come.'

Avi's eyes opened slowly. He rubbed his face and then put on his silver horn-rimmed spectacles and black trilby. Using his index fingers and thumbs as pincers, he tilted the two-inch fur-felt brim over his left eye. He nodded his head and muttered, 'Unterscharführer.' He was ready to face his tormenter.

Avi eased himself out of the car, opened the front gate, and crunched up the pea-gravelled path toward the Lehmanns' door. After a couple of rings of the bell, Miss Whelan, the maid, opened up and was greeted by Avi's sullen face.

'Good morning, madam. My name is Avraham Falco. I am from the Manchester Chronicle. I am here to see Mr Lehmann.'

'I'm afraid Mr Lehmann *won't* be seeing anyone today.'

'I'll come back tomorrow, then.'

'He won't be seeing anyone.'

'Then I'll come back the next day, and the day after that, and the ...'

Helmut Lehmann suddenly appeared at the door; his

left arm wrapped in his sling.

The maid sent Lehmann a look of concern.

'Do not fret, Miss Whelan. Not even an avalanche of roof tiles can stop Mr Falco in his tracks, or so I am led to believe.'

' "That which does not kill us makes us stronger," Herr Lehmann,' said Avi.

'Ah, a quotation from the great Friedrich Nietzsche. Perhaps you are a bit more interesting than you look.' With a sarcastic smile, Lehmann rubbed his chin. 'You can allow him in, Miss Whelan. We do not have anything to hide.'

Avi removed his hat and handed it to the maid, nodding politely. Lehmann led him through an ostentatious marble hallway, past a tall, 18th-century long-case musical clock. He opened the door into the spacious, oak-panelled lounge.

The high, vaulted ceiling assumed a size and scale that exceeded the modest exterior of the house. Avi sniffed at the pungent odour of beeswax furniture polish. A *Bösendorfer* concert piano commanded one corner beside a large antique bookcase filled with an impressive array of classical French poetry, English literature, and the complete works of great philosophers. Avi felt both jealous and impressed.

Above the majestic masonry fireplace, Avi's eyes were drawn to a full-sized reproduction of a classical 15th or 16th-century painting, where the three internal panels were on display. The left panel depicted the Garden of Eden, where God, the creator, introduces the innocent Eve to Adam, allusions to love and lust. The middle panel offered a complex orgy of sinful humanity living a life with moral abandon. The third illustrated the eternal damnation of humans suffering cruelty and torture for debauchery.

The Garden of Earthly Delights by Hieronymus Bosch, if I'm not mistaken,' said Avi.

'No, you are not mistaken.'

'Such a dark vision of Hell and the punishment awaiting nefarious sinners is an interesting choice to display with prominence, particularly if art is to be considered the window to man's soul.'

'I beg to differ. Rather than horrifying, I would describe this as intriguing. Interpretations of the work are often reduced to dire warnings on the perils of life's temptations or an illustration of a paradise lost. Which is it for you, Herr Falco?'

'Oh, I have led a sedentary life so far. I have little experience of life's perils and temptations, nor of paradise lost, for that matter. However, I should imagine that the demise of the paradise planned for the Thousand Year Reich after just twelve years must have been a bitter pill to swallow, Herr Lehmann. And your life's temptations are something I shall endeavour to uncover.'

Lehmann's self-assured smirk diminished as he guided Avi further into the room, where Julia Lehmann sat on an emerald-green Chesterfield couch with Patch, a streetwise mongrel guarding her feet. Sitting on a matching chair with a similarly rigid posture, Glenda Lehmann was positioned furthest from Julia. An elaborately carved Chippendale casing housed the splendid clock that hung on the far wall. Its pendulum emitted a dull, repetitive heartbeat.

Julia moved to rise. Avi smiled. 'Please do not get up, young lady.'

Glenda glared at Avi as Lehmann announced their

unannounced guest.

'Ladies, may I introduce …'

'Mr Falco, the reporter from yesterday. How wonderful,' said Julia with youthful glee.

Patch got up and wandered over to Avi, his tail wagging. Avi stroked the dog. 'I am sorry. We haven't been …'

'Of course, how rude of me,' said Lehmann. 'This is my daughter Julia, and my *liebchen* Glenda.'

Avi glanced at Glenda. He issued a wry smile and asked, 'And the dog. What is the dog's name?'

'Patch,' called Julia. The dog let out a friendly woof. Julia picked him up and sat him on her lap.

Avi grinned and made a mental note of stern-faced Glenda, whose posture and cold demeanour suggested that she would prefer to be anywhere else. He looked back at Julia. 'What are you reading?'

'We are learning about the Second World War at school.'

'I am impressed. History has a lot to teach us. We must always endeavour to find the truth about our past … no matter how difficult it may be to bear. Is that not so, Herr Lehmann?'

'The past is the past. What has happened has happened. It cannot be changed.'

'That is not strictly true. History has been manipulated throughout the ages. It was Winston Churchill who once said that "History is written by the victors".'

'Yes, but as you are aware, I was on the losing side.'

'Of course, but having lost a war doesn't necessarily mean that you are a loser.' Avi looked around the room. 'You have clearly done very well for yourself in such a short space of time. I would love to know the secrets of your success.'

Glenda looked away, Lehmann frowned, and then observed Julia's interest in the conversation. 'Julia, I must apologise, but we have some grown-up talk ahead.'

'But I would like to ...'

Lehmann interrupted once more. With narrowing eyes and a feigned smile, he added, 'Julia. I will not ask you again. Leave now, please. There's a good little girl.'

Intimidated, Julia composed herself. She put both her book and her dog down. She rose and, without further protest, addressed Avi.

'Mr Falco, it is my ambition to become a journalist.'

'Yes, Julia, I am sure you will be excellent,' said Avi with an encouraging smile.

On her way out, Julia returned the smile, but her shoulders were slumped forward. Patch's tail was also down as they both left the room.

'Please, Herr Falco, take a seat,' said Lehmann as he strolled to the walnut cabinet with the panache of a circus showman. Sitting on top of the cabinet was a solid silver tray accommodating a cut-glass decanter and a quartet of crystal glasses. He took out the stopper and poured. 'Sherry, Herr Falco?'

'No, thank you.'

'Of course not, how stupid of me. You prefer brandy.'

'You have impressive powers of observation, Herr Lehmann.'

'Call me Helmut, if you wish.'

'Speaking of the other night, Herr Lehmann, please tell me your version of events.'

Lehmann stroked his chiselled chin. 'Councillor Simpson's driver dropped me back home at around nine o'clock. I was tired and decided to take an early night.

Glenda woke me at around midnight. She heard noises in the lounge. I went downstairs to investigate.' Lehmann pointed. 'I walked in through that door and found a robber pushing my antique silver into a sack.'

'Was he wearing a black mask and a stripy top?'

'Do you choose to mock me in my own home, Herr Falco?'

Avi shook his head.

'I was shot in the arm. It could have been much more serious.'

'What did he look like?'

'He looked like a burglar. Is that not so, my darling?'

'I was upstairs. I heard the shot, and then a great commotion,' said Glenda.

'It must have been very distressing for you, Mrs Lehmann,' said Avi. 'It is strange that your neighbour, Elsie, did not hear the shot?'

Glenda issued a patronising smile. 'Do you mean Mrs Timmins? She is in her 80s. She is as deaf as a post.'

'How about young Julia? She must have been terrified.'

'She was distraught. Julia has spoken to the police. She will not be speaking to the press.'

Avi stood up then sauntered across to the sideboard. He studied the framed monochrome pictures laid on top. They included a shot of young Glenda standing in front of a lorry marked FRED TURNER FARMING. Another photograph from the same era showed Glenda hugging her smiling father.

Avi looked at the imposing oil painting of Fred Turner attired in Freemason's regalia, hanging on a nearby panelled wall. 'I am not surprised Julia was upset by these events. Such a nasty ordeal could certainly disturb a young girl.'

'She has an old head on young shoulders,' said Lehmann.

'How old is Julia?'

'She is fifteen.'

Avi looked at Glenda. 'So, she's not yours then?'

Glenda scowled and was about to reply, but Lehmann interjected. 'No, she is not. Julia was born in Munich during the War. Her mother, my first wife, took ill and died while I was away fighting. I found Julia in an orphanage in 1947. I brought her back to England just after her sixth birthday.'

'You are from Munich?'

'So many questions. Perhaps you will allow me one of my own?'

'Fire away.'

'Who was it that sent you up to Manchester, Herr Falco?'

'Nobody. I filled a vacancy caused by the death of a journalist who drowned in the local canal.'

'I read about that in your newspaper. A promising young man. A pity that too much drink can lead to such a tragic accident.'

'He was murdered. Speaking of tragedy, how did you know the man who was found stabbed to death in the park on Friday?'

'I did not know him.'

'Really? You were both together, deep in conversation in the social club after the opening ceremony.'

'He was a former German POW down on his luck. I offered him labouring work, but he wanted money for nothing, so I sent him on his way.'

'A philanthropist with the locals but no charity for old

comrades, Herr Lehmann? Why was Tommy Green so hostile with you at the bar?'

'He doesn't like us Germans.'

'Like your fine grand piano, I am Viennese, Austrian.'

'Yes, of course. I employed Green as a carpenter for a while. He was good at his trade, but he was insolent and kept poor time.'

'Of course. You are accustomed to obedience and hard labour.'

'He was a bad influence on some of the workers, so I had to let him go.'

'Let him go?'

'I fired him. He carries a grudge.'

'So, you think the killer was Tommy Green? It could be seen as an outlandish coincidence that you get shot by a burglar on the night of the murder of a German with whom you had a disagreement just a few hours earlier.'

'What are you implying?'

'As your wife and daughter could testify, I visited here yesterday and noticed blood on the steering wheel of your car. Why would there be blood on the steering wheel of *your* car if you were taken home from the club in Norman Simpson's car? You were later carried out of the house, wounded on a stretcher? I do not accept that you discharged yourself on Saturday and managed to drive such a vehicle with just one arm, apparently still bleeding.'

Lehmann bit his bottom lip but retained his composure. 'I accept that as a journalist, you are tenacious. Such tenacity can lead people into deep water.'

'Like that of a local canal?'

Glenda suddenly spoke up. 'Excuse me, Mr Falco, I wasn't listening. Unfortunately, you don't command my attention. Perhaps that's because you don't appear to be very clever. There is a simple explanation for the blood on the steering wheel. If Helmut had been taken from here by an ambulance, his car would not have been at the hospital for him to drive home. I caused the blood on the steering wheel. I have a weak blood vessel and suffer from involuntary nosebleeds. They are quite regular. I had one yesterday morning, just before I collected Helmut from the hospital at Helmut's request. Those disgusting places make me particularly stressed … and stress can lead to a streaming nose. I used the Mercedes to pick him up. My little two-seater is too small to take Helmut, particularly with his injured arm and with Julia in tow. You saw me upon my return from a shopping expedition with Julia, later that day. That is my blood on the steering wheel. Not Helmut's. I am glad that you drew my attention to it. I shall ask Miss Whelan to clean it, forthwith.'

'So where was Mr Lehmann when I arrived yesterday?'

'He was upstairs in his bedroom, recuperating. May I remind you that he's just been shot. Where do you imagine he was? Up in Blackpool Tower Ballroom, practising his *pasodoble*?'

'That's extremely doubtful, Mrs Lehmann. The Tower Ballroom is currently being restored. You may recall there was a serious fire there last year,' said Avi with some private satisfaction.

'Thank you, Glenda. It is fine,' said Lehmann. 'Let us keep this civil. Mr Falco is a professional journalist. He has to ask questions that may appear stupid. It is part of his job.'

We'll see who is stupid, Herr Murdering Nazi Bastard,

thought Avi as he noticed the scar above Lehmann's right eye. With protraction, he picked up and studied a black-and-white framed photograph of Helmut Lehmann wearing a pristine Wehrmacht uniform. 'I see that you were in the Seventh Army.'

'That is impressive, Mr Falco. How do you know?'

'I recognise the insignia. Where did you serve?'

'Fair is fair. I will tell you my story if you tell me your story first. You must have an interesting tale as a surviving German Jew.'

'I remain an Austrian Jew. My family was trapped in Vienna after the *Anschluß*. Most of them were murdered in Auschwitz.'

'But not *you*.'

'Obviously not. I had already left Vienna to study in England. I ended up working for the British Army.'

'Doing what?'

'I was an interpreter in the signal corps. I helped trap all types of enemy spies. Identifying liars with secrets is very rewarding. That's why I went into journalism after the War.' Avi touched his facial scar.

The lack of reaction on Lehmann's face was noticeable, but his absence of eye contact gave Avi a clue about his growing discomfort. Avi glared into Lehmann's eyes once more and issued the mere hint of a knowing smile. 'Now it is *your* turn, Herr Lehmann. What did you do during the War?'

'My story is unremarkable.'

'Really? Try me.'

'I was just a regular soldier in the Wehrmacht.'

'So, you took the oath of allegiance to Adolf Hitler.'

'It was not an oath of allegiance. It was a personal oath of obedience. Of course, we all took the

Reichswehreid. I had no choice.'

'No choice?'

'I had no choice but to follow orders, one of which was to take the oath. Those who would not take the oath were sent to concentration camps. Others were executed. Some were beheaded.'

'So, you *chose* not to object?'

'I was young and fond of my head. When I was conscripted, I enlisted and took the oath of obedience. Those who chose to object were shamed as cowards. I was not a coward.'

'Oh, but you *were* a coward, Herr Lehmann. A reluctant soldier who blindly followed orders and wilfully closed his eyes to their consequences?'

'Perhaps the conscientious objectors were the bravest in Britain, but it wasn't an option in Nazi Germany. It is a philosophical argument that I am happy to explore. Perhaps I did take the easier way out. That doesn't make me a coward. Army life was harsh. Mortality rates were high. I was caught between two desperate options. It was a dilemma for me to join the army, but I enlisted for my own reasons. I adapted to the circumstances. In my young mind, I was going to die one way or the other, so I chose to take the oath of a soldier, and a soldier has no choice but to follow orders to carry out his duty.'

'Not if his duty is to commit murder and atrocities as the Wehrmacht did in the East. Once the killing started, the Nazis accelerated the violence. They aimed to wipe certain races from the face of the earth with the help of their willing disciples. Is that the real reason why you became a Nazi? To help enforce the Führer's murderous will at your discretion? "From fanaticism to barbarism is only one step".'

'I am aware of Denis Diderot's philosophical claim, but I did not take that step. Despite your insinuations, I was not a Nazi. The Wehrmacht was not the Einsatzgruppen, and I was fighting in the West, not the East.'

'The relative innocence of the Wehrmacht is a contrived German myth. You will know that they carried out numerous atrocities in both the East and the West.'

Lehmann held out his upturned palms and offered a smarmy smirk. 'It was total war. As the English playwright John Lyly observed many centuries ago, "The rules of Fair Play do not apply in love and war".'

'Just because he said such a thing, it does not make it so. Do you possess a moral compass, Herr Lehmann?'

'I do not concern myself with such unnecessary burdens.'

'Then by definition, you are capable of anything.'

'I did not ask to be born, therefore I am not indebted.'

' "I did not ask to be born". That is the petulant riposte of a child to his mother. You were born into the human race whether you like it or not.'

' "Man is born free and everywhere he is in chains".'

'But those chains are *not* yours, are they, Herr Lehmann? Rousseau also spoke of the "Right of the Strongest". Where the reign of inequality destroys man's original state of happiness and freedom. Humanity becomes alienated as the relationship between the rich and poor descends into a violent state of war. This is against the General Interest. But you wish to alienate yourself from the General Interest to be released from your chains. You also know that for the good of humanity, the General Interest must prevail over the individual will. Rousseau also claimed that "The fruits of

the earth belong to us all and the earth itself to nobody".
But that viewpoint is not for you, as it was not for Adolf
Hitler.'

'I do not suffer from delusions of grandeur. I live my
life as *I* see fit because life is a *fait accompli*. From the
moment we are born, we are destined to die.'

'It is how we act in between that determines the path
of our souls.'

'I am an atheist. I do not believe in the soul. We are
not souls who belong to some non-material world. We are
evolved organisms. We do our best to survive in a world
of which we are inescapably a part ... unless we choose
to detach ourselves through individual will or suicide.
Either way, there are consequences, and bleak. There is
nothing before you are born. You live. You die. There is
nothing afterwards. When you are dead, you are dead,
and that is the end — eternal sleep, without the capacity
to dream. We are animals, Herr Falco — no more, no
less. We have no divine right to expect heaven any more
than any other animal, from a lamb to a lion. Life is here
and now, and that life is dictated by the survival of the
fittest.'

'I understand, Herr Lehmann, but God will not judge
animals. Rousseau also claimed that the only difference
between humans and animals is that God gave humans
free will. Free will to choose the right path or not. The
Nazis exercised their free will and carved a pathway to
Armageddon. They became the ultimate protagonists of
man's inhumanity to man. They were worse than animals.
Animals do not torture and kill their own kind. Not even
the strongest and the fittest can survive shackles,
starvation, and slaughter. Your Darwinian theories are
predictably familiar. But it is up to the strong to help and

protect the weak, not to overpower and abuse them. We are all members of the human race. "Those who forgo worldly power will inherit the kingdom of heaven".'

'And what is the kingdom of heaven? I do not have to appease God through his perception of my good behaviour to fulfil an empty promise of a better life after this life. I do not believe in God, and if I do not believe in God, I cannot be accountable to him.'

'So, you have given yourself licence to behave as you see fit without conscience or consequence. Yours *is* the mind of an archetypal Nazi?'

'No. Mine is the mind of individual free thought.'

'Then where was your free thought when you joined Hitler's murderous forces within a totalitarian regime? You have just claimed emotional blackmail. Which is it to be?'

'My way of thinking is clearly different from yours.'

'By different, you mean superior. In your world, we know where that leads if we disagree or fail to conform. I agree with Newton: "For every action, there is an equal and opposite reaction". If God does exist, you *will* indeed be accountable to him.'

'My beliefs are my own, based on my experience. I saw enough carnage on the battlefield to know that God does not exist. Where was your God during the War? Your people have more reason than anyone else to doubt the existence and protection of a higher being. If God exists, then how could the Devil be allowed to run riot all over the world, and for so many years?'

'Who was it that won the War?'

'Yes, but at such a cost! Scores of millions of people — including Jews *and* Germans, good and bad. The key to life is to satisfy your own needs, not the needs of others. I agree with Sigmund Freud's 'Pleasure Principle'. To satisfy my biological and psychological needs, I seek pleasure and avoid pain. But first and foremost, I look after myself above all others. It is human nature. It is the nature of every animal. It is natural to survive.'

'Do your pleasures include inflicting pain? If that is natural, then you are not human ... you are a *monster*.'

' *"Homo sum, humani nil a me alienum puto".*'

Avi shook his head.

' "I am a man, nothing human is alien to me".' Lehmann observed rage brewing in Avi's eyes. 'That is not my quotation, Herr Falco. It is a line from Terence's play *Heauton Timorumenos*. It dates back to 163 BC. Human cruelty has existed since time immemorial and will continue to do so until mankind becomes extinct. You have seen what war can make people become. The brittle crust of human civilisation is shattered as it plummets to the depths of depravity in the struggle for survival during war.'

'The War also brought out the best in people. It is obvious that you did not experience true human compassion and love. My father always used to say, "There is no humanity without compassion".'

Glenda nodded.

Avi continued, 'The Nazis obliterated boundaries of human decency with their atrocities. There has never been such mass murder on an industrial scale. No mercy, just ruthless evil. Genocide is not natural human behaviour — it is unnatural and abhorrent. Human existence must be built on empathy and understanding, not intolerance and hatred. There is good and bad in all of us. The good must prevail for mankind to survive. Otherwise, mankind will destroy itself.'

'But wasn't it the Americans who dropped two atomic bombs on a defenceless, civilian population? And they were supposedly on the side of the righteous.'

'Had he developed nuclear weapons first, Hitler would have done the same and more besides. The Americans dropped those bombs to prevent even greater losses that both sides would have suffered in the event of an American invasion of the Japanese mainland. Hitler would have used nuclear weapons to obliterate people to impose his imperialist will.'

'Perhaps. But maybe the Americans were also flexing their muscles? Perhaps they were showing the world who really has power and that they are prepared to use it, both then and in the future. Were their horrific actions part of your General Interest, Herr Falco?'

'Yes, I would suggest that they were. The Germans had been defeated, and the Japanese had to be stopped at the cost of the fewest number of fatalities. Besides, like the physicist J. Robert Oppenheimer once observed, "The bomb might help to convince everybody that the next war would be fatal". Do not forget that if Hitler and his Nazis had not started the War in the first place, there wouldn't have been a Second World War and any of the carnage.'

'But you appear to have forgotten that the Second World War was already underway. The Japanese invaded China and massacred over two hundred thousand Nanjing civilians in cold blood at least two years before the Germans invaded Poland. All over the world, there will always be conflict, with each combatant believing that they are on the side of the righteous. You also forget that the Russians subsequently developed the H Bomb in '53. We are all at the mercy of the man with the little red button. Now the whole world looks over its shoulder with trepidation.'

'But such a state does not have to prevail. It goes back to a question of empathy.'

' "What is hateful to you, do not do unto others" — is that it, Herr Falco? Your Jewish Talmud? It is a simple rule, but one that is not applied universally … and never shall be.'

'It may well be a simple rule, Herr Lehmann, but genius is often nested in simplicity.'

'But as the deployment of nuclear weapons serves to show, human beings are too complex and diverse for such a simple theory to succeed. Hitler did not see his aggression as hateful. He considered it justified revenge for the Treaty of Versailles.'

Avi's expression turned to stone. He tilted his head to one side, straightened up, and stared into Lehmann's eyes. With slow deliberation, he said, 'Herr Lehmann, you should also remember that justified revenge can also be coveted by the best of men.'

Lehmann frowned. His eyes drifted toward Glenda. No comfort there. He took a much-needed sip of his drink. 'As you stated earlier, "There is good and bad in all of us". There will always be good, and there will always be bad. It is a constant struggle between two opposing forces. Perhaps this is what makes life so interesting? I can see that you are a dreamer. A dreamer who believes in heaven. A dreamer who believes in the providence of God. Have you not heard, Herr Falco? "God is dead".' Lehmann offered a patronising grin.

'I used to believe in heaven. Now I believe only in hell.' Avi looked at the Bosch triptych painting above the fireplace, one finger pointed at the right panel's vision of a Hellscape of eternal damnation. 'You should be careful not to let your life imitate your art, Herr Lehmann.'

Lehmann bowed his head.

Avi continued, 'As for the so-called demise of God, I understand why you would align yourself with Friedrich Nietzsche. Nazi philosophies were riddled with his twisted ideology.'

'Twisted ideology. Is that so? Perhaps you will enlighten me?'

'Nietzsche called for the eradication of Jewish-Christian morality. He believed that "Some are born to be slaves; some are born to be masters." He said, "If God is dead, we must become gods ourselves and create a new set of values," and that "Different biological natures dictate different moral codes." He saw, "The Overman as the blonde beast of prey with the spirit of the lion asserting his will on the weak" — "The *Übermensch* and the *Untermensch*: the superman and the sub-human." Need I go on? Despite the Master Race being smashed and humiliated during the War, do you still see me as the *Untermensch*, Herr Lehmann?'

'No, not at all. You are clearly familiar with Nietzsche's work, but you greatly misunderstand its meaning. When he proclaimed that "God is dead," it was not simply the death of a deity. It also signified the end of the so-called higher values that we humans have inherited — values such as the morality you so evidently cherish. If the present world is the real and only world, we should not limit ourselves to a promise of a future heaven that does not exist. Such values constrain our lives because we remain within their moral boundaries, hoping for something better in an apparent world. But like him, I believe that everything of value is within reach of this world.'

'And where are you without moral boundaries that limit your actions? said Avi. 'You are a Nazi superman running amok in a death camp. Mass murdering people with impunity, simply because they were members of alternative groups whose alien ways you find abhorrent enough to liquidate with contemptuous justification. Genocide without mercy or recourse.'

'No, my confused Austrian friend. It is not, and that is not what Nietzsche meant. His was not a twisted ideology. His was an ideology that was twisted. It was Nietzsche's sister, Elizabeth, and the likes of Alfred Baeumler who interpreted Nietzsche's philosophy as legitimising Nazism. Nietzsche was not a nationalist. He was not a socialist. He was opposed to racial thinking. His idea of a superman was a fundamentally life-affirming way of being. A bearer of meaning in this world. His Superman is the meaning of the earth. "A Caesar with Christ's soul". Nietzsche died 33 years before Hitler came to power. If you had cared to dig deeper, you would have found that Hitler denied Nietzsche's influence. You would know that Nietzsche chastised the "Anti-Jewish stupidity of the Germans". He saw anti-Semitism as immoral. He said, "The Arian influence has corrupted all the world". He claimed that he would "Have all anti-Semites shot!". He also said that, "The Jews are beyond any doubt, the strongest, toughest, purest race living in Europe". I have had time to cultivate my intellect since I was young. These musings of Nietzsche are my influences … not the misguided interpretations of the Nazi creed you recite to accuse me. Nietzsche did not teach me how to think. You assume that because I was a German soldier, I was also a committed Nazi. The two are not mutually inclusive.'

'My assumptions are also based on my previous experiences of the War, Herr Lehmann. To clarify, you are telling me that you attest to Nietzsche's claim that "The Jews are beyond any doubt, the strongest, toughest, purest race living in Europe"? If you believe that is true, instead of just quoting it, you should say it with true conviction. Go on, Herr Lehmann, say it. Recite those words with sincerity that will convince me as I look into your eyes.'

Glenda straightened in her chair.

The steady 'tick tock' of the grandfather clock's pendulum was the only sound in the room.

Lehmann's right eye twitched. He took a deep breath. 'Your juvenile provocations are becoming tedious, Herr Falco. You are firing blanks at the wrong target.'

Avi offered a smile of derision.

Glenda placed her right palm over her mouth to cover a smirk.

Lehmann cleared his throat. A swift glug of sherry rehydrated his palate. Avi took out a cigarette and lit it.

'I would prefer you not to smoke in my house,' said Lehmann.

Avi took a quick drag and blew it towards his host. 'Oh, I'm sorry, I forgot. You wouldn't like me smoking. Body purity and all that.' Before Lehmann could respond, Avi pinched out his cig. 'We appear to have strayed from your *story,* Herr Lehmann, and I am eager to hear it.'

'No, no. Let us continue with our debate. It was beginning to get interesting.'

Avi ignored Lehmann's request. 'You were saying that you were in the Wehrmacht?'

'Yes. I *was* in the Wehrmacht. I spent most of my war in France, and not Russia. I was captured by the

Americans while retreating into Germany. Somehow, I ended up in the hands of the British. They sent me to a POW camp up here.'

'Which one?'

'Snape Farm. A charming little place near Crewe. We were well treated.'

Avi's heart began to thump. His eyes narrowed. His fists clenched as anger churned in his stomach like a sheet in a washing tub, but still, he retained his calm exterior. 'So, you were worlds away from the Nazi death camps?'

'Yes, I was worlds away.'

'Worlds away?'

Avi recognised that this was the moment he had contrived. He removed his glasses and asked aggressively in German, 'What was your rank in the 7th Army?'

'Unterscharführer.'

'Unterscharführer?'

He strode towards Lehmann and stared into Lehmann's face from point blank range.

Lehmann stepped back ever so slightly.

'Unterscharführer was a paramilitary rank used by the ᛋᛋ. The corresponding Wehrmacht rank was *Unteroffizier!* Your charade is over. I know who you are. You tell a good story, Herr Lehmann and that is just what it is — a story. Your time has come Unterscharführer ... I know that *you are a liar!*'

Their faces were now mere inches apart. Lehmann gritted his teeth. 'I told you that I have nothing to hide from you! You are convinced I was in the ᛋᛋ?' Lehmann thrust down his sling and ripped open his shirt, exposing his bare left underarm above his blood-stained dressing. He shouted into Avi's face, *'Then where is my ᛋᛋ blood group tattoo?'*

Avi stepped backwards to see that there was *no ʰʰ* tattoo. There was *no* tell-tale scar.

Aghast, Avi was stunned into silence as Lehmann continued his offensive.

'I am a free-thinking individual, a hard-working entrepreneur, a capitalist, and an intellectual. These are the secrets of my success. I am everything that the Nazis despised. Contrary to the beliefs of Josef Goebbels, money has not enslaved me; it has granted me freedom— freedom to control my life and to be the person I longed to be during the oppressive years of Nazi rule in Germany. If I hated the Jews as you suggest, I would never have invited one into my home, especially one as stupid as you! *You absolute fool!'*

Glenda spoke up. 'Enough, Helmut, enough! Mr. Falco, may I remind you that you are no longer in the British Army. You are a reporter and a guest in our home … but now it is time for you to leave.'

'Yes, yes, I …'

'Are you satisfied now?' Asked Lehmann. 'How dare you come into my home and insult me with such gross accusations?'

Picking up a small bell, Lehmann rang it feverishly. Miss Whelan arrived at once.

'Show Herr Falco out immediately,' demanded Lehmann. 'His welcome has well and truly expired!'

Avi retreated from the room without delay.

The dust had settled. With trembling hands, Lehmann topped his sherry to the brim and downed it in one.

Glenda took silent pleasure as she savoured his undignified fluster.

Lehmann took out an expensively wrapped gift box from a cupboard and handed it to Glenda.

She opened it to reveal a lavish sable fur wrap. Glenda wrapped it around her shoulders and beamed a further smile of satisfaction.

His rage still smouldering, Lehmann glared through the front window. The lingering cloud of the Moggy's blue exhaust wasn't the only toxic residue of Falco's visit. Lehmann had accepted his confrontation with the audacious Jewish reporter without thinking it through. His impetuous decision had let Avi through the front door and then into his psyche. It was a decision he now regretted. Despite calling him a fool, Lehmann now knew that Avi was anything but. Lehmann also knew that he had an adversary with cunning determination and an intellectual calibre he must take seriously.

Chapter 23.
A Quiet Word

Deeply bewildered, Avi drove around the corner from the Lehmann residence and stopped his car by the kerb. The engine still ran as he wound down the driver's window. He filled his lungs with a deep breath. His hands were trembling, and it was also cold. The collected volumes in Lehmann's bookcase were not just for show.

In Avi's mind, the interview with Lehmann had not gone well. In boxing parlance, he imagined that he would soften up his opponent with a few sharp body punches, dizzy him with stern jabs to the forehead, and then hit him hard on the chin with a devastating uppercut. But it was he who had received the sucker punch.

Did you really expect the dragon to melt into submission by lighting its breath? How naïve and stupid you are! How foolish and vain. You know that you should never underestimate your opponent. And now you know not to overestimate your ability. He will fight tooth and nail to preserve his superior existence. An existence he clearly feels befits his stature. He must be clever to be in this position, to have got this far. Perhaps he is too clever for me. Perhaps he is too clever for his own good. He is an arrogant egotist, and there were signs of his true character and identity ... even if the lack of an ᚻᚻ *tattoo suggests otherwise. This will not be an effortless victory. What is it that Gaggs always says? "Nothing worthwhile is ever easy". You must use all the help you can muster.*

From the start of his assignment, Avi's pride motivated his resolve not to rely on his mentor's help, but he understood that "Pride comes before a fall" and decided to reconsider. His defeatist attitude indicated a revised plan of action.

En route to the Press Office, Avi stopped off at bustling Didsbury High Street, crammed with everyday people doing everyday things. He parked up and waited outside a telephone box. Forming a queue of one, he leaned against a high brick wall with his hands in his pockets, staring at his shoes. He looked like a man who had just lost his mother's life savings after a losing streak in a casino.

An elderly man in a flat cap approached, whistling a cheerful rendition of *Pack Up Your Troubles in Your Old Kit Bag.* He stopped beside Avi.

'Cheer up, lad. Might never 'appen,' said the chirpy stranger.

Avi looked up. 'It already has.'

'Well, don't let it get yer down. Whatever it is, I'm sure you'll find a way through. You can't undo what's been done. You just 'ave to make the best of what's left, lad. There are no problems, only solutions.'

'Finding the solution is one of the problems,' said Avi.

The stranger tipped his head with a wry smile.

I'll bet he's a tale or two to tell. I'll bet he's survived the worst of the War and is determined never to let anything bother him again. He's living bonus time without a care in the world. If only I could find that state of mind ... and yet there is no chance of that.

Both men waited patiently in silence as they overheard the final part of an old lady's call. She excitedly told her ambivalent daughter about big news: the price of haddock had been cut by a significant amount, a tanner per pound, at Sproggett's Fishmongers. The stranger grinned. 'Ah well, we'd best run over to Sproggett's and get 'old of some cheap fish then, eh, lad?'

Avi chuckled as the pristine red chamber finally became empty. 'I'll not be a moment.'

The stranger winked. 'It's fine, lad. You take yer time; I'm in no rush. I'm never in a rush. When you get to my age, it's a joy just to be alive, never mind anything else.' He resumed his whistling.

Avi grabbed the phone and made his important long-distance call. The phone beeped until Avi pushed a penny into the slot.

The Paxton House receptionist at Fleet Street took the call. 'Hello, London Chronicle, how may I help you?'

'Hello, it is Avraham Falco. Can you put me through to Mr Herbert Gaggs, please?'

Avi rubbed the back of his neck as he was connected to the owner of the newspaper.

'Shalom, Sir … She is fine, thank you. Could you use one of your special contacts to locate details of a Second World War German soldier named Helmut Lehmann … L-E-H-M-A-N-N … Possibly from Munich. He was Wehrmacht 7th Army in France. He served time as a British POW in Snape Farm near Crewe … uh, Cheshire, I think. Thank you, Sir. I shall be in touch.'

Avi strode into the press office at Kemsley House. He hung up his overcoat and asked Doreen, 'Has Mr Lewis asked for me this morning?'

'No, but your wife rang twice.' Noticing Spencer's presence, she added, 'Take your tablets.'

Avi dipped his head, straightened his tie, and headed for Lewis's goldfish bowl office. The Chief Editor was sitting at his king-sized desk. Avi tapped on the door and stepped in. Declining the offer of a seat, Avi got straight to the point.

'Last night I found a couple of files that David Adams had hidden.'

'Really? Have you had a chance to read them?'

'Yes. Thoroughly. They hold confidential information on Councillor Norman Simpson and Helmut Lehmann.'

Lewis lowered his forehead. 'Pray tell.'

'Adams knew that Simpson ran an illegal black-market meat trade with Fred Turner's farms during the War. It was highly lucrative.'

'That is common knowledge in this city. Some things are best forgotten. The War is over.'

'Indeed. But after the War, Simpson and Turner expanded their operation by smuggling foreign meat through the Manchester Ship Canal Docks. When food rationing ended, they had to find something even more lucrative to keep their henchmen sweet.'

'Henchmen?'

'Anyone with any power in this city is a member of the Freemasons. Adams thought Simpson was up to his old tricks. He questioned the swift rise of Lehmann's building company, particularly as he married Turner's daughter. Turner was also a Freemason. He died two years later.'

Lewis's bloated face turned pink. '*Fred* Turner died in his daughter's arms from a heart attack while Helmut Lehmann was in West Germany searching for his long-lost daughter.'

'That explains a lot,' said Avi.

'Pardon?'

'Nothing.'

Lewis rubbed his tense forehead. 'I have already explained to you that Helmut Lehmann's building company has a solid reputation.'

'Yes, but what if Lehmann and Simpson fixed the new housing prices between them? They could be skimming off money at either end.'

'Possibly.'

'Have you ever considered how a down-at-heel German POW became head of a highly successful building company in less than ten years without substantial financial help?'

'Fred Turner was a very wealthy man.'

'Wealthy enough to get a major building company started? If not, where did Lehmann's finances come from? Was Adams getting too close to the answer? Is that why he's dead?'

'Adams was a loner. I had no idea what he was investigating. Besides, I find a Jew chasing a story of black-market racketeers during the War somewhat ironic, especially as the Jews were the biggest culprits in Britain!'

'Blaming "The Jews" always conveniently shifted shame away from the selfishness and greed of the wealthy British elite. An elite which Simpson and his cronies appear desperate to join.'

'That is utter rubbish.' Lewis's blood pressure began to rise. 'If Adams had confided in me, I'd have told him to stop wasting his bloody time! You are aware of the hardened resentment towards Germans. People act this way out of hatred and spite. People like Tommy Green.'

'I do not believe for one minute that Tommy Green murdered Wolff. He was certainly pugnacious, but he was far too drunk to have been capable. The heavy footprints and length of stride at the murder scene were those of a much larger man. Besides, he didn't have an adequate motive.' Avi took off his glasses and wiped the lenses with a handkerchief. He returned them to the bridge of his nose. 'I went to see Helmut Lehmann this morning to clear up his side of the story.'

'You did what!?'

'I think he was being blackmailed by Wolff,' added Avi.

'Blackmailed? Blackmailed for what?'

'I don't know yet.'

'Then come back when you do!'

Lewis's phone began to ring.

'This will be Mr Lehmann with another complaint.'

Lewis picked up. 'Hello, yes … Mr Lehmann.' He motioned Avi out of the door with a dismissive flick of the wrist.

Chapter 24.
Visitations

The dull clump of the Moggy door announced Avi's arrival at the otherwise empty Labour Club car park on the new Wythenshawe housing estate. A rare shaft of sunlight beamed down from a crack in the blanket of grey clouds, spreading across the flat-roofed, pebble-dashed club building. Avi gained access through the open front doors and then into the unmanned foyer.

The club smelled of a potent mix of stale ale and cigarette smoke. Sparsely populated, the games room had a more relaxed atmosphere. A blend of contented young and older men entertained themselves with calm rounds of snooker, darts, and crib.

Amid the clash of misaimed snooker balls, a retired veteran rolled up a cig in his adopted second home. His plump, black mongrel rested in a familiar pose, sleeping at his feet. The old stalwart was sitting within earshot of the bar, also an off-duty bus conductor was sitting at an adjacent table.

Avi sidled over to the bar and addressed the barmaid. 'Hello. I should like to introduce myself. I am Avi Falco.'

'Hello, Avi, I'm Hetty. Very formal, aren't ya, love?'

Avi looked over to the veteran's table. 'Who is that older gentleman over there?'

'The cantankerous old git with the eye patch? That's old Billy One Eye. The other one is Dave the bus conductor.'

'Thank you.'

'The glamorous woman over in the corner sweeping up the fag dimps is Carol the cleaner. And Walter the window cleaner is outside, skiving by his ladder. Anyone else?'

'Uh, no thank you, Hetty. I think that just about covers it.'

Hetty handed Avi a membership form and smiled. 'Fill that in before yer go, there's a good lad. Members-only in 'ere unless you're signed in as a guest. But seein' as you're so polite, I'll let yer off for now. What can I get yer?'

Billy noticed Avi at the bar and couldn't resist a little dig at the foreigner. 'Bloody 'ell, you've got a nerve showing yer face in 'ere after that rumpus the t'other night,' he said in his seasoned Lancashire accent.

Avi smiled. 'Would you like a pint, sir?'

'Would I like a pint? No thanks, son. Not from a bloody German.'

'I'm not a bloody German; I'm a bloody Austrian.'

'That's even worse.'

'How could that be worse?'

'How do you think I became acquainted with Iris?'

'Iris?'

Dave the bus conductor, grinned.

Billy pointed to his eye patch. 'She's me glass eye! It were you bloody Austrians started t' Great War!'

Avi bowed his head.

'Give him a chance Billy,' said Dave. 'Grand bloke is this. He was on me bus t'other morning. Looked after a couple of old dears. Gave them his brolly for keeps. Proper gent is this lad and generous with it.'

'Aye, all right then. A pint o' best, lad … and a whisky chaser might loosen me tongue. Get yourself the same!'

Avi looked suggestively at Dave.

'It's all right lad. I'll buy me own.'

Avi winked and nodded at Hetty to pull another pint.

He handed her the cash. 'There's half a crown tip for you. Any other non-members been in asking questions?'

'Like who?'

'Reporters, investigators, the police …'

'Not as I know of. And I know all of it, lad.'

Strange, thought Avi, who looked across to the occupied tables once more. *I'd have thought that reporters from other papers would be drawn to this place like bees to a honey pot.*

Billy's frown turned to a smile. 'Reporter, aren't yer? Suppose you want to find out summat about Tommy Green?'

'Yes, please.'

Hetty pushed the tray full of drinks towards Avi who handed Dave a pint and then sat opposite Billy as he passed him his drinks.

Billy supped the head off his pint and then swiped the froth from his lips. 'Not much to say really that you didn't see for yourself. After he'd had his tango with Herman the German, Tommy left with Ronnie Hyland. That was probably when you were out the back o' the club heading Teddy Boy punches. You'd better ask Tommy's mum if Hyland took him all the way home. She's the end terrace on Saxon Street. The one next to Bobby Nobby's house. The one with the tree.'

The knowing bus conductor failed to conceal a smirk at the generous description of the "Tree". 'We're always ribbin' him about that pathetic, bloody saplin'.'

Avi focused on Billy. 'What does Ronnie Hyland do for a living?'

'A bit o' this, a bit o' that. He's got a big flash car. You'd have to ask him how he got it, but I wouldn't. He's pots for rags.'

'Pots for rags?'

'Yer know? He's potty — a right nutter. You don't want to annoy Big Ronnie. He's a nasty piece of work ... a proper baddie.'

Billy and Avi necked their shots in one and then took a gulp from their pints. Hetty approached, collecting glasses. Billy couldn't resist the opportunity for a tease. 'Here she comes, Happy Hetty, club's number one gal!' With a cheeky smile, he broke into song to the tune of *My Mammy*. "I'd walk a million miles for one of your smiles, My Hetty!" Come on, gorgeous, give us a kiss.'

'Bugger off, Billy, ya sad old codger,' said Hetty.

Billy and the bus conductor laughed as she cleared away the empties. Hetty winked as she retreated to the bar.

Billy noticed Avi's genuine smile. 'I saw him give you short-shrift the other night. Underneath it he's champion is Tommy. He likes the drink, but the drink don't like 'im.'

Dave agreed. 'It's not surprising he turned to drink after what happened to his family during the War.'

'I should like to hear, please,' said Avi.

Dave and Billy looked at each other with raised eyebrows and then nodded in unison. Dave took up the story.

'Tommy has several reasons to hate the Germans. Tommy and his younger brother, Eric, joined up together just before the start of the War. Eric was put in the Cheshire Regiment, while Tommy was sent off to join the 7th Armoured Division in the North African desert campaign. Eric was sent over to France with the British Expeditionary Force in 1940. It didn't go well, to put it mildly. The Germans completely overran our boys and were soon in retreat as France fell.'

Billy scratched his forehead. 'Churchill called it "A colossal military disaster", but it could 'ave been much worse.'

'Yeah,' said Dave. 'During the retreat to Dunkirk, Eric's unit joined with the Royal Warwicks, the Worcester Yeomanry, and the Royal Artillery. They'd been ordered to hold a town called Wormhoudt. It stood between the advancing Germans and the retreating Allied Army. Even though they were badly under-equipped, they managed to hold back the enemy and fought to the last bullet. Eric and the other brave lads bought precious time for the famous evacuation from the French beaches. God only knows how many lives they saved. They held Wormhoudt for two days, but by then, they had nothing left to defend themselves with. Even a day earlier, the disaster would have been even more catastrophic. It was a heroic rear-guard action.'

'Well over 330,000 managed to get away in the Miracle of Dunkirk,' added Billy.

'They certainly did,' said Dave with a nod. He took a slug of his pint and continued, 'Anyway, Hitler's crack Waffen ᛋᛋ troops rounded up about a hundred or so British soldiers in the town. They'd finally surrendered in the expectation of being protected by the Geneva Convention.

The Jerrys marched them about a mile to an isolated farm out in the countryside. The prisoners knew they were in danger. The ᛋᛋ had been shooting injured stragglers along the way. Despite protests from the British senior officer, they forced them all into the barn at gunpoint, together with some other French soldiers they'd picked up. The ᛋᛋ threw two stick grenades into the barn, attempting to wipe them all out as quickly as they could. Two brave lads dived on top of the grenades to try and protect the rest from the blast. When the dust settled, the SS noticed that their attack hadn't killed them all, so they ordered the prisoners out of the barn five at a time. They were executed at point-blank range.

But even that was too slow for the SS, so then they machine-gunned the barn. Tommy's brother was among the eighty men massacred, but fifteen were only injured and played dead until the SS left. A few got away out the back of the barn. I knew one of the lads who survived his injuries. He told me all about it after the War.'

'No wonder Tommy hates the Germans,' said Avi, shaking his head.

'That's not the half of it, lad,' Billy replied. 'Tommy were away, fightin' in North Africa when his wife and baby boy were killed durin' Christmas Blitz of Manchester in December 1940. Can you imagine that, lad? The whole thing were an 'orrible tragedy. He lost his big brother, his wife, and his baby in the space of seven months. Tommy never got over it. He can be a bloody nuisance at times. Those that know make allowances, but most people have burdens of their own to take care of. Life goes on, lad.'

Avi nodded. Billy took another drink of his pint. 'As if *that* weren't enough to cope with, Tommy was one of the troops from the 11th Armoured Division that liberated Bergen-Belsen in '45. Did you ever see the newsreels, lad?'

'Yes, I know all about it.'

Julia Lehmann was sitting in a blacked-out, darkened classroom in Altrincham Grammar School for Girls.

Light from the projector flickered across her face. An all-too-graphic history lesson distressed her and her classmates. Tragic music accompanied the sounds of a bulldozer amid the incomprehensible images of the monochrome film, narrated with upper-class English commentary …

"Everyday soldiers of the British Army 11th Armoured Division were given the grim task of clearing away emaciated bodies of the victims of the Nazi atrocities at Bergen-Belsen concentration camp. There were familiar scenes all over the fallen Third Reich as scores of Hitler's death camps were discovered. Names such as Dachau, Treblinka, Ravensbrück, Mauthausen, and Auschwitz are synonymous with the evil that is perhaps impossible to imagine without the harrowing proof offered by these vivid pictures. A tragic shame for mankind to endure."

Julia covered her weeping eyes.

A small Jack Russell Terrier yapped as Avi knocked on the front door of Millie Green's Victorian house. Avi watched the angry little dog urinate against the forlorn sapling in the tiny, weed-strewn front patch. It continued barking aggressively as Millie Green opened the door, dressed in her heavy coat, hair curlers, and tatty slippers.

The blue rinse under her hairnet blended perfectly with the cloud of blue smoke billowing from the corner of her mouth. She frowned as she struggled to keep her dentures in place. Millie observed the canine protest approvingly. 'That's right, Bruno, see him off!'

Avi looked at the little dog, which wasn't much bigger than his Size 9 shoe. He suppressed a smile.

'You pressmen are like bloody leeches,' added Millie. 'Well, yer can bugger off back to where yer bloody well came from right this minute!'

Avi crouched toward Bruno. The dog fell silent. Millie was amazed. Avi smiled. The dog stepped forward to sniff his outstretched hand, instantly licking it while wagging its tail. Then he tried to bite his tail with gyrating frustration.

Avi looked up with a bright smile. 'Please, Mrs Green, I met Tommy in the Labour Club the other night. I don't think he was capable of murdering anyone in his condition. I want to help him. Nothing more.'

She looked him up and down. 'Bruno's a good judge of character. You'd better come in, son.'

They entered the neat and tidy sitting room. The clean and fresh lace antimacassars resting on top of the threadbare two-piece suite were a futile attempt to keep up false appearances. The room was scented with a telling whiff of mildew, which clung to the rotting wooden window frames and the damp cornice mouldings running around the ceiling. A large black-and-white photograph dominated the main wall: smiling Tommy holding his pretty bride on their wedding day.

'A nice picture, Mrs Green.'

'Yeah, she was a good girl was our Rose. She was Tommy's wife. It's my worst regret in life that we didn't have the money to have a picture taken of baby Arthur before the German bomb killed 'em both. Tommy never got to see his son … not even from a photo. The poor little mite was only a week old. It's driving our Tommy bonkers.'

Avi shook his head as he realised why Millie wore a heavy coat indoors. The fireplace was dormant. The coal scuttle was empty. The house was colder inside than out. Millie was warmer outside than in. She tried to put Avi at ease.

'Sit down, lad. Go on love, it won't bite.'

Avi hesitated and then sat at the table by the solitary window. On the windowsill, a black-and-white picture of two smiling brothers in short pants, home-knitted tank tops, and short-sleeved white shirts was displayed. The taller Eric had his arm around his little brother, Tommy — a clear confirmation of the earlier stories. Avi chose not to comment.

'Cuppa char?' asked Millie. 'I think there's a biccy in the canister... Oh, perhaps not. I think I gave it Bruno this mornin' for chasin' off a not-so-brave reporter down the path.'

Avi smiled and looked at his watch. 'No, thank you, Mrs Green, I'm fine. I want to go and see Tommy before the afternoon has gone. I want to find out what happened when he left the club.'

Millie nodded. 'I don't know if anything happened between the club and 'ere. All I know is that Ronnie Hyland bought him home. He carried our Tommy indoors and laid him on his bed. Tommy was out cold. I saw him. He sleeps like a baby when he's pissed. I think that's why he does it half the time.'

'I understand.'

Millie looked into Avi's eyes and smiled. 'We all 'ave our burdens, son.'

Avi nodded.

She continued, 'I let Ronnie out and went to bingo about half-nine. It was good of Ronnie, but it wasn't really like him. Normally, he wouldn't give yer the fluff from his belly button, let alone the time o' day. Bruno was goin' potty in the kitchen. He hates Ronnie Hyland!'

'Did you ever see Tommy's ϟϟ dagger?'

'That bloody knife. I got back from bingo at about eleven. I was late in cos I was gabbin' with Madge next door by the front gate. Anyway, when I got in, I could hear Tommy snorin' his 'ead off. I went into his room to make him comfy. He was in exactly the same position as when I left. He'd pissed his kecks, again — God bless him — but there was no knife.'

Millie stubbed out her fag. Avi reached out with a fresh one. Millie shook her head and plucked the half-smoked stump from behind her ear. 'I'm worried about him, Mr Falco.'

'I could take you to see Tommy in Manchester Prison if you wish, Mrs Green?'

'Strangeways nick? Ooh, no ta, love. I couldn't stand to see him in there. It'd only make him worse. Besides, it stinks o' piss. Send him a kiss from me, will yer, love?'

'Yes, of course, Mrs Green.'

'It's true what they say about you Germans. Polite lot, aren't yer?

Avi smiled wryly as he fished in his coat pocket and handed her a fresh packet of cigarettes. 'Please take these, I'm trying to give up. I thank you for your time.'

Millie accepted with a grateful smile.

The unshaven wreck of Tommy Green stood barefoot in his stark, freezing cell, which was furnished only with a rickety table just about strong enough to take his weight should the need arise. The bare walls were interrupted by a barred, loaf-shaped window set into a tapered concrete block, out of Tommy's reach. In more ways than one, darkness was closing in. Prison Warder Sharpe entered the cell. 'Straighten up, Green, there's a reporter from t' Chronicle 'ere to see you.'

'Don't wanna see anyone,' said Green with a croak.

'He has a message from your mother.'

Sharpe threw down a pair of outsized hobnail boots for Tommy to wear and then guided the handcuffed prisoner with his head bowed along the landing and down two flights of metal stairs.

Avi was sitting at a table and chair in the otherwise empty room. The prisoner and escort entered. Sharpe unlocked Green's cuffs. As if in a trance, Green shuffled toward Avi.

Avi smiled encouragingly, but was shocked to see a man seemingly in the initial stages of pallor mortis. He caught a whiff of Tommy's stale body odour. His stubbled, drawn face told its own story. Green rubbed the sore, blood-red rings on his wrists from overly tight bracelets. He looked up and stared directly through his visitor as his eyes focused.

Sharpe directed the proceedings. 'Sit down, Green. You've got ten minutes.'

Tommy approached the table and sat opposite his visitor. Avi glared at Sharpe, who took the hint, checked his watch, and left the room with a frown.

Avi opened another fresh packet of cigs and offered one to Tommy.

He clasped it in his shaking hand; his fingernails gnawed to the bone.

Avi reached over with his lighter.

The rush of nicotine induced a rare moment of clarity in Tommy. 'Aren't you the bloke from t'other night? The *Austrian*.'

'Ah, yes … at last. Thank you. My name is Avi Falco. I've just been to your mother's house. She is worried but bearing up well. She sends you a kiss.'

Green nodded and then rubbed his eyes with his fists.

'I understand why you might despise me,' added Avi. 'I know of your experience of Belsen. I also have experience of a concentration camp. I was imprisoned in Dachau.'

'Show me your tattoo, then.'

'We were not tattooed in Dachau.'

'No?'

'No. I am here to try to help you, Mr Green. I do not think that you committed this crime, but I must ask some basic questions.'

'Go ahead.'

'Do you have a criminal record?'

'No.'

'Have you ever been in trouble with the police before?'

'Uh, once or twice. I've been arrested for being drunk and thrown in the clink in the local cop shop to sleep it off, but they always let me out without charge.'

'Why is that?'

'I am not violent.'

With a look of incredulity, Avi tilted his head to one side and raised his eyebrows.

'The other night was not normal for me,' said Tommy. 'I don't like that Lehmann bloke. I never liked working for him. There's summat not right about that man and not just that he's a Jerry. Besides, the sound of so many German voices rattled my cage. I'm not violent but I will defend meself if I 'ave to.'

Avi nodded his head. 'I understand, but I have to ask,

194

did you kill Jens Wolff?'

'No. I did not kill Jens Wolff.'

'If you are not violent, why do you carry an SS dagger?'

'Just in case.'

'Just in case of what?'

'Just in case I get attacked. Can't be too careful these days. Flick knives are everywhere. The local ruffians know I have it, so they tend to leave me alone ... that and a bit of bravado, if I'm honest. Besides, people are always asking to see it.' Green shook his head. 'I suppose it's a bit stupid to keep it on me, but it also reminds me of my *so-called* revenge.'

'Revenge? Avi rubbed his chin. 'How did you acquire the dagger?'

'Must I?'

'No. It is up to you ... but I am interested to know.'

With vacant eyes, Green flicked his ash onto the floor, sucked on his cig, and exhaled with pleasure. 'When we arrived at the gates o' Bergen-Belsen, I wouldn't 'ave believed it unless I seen it with me own eyes. It was Hell in barbed wire, set into a forest of Christmas trees. The place was enormous. There was 60,000 starving, dying men and women. Poles, Russians, and Hungarians. Lots of Jews, but mostly Germans: political prisoners. Living ghosts in ragged pyjamas. Filthy, dazed, riddled with typhus and dysentery and God knows what else. A dumping ground of 13,000 unburied corpses dropped all over the confines o' both camps ... 13,000 rottin' bags o' bones and plenty o' other poor souls joinin' 'em by the minute. The stench is stuck up me nose. I'll take it to me grave.'

Green took another lengthy drag on his cigarette. As

he exhaled, his eyes returned to focus. 'I saw some pretty bad stuff while I was in the army … but *that* ungodly place.' He rubbed his temples with both palms. 'Anyway, a few nights after we liberated the camp, there was rumours of a senior ᛋᛋ guard hiding out somewhere in Bergen town. I was in a bar drownin' me sorrows. I took a wrong turning for a piss. I found him in the cellar. Big bloke. Pulled the dagger on me. I was so mad I somehow got it off him.' Tommy revealed a hint of a smile. 'Then I stuck it up his arse and twisted it hard.'

'And that killed him?'

'No. That was when I blew his bastard brains out wi' me gun. But first, I made the bastard suffer.'

Avi smiled with wryness.

'I gave him a lot more of a chance than the ᛋᛋ gave our kid.'

'So I heard. You have my sympathy. Unfortunately, everyone saw you pull the dagger on the German in the club. It doesn't look good.'

'Yeah, but I thought better of it and dropped it before I went for him … remember?'

'Yes. Yes, you *did* drop it. I'd had a few myself. I hadn't realised.' Avi shook his head at his own ineptitude. 'I'd forgotten. That could really help your case. You showed no intent to use it, and you have no criminal record. Did you mention this to your solicitor?'

'Solicitor? That joker.'

'What is his name?'

'Uh … Mr William Rodwell.

Avi took out his pad and pencil.

'I couldn't afford a proper one, so I was appointed a state solicitor. I only saw him for a few minutes in the cop shop. I'd barely told him anything before he said he had to leave.'

'Can you remember what he said about your case?'

'Yeah. The cheeky bastard advised me to plead guilty due to the weight of evidence against me. He said I'd have a better chance of avoiding the swing if I admitted it. I told him to fuck off, and he did. He returned a couple of days later to tell me there'd been a hearing and that it would be taken to trial at Crown Court at a date to be determined. His motion for bail was denied due to the seriousness of the accusation, so I was remanded here.'

'You weren't at the hearing?'

'Mr Rodwell said it was heard in *absentia* … wherever the fuck that is?'

Avi closed his eyes, scrunched up his nose, and shook his head.

'I'm sorry, but I wasn't in a fit state to attend. I've been comin' down off the booze and the guards have been slapping me around a bit.'

Green looked behind him towards the door and lowered his voice. 'They worked me over good in the police cell, but I admitted nowt. Then they transferred me here. I'm sure they keep putting drugs in me food. I keep on seeing things. They're trying to soften me up. The other night, a guard came in and left a length of rope in me cell and a table to climb on. They want me to top meself, but they're wasting their time.'

Avi shook his head. 'I'll have a word with your solicitor tomorrow.'

'Well, the best of British for that.'

Avi took a glance at his watch. 'Going back to the night of the murder, I saw Hyland pick up the dagger in the club when the barman restrained you. Did you have it when you woke?'

'I was so far gone I could 'ardly remember how I got home, let alone the fight. I just about remember Big Ronnie carrying me … but it's strange.'

'What is strange?'

'I've been rackin' me brains. Me memory's in and out, but I could swear he gave it back to me when we got outside the club. In fact, he made a big of a show o' it, that's why I remember. I thought it might have fallen out o' me kecks when he carried me 'ome.'

'Or Big Ronnie might have taken it back?'

'Oh yeah, he could easily 'ave nicked it … *easy*. D'ya think he'd do it … the bastard?'

Avi shrugged his shoulders. 'Does Big Ronnie do business with Helmut Lehmann?'

'Maybe he has since I lost me job. He tells me nowt these days.'

'I understand. I have just one more question.'

Green nodded.

'When you told me your story of the German guard, why did you call it your *so-called* revenge?'

'Killing that Nazi bastard gave me some satisfaction. I try to cling on to it, but it never lasts. My wife and the little un are still buried in Southern Cemetery. They always will be and there's nowt I can do about that.' Green looked down. 'I also used to carry that dagger just in case I ever decided to cut me own wrists … but I could never go through with it. I 'ave to try and look after me mam. I can't leave her on her own. That's why I didn't use it on that German bastard in the club. I'd 'ave liked to kill 'em all, particularly the ϟϟ, but where'd that 'ave got me?'

Avi shook his head as the door opened and Warder Sharpe returned.

'I believe that you didn't commit this murder and I will

do my best to find out the truth, Mr Green,' said Avi.

'It's Tommy. I'm sorry about the other night, Mr Falco.'

'It's Avi and no offence taken, Tommy. Sit tight.'

Green nodded. 'I would do, but there's fuck all to sit on.'

Chapter 25.
Strange Ways

A group of grey-haired, distinguished-looking locals trooped toward the oak doors set in the Portland Stone façade of the Bridge Street Masonic Hall. Councillor Simpson, Chief Inspector Collins, and Bernard Lewis were dressed in civilian clothing for their morning meeting. They passed beneath the square and compasses motif, unaware of a Leica M3 camera's telephoto lens zooming in on them from a stationary black Riley saloon across the road.

Denis Davenport, the Governor of Strangeways Prison, brought up the rear of the party. The group brushed past an officious-looking concierge without acknowledgment as they entered the brightly lit hallway with its majestic barrel-vaulted ceiling supported by stout ionic columns.

As the men disappeared into the main cloakroom with a whiff of expensive cologne, a white Mercedes-Benz pulled up to the kerb. Helmet Lehmann stepped out, prompting another burst of clicks from the Leica M3's shutter.

Inside the grandiose building, the oak-panelled meeting room displayed portraits of prominent Freemasons on high walls. They included the original of Fred Turner, who presided over Helmut Lehmann's lounge.

Simpson, Collins, Davenport, and Lewis had changed into Freemasons' regalia and were seated around a polished mahogany table. The glossy reflection redoubled the shifty images of these flamboyantly, if strangely, attired occupants. There was pressing business to discuss.

As ever, Norman Simpson couldn't wait to impugn Lehmann's character behind his back. 'We need to get shut of that bloody German; he's bad news. This is the second time he's put us in this position. He'll bring us all down, mark my words.'

'It was you and Fred Turner that brought in that "Bloody German" in the first place,' said Collins.

'Maybe so, but he's not fit to be with us now.'

'Not fit to be with us? Don't get all self-bloody-righteous on me. You and Fred Turner were selling condemned meat to local schools when Lehmann arrived on the scene.'

They both looked up at Turner's portrait.

Simpson said, 'I need a payment. I have overheads. We're making at least fifty quid per house on 5,000 houses, but he's the one with all the bloody money.'

Lewis became pragmatic. 'Listen up, brothers. We can't do this without Lehmann or his money. We must be patient. The plan is coming together nicely.' He strolled over to a table and poured four neat single-malt whiskies from a lead crystal decanter, adding a splash of water to each from a Montessori jug.

There was a knock at the door. Collins put his finger to his mouth, shushing his companions. At that moment, Lehmann entered. Lewis offered him a fake smile and a real drink. Lehmann declined the latter as he sat down casually.

Collins was first to assert his authority. 'As your associates, we are keen to learn the story about your German adversary before we might act in your interests once again. Jens Wolff was a former member of the ᛋᛋ. Green wasn't the murderer. Helmut, please tell us what is going on?'

'Wolff was a blackmailer. He thought I was some sort of former top-ranking Nazi.' Lehmann noticed each individual looking at their reflections in the table, avoiding eye contact. He continued, 'Wolff came at me with a scurrilous accusation which would have put all our plans in jeopardy. So, I dealt with him.'

Lewis asked, 'Are you sure there are no more Wolffs to emerge from the forest, Helmut?'

'Yes. I am certain, Mr Lewis.'

Collins looked at Lewis. 'What about your Jew reporter? Even a blind dog finds a bone once in a while.'

'He'll have nothing once this murder goes away. I can control him.'

'Then please do a better job ... or I will do it for you!' said Lehmann.

'Not until I say so,' replied the Chief Inspector indignantly. 'That's the last action you take without clearing it with me. This is my town, Helmut Lehmann, my town. Do you understand me? Your killing of Wolff was slipshod. You should have contacted me before deciding to dump him in the park. I could have made his body disappear without a trace and with no questions asked. Then we wouldn't have to go to such lengths to clear up your bloody mess.'

'Just like how *you* handled the David Adams killing. Why didn't you make his body disappear then? Your cover-up is full of holes, and that Jew reporter won't let it drop. You let your pair of bungling idiot Keystone Kops start this *bloody mess* ... not me!'

With homicidal menace on his face, Collins' eyes widened as he clenched his fists.

'Stop this now!' said Davenport. 'The lodge will not tolerate such language.'

'Calm down, Denis,' said Simpson. 'It *is* a bloody mess. We have much more to worry about than mere profanities, and minor ones at that.'

Lewis saw the threat raging in Collins' eyes. 'Yes, well, perhaps we have all made mistakes, but solutions are in hand. Maybe this is a good moment to take a step back. As I said, I will control Falco.'

Simpson, Lewis, and Davenport took a drink. Simpson went back to the money. 'What about a goodwill payment to keep us happy? There are palms that need greasing.'

'Of course,' said Lehmann. 'I have continued to purchase the necessary properties. You will all be paid very well and very soon, but these things take time. Please be patient. Believe me, my good friends, the rewards will be much greater than you can imagine.'

Collins, Simpson, Davenport, and Lewis looked at each other. Davenport nodded.

'Are the arrangements in place Mr Davenport?' asked Collins.

'Yes. It will be tonight.'

Meanwhile, Avi had arrived early at the office. He had spent most of the morning with his nose buried in Douggie Fowler's cobweb-covered case files, buried in the Kemsley House basement. Although he was disappointed that nothing groundbreaking had come to light, the exercise provided plenty of food for thought. Before leaving the dusty dungeon, he had reflected on his conclusions.

Fowler's style of copy was more tabloid than broadsheet. His often sensationalist stories were popular with a large group of readers and equally popular with the company accountant. From Lewis's point of view,

Fowler's scoops were high in entertainment, on the money factually, and on the newsstands at the kind of breakneck speed Donald Campbell would have admired. Fowler was an efficient old bear instrumental in keeping The Chronicle in the black. Any deviations from journalistic standards worthy of the paper were overlooked.

Avi realised that Spencer might be right. There was something devious about the relationship between Fowler and Collins. Still, there was nothing in the files to suggest a more sinister collusion that had amounted to anything more than mutual backscratching.

Collins had never been the subject of negative comments within Fowler's copy. As Peter Spencer had said, Douggie Fowler's sycophancy reared its head at every opportunity, and this was backed up with positive results. The local crime statistics, to which Fowler had often referred in his articles, had shown that the clear-up rates of crime in Manchester were remarkably efficient during Collins' six-year tenure as Chief Inspector. But if the police were actively involved in the crimes themselves, that was a different story.

The Adams case was now over six months old. In that period, local crime statistics had detailed thirteen murders in the Manchester and Salford conurbation. Twelve had been the result of domestic and alcohol-fuelled disputes, aggrieved wives throttling cheating husbands, aggrieved husbands throttling cheating wives, aggrieved drunkards throttling each other. Each was straightforward. Each was processed efficiently by the police. The armed robbery at Fenton's Jewellers in Piccadilly had left one unlucky shop assistant mortally wounded, but the culprit was soon apprehended. He was a former World War 2 soldier. Had this reflected a taste for violence? To kill was a thrill, an aberration from the banalities of his post-war everyday life. But beware, Avi, beware. The guilty man awaited 'the swing' on death row, sharing a cell in the same wing as Tommy Green in the regimented wrought-iron landing of Manchester's Victorian prison.

Collins' advice in Wythenshawe Park had played on Avi's mind ... *"The easy way or the hard way"*. It wasn't a huge leap of faith to suggest that the Chief Inspector was a manipulator of facts, figures, and the people around him. That was how such men made it to the top of their professions.

It was also clear that Fowler had benefited from a good source of information within the police, and that source was the top brass. Avi realised the need to tap into Collins, either "The easy way or the hard way", preferably the first. A delicate conundrum to solve and to solve quickly. The Adams case was getting colder, and the Wolff case was going nowhere.

Collins was efficient at making problems disappear, but was he the cause of the problems in the first place? Avi knew that he had to ensure he didn't become a problem while somehow advancing the investigation.

Avi arrived back in the office. He went straight to his desk, intending to track down Tommy Green's solicitor. He took out his notebook, but before he could make any calls, Doreen parked a cuppa on his desk.

'Your wife rang. She doesn't sound too well. I'd go and see her if I was you,' said Doreen.

'Yes, but first I need some information.'

'Why don't you get gone and leave it with me. Us girls need a bit of pamperin', particularly when we're ill.'

'Uh, okay. You're right. I'll nip home. I need the details of Tommy Green's solicitor. His name is William Rodwell. Address and phone number if you can.'

'Do you want me to ring it on to your house?'

'No, I'll be back here later. Just leave the details on my desk, please.'

On his way to his car, Avi managed to catch Helen, the flower lady, at the lonely corner outside Kemsley House. So, he was clutching a bunch of Kathy's favourite red roses as he sauntered through the front door. An optimistic 'Honey, I'm home' brought no response.

He searched the house, failing to notice the kitchen's newly finished decoration. From the bottom of the stairs, he heard a stir. He climbed the wooden steps and crept into the master bedroom. It was darkened by the closed curtains hiding Kathy's swollen face, puffed up by sleep and a viral infection. Kathy was tucked in bed. Fresh paint fumes had worsened her condition.

Avi's concern was genuine. As Kathy's eyes opened, his approach was gentle. 'What is wrong, my angel?'

'Don't come near, sweetie, it might be infectious,' she whispered. 'My tummy is rumbling. My head is whirring, and I've been sick a couple of times.' She saw the flowers and smiled. 'Are those for me? Best go downstairs. There's an empty vase in the cupboard under the sink. Put them in some water.'

Avi sat at the end of the bed. 'Never mind, don't come near. You're worth the risk. I was going to go back to the office, but now I'm staying with you.'

'No. Please.'

'If you're still ill tomorrow, I'll phone Doreen in the morning and take a day's leave. I've worked every day since I started, so it shouldn't be a problem. Let me look after you. A day of my special pampering will soon get you right. I'll sleep in the spare room tonight.'

'You have your job to do. Make a good impression. I don't want you taking time off sick. Please stay back. You must go in tomorrow.'

Avi felt a fleeting pang of guilt about his bluff. He'd known that sacrificing the afternoon would prompt Kathy to insist he should put in a full day the next day. What he couldn't have known was that the next day was one Tommy Green would not live to see …

Chapter 26.
Tommy Goes to War

Tommy Green hadn't been immune to the abuse he endured during his time in HMP Manchester. Being an innocent man framed for reasons beyond his understanding was torment enough without facing further victimisation. His broken body had slipped into chronic illness. He had been roughed up several times. The bright lights in his cell had kept vigil at night as the guards rattled his cage, banging a cricket bat against his cell door when he tried to sleep. His nervous system had been on the verge of collapse ever since his arrest.

During Tommy's alcohol withdrawal, Governor Davenport ensured the guards denied him medicine for his severe headaches, vomiting, fever, nausea, and tactile and visual hallucinations. All they provided was a table and a rope, the latter hanging from a conspicuous height. Depression might tempt him with the noose's comforting embrace. But that was their intention, so why make it easy? Besides, he must not give up the fight for survival, especially for his mother's sake. Avi's visit renewed his determination.

Tommy would cling to life at any cost. He had someone in his corner who believed in his innocence. Avi had given him hope, and a bond of trust had formed between them. Tommy would grit his teeth, tighten his fists, and revive his old British Bulldog spirit.

Cut off in solitary confinement, Tommy had lost track of time. Too weak to attempt press-ups, his only exercise was the brief walk from his cell to the visitor's room and back. After his return, the prison guards noticed an improvement in Prisoner Green's demeanour. They reported this back to the Governor. The wooden table and rope were soon removed.

With a sudden official visit from a bona fide reporter, Tommy realised that his captors had decided not to be so brazen in victimising him. They had even left a blanket. Maybe things were beginning to look up?

Tommy had two positions in his cell. The first was to sit on the floor with his back propped against the farthest corner from the heavy metal door, keeping his nose as far as possible from the stench of his two unemptied slop buckets. The second was to curl up on the cold stone floor as he tried to enter a restful sleep. He took comfort in knowing that his conditions were nothing compared to the overcrowded, disease-ridden death camp of Bergen-Belsen. At least he had a room to himself and was fed and watered, even though rations were barely enough to survive.

If the guards had thought that forcing Tommy to lie on the cold floor would cause him undue hardship, they were mistaken. A consummate soldier, Corporal Tommy Green had endured many a night in a frozen slit trench or on a bedroll beneath thirty-two tons of Sherman Tank.

Tommy was always eager to share his War stories with attentive ears, but he couldn't remember most of the incidents or many details while his mind was soaked in alcohol. However, as he gradually freed himself from his self-induced amnesia, his memory improved. With newfound clarity, he spent the lonely hours reflecting stubbornly on his adventures from his army days, muttering to himself like a hermit on a desert island.

It had been twelve years since Tommy had worn his demob suit. He had done more than his fair share for

King and Country. Both he and his brother, Eric, recognised that another world conflict was imminent. A few weeks before Britain declared war on Germany—and despite Tommy being a newlywed—the Green brothers kept their boyhood pact and joined the army together in 1939, but they were sent their separate ways. Tommy's combat service started in 1940.

After six months of desert training, he was sent to the 7th Armoured Division reinforcement camp during the Western Desert Campaign in North Africa. There, he joined the Light Armoured Brigade, the 11th Hussars, known as The Cherry Pickers. Proudly wearing the Desert Rat Jerboa emblem, Tommy remembered writing love letters to his pregnant wife beneath a panorama of stars. Each night, he prayed that God would protect her as their child's due date approached, and that He would keep them safe so he could reunite with them. His prayers were answered. Tommy's childhood sweetheart gave birth to the son they had longed for.

Courageous but not reckless, and as tough as his army ration dog biscuits, Private Green soon lost his fighting virginity amid reconnaissance missions through the wire and into Italian-held territory. He became adept at attacking convoys and ambushing Italian patrols while sending numerous prisoners back to base.

The news of his son's birth reached Tommy by the time of the first 'big show" — Operation Compass, which started on 12th December 1940. Along with 30,000 men from the 4th Indian Division and the Selby Force, Tommy was caught in intense fighting during the effort to recapture the port of Sidi Barrani and the six fortified camps of the Italian Army nearby. The bullet that curved into his right arm wasn't life-threatening, but it delivered a sharp blow to his youthful naivety about his ability to survive, despite the chaos around him. Tommy was a new father trying to stay safe and complete his duty without compromise. Still, the painful wound starkly revealed the cruel randomness of death.

At the end of the four-day conflict, Tommy was being transported from a field hospital when he saw the captured herd of 38,000 Italian and Libyan prisoners languishing in an enormous makeshift compound. He'd only seen such numbers gathered together on the football terraces of Manchester, but this crowd wasn't jubilant. It was a stunned swarm, wearing mixed expressions of fear and relief. They were at the mercy of their captors but also grateful to have stopped fighting. Although he was one of the 624 British forces who were wounded or missing, Tommy began to see the foolishness of all these men, both friend and foe, being sent by politicians to an alien world to fight and kill innocent strangers while their own children, wives, and families waited anxiously back home for reassuring news.

While recovering at the El Arish Convalescent Camp, his new awareness of the overwhelming size and scope of human suffering caused by war had lessened his aggression toward the enemy. But on the night of 22/23 December, Tommy's wife and baby were among the 684 killed in the Christmas bombing raids over Manchester. He was informed of the news by his CO through a delayed message from his mother. The Lord gave, and the Lord has taken away. Tommy's heart died.

Now an empty vessel, he was lost and alone within an army of thousands.

Tommy chose not to be shipped home. The burials of his loved ones had already taken place. North Africa would be the theatre to kill the enemy and seek the vengeance that would sustain his will to live, at least temporarily. Once more, his attitude had shifted. The Italian and German people had allowed fascism to prevail, and their dictators now waged an imperialist war, a war that had already taken away those they had loved and lived for. The enemy was *not* innocent strangers, and they would pay the price for their compliance.

The poor performance of the Italians prompted Hitler to act, sending the Desert Fox, Erwin Rommel, and his Afrika Korps. The Germans offered more vigorous opposition than the Italians. While riding with his unit's light-skinned armoured cars, Tommy was both chased and the chaser in many battles back and forth to Benghazi, a Libyan city that changed hands five times in the next two years between the British and the Germans.

As if fighting the Germans wasn't challenging enough, on 27th June 1942, newly promoted Corporal Green was lucky to survive one of the worst friendly fire incidents of the Second World War, when bombs dropped by RAF Wellington Bombers pounded helpless soldiers for over two hours near the coastal port of Mersa Matruh in Egypt. Since both sides used each other's captured transport, it wasn't easy to distinguish between them. Amid the chaos of the intermingled British, New Zealanders, South Africans, French, Germans, and Italians, Rommel observed, "Even the German units had fired on each other".

In this turmoil, 359 British & Commonwealth troops were killed and 560 wounded. Tommy recalled the terror of being buried alive amid the chaos of bombs and bullets and of being rescued from his shallow grave by a brave

Kiwi soldier who had spotted his plight. He shuddered at the memory of the sand in his eyes and the sand he had swallowed. The gritty remnants crunched in his dry mouth for the rest of the campaign—an excuse for the constant thirst that persisted beyond the War.

Tommy had emerged physically unscathed from the hand-to-hand fighting. But now he remembered killing a German soldier with an attached bayonet, which pierced through the victim's mouth and out the back of his head, and how he had stamped on his foe's face to release his blade. It was a gruesome image he now recalled with a sense of disbelief. How could he have done such a thing without a hint of compassion? From a carefree carpenter to a ruthless killer.

Deep down, he knew. It was one of many animal instincts that had overwhelmed during the struggle to survive. Instincts he had discarded upon returning to Civvy Street, where he had made no effort to put away the past and try to resume a 'normal' life. Tommy Green wasn't consumed by self-pity. He was devoured by despair.

During his time in North Africa, Tommy survived ground battles, artillery fire, and air attacks from needle bullets and bombs dropped by Messerschmitt 109s and 110s.

He toiled in the intense heat of the day and the bitter cold of the night.

He fought in the exposed, corpse-strewn desert terrain.

He endured the scorching sun, burning blisters, melting bully beef, and long stretches of boredom.

He coped with relentless swarms of flies, scorpions, and vipers and suffered frequent diarrhoea.

He cowered in the blinding hot fog of depressing

Khamsin sandstorms, which could howl for days and penetrate every bodily orifice. But Tommy was in his element. The desert also offered numerous opportunities to kill Germans.

After more than two years of desert combat, he became involved in the Second Battle of El Alamein, which began on 23rd October 1942. He took pride in surviving eighteen days of fighting, having charged through a vast German minefield amid machine gun, anti-tank gunfire, and mortar attacks. It was the "Messy, horrid, killing match" that Commander of the 8th Army, Bernard Montgomery, had predicted.

The mass Axis retreat marked a decisive victory for the Allied forces. The Germans alone lost 1,149 dead, 3,886 wounded, and 8,050 men captured. Church bells rang out in Britain for the first time since the disaster of Dunkirk. When Tripoli fell back into Allied hands in mid-January 1943, the victory parade through the Libyan capital was something Tommy's 7th Armoured Division savoured to the full.

Tommy was always grateful to have avoided life-threatening injuries. But in March 1943, he was severely wounded in Tunisia while on the westward pursuit of retreating Germans. During an enemy counterattack in the southeastern town of Medinine, he was struck when an 88mm shell exploded near his position. Pieces of flying shrapnel pierced his chest, luckily missing his vital organs. But when his wounds became infected, he was a camel's eyelash away from death.

After several weeks in a field hospital, he was finally strong enough to fly back home on an army transport plane. He didn't recover in time to join the 7th Armoured Division's landing at Salerno in Italy's "Soft underbelly" in September 1943.

After nearly three years of hiding his emotions in the desert, Tommy Green returned to England to confront the loss of his family. Once a teetotaller, his turning to heavy drinking began the night after visiting the grave of his wife and son.

In January 1944, having finally recovered from his injuries, he was ordered to join the 23rd Hussars of the 29th Armoured Brigade in the 11th Armoured Division in East Anglia. The focus was on preparing for the D-Day invasions and the route to France, where his brother, Eric, was buried in a mass grave at La Plaine au Bois.

Under his Desert Army maxim of 'An old soldier is a cautious soldier, that's why he is an old soldier,' Tommy prepared for 'The Big Push'. With the landing area already secured, he arrived on Juno Beach in Normandy on 13th June 1944, D-Day + 7.

His new division was soon engulfed in the *brocage* of Normandy countryside, with the British Army engaged in a rematch with Field Marshall Rommel in a terrain that couldn't be more contrasting than the desert. The 11th Armoured quickly faced intense German resistance from several elite Panzer Divisions, including the infamous Der Führer Regiment of the 2nd Panzer Division, Das Reich — just two weeks after its troops had massacred 643 residents of Oradour-sur-Glane, including 247 children, then laying it to waste.

The Allies' failure to execute Montgomery's plan to take Caen on D-Day led to fierce battles in and around Caen, Saint-Lô, and Falaise, before the British 2nd Army broke out into the Falaise Plain. The area on the high ground southwest of Caen, between the Orne and Odon rivers, witnessed some of the most intense fighting in Normandy. Once again, Tommy was at the heart of it, advancing against an often-invisible enemy as snipers, machine guns, and distant mortar fire picked off many around him.

While inexperienced recruits often cowered and froze, Tommy had to manage the rush of adrenaline and prevent hesitation that could lead to disaster. The little Mancunian joiner discovered depths of leadership he hadn't known he possessed when cast as a role model to a close-knit group of reluctant young soldiers, offering them guidance, comfort, and support. A paternal role that the Blitz had previously denied him.

Spearheading 'Operation Epsom,' on 27th June, the Scottish Division fought their way to an unblown bridge over the River Odon at Tourville. The Cream of Caledonia suffered heavy losses but bravely created a corridor leading to the lower reaches of what became the infamous Hill 122 — the "Hill of Cavalry" — which dominated the landscape and, more importantly, the approaches to "The Crucible" of Caen. The following day, the 11th Armoured Division took over and faced fierce resistance while advancing beyond the Odon River towards the lower reaches of the coveted slope.

Over the next three days, a series of desperate attacks and counterattacks raged as control of the crest remained elusive. Pinned down amid a hail of mortar bombs and machine gun fire, Tommy briefly felt euphoric invincibility as he took the lead in sneaking up on the machine gun nest that was blocking their advance while causing chaos in the enemy ranks.

With the stealth of a prowling tiger, he crawled around the covered flank of the position, then lobbed a precise grenade that routed the German crew. With a wry smile, he imagined how his accurate spin bowling skills as a schoolboy cricketer had come in handy that day. But his smile soon faded as he recalled the bloody chunk of human flesh he picked from his helmet once the dust settled.

On June 29th, British forces were forced to withdraw from their positions at the summit. In the small hours of June 30th, Tommy and his four fledglings were sent on a reconnaissance mission in the dead of night to assess the German positions.

As dawn approached, his group moved forward, but the weight of a hailstorm of *Nebelwerfer* fire caused his young comrades-in-arms to disappear under a single blow. Tommy was the only survivor. Disoriented with blast concussion and most of his right ear missing, he staggered through the carnage, his head ringing with tinnitus.

A German counteroffensive was soon to retake the hill as troops swarmed forward, but not before Tommy was pulled to safety from the southern face by the 11th Division's motor battalion. Tommy shed a tear as he remembered wishing that he had been killed along with his brave young protégés.

Often sent on reconnaissance missions, Tommy was usually at the front lines. He recalled the many signs of chaos within the whirlwind of battle. The raking hail of machine-gun fire and the flames from flamethrowers spewing deadly bile. The snipers who took a man down silently. The zinging of shrapnel. The deadly shells and tree splinters slicing through the air. The blinding flashes of explosions. The relentless, ear-bursting pressure of exploding bombs all around, of ground-shaking, soul-rattling grenades, mortars, *Panzerfausts*, and shells.

He cowered in memory of the sheer terror of screeching salvos of 'Moaning Minnie' rockets that fuelled the inferno and unleashed violent fountains of earth and stones.

He panicked in the blast's concussion, with men wandering dumbstruck and on the brink of insanity amidst fluttering showers of falling leaves.

He shrank from the screams of flaming comrades climbing to escape from 'brewed up' burning tanks.

He trembled amidst the scattered remains of shot-down planes and was terrified for their crews as he watched them fall to the ground with fuselage and wings ablaze.

He brooded in the aftermath. The eerie silence after the explosions. The helpless tangle of trees. The churned-up landscape littered with half-clothed torsos, butchered limbs, and eyeless sockets in mutilated heads that had once frowned and laughed and smiled and kissed.

He retched at the slaughtered farm animals, and the rancid smell of dead horses covered in flies.

He revisited his battle-hardened state, feeling nothing for those he had killed or for the limp, anonymous bodies of the young dead soldiers from both sides, barely recognisable as his own species, obliterated by booby traps or caught in the innocent-looking harvest fields sown with Teller or Schü mines.

He shivered in the wilderness among abandoned, rusting machinery and the mangled, burnt-out wreckage of smoke-blackened tanks, including Shermans, Cromwells, Panzers, and Tigers.

He tasted clinging dust, dirt, smoke, and diesel.

He smelled the abhorrent reek of raw sewage, of gangrene, of burning rubber, of gunpowder, of cordite, of charcoaled flesh rigid amid a cloying, sickly-sweet stench of death.

He bowed to the bravery of everyone, including his friends who had served with him, but had died alone.

He despaired over the wide range of civilian victims, from children to pensioners.

He regretted intruding into an ordinary French townhouse, the scene of a family sitting impassively at a dinner table, long since dead but without a mark on them. Their untouched corpses frozen in time as if carefully arranged by Satan's window dresser.

He smiled at the passionate renditions of *La Marseillaise*, the flowing Champagne, the *vin rouge*, and the *Calvados*.

He embraced the excited, chest-thumping, flag-waving, flower-throwing, triumphant crowds, expressing undying gratitude in languages he couldn't understand but with joyous expressions that spoke for themselves.

He indulged in a swell of proud Frenchmen and the adoring women with liberal affections. He pitied the denuded harlots with their brutally shaven heads, shamed for their *"Collaboration Horizontale"* during the invaders' occupation, branded by those without sin willing to shave the first head. Many of them deliberately deflected attention from their own inglorious lack of *Résistance*.

He relived "The Great Swan" through France and skirted past the newly abandoned flying bombsites, just as London exhaled a collective sigh of relief.

He remembered passing through Ypres and heading towards the seemingly endless procession of Great War cemeteries, incredulous at the many unheeded lessons of the past.

He retraced the long advance of the infantry and machinery of the 11th Armoured Division as they fought from France to the Low Countries.

He reflected on the bloody capture of Antwerp in Belgium and the march to the German-occupied Netherlands, then through the Ardennes to Germany's Lower Rhine region.

He recounted crossing the mighty Rhine River into Germany after nine chaotic months of combat on foreign soil, where he detested the accusing faces of the 'Master Race' of embittered parochial German civilians and their indignant response to the Allied invasion of their sacred Fatherland.

He loathed their false expressions of innocence, especially after the harrowing liberation of Bergen-Belsen and the man-made horror that lay inside the barbed wire.

He despised those who had looked the other way and buried their heads in Nazi propaganda while living in denial: no eye contact, no admission of guilt, no awareness of the Holocaust, despite the presence of over a thousand concentration camps in Germany and Nazi-occupied Europe. No responsibility for the starving, brutalised hordes of 11,000,000 slave labourers from subjugated countries, which swelled the populations of German towns and cities.

He abhorred those who had stuck out their arms in fascist salute and yet admired the courageous minority who had stuck out their necks: 150,000 brave Germans imprisoned or executed for political resistance.

He rebuked the ᛋᛋ officer in the cellar, having told

him to surrender, and then having no choice but to kill or be killed.

He re-crossed the River Elbe at Artlenburg, renewing his division's task of rounding up over 80,000 Prisoners of War, including twenty-seven Generals, wriggling like sardines in the trawler's net.

He wept at the news of his brother's cold-blooded murder while an unarmed prisoner, and how it broke his mother's heart.

He found comfort in his own humanity, refusing the many opportunities he had, due to shifting circumstances, to take vengeance on the numerous German Prisoners of War.

He collapsed upon hearing the news of his beloved wife's and baby son's deaths, the latter's existence only verified through memories of Tommy's mother and the name carved on a headstone with no recorded age.

Finally, he scolded himself for his many weaknesses, for turning to drink and letting the "Poison of Hate" consume his soul and ruin his life.

It was the end of another exhausting day. With hooded eyes and minimal movement, Tommy grunted as he dragged himself up from the corner and then curled into a ball on the cold floor in the centre of his cell. He carefully draped the old army blanket over his bare feet before closing his eyes.

Tommy was slow to find the relief of sleep, but when it came, it was intense and vivid. His mind drifted into one of the strange dreams that had been most common during his time in detox at Her Majesty's pleasure. Once again, Tommy was lost in the bitter battles of his army days. Last night, it was North Africa ...

... Tonight, in Northern France, for the first time, Tommy had successfully fought his way to the top of the coveted Hill 112. With victorious arms outstretched like Christ the Redeemer towering above the summit, he took on a superhuman appearance that pushed away the dense black cloak of smoke and debris enveloping the war-torn surroundings. But instead of a victorious ascension, the sweeping view had made his heart pound with fear and anxiety.

To the northeast, he observed the vast footprint of the Carpiquet Aerodrome. He heard the drone of a queue of British fighter bombers charging down the runway and then climbing into a shroud of low clouds, poised to unleash furious fire.

Further to the east, he admired the great chimneys of the Colombines Steelworks, standing proud amid their likely destruction, towering above the rubble of Caen, a historic Norman town devastated by waves of Anglo-Saxon bombers, whose airspace had been obliterated amid an exploding blanket of German flak.

To the south of Caen, he saw a sweeping view across the River Orne into the flat, featureless Caen-Falaise Plain, where vast armies of Allied and Axis soldiers advanced toward him like swarms of locusts devouring the ground as they crawled toward the base of Hill 112.

Turning westward, he gazed over Villers Bocage and the hilly, wooded area that sheltered the heavy artillery, with colossal cannons aimed at the distant 1,200-foot-high Mount Picon. They pointed directly at Tommy like accusing fingers, ready to mete out punishment. Menace loomed from every angle. Gradually, the Germans and the British trained their weapons on the top of Hill 112, all targeting Tommy.

Suddenly, a distant flash illuminated the sky as the mighty naval guns on British warships fired from the English Channel. Three enormous silver warheads speared toward him like arrows from an angry tribe of Apache warriors. They enlarged as they neared, threatening to obliterate him and send him to kingdom come ...

... At the moment of impact, Tommy's eyes opened as three prison guards rushed into his cell. Slamming a mattress on top of his prostrate body, the first two guards forced him to the floor.

As they pinned him down with all their strength, the third guard gripped Tommy by the throat and, with merciless hands, choked the living daylights out of him.

Tommy Green's nightmare was at an end.

Chapter 27.
Dubious Demise

Never the world's greatest cook, Avi was struggling to juggle scrambled eggs on toast as breakfast-in-bed for Kathy when the phone rang. He snatched the receiver but managed to retain his composure as the eggs began to overheat and curdle. 'Good morning, Avi Falco speaking.'

'Oh, good,' said Doreen. 'Listen, Avi love, you need to get over to Bootle Street nick right now. There's a press conference at ten. A big announcement or summat. Mr Lewis says you 'ave to be there.'

A whiff of flaming toast made him snatch it from the grill. Just after the eggs had welded themselves to the bottom of the pan, he grabbed his jacket and left in a hurry.

The heavy slam of the front door woke Kathy from her all-too-brief slumber.

Avi charged up the garden path, noticing his next-door neighbour, Mr Wilkins, polishing his pride and joy car. 'Morning,' called Avi. Wilkins ignored the greeting and kept polishing.

Avi had deliberately parked the Moggy out of sight of the police station. He pushed through the heavy double doors into the makeshift conference room, obtaining a good view from the back row among a muttering mob of male reporters. The cramped Bootle Street police station canteen was buzzing with anticipation.

Plain-clothed CI Collins entered with the jowly-faced civilian, Denis Davenport. Both were flanked by uniformed PCs, Taylor and Brookes.

The sound of scraping chairs against the polished wooden floor grated on the ears as the men in charge settled at the top table to face the gallery of inquisitive journalists.

Collins addressed the microphone and began the formalities. 'Good morning, gentlemen. You know who I am. To my right is Mr. Denis Davenport, the Governor of Strangeways Prison. My formal announcement is as follows.'

Collins hooked on his reading glasses and read from a script … 'In the early hours of this morning, Tommy Green — the chief suspect in the Wythenshawe Park Murder Case — was found hanged in his cell. We have no reason to suspect anything other than suicide. The evidence in the case of the murdered German, Jens Wolff, suggests that Tommy Green was guilty. We have therefore decided that the case is now closed.'

Amid the buzz of inquisitive journalists, Collins stood up to leave. With a sudden rush of blood to the head, Avi arose and called, 'Chief inspector, I was led to believe that this is a press conference, and not a press announcement. Surely you will allow us some questions?'

'Make it brief,' said Collins, sitting back down. Davenport looked down at his sweaty palms and shuffled in his seat.

'Please tell us how and why Tommy Green hanged himself?' said Avi.

'Did you say "Why"?' asked Collins, tempering annoyance. 'I should have thought that was obvious. He hung himself because he was guilty of murder. That is *why*. As for *how*, that's more appropriate for Mr Davenport.'

Davenport cleared his throat. 'Uh, he tied his bedsheets together and hung himself from the bars on the cell window. He was extremely depressed.'

'I visited him in prison two days ago,' said Avi. 'The subject of suicide came up. He told me that a length of rope and a table had been left in his cell to try and encourage him to kill himself.'

'That is an outrageous lie!' cried Davenport.

Collins pinched Davenport's arm.

Avi continued, 'He also told me that he would never kill himself because of his duty to look after his mother. That is why he would have never murdered the German. He knew he couldn't look after her while locked up in jail.'

'I think that you are being rather naïve, Mr, uh …'

'Falco,' said Collins.

'Well, Mr Falco,' added Davenport, 'What we say and what we do are often different things. He was under great pressure. An alcoholic without access to drink. He was at the bottom of the barrel, quite literally. His depression was obvious. He knew he was the murderer, and his remorse over his mother on account of his crime must have been overwhelming. Would you not agree?'

'No, I would not agree,' said Avi. 'He told me that he'd received several beatings at Bootle Street by the police and in Strangeways Prison by your officers, Mr Davenport. He said that drugs had been laced in his food. So much so that as a consequence, he missed his legal hearing.'

'There is an easy explanation for these outlandish accusations,' said Davenport with a patronising smile. 'Understandably, in his desperate predicament, Green was agitated and rather paranoid. He attacked a prison guard and had to be restrained with force. There was some unavoidable collateral damage. The accusation about putting drugs into his food is preposterous. He didn't attend his hearing because he was hallucinating at the time, not because of any disguised medication but because he was an alcoholic in the process of detoxification. Keeping him in his cell was doing him a favour. He was in no fit state to attend his hearing. He would have only made matters far worse for himself.'

'Well, that's not what he told me.'

'Well, he wouldn't have told you the truth, would he? He was looking for a gullible ally. So, congratulations on providing him with one.' Chuckles echoed around the room as Davenport continued, 'Given what you've said about his mother, Green's suicide is even more understandable. He knew his situation was hopeless. His course of action was of no surprise to us.'

'If his suicide is no surprise, why wasn't he kept under surveillance?'

'I don't have enough staff to carry out overnight vigils on murderers!' said Davenport.

'So, not innocent until proven guilty?'

With drawn eyebrows, Collins spoke again. 'This horse is dead, Mr Falco… but still you continue to flog it.'

Another collective chuckle made Avi glance at his shoes.

Collins looked at Brookes. Brookes got to his feet and said quickly, 'Thank you, thank you. I think that is enough. That'll be all now, gentlemen. I thank you for your indulgence.'

As if being chased from the room by the truth, Collins, Davenport, and Taylor retreated without delay. The towering Brooks also departed with a lurching gait very familiar to Avi.

Avi took a brisk walk back to his car. He climbed in and tried to assess the various revelations. Once again, he was dissatisfied with his performance. He hadn't intended to confront Collins and his associates so aggressively or so publicly.

Well done. You let your emotions get the better of you at a time when restraint was needed. Now those bridges are well and truly burned... It will be the hard way, after all.

Avi took a deep breath and swallowed another yellow tablet. Once calmed down, he was able to see things more objectively — but the press conference raised far more questions than answers. Why was Avi the only reporter brave enough to push for answers? He didn't believe a word about how Tommy had died, and surely, he wasn't the only one? The lack of press interest was unbelievable.

Was Avi the only journalist seeking the truth? The others seemed like a bunch of spineless sycophants. Maybe Collins' involvement explained the press's apathy. Did his influence reach that far? Were they all in his pocket? Had they been bribed or threatened? Did he really mean that he and Avi could have a mutually beneficial relationship, both professionally and financially? Was Avi supposed to jump on the Collins train to Corruption Central?

This is England, dammit. Do such things happen here?

Avi took out a handkerchief and blew his nose. Green's death was sinking in. Despite their difficult introduction, Avi had taken a shine to the tough little trooper. He had recognised his courage and plight. He empathised with Tommy's experiences at Bergen-Belsen and the callous death of his brother. He was especially moved by Tommy's story of his wife and baby Arthur, and admired his paternal bond.

Avi's eyes welled with tears as he pondered yet another of life's tragedies — the catastrophic loss of his wife and baby son, a son he never got to meet, hold, raise, love, or cherish — the darkest of burdens to bear. There was not even a picture of his baby to cherish. He had no memories of his son's existence whatsoever. What if the bomb had been a dud or missed the house entirely, and his wife and son had survived? The baby would now be nearly eighteen years old. Tommy might have taught him his trade. They could have started a business together: *Green & Son, Family Joiners*. Tommy could be thriving with a happy, loving wife. No need to drink, no pain to soften. Three wages coming into one household. A comfortable and productive life. Millie Green would not have to eke out a meagre existence on a tiny pension.

Tommy did not kill himself. Now, the Green family is lost to the world, except for poor old Millie, left alone with just a dog for company. How can she survive without her only remaining son? More dark burdens to bear.

Surely this is not how life is meant to be? Those bastard Germans. Nobody wanted a war except them, and look how it all turned out. They've ruined the lives of generations to come.

Tommy Green was the innocent victim of circumstances that shaped his unhappy life. He was also the innocent victim of the circumstances that influenced his untimely death ... and I am going to prove it.

Chapter 28.
Cold Call

On his way back to the office from the press conference, Avi took a detour to check on Millie Green's well-being, but she wasn't home. The police had sent an officer to her terraced house to deliver the grave news about her youngest son, Thomas Stanley Green. Distraught and inconsolable, Millie had taken an early bus to find sanctuary at her sister's house, up in Bury. A group of reporters and neighbours gathered outside her wilting tree, but they were too late to point a finger of guilt. They were disappointed by her absence.

Avi was soon back in the Kemsley House press office. Spencer and Doreen were flirting with each other when he walked in unannounced. Doreen dropped the smile from her face as she said, 'Tommy Green topped himself, eh? They're all sayin' he was as guilty as Crippen.'

'Did you manage to get the details of Green's Solicitor?' asked Avi.

'Yeah. William Rodwell. I've got his details here.'

Doreen passed Avi a note.

'Is the address on Oldham Street?' asked Spencer.

Avi adjusted his glasses. 'Uh, yes, 77a Oldham Street.'

'That'll be Willie Rodwell. When I first heard of him, I thought his name was a joke question that a virgin might ask on her wedding night. When I met him, I realised that he *was* a joke. He's a right slippery character and not worth a piss. Douggie Fowler used him when he got in a couple of scrapes. Why d'ya ask?'

'He was Tommy Green's solicitor.'

'Yeah, well, he might as well 'ave had Stan Laurel as his solicitor. He's next to useless. Another member of the funny handshake brigade.'

Avi shook his head. 'A Freemason. The legal system is riddled with 'em.'

With a look at his watch, Avi rang Rodwell's number. His secretary informed him that Mr Rodwell was out of the office and would be unavailable for the rest of the day.

Doreen took an internal call. 'Yes, Mr Lewis. I'll send him right now.'

Avi looked into Lewis's office and saw a curly finger and an expression of menace. He entered with apprehension. As usual, Lewis was not amused. 'This time you've managed to upset not only the Manchester Constabulary, but also Her Majesty's Prison Service!'

'I was only …'

'Don't you dare interrupt me! Chief Inspector Collins has informed me about your behaviour at the press conference. You will write a functional piece for the headline of the evening edition. It will focus on the verified facts. Green was found hanging in his cell. Suicide is presumed. The Wolff murder case is considered closed. I don't want any reference to your list of unsubstantiated accusations. I'm sure that even Mr Gaggs would not tolerate the numerous litigations he would have no hope of winning. Now get out of my office and make sure you get my approval before you even consider sending your article to print.'

It took little time for Avi to write the front-page article, but it was over an hour before he remembered to call and check on Kathy's well-being. She had just about managed to reach the phone in the kitchen from her sickbed, but he had hung up and left the office by the time she called back.

Avi had taken a short trip across town to Oldham Street to verify Rodwell's secretary. When he arrived, the lights were off, and the office was locked for the day. On his walk back to the car, he saw a street vendor's Chronicle billboard with the headline, MAN CRUSHED BY BELLE VUE ELEPHANT! Avi's report on the Green murder had been downgraded as the main story.

With a wry smile, Avi shook his head. Despite Lewis's bluster, Avi's piece on Tommy Green's "Suicide" was never meant to be the headline story, even if he had followed his instructions perfectly and omitted all his controversial accusations.

He should have known from Fowler's files that Lewis would never risk crossing Collins. From the way he handled the press conference, it was clear that Collins wanted to keep this low profile. Lewis was happy to comply. It was time to explore Lewis's relationship with Collins further.

Back in the driver's seat, Avi fished into the glove compartment and looked at his watch. There was just enough time for one more visit before heading home. Sitting in the Moggy with a white badge marked Courier pinned to his lapel, Avi took out a yellow pill and swallowed.

He finished reading Spencer's headline article in the evening edition and lifted the small brown paper package from the passenger seat. He took a deep breath and stepped out of his second-hand car.

The COUNTY MORTUARY sign was lit up in a glamorous blue neon. Carrying the small package wrapped in brown paper, Avi entered the bland but expansive two-storey brick building and headed toward the burly desk clerk whose name badge read SPIKE MULLINS.

Avi's eyes were drawn to the tattoos crudely jabbed into his knuckles, which suggested a dalliance with the Navy or a familiarity with prison life. On the left hand, it said, 'LOVE' and on the right 'HATE'.

Avi adopted a thin Southern English accent. 'Evening gov'. I'm looking for the Coroner's Office.'

Without looking up from his studying of the horse racing form in *Sporting Life,* Mullins replied, 'Give it 'ere. I'll see he gets it.'

'Can't, mate. He needs a specialist surgical tool urgently. More than me job's werf if I don't get a personal signature from the 'ead man.'

Mullins finally conceded an upward glance. 'All right then,' he snapped. 'Left at the end of the corridor, then turn right at the top.'

'Thanks a lot, gov' replied Avi as he strode to the end of the corridor.

A hand-painted calligraphic sign read CORONER'S OFFICE with an accompanying arrow pointing to the left. Underneath it, another sign was marked MORTUARY with an accompanying arrow pointing to the right. Avi turned right. Eagle-eyed Mullins spotted the deviation, picked up his phone and dialled.

Avi trod lightly as he approached the mortuary. The office behind the door was dark and deserted. He pulled out a Swiss Army knife from the package, prised out a hook-shaped pick, and unlocked the door.

PCs Taylor and Brookes stood at ease in front of Collins'

desk, awaiting their Chief Inspector's unofficial instructions. Finally, Collins obliged. 'Get yourselves over to the mortuary. A man fitting Falco's description is snooping around. Make sure you don't kill him. We don't want another dead reporter on our hands. Do you understand?'

'Yes, Sir,' replied Taylor and Brookes in gruff harmony.

Avi edged into the bleak mortuary tainted by astringent odours of formaldehyde and death. The room was partially illuminated by the electric blue glow of a humming fly-zapper with its collection tray.

A mini morgue for flies, thought Avi, who took out his hand torch and flicked it on.

Two covered corpses were laid on separate tables. Failing to notice the name tag tied to the first cadaver's left toe, Avi screwed up his face in revulsion as he lifted the cover of the cyanotic corpse of a middle-aged male of no previous acquaintance. He nodded in recognition of the story that had stolen his headline.

This was the wreckage of the impetuous alcoholic who had managed to get his head caved in, throwing himself under an elephant's ride for children at Belle Vue Zoo, in a vain attempt to rescue his expensive Failsworth Fedora hat from being crushed after a gust of wind had blown it off.

Avi wished he'd covered that gem instead of Pete Spencer; then he wouldn't have rubbed up Collins and his cohorts the wrong way. But at least it spared the tricky interviews with the traumatised children and their equally traumatised parents.

Dropping the cover swiftly back down to rest, Avi

moved on to the next table. He lifted the rubber sheet from Tommy Green's torso. His eyes were drawn to the heavily marked throat. Carefully, he lifted the head, exposing the back of the neck.

Using the same tool on his Swiss Army knife, he had no trouble breaking into the adjoining mortuary records sub-office. He opened a cabinet and flicked through the files, quickly locating those marked David Adams and Jens Wolff. He aimed his torch and hurriedly examined their contents.

Taylor and Brookes strutted over to Mullins' desk. After a brief altercation, Taylor handed Mullins a payoff. He rejoined Brookes, and they marched through the open double doors toward the end of the corridor. Turning right at the top, they yanked fawn silk stockings over their heads and took out large handguns.

The rogue policemen sneaked into the mortuary with unusual stealth. They crept toward the faint light in the mortuary records sub-office, but a creaking floorboard betrayed them.

Avi switched off the torch and frantically searched for a place to hide. The best he could find was a metal filing cabinet. A flip of the switch made the flickering main lights turn on. A dull, monotonous buzz filled the room.

The disguised pair moved silently, their guns pointed at the lone hiding place.

'Come out and put your hands up right now, sunshine.'

Avi obliged with raised hands.

'Now turn around.'

Avi turned. A crack on the back of the head with the butt of a gun, and he was out cold as his head hit the floor. Brookes bared his teeth as he kicked him hard in the stomach — payback for Avi's similar kick on Adams' driveway.

Chapter 29.
Torturous Times

The jet-black Humber Hawk pulled up outside an abandoned cottage, which was within view of the Ringway Airport control tower. Strings of distant runway lights twinkled in the dark as Avi's car arrived seconds later. Taylor got out of the Moggy and then helped Brookes drag Avi's limp body from the blackbird.

Unconscious and bloodied, Avi was tightly bound at his ankles and wrists with the same hemp rope that anchored him upright to a heavy wooden chair. The long-abandoned bungalow was in a severe state of decay.

Rain dripped through the hole where roof tiles were missing, beyond the open ceiling, and into a rusty upside-down pan. It maintained a steady drip until a passing Bristol Britannia turboprop plane screamed overhead, eclipsing the sound.

The angry noise stirred Avi into a nauseating semi-consciousness. The back of his head throbbed from the knockout blow. The lump felt like a golf ball embedded in his skull. A bright light shone directly into his face. His brain felt as if it were out of sync with his body. His glasses had been fixed around his ears, but his vision was retarded, as if he were peering through a floating purple jellyfish. He could only make out the strange motion of two flowing human shapes.

Unaware that he was also cuffed and wired to a car battery, Avi could sense a presence lurking behind him. Two hypodermic needles resting in an enamel tray were just out of his reach. With submissive disorientation, he tried to focus but failed to notice a fountain of liquid spouting from one of the syringes. Then his stocky assailant jabbed the needle into his arm. Avi immediately became more alert but still felt confused.

The masked captors were relieved to begin their interrogation.

'We've been looking forward to your return, sunshine,' said Stocky.

'We are going to ask you some questions and you are going to give us some answers. If they aren't the right answers, we are going to hurt you very badly,' added his lofty companion. 'You understand, Jew boy?'

Avi drifted into what felt like a schizophrenic state, consumed by twisted images that invaded his mind. Nothing was real. Everything was real. Past and present merged into a vivid, tangled nightmare...

Dachau Prisoner Baths 1940: minus his glasses, barechested Avi was suspended. His wrists were twisted behind his back as he pole-hung from metal hooks attached to wooden beams. The excruciating pain tested his will to live. The ᛋᛋ Unterscharführer entered the area with a short, stiff wooden whip. As he convulsed with fear, Avi could only make out the blurred shape of the guard.

'Why were you in the mortuary?' asked Stocky.

'Who are you, why am I ... here?' replied Avi.

'I'm asking the questions, sunshine.'

A brief electric shock charged through his body. Avi screamed in agony.

The Unterscharführer began his interrogation in German. His whip tore into Avi's back. 'I want the other names of your "friends" at the university ... now!'

'No friends,' croaked Avi.

The Unterscharführer moved around and lashed Avi across the chest. It allowed the victim to see his torso being torn to ribbons.

Avi craved the relief of a protracted scream, but his lungs were so stretched that his larynx was unable to muster the sound.

'Once again, why were you in the mortuary?' asked Stocky.

'I was lost ... I wandered into the wrong place.'

'Then why pick the lock, you stinking, Jewish liar?'

A longer electric shock ratcheted his pain. Avi's body contorted as every sinew tightened to the point of implosion.

The Unterscharführer smirked at the sight of blood seeping from Avi's chest. His gravelled voice barked out, 'I want the names of all of the subversive students, right now, or I will beat you to death!'

Avi was unable to put the words together as he spun around, back and forth.

The Unterscharführer worked up a sweat as he whipped Avi's torso into a ravaged, bloody mess.

Avi gasped for breath.

'How did a Jew like you survive the War in Germany?' asked Stocky.

'I was in England, not Germany!'

Another stupefying shock travelled his body as Avi's throat grated in a high-pitched screech.

A Jewish Kapo prisoner entered the Prisoner Baths. Head bowed, he said, 'Unterscharführer, you are summoned to see Obersturmführer immediately.' Avi's head dropped as the Unterscharführer marched out of the area.

The pressure was relentless. 'Why were you in the mortuary?' cried Stocky.

Avi's head lifted.

'You're a long way from home, Mr Falco,' said Lofty. 'Manchester isn't London. You are a fish out of water, and so is your wife. I'm sure you get my meaning.'

The second syringe shot liquid into the air before the needle was once again sunk into Avi's arm. Finally, he passed out.

The Kapo was covered in Avi's blood as he lifted Avi by his armpits up and off the hook. He carefully cradled Avi's limp body out of the Prisoners' Baths area and back to his hut.

The sound of rain drumming against the soft roof woke Avi in his parked Morris Minor. As he stirred, his reflexes caused a twinge in his tender stomach. His captors were long gone. Another propeller plane flew low, landing on the glassy runway of Ringway Airport.

In his weakened state, Avi opened the driver's door and staggered out of the car. He pulled himself upwards and recognised the airport control tower peeping through thick perimeter bushes.

With bubbling lungs, he looked up at the night sky for the North Star to confirm his bearings, but blackened clouds obscured his view. The rain splashing against his face helped stimulate his senses. He dropped back into the car and propped himself up in the driver's seat.

A glance at his smashed watch showed the time frozen at 12:15 am. He pulled out the choke halfway and started the Moggy, which was conveniently aimed toward the only exit leading to a solitary country lane.

Shivering from cold and shock, Avi tried to compose himself as he drove into the darkness beyond the overgrown bushes.

The effort of driving the five-mile trip safely and competently to Didsbury further exhausted Avi. Mindlessly, he parked the Moggy five yards behind Mr Wilkins' car. He let out a deep sigh of relief, closed his eyes, and rested his weary head on his stiff white hands gripping the steering wheel.

With his guard down, he failed to notice Mr. Wilkins' car starting up and reversing quickly. It then slammed directly into the front of the Moggy. The loud crash jolted Avi in his seat.

He lifted his head just in time to see a dark figure get out and run into the night like a startled badger.

Avi was in shock as a police patrol car pulled up beside the Moggy. PC Taylor was at the wheel. He got out and dragged Avi from his car onto the pavement.

Concerned about the noise from the crash, Kathy came out of her front door in her dressing gown.

'You're under arrest,' said Taylor, who grabbed Avi's collar and lifted him like a rag doll. Making a deliberate show of cuffing his prisoner, Taylor forced him into the patrol car and slammed the door.

Avi was taken to the police station before any of the watching neighbours realised what had happened.

Chapter 30.
Slippery Slope

It was turning out time in Didsbury Police Station. The bravado in last night's sleep-it-off drunkards had shifted into sheepish looks of embarrassment. During the night, Avi had been awoken every thirty minutes by Collins' attentive officers. It was 6:29 am when he was escorted from his draughty cell.

A ghostly pallor revealed his fragile state. Woozy and dehydrated, he rubbed his half-hooded, glassy eyes with his palms. He tried to focus, but that was impossible without his glasses. For a moment, he lost his balance and reached out for support from the nearest wall.

Avi listed starboard as he shuffled towards the reception desk.

The desk sergeant placed Avi's spectacles and smashed watch on his reception counter. Struggling to put his specs back on, Avi poked himself in the eye with a coiled arm of the frame. The desk sergeant smirked. Avi shook his head and noticed Lewis loitering with intent by the exit, wearing a stern frown.

Just what I need, thought Avi with a similarly negative expression.

Neither man had spoken since they left the police station fifteen minutes earlier. As they drove through the modest morning traffic towards Kemsley House, Lewis's rage was evident from his constant tapping on the steering wheel.

Propping up his forehead, Avi's left arm sank deeply into his left thigh. His right arm clutched his tender stomach. The repetitive tapping was irritating. Avi's patience was finely balanced, but his dark mood was barely under control. He thought it wise not to ask Lewis to … *stop tapping just now, or I'll break all your fingers, you annoying bastard!*

Apart from that, given how he felt at that moment, he suspected he might not have the strength to carry out such a simple threat. He suspected that the percussion was a precursor to more condemnatory rants. As it turned out, he wasn't mistaken.

As they approached another queue of stationary traffic, Lewis finally lost his patience. He looked in the mirror and brought the car to a halt with a purposeful jolt. 'You look like you have been dragged through a hedge backwards. Numerous Jewish tailors in this city will offer you a good deal. Perhaps it's time to treat yourself to a new suit and, while you're at it, buy a single ticket back to London, Mr Falco!'

Avi opened his mouth in a bid to issue a riposte, but Lewis was in full flow. 'The newspaper has paid your bail and will also pay for your neighbour's car. You can pay it back from your redundancy package … unless you give me an explanation as to why you were found drunk in your car last night!'

Lifting his head slowly and in a hoarse voice, Avi said, 'I wasn't drunk.'

'Not drunk? Then why do you have an obvious hangover?'

'I saw Tommy Green's body. They got me and drugged me. I told them nothing.'

Raising an eyebrow, Lewis lowered his voice and, with a less aggressive tone, he added, 'Told who nothing? The police think you were out drinking all night. Can you get anyone to corroborate your version?'

Avi shook his head. Cogent responses were difficult to grasp. 'Uh … perhaps the clerk at the mortuary?'

'The police have spoken to him. He denies any knowledge.'

'The police …' Avi stopped again, preferring not to elaborate. He rubbed his forehead and puffed out his cheeks. With an outdrawn whisper, he said, 'Tommy Green's body was on a slab. I inspected the markings on his neck. It was not suicide. I saw plenty of suicide hangings in Dachau. If he'd hung himself, there would have been ligature scars, not strangulation bruises around his throat. He was choked to death.'

Lewis suppressed a look of surprise.

Avi failed to recognise his mistake. He took off his glasses clumsily and rubbed the foggy lenses with the grubby handkerchief he'd pulled from his trouser pocket. His eyes vacant, he continued, 'I also saw the coroner's report on David Adams. His injuries suggested he had been in a heavy brawl. His hands and wrists were lacerated. His face and body were covered in bruises. He'd sustained a collapsed lung and six broken ribs … *Six broken ribs!* From the strike wounds on his hands, he put up a hell of a fight. He was an amateur boxer — "A tough little nut to crack".'

'Yes, I am aware that he could handle himself.'

'He didn't drown in the canal. He was beaten to death and dumped in the water.' Avi fondled the back of his ear for a cig without success. He found a half-smoked dimp in his trouser pocket and placed it shakily in his mouth. 'Chief Inspector Collins signed off on both reports.'

'Well, I … That wasn't released to the press,' said Lewis.

'The police know the truth … but they are not telling.

Why would that be? They've pulled the wool over your eyes. Do you blindly accept everything that Collins tells you?'

'I beg your pardon. What on earth are you suggesting?'

'I'm not *suggesting*. I'm *telling* you that whatever Collins says goes. Nobody ever questions his integrity. Why would that be, Mr Lewis?'

'If you ever aspire to my position, you will soon realise that, as a chief editor, you need to adopt a more diplomatic approach than the gung-ho style you use unreservedly. It is not beneficial for a newspaper to antagonise the police in the same city. Therefore, I must respect the word of the venerable Chief Inspector... unless I have irrefutable evidence of foul play. Besides, Collins' crime figures speak for themselves.'

'I think the Wolff murder is connected to David Adams. Was his murder a warning that was taken too far? Is that why people are afraid to confront the powerful Chief Inspector, for fear of ending up floating in the canal?'

'From what I heard, you questioned his integrity quite aggressively in public at his police station. But I see you weren't found floating in a canal this morning, were you?'

A brief silence. Avi had the sense to withhold his suspicions about the perpetrators of last night's events.

His doubts fading, Lewis stroked his jawline. 'Perhaps you have a point or two worth further consideration, but experience shows me that it's very easy to jump to wrong conclusions until the pieces of the puzzle fit together. I need you to find the whole story before I can publish anything. This might be something more than a fanciful conspiracy theory, but I must only deal in facts.'

Avi managed a slight nod of the head.

Striking a match, Lewis lit Avi's cig and continued, 'Fair enough, Mr Falco. It is my opinion that you might be onto something. You appear to have made progress, and you need to keep me informed of any developments. I will give you the benefit of the doubt and the time you need to dig deeper. Get me some facts, and please make a greater effort to remember that discretion is the better part of valour.'

Avi and Lewis slouched into the press office. Both were out of breath from climbing the stairs. Avi's physical fitness was decreasing in tandem with his mental health. Lewis split away and went into his office.

Avi pulled up his necktie.

Doreen's sarcasm was primed and at the ready. 'Oooh look, 'ere he is, the Austrian piss pot. Crashin' yer car while drunk? I'm amazed Mr Lewis 'asn't blown a gasket.'

Avi tried to give a reply, but was interrupted when Doreen picked up the ringing phone and answered. 'Yes, hold on please.' She cupped her hand over the phone and whispered, 'I thought it might be your wife, she's been ringing all morning.'

'Then who is it?'

'Some bloke for yer. He's rang a few times as well. One of yer drinking buddies, is it?'

Doreen patched through the call to Avi's extension.

'Hello … yes, thank you, I'm fine … yes, I'll be there within the hour.' Avi grabbed his overcoat from the coat rack.

As he left, Doreen commented with dry sarcasm,

'Oooh, very cloak and dagger!'

Lewis was tucked in behind his oversized desk. He dialled a well-rehearsed arrangement of circles on his brown Bakelite telephone. Collins was sitting at a more modest desk as the phone rang.

'Collins? It's Lewis, can you talk?'

'Yes, of course, carry on.'

'I've just discovered something interesting. Falco let slip that he was a prisoner in Dachau Concentration Camp. I strongly suggest we need to find out who Mr Avraham Falco really is. Can you contact our worshipful brother in MI5?'

'Yes. That would appear to be necessary. Is Falco a man to take a hint?'

'Maybe … maybe not. If he's been in Dachau, he's probably a lot tougher than he looks, and I think he's getting too close for comfort.'

'I agree.'

'Stay calm. Mr Falco's interrogation and arrest are just part of my process.'

Avi reached the top of the stairs of a dark, dilapidated backstreet building on Tib Street on the seedier edge of the city's rag trade area. The three-story establishment provided affordable rental space for the shady businesses operating within. The sign etched onto the office door window read, J. McCLAY PRIVATE DETECTIVE.

The sound of high-pitched voices and raucous laughter drowned out the knocking noise of Avi tapping on the window. Avi knocked louder. The laughter persisted. He took matters into his own hands and entered the small waiting area, advancing into the office, where Joe

McClay sat alone, in hysterical tears, with his feet on his desk.

McClay looked up and wiped his eyes, then reached over and turned off the wireless. His laughter slackened to a chuckle, then to just a smile.

With a pale, washed-out complexion, two days' stubble, and a greasy suit that looked two sizes too large, Avi resembled a helpless vagrant as he hauled an empty chair toward his companion.

The movement disturbed a cloud of blue smoke hovering above McClay's desk. On one side of the room was a door marked DARKROOM, with an unlit red bulb hanging above the sign.

McClay lifted his feet off the desk, reached over, and shook Avi's hand, and then slumped back down and observed, 'Bloody hell, lad, you look like you could use a large stiff 'un. You're shakin' like a bald polar bear.' Pulling out a bottle of whisky and two shot glasses from his drawer, he asked, 'Kill or cure?'

Avi shook his head.

McClay smiled and poured one for himself.

Avi returned the smile and then nodded.

McClay poured and handed him a full-to-the-brim measure.

'I like to see a man enjoying himself,' said Avi. 'What was so funny?'

'Oh, just the latest episode of *The Goon Show*. I swear, that Spike Milligan is going to make me laugh me bollocks off one day.'

Is that even possible? Avi pondered, wisely deciding not to ask. Instead, he said, 'I haven't laughed like that in years.'

'Yeah, Avi? That's what life is all about. Having a

laugh and enjoying yourself.'

'Yes … you are right,' he replied.

'Perhaps you owe it to yourself to make sure that you laugh more often, Avi? We're only here the once, so best to make the most of it.'

'Yes, you are right. Maybe I will once we have cracked this case.' He raised his glass and proposed 'A *L'Chaim.*'

'A Lehigh what?'

'Luh-khah-yim. A toast to life.'

'A toast to life? You look more like death warmed up!'

They both downed their shots in one.

Avi winced. McClay remained impassive as he continued, 'You're here for an update. Well, I've been keeping an eye on Helmut Lehmann. I crept into his depot late last night and found out he's one o' them 'omo's.'

Avi shook his head.

'You know, 'omo's? He were kissin' wi' another bloke.'

'I'll have you know that there were lots of "Them 'omo's" sent to German concentration camps to suffer and die. Thousands of beautiful, innocent people just trying to live their lives in peace.'

'Bloody 'ell, keep yer 'air on, Tarzan! Not judgin', just tellin'.'

'Have you any evidence?'

'I couldn't take a close-up at night without a flash, but I developed this, this mornin'. This were the bloke he were kissin'.'

McClay passed over a photo of big Ronnie Hyland leaving the depot.

'Blimey. Are you sure?'

'I'm positive, lad. He had a flash attaché case when he arrived.'

Avi took a second look at the photograph. 'Where did you take these shots?'

'The empty factory opposite. Room 27 is one flight up. A great and discreet angle. That's where I took this.'

He handed Avi a picture of CI Collins leaving Lehmann's depot disguised in civilian clothing.

'Collins?'

'I've seen him coming in and out of there a couple of times … and that's not all.'

'Go on.'

'When I first started investigating the case, I suspected that Collins might be a Freemason. Senior policemen are traditional recruits. Any club that has Collins as a member is up to no good. The Freemasons are a secretive bunch with power and influence. So, I mooched on over to their city centre lodge and had a stroke of luck.'

'Go on.'

'I used to go to school with Ralph, the — and I quote — "Underpaid and overly patronised doorman". After his shift, I took him for a pint in the Bridge Street Tavern. I tried to bribe him into getting me a membership list, but nowt doin'. But after a few pints of Hydes and a few Fiery Jack chasers to lubricate his tonsils, he confirmed that Collins was a Mason. I stuck a few beer tokens in his back pocket and he promised to tell me if anything out of the ordinary was going on at the lodge, involving the venerable Chief Inspector.'

'And?'

'And, a few days ago, Ralph tipped me the wink that a meeting was due to take place between Collins, several senior brothers and a certain local businessman. I thought it might be worth a little gander, so I took me camera along to keep me company.'

McClay handed Avi two pictures of Collins, Simpson, and Davenport entering the Freemasons' lodge.

Avi lurched forward. His eyes widened. His eyebrows arched. His jaw dropped … as also present in the sharply focused picture he spotted … 'Lewis! You hard-faced, treacherous bastard! No wonder both cases went stale. He's led me on a merry dance ever since I got here.'

'Looks like they are in cahoots over something.'

'Yes indeed. They're all at it. Tommy Green's useless solicitor was a bloke called William Rodwell. Peter Spencer told me that Rodwell is also a Freemason.'

'Spencer's right, I've dealt with him before. He's just a bit-part player, but a very canny bloke. You'll get nothing worth having from him. He's one of Douggie Fowler's old cronies.'

'And Douggie Fowler was in cahoots with the veritable Chief Inspector.'

'Correct. You win a toffee apple.' McClay smiled as he produced yet another picture. 'I took this a few minutes after the others arrived.'

Avi examined the photo and saw Helmut Lehmann entering the Freemasons' building. He smiled as some of the colour returned to his cheeks. 'Now it is beginning to open up. I interviewed him a few days ago.'

'And what was his story?'

'He claims to have been a soldier in the Wehrmacht, but I didn't believe a word he said … well, perhaps one thing?'

'Pray tell.'

'No, it's not relevant.'

'Try me.'

'He's an atheist. He believes that God is dead.'

McClay rubbed his chin thoughtfully. 'That was Nietzsche's theory, but of course, "Once God is dead, all sources of authority are abolished. Hence, in a world given over to human appetites and designs, all is permitted," … and you know where that can lead.'

Avi gasped in amazement.

McClay continued. 'Not my own thoughts, of course, but observations about the deductions of a character from Fyodor Dostoevsky's final novel, *The Brothers Karamazov.*'

'Are you referring to Ivan Karamazov?'

'Yeah, that's him. Ivan was the intellectual brother. The other two played up front for Dynamo Moscow!' McClay smirked as he winked.

Avi shook his head. 'You Mancunians never cease to amaze me.'

'Yeah, well, perhaps we all have hidden talents.'

'It would appear that Mr Lewis has hidden talents and he's not on his own.' Avi picked up the photographs. 'Well, you certainly know how to take the right picture. These are absolutely first-class, Mr McClay. Absolutely first-class.'

'Swell. I thought you'd be chuffed to little mint balls wi' them.'

'Chuffed to little mint balls?'

'Yer know … really, really pleased!'

Avi nodded. He handed McClay his fee.

'Does that cover it?'

McClay didn't bother to look at the money. 'In the words of the great Oliver Norvell Hardy, "Why certainly",' and then he twiddled his tie.

'Thank you. That is nice work, Mr McClay … really nice work.'

McClay winked. 'Happy to oblige, pardner. You can call me Joe.'

The Moggy arrived behind the abandoned factory opposite the F&G Construction depot, its rusty front bumper badly dented. With a tired grunt, Avi hauled himself out of the car. He looked around as he made his way towards the factory. When he reached room 27, he opened the door and stepped into the deserted, decaying former accounts office.

The ragged room was filled with filthy furniture, all of which was covered in mould. The uneven floor was strewn with discarded papers, and dust settled in thick layers. Several used condoms lay beside a sturdy but unfashionable desk.

Deflated evidence of inflated pleasure.

A rickety chair faced the only window, set in peeling paint on a rotting frame. An empty whisky bottle lay prostrate on newspapers strewn on the floor beside another upright bottle, with a finger of whisky remaining.

From a certain vantage point at the grimy window, Avi had a perfect, discreet view of the front of Lehmann's depot. Drawn to the dregs in the upright bottle, he stooped and picked it up, unscrewed the top, and slugged down the pitiful remnants. He heaved and spat out watery saliva. He dropped to his knees and then retched up bile as tiny stars circled in his bloodshot eyes.

Avi pulled up outside his house, parking the Moggy at the scene of last night's disturbance. He dragged himself out of the car and, with a weary sigh, examined the heavy dent on the rear of Mr Wilkins' car. He glanced at his neighbour's house. The curtain twitched.

Sorry Mr Friendly, but it wasn't me. I think you would find that the local constabulary might have had something to do with it.

Trudging up the garden path, carrying his overcoat, Avi rummaged in his pocket, pulled out his house key, and entered. Kathy was standing in the hallway, wrapped in a grey army blanket with her arms crossed. 'Look at the state of you, Avi. You look like something the tide washed in. Well, just so you know, since you're clearly not bothered, Mr Wilkins came round to complain about his car. He's devastated. It's his pride and joy.'

'At last. There we have it. I've been wondering what might make him finally talk to me.'

'Oh, that's right, Avi. Make light of it. I apologised twice on your behalf. I didn't think you would be bothered enough to say anything. How could you do that? What were you thinking?' Her sore red nose sniffed. 'And your breath stinks! Have you been drinking again? Does that account for your facetious attitude?'

'The paper is paying for the damage. It wasn't what you think. Can I at least take off my coat, sweetheart?'

'Don't sweetheart me, Avraham Falco. I've been worried sick. The police said that you were bailed out this morning — but not a word from you! What am I supposed to think? What am I supposed to do?'

'I will explain in the morning,' said Avi in a casual tone that revealed a lack of concern Kathy had expected. 'I just need to get some sleep and I'll be fine. I am sorry.' Avi turned his back on his forlorn wife. He dropped his overcoat on the banister and trudged up the stairs. Halfway up, he remarked, 'I'll take the spare room again.'

'Thanks… that's very big of you, my kind-hearted husband. And how are you, my darling? Feeling any better? Yes, oh good. Must be all that pampering I gave you,' Kathy muttered to herself.

Exhausted, Avi struggled into his pyjamas before flopping into bed. Before long, he was tossing and turning beneath sweat-soaked sheets. His flashbacks had become more frequent. The dreadful events he had once managed to suppress were resurfacing with alarming regularity. His defences were crumbling. There was an increasing toll to be paid …

… Young Avi awakened to the muted moans of suffering that tormented his ice-covered Dachau hut. He was surrounded by ravaged, shivering prisoners. They lay sick, perishing, and exhausted on piteous wooden beds, trying desperately to locate the fleeting sanctuary of sleep.

The hut door opened. Torch in hand, the dark-hearted devil entered dressed in the black of the Grim Reaper. He shone a light around the cramped victims wallowing in the stench of vomit and diarrhoea.

Savvy prisoners turned a blind eye to the intrusion. In the pretence of a spurious bed-making infraction, the Hasidic Jew was yanked from his rack. He was slapped around the splintered wooden hut by the tall black figure of the ᛋᛋ guard.

Through the haze of blurred vision, Avi had seen the shaven-headed young Hasidic Jew being dragged out by the growling silhouette that was the ᛋᛋ Unterscharführer.

Avi was shuffling between Jewish barracks,

distinguishable from the rest of the camp by painted-over windows that deprived the prisoners of natural light. His head was bowed forward. He gazed blankly at his lice-infested trousers as he made his way to the lengthy roll call in grit-smeared snow. With an unwelcome shift in his peripheral vision, Avi caught a glimpse of jaundiced flesh immersed in a pile of snow beside a hut.

He stopped. He advanced for a closer look at what appeared to be a face-down corpse. He crouched. The abused and broken body was naked from the waist down. There was a large bloodstain on the buttocks. He carefully turned the shaven head by its snapped neck. With his red, chilblained hands, he felt the rigid contours of the contorted death mask of the young Hasidic Jew, frozen in eternal terror.

Avi screamed like a mating fox. He was bolt upright in a frantic state when Kathy rushed into the room. She fumbled to turn on the bedside lamp and then moved to comfort him, but he unconsciously pushed her away with a firm shove. Her slight frame careered off the side of the bed. Her head hit the base of the wardrobe. She picked herself up from the floor and gripped her throbbing forehead.

Her presence didn't register with Avi. He lay back down, staring beyond the ceiling. Kathy left the room, quickly returning with a slopping glass of water and a yellow pill. He sat up and took the pill, and then lay back down as if nothing had happened. Now swollen above her right eye, Kathy maintained a devoted vigil with the lamp still blazing.

Daylight seeped through a small slit between the brocade

curtains as Avi awoke from his sleep. He scrunched his nose at the smell of stale body odour. His first thought was of the callous murder of the Hasidic Jew. He shook his head, burdened by guilt for passively accepting the futility of intervening.

Blessed are the meek, for they shall inherit the burden.

The alarm clock showed 3:05 pm. He rolled out of his ruffled bed and began getting his act together.

For hours, Kathy had been in the kitchen pondering her plight and contemplating their future. She realised that since their move to Manchester, Avi's anxiety was getting worse instead of better. She had dismissed some of her old colleagues who warned her not to marry a Jew. While some were anti-Semites, she wondered if the others might be right. All those negative stereotypes, justified in the name of wisdom, portrayed them as too self-centred, too insular, too controlling, and too overly attached to their mothers, but what did they really know? He was extremely self-centred, but then again, aren't most men?

Kathy never converted to Judaism, and Avi had never asked. She had always appreciated his encouragement to follow her own beliefs, religious or otherwise. He was a generous soul, certainly with money if not with his time, and besides, his mother was dead. He missed her badly, but Kathy was sure that her loss wasn't the root of his problem.

Kathy tried to understand his behaviour, but he always kept everything bottled up inside. But hadn't she done the same thing? He knew nothing of her traumatic past, though he'd never thought to ask. Perhaps it was her fault? She knew he was damaged goods when she married him. The only advice she had ever listened to came from her mother. She also remembered their recent chat, which had made her feel better, albeit briefly.

"Come on, Kathy darlin'. Where's your East End spirit? You went through a lot to marry 'im. Stick with it. He's a good lad underneath it all, and you're a good judge of character. I know you're not practising any more, Kathy, but for a Catholic, marriage is sacrosanct. The success of any marriage should not be taken lightly. People give up too quickly and too easily these days. We all have our ups and downs. You have to work things out. You must fight all the way. But don't make it too easy this time, that's for sure. Have a good talk when he steps off the straight and narrow. Lay your cards on the table and clear the air. It's the only way."

Clean and dressed, Avi lingered at the bottom of the stairs. His overcoat remained draped across the banister. He gave it a second glance, then realised he was once again in the doghouse without a bone.

He stepped into the newly painted kitchen. Kathy had her back turned while putting the kettle onto the lit stove. He tried an optimistic icebreaker. 'I slept all day.'

Kathy carried on regardless.

He tried again. 'I am sorry, Kathy.'

Finally, she turned around. The swollen lump above her eye was prominent and shaded with a bruise. She rubbed her hands on her apron. 'You said that last night. You're always saying that. Your boss rang... Mr Lewis? I told him you were out so that you could sleep it off.'

His voice was cold as Avi said, 'I have other things to take care of before I deal with him.' He swallowed the yellow pill she had left on the table.

Kathy handed him a gift-wrapped box and said, 'Open

it.'

Puzzled, he shook his head, having no idea what the package could be.

'Go on, Avi, open it.'

He tore off the striped wrapping paper to reveal a luxurious box that contained a Rolex Tudor Gold watch. 'Wow. This is for me?'

Kathy nodded. 'In case you've forgotten, your old one was smashed beyond repair when you sauntered home last night. It's in the bin. We've been saving up for a while to buy you this for your fortieth birthday. My mum went halves on it. She insisted. I thought you might as well have it now, since you need it.'

Avi shook his head, smiled, and slipped on the watch. 'I absolutely love it. I can't believe you ... it must have cost a fortune. I really don't deserve it.'

'No. No, you don't, Avi. You certainly don't deserve it. This isn't what I had in mind when we bought it. Please listen. I want you to stay and talk. We have things to sort out, and quickly.'

Avi got to his feet. 'I'm sorry, but I haven't got time for that now, Kathy. I've already lost most of the day. We'll have a chat when I get home. I promise. I absolutely adore the watch. Thank you so much.' He moved to kiss her, but Kathy backed out of reach. He flipped on his trilby hat and grabbed his coat. 'We'll talk when I get back, I promise you.'

Kathy was churning inside. Her annoyance felt grossly compounded.

He liked the watch all right, but didn't even comment on the new paintwork ... never mind the black eye he gave me.

Chapter 31.
Dirty Deeds

Avi arrived at the Lehmann residence, ready to stir the pot once more. Two soot-covered, beady-eyed chimney sweeps left the front door. Glenda soon followed them with her usual hauteur. 'And I want all that horrible mess cleaned up properly by the time I get back.'

She saw Avi approaching along the garden path and tried to stop him with a pre-emptive strike. 'Not you again? Well, he's not in.'

Avi carried on moving. 'I came to speak to *you*.'

'You want to speak to *me*? Well, I haven't got the time.'

'Please, it's just one small question.'

Glenda's curiosity prevailed. 'Well, if it's only the one.'

'Thank you. I was just wondering how your husband managed to father a child, given that he is a homosexual?'

'Well, aren't you the great detective? How did Helmut put it? "You absolute fool"!' Glenda brushed past him, towards her car.

Steady on, Glenda, love. You wouldn't want to trigger one of your famous nosebleeds.

He cupped his left hand as he lit the fresh cig that dangled from his mouth, then headed back down the path as Glenda's car pulled away with a deliberate spin of tyres.

Before he reached the front gate, Julia Lehmann appeared at the front door and shouted, 'Mr Falco, please wait.'

The familiar sound of the distant childish voice made

him stop in his tracks. He pinched out the cig, wedged it behind his ear, and turned as the mongrel Patch darted into the house from his unrestricted roam of the streets.

'Ah, hello, Julia. What can I do for you?'

Julia looked around, her face tense with paranoia. 'Please come inside, Mr Falco. I want to show you something.'

Avi turned quickly. His friendly approach had unintentionally paid off. Julia was eager to confide in the reporter she admired. He stepped into the hallway, and they sat together on the tartan couch.

'Julia, just before you begin and before I forget, can I ask you if Glenda suffers from nose bleeds?'

'Not that I'm aware of.'

'Did you go to the hospital with Glenda in the Mercedes to pick up your father from the hospital the morning after the burglary?'

'No. She went on her own in the sports car. I would have gone with her, but I wasn't invited. She came home on her own about an hour and a half later, and he followed on in a taxi not very long after that.'

So now we know that they are a pair of lying bastards, thought Avi, who started to pluck the cig from behind his ear, but then recalled the reason he'd put it there seconds earlier. He shook his head. 'Uh, what was it that you wanted to show me, Julia?'

She handed him a fragile wedding picture. 'These are my parents in Germany before the War.'

Avi looked closely at the tattered picture and saw her father boasting a pronounced scar above his right eye. 'A nice photograph.'

Julia's eyes welled up. Avi began to put a comforting arm around her, but then hesitated and pulled back.

'What's the matter, Julia?'

'Look closely, Mr Falco. I saw my father for the last time when he went to War. I don't think he's the same man.'

'Unfortunately, the War changed lots of people in lots of ways.'

'No, I mean literally. I don't think that he's the same man.'

'How old were you when he left?'

'I was three years old.'

'We do not generally remember things well until we are at least six years of age.'

'Young as I was, I still remember my father. He was kind and loving... never cruel. When both of your parents are gone, you think a lot at night, especially in a scary place like the orphanage.'

'Yes. The orphanage. Can you remember its name?'

'Always. The Spangell Orphanage.'

'Why Spangell?'

'Spangell was the name of the owner.'

'Did the owner have a first name?'

Julia's eyes narrowed. 'He made us call him Uncle Felix.'

Avi took out a pen and a pad and wrote down *Felix Spangell*.

Julia placed the picture on Avi's palm.

He studied it more closely. 'Julia, I understand your doubts, but your mind plays tricks when you are young. What we think we remember and what is the truth are often far apart. It is not a good likeness, but let us keep it our secret, for now, at least.'

'It's not just the picture. The story about the burglary isn't true either. When I asked him about it, he said he would beat me again if I ever mentioned it.'

'Beat you again?' Avi handed Julia his calling card. 'If ever you need me, I am only a phone call away.'

Julia nodded and slipped the card into the side pocket stitched into her cotton dress.

'Listen to me carefully, Julia. You'd better not mention any of our conversation to anybody, particularly your parents.'

'No, I definitely won't.'

He turned to leave. 'Goodbye, Julia … Oh, I forgot. Just one last question, please. Do you ever remember your father playing the piano for you in Germany?'

'Yes. We had an upright piano in the hallway. Daddy used to play well. He still does. But not the same childish tunes anymore.'

'That is a pity,' said Avi.

As Julia opened the door, Patch ran out into the now pouring rain, barking at ruffled chimney sweeps. Avi smiled — *crazy dog.*

Chapter 32.
Intimidation

Avi killed the headlights as he parked the Moggy across the street from the illuminated mortuary entrance. A young couple exited an empty fish-and-chip shop. Avi's nervous hands writhed like snakes in a bag. He removed his gleaming new watch, wrapped it in a handkerchief, and stuffed it out of view behind his seat. He took out a yellow pill, swallowed it, and pulled himself out of the car. It was just a few steps into the inviting chippy.

The assistant handed Avi an open bag of chips wrapped in the front pages of an old edition of the Manchester Chronicle. The covering headline read, MAN CRUSHED TO DEATH BY BELLE VUE ELEPHANT! The hot chips warmed Avi's hands, and the aroma of salt and vinegar made him salivate as he shuffled toward the steamed-up shop window.

Wiping a peephole, he looked across to the mortuary entrance and saw the desk clerk, Spike Mullins, exiting at the end of his evening shift.

Avi stepped out of the chip shop with his open bag of steaming chips.

Oblivious to his stalker, Mullins walked with his head down and his hands in his pockets on the other side of the street.

Avi dropped the bag into a gaping bin. He broke into a trot as he crossed over, closing in behind Mullins at a fast pace. Avi's breathing was heavy. He could feel his senses sharpen as he homed in on his prey.

As Mullins approached a secluded alleyway, Avi drew level and shoulder-charged him into it.

Mullins stumbled but then regained his balance. He

turned, recognised Avi, and took a couple of wild swings. Both punches missed as Avi rolled his head out of reach and moved forward, left jabbing twice, fast and hard, at Mullins's mouth. Mullins was bloodied and dazed. He shook his head, wiped his gashed lips, and pulled a flick knife in his right hand, tattooed HATE.

He released the blade and smiled with menace. 'Come on then, ya Yid bastard. I'm gonna carve you up bad,' said Mullins as he crouched and jabbed the knife at Avi a couple of times as they circled on their haunches. At the third circle, Mullins lunged forward.

Avi evaded the knife and grabbed Mullins' leading arm, gripping it behind his back in one slick move as the knife clattered onto the floor. 'Be still, *be still!*' Avi jerked his grip tighter and cocked his free fist, ready to rearrange Mullins' face.

Grimacing with pain, Mullins stopped struggling. 'Wadda ya want?' he spluttered through gritted teeth.

'Why did you do it?'

'Just doin' me job. I knew you was no courier.'

'So why deny seeing me?'

'The copper in the fancy uniform.'

'Collins?' Avi pulled the arm up tighter.

'Aaargh, yeah, yeah, it was him, Collins! You do what the filth ask in this city or you end up in the infirmary.'

Avi extended a leg and threw Mullins to the ground. He picked up the knife. He put his right index finger to his mouth, then pointed at Mullins. 'Not a single word of this, or you will end up in the cemetery. Understand?'

Mullins nodded as he wiped dripping blood from his swollen lip.

Meanwhile, Kathy was in her bedroom, dozing in bed

while dressed in her nighty and a dressing gown with an open copy of *Moby Dick* resting on her lap. She sneezed and returned to her senses. As she wiped her sore nose, she heard the shattering of glass and clumping noises. She jumped out of bed and darted to the top of the landing. More crashing and banging noises came from downstairs.

Oh, my giddy Aunt!

She retreated into the bedroom and quickly moved to the window. There was no sign of Avi's car, but she noticed a black Humber Hawk parked behind Mr. Wilkins' car in front of the house: big car, big trouble. Kathy looked around the sparse room, desperately searching for somewhere to hide.

The wardrobe!

She pulled it open, but it was crammed full of clothes. Panic took over. She turned off the lamp.

Slow, heavy footsteps creaked up the stairs. She crawled under the bed, her heart pounding fiercely as memories of her childhood flooded back.

The gaunt, terrifying face of dirty John Winnot appeared in her mind. With her eyes squeezed shut, she pinned herself down, her fingernails tearing at the carpet as her left hand clawed. She bit down hard on her right index finger. Not a breath. Not a sound. Kathy was screaming inside.

The footsteps stopped.

The door opened.

Brookes entered.

He swaggered across to the wardrobe and opened it. He looked around the room and saw Kathy's slippers by the bed, catching a glimpse of her bare right foot. He smirked as he stood next to the bed, just inches from

Kathy's screwed-up face. He undid his fly, took out his penis, and urinated.

Kathy suppressed her shudder as she heard the seemingly endless patter of urine falling on the heavy quilt, like rain on a canvas tent.

Brookes zipped his fly back up, tapped his foot, and left the room.

Brookes met Taylor at the bottom of the stairs. They exchanged a knowing glance, smiled, and left.

Kathy stayed under the bed, curled up in a ball of pure terror.

Chapter 33.
The Final Straw

Avi parked the Moggy behind an empty Ford Anglia Police patrol car. He eased himself out to see a wooden-top police officer standing guard at his front door, like a well-polished sentry. Fearing the worst, Avi hurried past the rigid officer and into the house.

With bloodshot eyes, Kathy was sitting on the couch beside another, older policeman, who was slurping on a steaming brew, his Custodian Helmet proudly balanced on his lap. The room was ransacked, as was Kathy's mind.

The experienced sergeant put down his tea, stood up, and offered a calm, 'Good evening, Mr. Falco. Nothing appears to have been taken, and your wife wasn't attacked. She did the right thing.'

'When did this …'

'It took them over two bloody hours to get here!' cried Kathy.

Retaining his decorum, the sergeant continued, 'I would take good care of her, lad. The little lady has had a nasty ordeal. The same thing happened a few months ago. A pretty woman left home alone. She wasn't so lucky. We found her mutilated, dead body bound and trussed, with a telephone flex wrapped around her …'

'… Yes, yes, well, thank you, sergeant. I read the reports on that one. That was the one murderer you actually managed to catch,' said Avi.

Kathy shook her head. 'There were two of them. I could hear noises downstairs while the other one was in my bedroom.'

'Have you any ideas on who might have done this,

sergeant?' asked Avi.

'Uh, no. It's probably just a burglary. There's been a few in the neighbourhood lately. These new-fangled television sets are in big demand with the criminal fraternity. They're so bloody heavy, it takes two of the buggers to carry 'em off.'

'But we don't even have a telly!' called Kathy.

'Don't worry, madam. We'll be keeping a keen eye on you and your 'usband from here on in,' said the sergeant with ambiguous menace in his voice registered only by Avi.

'Thank you, officer. I will take over from here,' said Avi, finally recognising the sergeant from desk duty on the morning after he was arrested.

The sergeant noticed Avi's recognition, scowled, and then tightened his helmet under his double chin. As he exited the room, he clipped the metal rose top of his helmet on the door frame, nearly strangling himself on his leather strap.

Avi suppressed his smile as he went across to comfort Kathy.

As he approached, she stood and raised her hands for him to … 'Back off!'

He raised both hands in surrender. 'What happened?'

'Two men came and broke into the house. I had to hide under the bed. One of the dirty buggers urinated on the bedding!'

'Did you get a look at him?'

'From under the bloody bed? You brought those men to this place. You brought me to this place. We don't belong here. *I* don't belong here.'

Avi moved towards her once more.

'Please stay back, Avi. I want to know what is going

on. Why would two men break into this house? We have nothing worth stealing!'

He took off his trilby and inhaled deeply. 'I am working on a case. A dangerous case involving dangerous people. The man I replaced at the paper was murdered because of it.'

'And you left me in here on my own?'

'I didn't think …'

'That's exactly right, Avi. You didn't think of me or anyone but yourself.'

'But I …'

'Don't interrupt! I left my mother all on her own in Croydon for you. There's no point in both me and mum being alone and miserable. I agreed to come up here for a new start for us. To try and work things out to save our marriage, but it turns out you're here for something else entirely. I should have known you'd have an ulterior motive.'

'It wasn't like that. I had no idea of any of this when we left London.'

'You have no idea, full stop! We've only been here five minutes and you're already consumed to the point of obsession … and you're drinking again!' Kathy sat back down and dropped her head into her hands. 'You left me to fend for myself. I've had it here, Avi. There is no reason for me to stay. You have no idea what I've been through. No idea. This is the final straw. I'm going back to my mum's in the morning.'

'Perhaps it is for the best under the circumstances. I will take you back to London.'

Yes, you will, Avi. Len would never have left me alone and in danger like that …

Chapter 34.
Disaster Strikes

In 1939, eighteen-year-old Leonard Bracegirdle worked as a young stevedore in London's East End Docklands. A muscular, handsome, and level-headed young man, Len was an essential worker with a reserved occupation and was therefore exempt from conscription into the armed forces. He was also prohibited from enlisting on his own initiative.

Just after the War began, Len became a volunteer Air Raid Patrol warden to "Do his bit" for king and country. During the first year of the War, Len's main task was to help maintain the blackout, which had caused more casualties on the British mainland through accidents than from any form of German attack.

Black Saturday, 7th September 1940, marked the first night of the Blitz of Britain, when 967 German and Italian fighters and bombers attacked the capital at 5:00 pm. They left 430 dead and 1,600 injured. It was the first of fifty-eight successive nights of the London Blitz. By November 11th, four out of every ten houses in Stepney were either destroyed or damaged.

Almost 200,000 people lived in the area, with an average of twelve people per dwelling. Len and his fellow volunteers were tasked with maintaining order during harrowing times for so many. However, while ordinary people were left to fend for themselves in the best way possible, wealthy and privileged members of the establishment had different experiences. They were able to buy their way out of London, migrating to comfortable country residences or taking safe refuge in expensive, reinforced basement clubs in the city.

Before the bombing had commenced on that fateful first night, Kathy and her mother had taken shelter with an eclectic mix of frightened refugees, 'dollymops' and crying infants. They were marooned at the mercy of the infamous improvised Tilbury Air Raid Shelter, located beneath the Stepney railway arches.

The refuge was intended for 3,000 refugees but bulged with three times as many. Terrified civilians were shoehorned into the dank, urine-smelling cavern, awaiting the lottery of fate. One and all shook with fear, cold, and the dull and heavy shock waves of numerous bomb blasts that rocked the city's foundations. The sheer terror of helplessness inside the crumbling complex of cells and vaults was expressed through screams and tears from both the young and the old alike.

Having responded to numerous false alarms, Kathy's grandparents decided to stay in bed at home, despite protests from their daughter and granddaughter. This was no night to cry wolf, as Stepney was battered, especially Lydia Street. At the sound of the all-clear, Kathy and her mother pushed their way through the crowd.

They raced back home. Amid the flaming carnage, they found their house and surroundings destroyed by a high-explosive bomb. Kathy's grandparents lay stricken in the street, having been pulled from the rubble by a young ARP Warden, Len Bracegirdle. The valiant young hero had dug them out of the blazing wreckage as water from inadequate fire tenders showered down to fight the ferocious flames.

As Kathy and her mother arrived at the scene, the charred, exhausted elderly couple was rushed to Mile End Hospital. They died of their injuries, holding hands while lying prostrate in the ambulance. It was a comforting, if gruesome, end to forty-two years of a loving marriage.

The next day, Len was still at the scene, guiding the public away from an unexploded bomb buried in the smouldering wreckage of Lydia Street. Kathy and her mother arrived from a nearby refugee station, where they had spent the rest of the night in shock.

The compassion demonstrated by young Leonard left a lasting impression on Kathy's heart. This was Len's first experience with violent death, and he took a keen interest in the vulnerable Kathy Cranighan and her mother. He became well-acquainted with them while attending their brief family funeral at the Roman Catholic Church of St Mary and St Michael.

With Derek Cranighan's enforced absence from the army, Len took the female Cranighans under his wing, helping to secure nearby accommodation for them at his Auntie Mabel's house in Bethnal Green.

Kathy and her mother settled into their new lodgings as inconspicuously as possible. They were fortunate to find refuge and even luckier that their new sanctuary wasn't hit by the falling bombs, which continued to pound the East End.

Their stay allowed Kathy's relationship with Len Bracegirdle to develop from platonic admiration into true love. Kathy had fallen for the selfless young man, who offered her unconditional devotion and understanding with a maturity beyond his years.

Len became her soulmate and confidant in every aspect of her life, including the pain of her abuse at Winnots' Farm. Kathy was damaged, but Len remained devoted. Time and love would heal her wounds. He was determined to ensure that Kathy's life would be free from the scars of her past.

Despite the dark days still looming in Britain, Kathy and Len's love continued to grow. They became engaged and planned to marry as soon as Kathy turned eighteen. In keeping with traditional customs, Len was happy to ask her father for her hand in marriage.

The young couple waited for Kathy's father to return home from Southeast Asia before marrying, but Derek Cranighan never came back. He was killed on 14th February 1942 while serving in Singapore. On 16th February 1942, Eileen and Kathy received a telegram. They both expected a message of love from Derek to celebrate Kathy's eighteenth birthday. Instead, they received a devastating 'Regret to Inform You' official War Office telegram handed to them by a meek and nervous 'Angel of Death' telegraph boy.

Thoughts of marriage were postponed until Kathy and her mother observed a year of mourning for their beloved Derek. After that year of sorrow, Kathy and Len began to step out once more. On the drizzly evening of Wednesday, 3rd March 1943, the young couple left the matinee re-run of Noel Coward's *In Which We Serve* at the local bughole Empire Picturedome in Roman Road. The show's ending was marked by sinister, steady Civil Defence Air Raid sirens — the wailing of the dead — signalling potential danger ahead.

Outside the cinema, a lone shaft of searchlight raked the hostile skies in search of enemy bombers. ARP warden Len jumped into duty. Leaving Kathy behind, he ran on ahead towards the mothballed Bethnal Green Tube

Station, which served thousands as an improvised communal air-raid shelter during the onslaught of the Blitz during 1940-41. With a capacity of 5,000 people, the newly built station was an obvious choice for the masses to find sanctuary. The Central Line track was still being laid, so the labyrinth of tunnels had no trains, allowing its complete conversion into a subterranean town.

Despite the continuous call of the siren, there was no panic on the streets. The seasoned campaigners of the East End knew it could take up to forty-five minutes for a raid to commence. However, an unusually large crowd had gathered outside the tube station in the blackout, anticipating a German attack. Londoners were aware of the large air raid that had taken place over Berlin two nights earlier and feared reprisal attacks from the Luftwaffe.

Within ten minutes of the sounding of the siren, approximately 1,500 people had already entered the underground cavern, lit only by a solitary 25-watt bulb.

Len arrived amid a burst of sixty brightly coloured Anti-Aircraft Z Battery rockets launched from nearby guns at Victoria Park. They exploded into the night sky, their unfamiliar, deafening roar causing panic among the people, who mistakenly thought a full-scale raid was underway.

With no other ARP Wardens present and wearing civilian clothes, Len tried to gather the refugees in the dangerous, uneven stairwell leading down into the station. He was quickly overwhelmed. In his effort to push back the crowd, he was caught in the centre of the stampede.

A woman with a baby in her arms tripped near the

bottom of the stairs. Since no central handrail was installed, the crowd surged forward without any way to stop them. A domino effect followed. Within thirty seconds, about 300 people were packed and compressed into the space between the nineteen steps and the ceiling, which measured fifteen by eleven feet. A "Herd of Humanity" five to six people deep, piled on top of each other as the frightened crowd continued to surge forward from behind. It was a disaster on a massive scale. Those who were not overcome by claustrophobia were immediately overwhelmed by heat and a hysterical sense of helplessness.

Len Bracegirdle was asphyxiated within two minutes amid the groaning pile of tangled limbs, crushed torsos, and purple and mauve faces. A total of 173 victims, comprising 84 women, 62 children, and 27 men, were killed — the highest loss of life in a single incident in Great Britain during the entire Second World War.

When Kathy arrived at the scene, she was unable to help any of the sixty or so casualties whom rescuers eventually ferried to the nearby hospital. It took over an hour of frantic searching before she spotted the limp corpse of her dead fiancée slumped beneath a pile of lifeless bodies, stacked by the kerb.

Not a single bomb had fallen within two miles of Bethnal Green.

Along with the rest of the national press, Herbert Gaggs' Chronicle reporters investigated the tragedy at Bethnal Green Tube Station. Witnesses were offered lucrative bribes of up to £5 each to share their stories, but silence prevailed. Prime Minister Churchill suppressed the truth about the catastrophe to prevent a propaganda victory for the Nazis and to maintain British morale.

Subsequent reports claimed that a German bomb had directly hit Bethnal Green Tube Station.

The next day, the station stairs had been washed clean. The only signs of the disaster were a pile of discarded shoes and a lonely, abandoned pram. Crestfallen, Kathy spent that morning wandering around the makeshift mortuary at St John's church, trying to make sense of and cope with yet another loss of a loved one — a loss she would have to bear with stoicism.

The helplessness Kathy Cranighan felt during the disaster was the catalyst for her decision to train as a nurse, which she began just one month after Len's death. She would never seek refuge in a tube station again.

Both Kathy and her mother took their chances during future air raids, cowering under the fragile protection of the Anderson shelter dug into the bottom of Len's auntie's small garden in war-torn Bethnal Green.

Life carried on regardless.

Chapter 35.
Revelations

Adding a colourful splash of glamour to the otherwise dull and functional press office, Doreen Colman shrugged on her chic but imitation Coco Chanel knee-length pink 'swing' coat as Bernard Lewis burst into the press room. His folded umbrella dripped a small puddle onto the floor of the Press Room.

'Oh, Mr Lewis, I've got to nip out. Julia Lehmann just called for Avi. Third time this morning,' said Doreen.

'Thank you, I'll let *him* know,' replied Lewis.

Julia was fidgeting by the phone in the Lehmann residence hallway, sporting a throbbing fat lip, while hoping Avi would return her call — but Avi was hanging on the kitchen telephone, awaiting a connection to London.

Finally, his call went through. 'Shalom, Sir, it is Falco. I have several major problems, one of which is Bernard Lewis. I will arrive in London this afternoon. Can we meet... Good.'

Kathy turned her head toward the door. 'Please get a move on, the taxi is waiting.'

'Just a minute. I have to make one more quick call.' He dialled McClay as fast as the contraption would allow. 'Hello, Joe? It's Avi. I am going away for a few days. Could you keep an eye on Helmut Lehmann while I'm away? ... Excellent. I'll be in touch as soon as I get back.'

From a hidden vantage point at Central Station, PC Brookes watched Avi and Kathy loading their cases onto an express train bound for London. As the train pulled away, he slipped his hands into his overcoat pockets and sidled off with a contented smile.

The journey had been long and quiet. Avi and Kathy were sitting in a Second-Class compartment opposite a young married couple. The woman was heavily pregnant. The cracked NO SMOKING sign stuck to the carriage window served as a clear warning.

As the train devoured the track, Kathy had noticed the weather becoming increasingly brighter the further south they travelled. The greater the distance from Manchester, the more relaxed she became.

The soporific blend of abject fatigue and the gentle rhythm of the train had sent Avi into a deep sleep. Kathy finished her book and then glanced out of the window. Smiling at the pregnant woman, she asked: 'When's the baby due?'

'Should be any day now, with a bit o' luck.'

'Is this your first?'

'No, this'll be our fourth.'

'Blimey. You must have your work cut out.'

'You can say that again … but it's worth it. You got any?'

'We'll be pullin' into London soon. We've just got time for one last ciggy,' said her eager young husband, looking anxiously at his watch. His wife nodded. He prodded out two Park Drive untipped from his metal cigarette case and handed one to his wife. She smiled as they arose and left the carriage, without waiting for Kathy's reply.

Kathy looked over to Avi, but he was sound asleep. His dream was one of rare comfort. He was nine years of age, back in Leopoldstadt, Vienna, in 1928 …

... Avi's father, his older twin sisters, four grandparents, two aunts, and two uncles were sitting around a table in their family-run restaurant, chatting and laughing with gay abandon. Avi was sitting on his mother's knee. She rocked him while humming a soothing lullaby. He clung to her slim waist, tucked in against the warmth of her bosom, and the steady pulse of her reassuring heartbeat.

Meira was beautiful and completely relaxed with her only son. Her beaming smile reflected her happiness. Her heart was as pure as the white dress she wore. The close-knit family gathered to celebrate the Sabbath together. They broke Challah bread as Avi's father, Victor Falco, served the bountiful food.

The clatter of the carriage door slamming shut gave Avi a rude awakening. Kathy had again been pondering her plight since she'd left Manchester. Noticing Avi's jolt into consciousness, she asked, 'How long have we been married?'

Avi took a deep breath. He rubbed his eyes, stretched his arms, let out a loud yawn, and then patted his face. 'You know how long. Three years.'

'Yes, three years. In all that time, we've never discussed starting a family of our own.'

'We *have* discussed it, Kathy, but I'm just not ready to take on such a burden.'

'A burden? A family is not a burden; it is a blessing. I know that your family is no longer with us, but you've never told me of their circumstances. When you are a child, you always think that your parents will be there throughout the journey of life. To guide you and coach you and provide the unconditional love that a good mother and father will give. But to expect them to live forever is childish. That is not how it works, and now we both know the reality. People fall by the wayside, especially during a world war. The War took away not just yours, but millions of other parents, friends, or foe. Now the world is full of orphans who are left behind to cope. They gather strength and move on with their lives. We all die, Avi. It is part of the cycle of life. That is the risk we take when we bring new people into the world, but the positives will always outweigh the negatives.'

Avi shook his head. 'You are right, I was blessed with a family.'

'Yes, but you never talk about them. I've put up with this for far too long. How can I help you if you won't help me to understand your past?'

He stared beyond the window as if the question had never been asked. The train had sped along to the built-up suburban gateway into London. Its whistle squealed, and the carriages rattled as Kathy wiped her eyes with her handkerchief.

Agitated, she staggered to her feet. 'I have tried everything I know to get through to you, but you just won't let me in. This can't carry on. I can't carry on. I have seen enough misery to know that you must be happy in life, if not happy, at least contented, and I am neither. Life is too short. I don't want to be with you anymore, Avraham.'

The paunchy ticket inspector's head popped into the carriage. 'Approaching St Pancras. This is the end of the line.'

Shaking his head at the verbal irony, Avi recognised the gravity of the situation. He closed his eyes.

'Sit down, Kathy … please sit down and I will tell

you.'

Kathy brushed her dress as she complied.

He took a deep breath and puffed out his cheeks. 'I was eighteen years old when my father paid for me to attend the *Ludwig-Maximilians-Universität* to study Philosophy in Munich. He had saved up his money. He wanted his children to realise their dreams. I was one of the last Jews to be admitted. It was a great opportunity, but Munich was a political cauldron, a treacherous place. We had little idea of how bad it was until I arrived. There was no going back. I had to melt into the background and keep myself to myself. I didn't look typically Jewish, and nobody asked. I had one friend, my roommate Günter Kraft.

He was a big, strong mountain of a man, but also clever and resourceful. A really good man to know. But he had a quick temper. One lecture turned into a political debate. Several students spoke out against the Nazi regime, including Günter. I'd told him to keep his views to himself, but he got carried away — just that one time. There were all sorts of Nazi sycophants in the room. He was denounced to the authorities. I was guilty by association.

That night, we were summoned to report to the nearest police station. My papers showed that I was Jewish. I was arrested on a trumped-up charge. We were both sent on to Dachau Concentration Camp without a trial … without a prayer. We arrived in the dead of night. We were split up on the bus. I thought if I could get to him, it would all be all right, but once we got to the camp, it was brutal. It was chaos.

A guard rammed his rifle butt into my face. That is when I got this.' Avi touched the facial scar. 'My glasses were shattered and lost for good. The Nazis frowned on people who wore glasses. They were suspected intellectuals — a threat to the Reich. I couldn't see anything, but I could hear.

We were thrown into line. There was a scuffle. A prisoner was shot at point-blank range. I couldn't see the victim's face, nor that of the guard who murdered him … but I heard the voices. I knew it was Günter who had been shot. I've never forgotten the voice of the man who shot him.'

Back in Helmut Lehmann's dingy Site Depot office in Manchester, CI Collins entered as a buzzing fly swung around the room and landed on Lehmann's desk. Lehmann crushed it without shifting his gaze. 'Whisky, Chief Inspector?'

'Yes. I think I deserve a drink.'

Lehmann rose from his tattered chair and prepared two glasses. 'How so?'

'My contact in MI5 has replied. Falco was an SOE operative during the War. He undertook a series of assassinations of key ⁴⁴ personnel. He was highly efficient. When the War ended, he was given British citizenship and became a journalist. Lewis told me that Falco was sent up here from London to investigate the murder of David Adams. His father was Moshe Adamski.

Towards the end of the War, Adamski was a founding member of the Nakam, the so-called Jewish Avengers. Herbert Gaggs is the Chief Editor of the London Chronicle. He is a committed Zionist and has known links with the Nakam. They are sworn avengers of Nazi crimes against the Jews. They are not to be taken lightly.'

Lehmann's hand trembled slightly as he handed

Collins his nip.

'Does Falco have anything on you?' asked Collins.

'No. My tracks are covered.'

'Good. One of my men watched him board a train to London with his wife this morning. Falco spent six months recovering in Cane Hill Asylum in Croydon after he'd suffered a complete mental breakdown. While he was in Dachau, he was tortured to within an inch of his life. Do you know what they did to prisoners in Dachau?'

'No. I have no idea.'

'My MI5 man told me all sorts about that place. He said that *special* prisoners were condemned to serve time in medieval *standing cells,* with brick walls bolted in behind thick wooden doors. Each was two feet by six inches square with a small hatch at the top for air. Can you imagine? A prisoner was put into a standing cell for seventy-two hours at a time with no light and stale air to stifle the lungs. Always touching the walls, he couldn't sit down or crouch. He had to sleep standing up, usually locked up for three days and nights with just bread and water. Every fourth day, he was taken out and put into a normal cell. He was given standard prisoners' rations and allowed to sleep one night on a plank bed. Then the three-day standing period began again. It must have been like being stuck up a tight chimney stack, not knowing if you would ever come out alive … survival dependent on the whim of twisted torturers. Can you imagine what that would do to a man?'

Lehmann altered his gaze to avoid eye contact.

'If Falco suffered such blind terror, it's no wonder he went doolally.'

Lehmann broke into a satisfied smirk. 'I can imagine.'

'His nurse at the asylum became his wife, and his wife

is scared out of her wits. If he loves her, he won't be back. Who wouldn't love a woman who looks like that?'

Lehmann shrugged his shoulders as he looked out of the window.

In Avi's London hotel room, Kathy was sitting on one of the twin beds, her eyes fixed on the battered leather suitcase resting at her feet. Avi was sitting on the end of his adjacent bed, his face glistening with sweat.

'Please continue, Avi,' said Kathy.

He rubbed his brow. 'Five months in Dachau was like a lifetime. Early in 1940, my father risked everything by bribing the Gestapo to let me out. They agreed, providing I left Nazi Germany immediately.'

'What happened to your family?'

'They were left behind. The British would only take a limited number of Jews. I was young. My father's actions drew attention to the family, and their lives became a living nightmare. They lay low with the help of friends, but they were betrayed by neighbours anxious to please the authorities. They were eventually transported east in cattle trucks. My mother and father, my twin sisters, and my Grandparents. They were gassed in Auschwitz. All of them annihilated … except for one uncle and aunt who made it into Palestine just before the War began. They understood what was happening. They had money to get away, but my father had built up his restaurant. Despite his brother's pleas to join him, he wouldn't leave it behind. It was his life. Amid the vivid persecution, he still could not believe what he was seeing in front of him.'

Avi dropped his head and stared at the fraying carpet. 'During the Great Depression, my father and mother often provided free soup outside their restaurant. Long queues of grateful, hungry people. The same people who turned on him and my family once Hitler came to power. I always remember my father's words to those who thanked him for his kindness. He would say, "There is no humanity without compassion". My pappy had a generous heart.'

Kathy's empathy rose. She reached for a handkerchief.

'I made it into Switzerland, then on to Britain. My safe passage was arranged and sponsored by an old family friend. Now he's the owner of the Chronicle Group.'

'Herbert Gaggs? You go *that* far back with him?'

'He has contacts in high places. He secured my visa. My linguistic skills and hatred of the Nazis were of great interest to the Ministry of Ungentlemanly Warfare.'

Kathy shook her head in puzzlement.

'Their official title was *The British Special Operations Executive*. It was a covert unit set up to coordinate all action by way of subversion and sabotage against the enemy overseas. I was an early recruit. They trained me as part of a handpicked hit-squad that eliminated senior Nazis.'

'Eliminated — as in killed them?'

The rattle of the train and the familiar smell of the musty carriage helped in opening the door to the horror that haunted Avi's memory. He never wanted to return and recount his harrowing story, but he knew he must ...

... Avi waited as a whistling express steam train cut a determined dash through a winding, snow-bound, mountainous track, shaded with frosted green pine trees swaying in the stiff alpine breeze.

A spruced-up waiter weaved down a tight carriage

corridor towards a shuttered First-Class compartment. He carried a bottle of vintage champagne, chilling in an ice bucket on a round silver tray. He rapped the window three times and entered to the sound of raucous laughter.

The door opened as the waiter left to a belittling shout. 'We ordered two bottles. Get out and come back with the other bottle, schnell, schnell, you stupid fool!'

The waiter stepped back into the tight, rattling corridor. He exchanged a nod with young Avi, whose loaded gun was concealed under a towel draped over his tray.

Dressed in a waiter's white apron, Avi balanced the extra bottle of bubbly as he waited for the exact moment. Timing was paramount. He was focused and ready for the kill. As he advanced, he failed to register the passing compartment, populated only by a single mother holding hands with her timid young son.

Both dressed in black ᛋᛋ uniforms, middle-aged Commandant Bauer and Gauleiter Völler behaved like naughty schoolboys. Open-bloused, voluptuous young Heidi was perched on Völler's knee, her pencil skirt riding up her seductive thighs. Her stocking tops were on full view. The honey trap was set.

Three raps at the door. Avi entered as the train darted into a timely tunnel. Heidi dived to the floor. A rapid volley of shots illuminated the darkness. A woman screamed. The train emerged back into the light. The screams continued, but not from Heidi. Avi looked around. Both ᛋᛋ were dead. A shot had blasted through the wooden wall panel.

Rushing into the adjoining compartment, gripping the smoking gun, Avi was horrified to see a hysterical mother clutching her precious boy, limp from the gaping wound in his neck as blood spurted into her face and onto Avi's apron.

The shrill of the train's whistle jolted Avi back into the present. He bit down on the outside of his right index finger and then vigorously rubbed his forehead as if trying to erase the moment that had pushed him to the brink.

He glared at Kathy with despair etched on his face. He ran his fingers through his mop of hair. 'I killed an innocent child. I can't ever take that back… are you happy now?'

Kathy looked down at her shoes. She took a deep breath and whispered, 'I have always known your pain. I understand its roots. I have never doubted that you could make me happy. I was by your side while your demons tormented you. I pieced together what happened during your tirades, your hallucinations, and your nightmares. You were in such a state.

The doctors thought you would end your days trussed up in a straitjacket. I knew your history. Not in such detail as now, but I knew about the child on the train. I have always waited for you to tell me in your own time and your own words. I cannot possibly imagine your burden, but it wasn't your fault. You were a victim, Avi. A victim of circumstances. We were *both* victims of the War.'

Avi was too consumed to recognise and accept her subtle invitation.

Kathy offered her hand. 'I love my mother as you obviously loved yours. I've sacrificed mine to be with you … but there is no point. I am pleading with you not to continue with this, Avi. You will either end up dead or in a padded cell. I won't bury you, and I won't be a slave to your demons. You have to banish them or let them go … here and now.'

Kathy wanted to get close. To rub her cheek against his face so that he could smell her scent and feel the touch of her tender skin, so that he could know exactly what he would be missing if she walked out the door and out of his life. But his eyes had grown aloof, a vacancy she had seen many times before.

He let go of her hand and clenched his fist. 'When I was in Dachau… there was one particular guard. The prisoners called him Der Folterknechte.'

Kathy shook her head.

'*The Torturer*. A complete sadist. He tortured anyone who took his fancy … including me. He was the same guard who murdered my friend, Günter. I think he is the German I have found in Manchester. I have to find out for sure.'

'By putting *me* in danger?'

'I didn't think they would come after you. They came after me.'

'And then it was my turn. You didn't protect me, Avi.'

'I am so sorry, but he cannot be alive when my family is dead. He tortured me. It wasn't just physical. You have no idea.'

Silence prevailed. Kathy's brain was racing. She teetered on the verge of revealing her anguish.

I do have an idea of mental torture. A very clear idea. The torment from John Winnot was terrifying … Tell him, Kathy. Tell him what happened. Tell him how that pig toyed with you every night. Tell him how that pig toyed with you every night, and then finally raped you. Tell him about the torture, Kathy. Tell him about the rape. Now is your chance. Tell him now. A burden shared is a burden halved. But what are two burdens shared? Double the anguish? Keep it buried. Don't dig up the past. He already has too much of his own to cope with. Live for the future, not for the past.

Her burden was one she would shoulder without him. It had been determined from the onset of their relationship. 'Please tell me what happens after you've killed him? Will your family come back? You know it will never be enough. Please stop, Avi. You must forgive yourself and others for their past. They will be judged, Avi. Oh, they will be judged all right, but not by you. You *have* to stop.'

'*He* cannot be alive while my family is dead. He killed the only friend I had on this earth.'

'I am your friend here and now, Avi. The past is the past. What is done is done.'

'Not until I have finished. Then it will be done.'

Kathy's chin quivered as she choked out the words, 'Then you have to let me go. I can't live like this anymore.'

Avi reached out, but she pushed him away. Their eyes did not meet. They both knew that every word they uttered from now on would be vital. They could both hear the noise of new guests trundling down the hotel corridor until Avi spoke with increasing passion.

'I interviewed him in his home, Helmut Lehmann. He sat there lying through his teeth. Oh, he was clever. Very clever. He had all the answers — but I was not convinced. I have to find out for sure. What if there is no God, Kathy? What if there is no God and no afterlife? What if there is no Hell? He was the devil who helped create my Hell on earth. When Lehmann dies, you say that he will be judged... but by whom? He won't be punished, and I suspect you know it. He will get away with all his crimes. That must not happen. I must make sure it does not. You are right, he will be accountable — but not to God — he will be accountable to me. I will cut his life short more than good health allows. I will avenge my friend's murder, and I will gain revenge for the dreadful acts he committed.'

Kathy held back the tears. 'I hoped you would commit to something good. Just so you know, Avi, the War was over years ago, but the war inside your head will never end if you don't let it go. He may be accountable to you, but you are obviously not accountable to me.'

She fished out a piece of paper from her coat pocket. 'You had better take this.' She handed him the prescription for his medication. 'You don't want to lose both crutches in one day. I've had it, Avi. I'm sorry, but enough is enough.' She picked up her case and walked out the door.

Avi buried his head in his hands. His marriage was crumbling along with his sanity.

Kathy faltered up the hotel corridor. From her coat sleeve, she took out a handkerchief, wiped her eyes, and stepped into the waiting lift.

An hour or so had passed. Avi sustained a statuesque pose at the end of the bed, oblivious to his surroundings. The magnitude of Kathy's departure began to sink in. Tears of despair wet his cheeks as he fell into a deep crisis.

The hand of fate is pushing me into the abyss once more. The same hand that killed my family. The same hand that killed my friend. The same hand that slew the little boy. My punishment will never, ever, end.

An indelible image of Kathy framed his torment as she stood in her lily-white wedding dress on that heavenly spring day. A glittering treasure he'd allowed to slip through his fingers. It was he who had pushed her out of that door. His gloom had descended. Bereft and alone in the dark, Avi finally lifted his head from the palms of his hands.

When I met you, I was dead, inside and out. It was you who brought back my emotions ... Your faith, your devotion, your love ... You were my only reason to live ... My sweet mother ... my sweet Kathy.

Avi's sweat-stained vest pressed against his pounding chest. His body and mind were overwhelmed with pain, a pain that suffocated his very existence. He was utterly exhausted, his body and soul drained by fatigue. Tangled thoughts tormented his mind. It was a burden he could not carry alone. His vacant eyes swelled with tears.

So tired. So tired. If only I could sleep. Let my mind drift away to a place without burden ... a place without pain.

He looked at his shaking hands. *Falco the Failure.* He removed his wristwatch, placing it carefully next to him on the bed. He rummaged through his suitcase and pulled out his Swiss Army knife. The phone began to ring. He tugged out the knife's biggest blade and rested it against his scarred left forearm. He ignored the ringing bell as he slashed through his flesh.

Warm claret coursed over his goose-bumped skin.

The phone stopped ringing.

Avi flipped his arm over and moved the knife towards his wrist and all the life-supporting cables pulsating within.

A loud bang at the door. 'Cleaning woman ... please

let me in, mister.' More banging, and then keys rustled in the lock. 'Sorry, but I 'ave to cam in. I fink I've left me mop in yer barfroom.'

Her entrance pulled Avi back from the cliff edge. He quickly covered his injured arm with his shirt. The cleaning woman returned with the mop, taking an unconcerned glance on her way out. The phone rang once more.

Avi wrapped the shirt around his wound, staggered to his feet, and picked up the receiver.

'Uh, yes, yes, it's Avi … I'm sorry, sir, I will be there in thirty minutes.'

He rummaged through his suitcase and located the medication bottle. He took out a yellow pill and swallowed hard, and then strapped his watch to his right wrist.

Chapter 36.
Decisions, Decisions

The aging newspaper mogul Herbert Gaggs waited patiently outside the towering, late 17th-century Bevis Marks Synagogue. His olive-skinned Iberian features and continental good looks blended well with the physiognomies of the Spanish and Portuguese founders of this revered place of worship. Now in his mid-sixties, his face told a thousand stories. His bespoke Savile Row suit befitted a wise man of distinction who commanded the attention and respect of those around him.

Genuinely pleased to see Avi approaching, Gaggs greeted him with a warm, firm handshake, which was reciprocated by his former protégé. The erudite magnate exuded a confident and calm manner. While exchanging a respectful 'Shalom,' Gaggs looked at Avi from shoes to hat. 'You are thinner.' He flipped Avi's hand, noticing his nicotine-stained fingers, he made a tut. 'Still smoking like a chimney.'

'Still trying to look after me?'

Gaggs placed a paternal hand on Avi's shoulder. 'Of course, Avi. I always want the best for my favourite sons.' Gaggs noticed that Avi was wearing his watch on his right wrist and observed the tell-tale bulge under Avi's left overcoat sleeve, where a hastily made bandage concealed the painful, self-inflicted wound. He decided not to draw attention to the bulge; instead, he commented, 'What an exquisite Rolex.'

'Yes... a present from my wife.'

'Your wife has always possessed excellent taste.'

Avi handed him a photograph and got straight to the point. 'This is Chief Inspector Collins from the

Manchester Constabulary. He's entering the Freemasons lodge with his associates. I am reasonably certain they are responsible for the murder of David Adams. I strongly suspect they also murdered Jens Wolff and Tommy Green. Bernard Lewis is one of them.'

'*Lewis*. I was right not to trust a gentile.'

'My wife is a gentile, and I would trust her with my life.'

Gaggs issued a wry smile. 'I am sure you would. It still disturbs me that God did not witness your plighted troth. There is still time for him to bless your union with Kathy.'

'I should doubt that very much.' Avi handed Gaggs another picture. 'This is Helmut Lehmann entering the same lodge several minutes later. Lehmann is behind whatever plot they are scheming.'

'Helmut Lehmann? This is the man you suspect could be a guard who gave you special attention during your time in Dachau?'

'Yes.'

'I don't wish to question your judgement, Avi, but it is nearly twenty years ago. There were thousands of ᛋᛋ guards at Dachau during your incarceration, and without your glasses, you were virtually blind … you told me yourself. However, to quote the French philosopher Denis Diderot, "Scepticism is the first step towards the truth".'

'I understand your scepticism. It is true. Guards were mostly anonymous to me, but the odd one stood out from the pack. You always remember the dog that bites you, and this one had a very distinctive bark.'

'Perhaps we should find out if this old dog is up to the same old tricks?'

'I have already questioned him about the murder of Jens Wolff.'

'And what was revealed?'

'Nothing of real significance, but I do believe that his character was exposed. He sees life as something to be exploited for his own gain. He sees his life as superior to that of all others. He is arrogant, selfish, and ambitious. A self-proclaimed superior being. He has all the trademarks of the man I suspect him to be, but I cannot explain his rise from obscurity to prominence in such a short space of time.'

'Perhaps he has made a Faustian pact with the Devil?'

'No. If he is Der Folterknechte, he is the Devil incarnate.'

Gaggs shook his head. 'His solipsism is his weakness, not his strength. It will lead to his downfall *if* he is played with care.' He produced a copy of the picture of Lehmann receiving the Iron Cross while in the 7th Army. 'The German War Records Commission confirmed that Helmut Lehmann was a decorated soldier. They supplied this picture of him receiving the Iron Cross in Wehrmacht uniform in 1942.'

'Lehmann has already shown me this photograph.'

'My man in MI5 investigated your request. Helmut Lehmann's battalion was obliterated by the Americans while on the retreat into Germany. Before the War, Lehmann had a scar above his right eye. Your man had an identical fresh scar when he fell into British hands.'

'It is too much of a coincidence. Lehmann is not the man he says he is.'

'Perhaps. Perhaps not. When he arrived in England, there were only two surviving soldiers from his battalion: Helmut Lehmann and a young Senior Private named

Bonhoeffer. *Oberschütze* Bonhoeffer, to be precise.'

'Bonhoeffer?'

'Eldred Bonhoeffer was murdered in Kempton Park Transit Camp on 25th June 1945, not long after Lehmann was transferred there. Lehmann was questioned, but investigations into such matters were slack. British officers preferred to let the prisoners fight it out among themselves.'

'So, if Bonhoeffer knew the real Lehmann, he would have known he was an imposter. Perhaps Wolff uncovered this and was blackmailing him? I think Lehmann is ᛋᛋ... but he doesn't have the ᛋᛋ tattoo.'

'Not all ᛋᛋ were tattooed.'

'Pardon me?'

Gaggs raised his eyebrows. 'The blood group tattoo was mostly for combat ᛋᛋ. High-ranking ᛋᛋ and ᛋᛋ camp guards were often able to avoid the inscription as it was far less likely they would need a transfusion on the battlefield. You didn't know?'

'I only saw pictures of their faces. They didn't ask me to rip their shirts off to check before I killed them.' Avi took out a packet of cigs.

With a shake of the head, Gaggs glanced down at the cigarettes. Avi put them straight back into his pocket. Gaggs gave a sardonic smirk and commented, 'The Bavarian Kinder Refuge Agency signed off on Lehmann's daughter's citizenship.'

'His daughter has also expressed several doubts about her father to me.'

'How old is the daughter?'

'She is fifteen.'

'Then she is still a child, and everything we have on him is circumstantial. If you think this man is ᛋᛋ you must prove it.'

'I'm not Nakam anymore. I left that life behind, years ago.'

'I understand. I also understand the personal toll it has taken.' Gaggs placed his hand on Avi's shoulder and continued, 'As you are aware, I am a great believer in the concept of *middah k'neged middah.*'

' "Hail the just man, for he shall fare well; He shall eat the fruit of his works. Woe to the wicked man, for he shall fare ill; as his hands have dealt, so shall it be done to him". Isaiah 3-10-11. I am aware of your philosophical allegiances, Mr Gaggs.'

'It is also my firm belief that measure-for-measure retribution doesn't go far enough, particularly when one is forced to implement divine justice. This is a difficult situation. The wise are those who hold back. You must balance the advantages with the disadvantages of any action that you may take. Remember, Avi: *Fools rush in where angels fear to tread.*' Gaggs' eyes narrowed. 'I must emphasise that this is a key investigation, and it must be settled. It would be a pity not to have you on board, Avi, but if *you* feel that you cannot close this assignment, I will appoint an alternative. If *I* feel that you cannot close this assignment, I will appoint an alternative. It is not too late to bring in a replacement.'

'No, this one is mine,' said Avi.

'Good. Then remember your training. Keep calm. Stay focused. If you are going to try to track down the ᛋᛋ, the Russians possess most of the surviving ᛋᛋ files at their War Crimes Commission in Vienna. It was supposed to be shut down at the end of the four-power occupation in '55, but they stubbornly retain a few footholds in the West. The Red Army lost over 18,000 soldiers when they fought the ᛋᛋ to take control of the city in 1945. They like to remind the locals who *really* drove out the Nazis. We will finance your trip.'

'I have to go to Munich first. I shall require passports and currency.'

'It is already in hand.' Gaggs' outstretched hand had guided Avi's eyes towards the synagogue. 'Perhaps you should seek guidance from the Lord before you set off on your mission. You might have lost faith in Him, but He has not lost faith in you.'

'As I recall, Diderot also said, "If you want me to believe in God, then you must make me touch Him".'

'One never knows, Avi. You may do just that.'

Returning to his hotel room, Avi found a small leather bag resting on the bed. He paced back and forth, his mind whirling. All options remained open. Despite his reassurances to Gaggs, he still hadn't decided which way to go at the fork in the road.

I'll have to live with this decision for the rest of my life.

Finally, he sat down on the sheet. He picked up the phone and dialled. There was a ring tone, and then he said, 'Hello, operator. Croydon 2472 please.'

'Thank you, sir. Hold the line, please.'

Avi opened the bag. Inside were a blue British passport in the name of Julian West, a green West German Federal Republic passport in the name of Julius Perl, and a buff Austrian passport in the name of Michael Knoller. There was also a generous wad of mixed currency.

He studied the passports.

The operator returned. 'Connecting you now, sir.'

A sudden, overwhelming urge took hold. After a moment of hesitation, he said, 'It is all right, I will leave it, thank you.' He hung up the phone and, with a deep sigh, removed his wedding ring.

Chapter 37.
Contrived Convalescence

Herbert Gaggs and the eminent psychiatric consultant, Matthew Burrows, lingered behind the tall patio doors of the functional conservatory, which overlooked the well-kempt garden in the sun-drenched grounds of Surrey's Cane Hill Asylum. The summer of 1953 was especially hot in Southern England.

The songs of delicate birds serenaded the idyllic scene; their feathers lifted gently in the cool summer breeze. The leafy branches of a generous thicket of deciduous trees shielded troubled residents from prying eyes.

Mid-afternoon sun poured down on the convalescing Avi Falco, who rested on a cushioned wicker chair with a small wooden table by its side. The patient was oblivious to the hum of pollinating bumble bees that hopped from one luscious flower to the next. Nor was he alert to the sweet aromas of freshly cut grass and arching honeysuckle, all congruent with the colourful scenery.

Avi was dressed in blue paisley pyjamas, a maroon dressing gown, and well-worn, navy-blue corduroy slippers. Despite the glorious weather, a folded plaid blanket resting on his lap protected his legs from goosebumps. He cut a casual and relaxed figure from afar, but closer inspection revealed gaunt and sallow features with bloodshot eyes encircled with sunken rings. The book sitting on the adjacent wicker chair remained unopened as he stared vacantly into space.

A trim nurse in her late twenties, Kathy Cranighan, eased across the lawn, carrying two glasses of freshly made lemonade. An English rose at the crest of her bloom; Kathy lay the tray down on the table. She tucked Avi's woollen blanket neatly under his thighs and handed him a drink. Dressed in a standard all-white uniform, she eased into the small upright chair by his side while radiating her warm disposition.

Avi stirred from his trance-like state. He perked up and smiled in her direction. Kathy opened his bookmarked Charles Dickens novel, *Great Expectations*. She nodded and then continued her recital as she gently stroked the top of Avi's right hand with her thumb.

Both were unaware of the watching duo.

Gaggs was impressed. 'He is obviously less agitated than during my last visit, Dr Burrows. You appear to have made remarkable progress.'

'Slowly but surely, he is coming back from the brink, but the neuro psychoanalytical process requires time and patience. This particular therapy is a pioneering new treatment. A lasting, positive outcome is far from guaranteed, but I believe it is the right direction to take. A chronic dependency on alcohol exacerbated his traumatic state. This appears to have desisted. CNS depressants have been retained in line with the treatment guidance. Now that his body has been largely detoxified, I believe that the chances of his mind making a meaningful recovery have improved significantly. There is no discernible liver damage. His self-inflicted flesh wounds are healing nicely. At this point, his hallucinations appear to have ceased. Even his appetite is beginning to return.'

'What about the night terrors?'

'Alas, they persist, and more so than before. There is substantial pain inside that broken mind. He must take ownership and control of his thoughts and the emotions they generate. But he must also find a much stronger will within himself to make this happen. What occurs at night is beyond his control. I suspect that Mr Falco's nightmares are the complex manifestations of a deep torment of conscience, rather than the impulsions of alcoholism or drug abuse. Inside his subconscious mind is the brake that restricts his progress. It is a brake that somehow must be released for him to have any prospect of a return to normality. "And his eyes have all the seeming of a demon's that is dreaming".'

'A line from 'The Raven' by Edgar Allan Poe if I'm not mistaken. Another man tormented by his inner demons.'

'Indeed, Mr Gaggs.'

'Indeed, Dr Burrows … and *I* am reminded of a particularly poignant poem.'

'Pray tell, Mr Gaggs, for I am a keen scholar of fine poetry.'

'As you wish.' Gaggs scratched his chin and released a brief cough before reciting.

'To overcome the mountain steep,
To cheat the Devil's toll not cheap.
Banish them true, so as not to weep,
Dig a great hole and bury them deep.

Released from shackles when his sleep,
Dark memories that are his to reap.
Pray to the heavens when nightmares creep,
No shelter to find, his conscience to keep.'

'Not a poem of which I am familiar, Mr Gaggs. One of your own, perhaps?'

'That bad, was it?'

'Not a classic … but poignant nonetheless.'

Gaggs exhaled a lengthy sigh. 'We all have our burdens to bear. Mine is amateur poetry, and alas, it would appear to reveal a lack of natural ability in that particular form of literary expression.'

Burrows' smile was one of duty.

'At least you are doing sterling work, Dr Burrows.'

'We have yet to confirm the catalyst of his mental breakdown. Until this main trigger is identified and confronted, he could relapse into a suicidal state at any moment. Getting him to part with his emotions instead of turning them on himself is key to this process.'

Gaggs looked up to the heavens. 'What is your supposition of this root cause of his decline?'

'Since the expiration of his secret Wartime activities, settling into the banalities of post-war life has led him into a circumspect existence. He believes that his life has little or no meaning. He is consumed with guilt – perhaps the guilt of being the only survivor of his family, but I suspect that there is a more profound event that has caused his depression. Perhaps a wrong has occurred, he cannot possibly make right, something he has no power to change, Mr Gaggs?'

'Perhaps only revenge or atonement will lighten his burden. With God's help, I may find an opportunity to lead him to both. It is my opinion that true enlightenment is only attained through painful experience.'

'Do you know more about Mr Falco than you have told me, Mr Gaggs?'

'Absolutely not. Please forgive me. I was only thinking out loud.'

'Hmm. These are still early days, Mr Gaggs. With due diligence and the right medication, we might just persuade him into a state of permanent calm contentment.

'Perhaps we can find him a little more than that. Who is the delightfully pretty and attentive nurse at his side?'

'Miss Cranighan,' said Burrows.

'Cranighan!' replied Gaggs, who then tried to cover the intonation of his surprise by continuing with a deeper tone. 'I was once led to believe that Cranighan is an extremely rare, gentile surname. Her first name is not Mary, Mary Cranighan from Bexley, perchance?'

'No, it is Kathy. *Miss* Kathy Cranighan, originally from Stepney, according to her file.'

Gaggs offered a wry smile.

Burrows raised a fist to his mouth and cleared his throat. 'Nurse Cranighan is a dedicated and talented individual. She is one of our best nurses. Your perception appears to be accurate, Mr Gaggs. Come to think of it, she *has* taken a shine to your Mr Falco. Her personal devotion has certainly strengthened over the past months, and for that, I do apologise. We actively discourage any sort of fraternisation between staff and patients.'

'More's the pity. The sainted angel nurtures the injured bird, clasping it gently to her breast. She caresses it with the tenderness and devotion afforded by her love without condition. Soon the bird will fly once more, and the awaiting flock in heaven will rejoice.'

'You appear to be a hopeless romantic, Mr Gaggs. Unfortunately, this bird may be beyond repair, even with the love of a good woman.'

'Perhaps. Perhaps not. They look good together. Maybe there is potential for something more. Something special.'

In the distance, they could see Kathy taking a gentle grip on Avi's hand as the white bandage, tightly strapped to his wrist, was inadvertently exposed. Gaggs went on. 'You have just said that getting him to part with his emotions, instead of turning them on himself, is key to this process. Nurse Cranighan could be just the person to facilitate this objective successfully, and that would be of benefit to all parties involved. That is the first time I've seen Avraham smile in a very long time. Perhaps there is something more than just coincidence that has brought these two together. She could be a beacon of light shining out from his darkness.'

'I'm sorry, Mr Gaggs?'

'God moves in a mysterious way.'

'His wonders to perform,' said Burrows, who rubbed his fingers nervously against his chin as both men collected their thoughts.

A cheeky red squirrel scurried up to the door behind which Gaggs and Burrows were sheltered. It sat on his haunches, glanced at the pensive duo, before darting up the nearest oak tree in search of a tasty nutty snack.

Gaggs broke the silence. 'You mentioned earlier words to the effect that his mind and his body must reacquire strength before he can leave this facility. However, he must develop a much stronger will to make this happen. In my humble opinion, he needs a more tangible incentive than mere self-preservation.

I see an angel. A sainted angel dressed in white who can give him that will. I should like Nurse Cranighan's personal care of Mr Falco to be maintained, perhaps even extended. She looks at him in the loving way my wife used to look at me, God bless her soul. We all need to be loved, Dr Burrows. She is perhaps just what the doctor should order?'

'Unfortunately, Mr Falco's precarious emotional state

is not one to be trifled with, particularly in terms of those of the opposite gender. We have treated many recovering soldiers in this institution over the years. If they get the wrong idea about professional female kindness, it can easily send them straight back to the dark places from whence they came.'

' "Cupid is a knavish lad, thus, to make poor mortals mad!" ' said Gaggs with a smile.

'Ah, William Shakespeare,' said Burrows. 'A genius with an unadulterated comprehension of the meaning of tragedy.'

Gaggs and Burrows continued to study the subjects of their conversation, congenial in each other's company. Burrows resumed, 'Nevertheless, I do think that perhaps it is time for a new nurse to attend to Mr Falco's needs. He is an extremely vulnerable man.'

'That would be such a pity, Dr Burrows. Perhaps another nought on this month's cheque or a cash advance might assist with the continuation of his gentle female therapy?' said Gaggs.

'Your judgement on this matter does not entirely convince me, but you are paying his bills, Mr Gaggs. You are also playing with fire, and besides...' Burrows hesitated, careful not to overstep the mark.

'Besides what, Dr Burrows?

Burrows' silence continued. He shifted his gaze down to the floor.

'Pray tell. I shan't be offended,' said Gaggs.

'They aren't *religiously* compatible.'

Gaggs shook his head and smiled. 'Don't tell anyone, Dr Burrows, but my late wife was also a gentile. It is my experience that when you meet the right woman, you meet the right woman. God understands. Arrangements can be made. Some matches are made in heaven, not on earth.'

'Perhaps you are getting ahead of yourself, Mr Gaggs.'

'Perhaps I am, indeed. However, I always find it prudent to plan well ahead. I find it makes life so much easier.'

Burrows stroked his chin. 'An additional cash payment will suffice in this instance. As you are aware, his treatment is unofficial, and I shall deny any collusion if your chosen course of action causes him to relapse into his previous self-destructive mode.'

Gaggs produced his wallet and plucked out several large-denomination notes, offering Burrows the bonus. 'You have my money and my gratitude, Dr Burrows. Sometimes there are instances in life when the latter can be of greater value than the former.'

Burrows pocketed the money. 'Not in my world, Mr Gaggs.'

Gaggs offered a wry smile. 'I understand your concern, Dr Burrows, and I remain grateful for upholding my anonymity in this matter. I shall maintain my responsibility for Mr Falco's care. I would prefer that you nurture their relationship and allow them extra space. His future well-being is my primary concern, and in consideration of Nurse Cranighan's positive involvement, perhaps I am no longer alone in this regard. I have always been confident in my judgement of a person's true character. Sometimes key events in life require a gentle nudge in the right direction to obtain the best possible results. As I am sure you are aware, "Great oaks from little acorns grow".'

Chapter 38.
Cold Shoulder

The propellers whirred in a blur. The BEA Airspeed ambassador passenger plane was buffeted as it cut through thick grey rain clouds hanging over Western Germany. Through the edges of his tiny window, Avi saw a scatter of disparate buildings as the earth approached with a disconcerting lack of equilibrium. He felt for his absent wedding ring for the umpteenth time, although his new watch offered much-needed reassurance.

The constant drone of the two twin-piston engines muffled the prim English voice announcing their imminent landing. Her message triggered an involuntary response. Avi struggled to keep his stomach contents as a wave of panic swept over him. A foreboding not borne from fear of crashing, despite the fuselage tilting caused by heavy crosswinds on the approach. Instead, it was his dread of returning to the country of people he loathed that caused nausea.

As his nerves continued to fray, Avi's stash of small yellow pills had shrunk. His decision not to protest the separation from Kathy was never more doubtful than during the descent into Bavaria.

Despite the weather, the silver propeller plane landed safely on the Munich-Riem Airport runway. Avi watched as the aircraft was guided into the arrivals' terminal by an aircraft marshaller wielding the customary red table-tennis bats.

Stepping out onto the mobile staircase, Avi's lungs were filled with his first breath of German air since the poison of the Third Reich had been dispersed. He managed to snatch his trilby hat before it blew into the distance, thus preventing a poor start to his return to a country guilty of countless crimes against his people.

Cold and weary, Avi schlepped into the airport arrivals lounge, an inconspicuous traveller among an anonymous herd. His black trilby hat was perched back on his head. His grey overcoat was draped over his left arm. His lightweight leather suitcase was held in his right hand, and the heavy weight of his self-imposed decision pressed down on his shoulders.

He hadn't spoken German fluently for a while, but he slipped back effortlessly as he joined the queue for passport verification. With Julius Perl's green West German passport at the ready, he blended with his stone-faced contemporaries as they waited in the long queue for the usual red tape to be cut.

Avi knew he would have to suppress his hatred for the Germans ... for now, at least. His lips tightened as he couldn't help but stare at all those *contented-looking, middle-aged sour Krauts growing fat on Western charity.*

He had hoped that the War and its aftermath would have caused as much suffering as possible for those *servile, murdering, Nazi bastards,* but to his bitter disappointment, normality dominated his initial impressions.

How many of these fickle, cold-hearted hypocrites seized the helping hand offered by my father and many other generous but misguided Jews during the famine before the War? Now that the War is over, they're at it again. The British, Americans, and French have extended a helping hand to restore their country's stability. No oppressive treaties this time. No reparations for the guilt-

ridden nation. Crimes unpunished. It wasn't just the leaders who should have been hanged. They should have weeded out all the Nazis, put them against the wall, and shot the lot of them... at least this queue would have been a lot shorter, thought Avi, trying to lighten his dark mood. After a cursory check of his passport, Avi crossed the main terminal into West Deutschland without incident.

In the clear, raw evening, Avi paid the taxi driver from the airport and then crossed the busy Munich city centre street toward the three-star Hotel Treff on *Residenzstraße*. The hotel was just a stone's throw from the floodlit *Feldherrnhalle*, the iconic 19th-century memorial to the Bavarian Army and shrine to the sixteen martyrs killed in Hitler's failed 1923 Beer Hall Putsch.

Avi smiled wryly. From his time at university, he recognised the sacred shrine of many ostentatious, torchlit Nazi ceremonies. He suspected Herbert Gagg's curious sense of humour had played a part in the ironic location of his first hotel booking.

Adhering to his training, Avi circled the hotel. He cased the building for potential escape routes in the event of a need for a quick getaway. Each of the rear rooms had an iron landing leading to fire escape staircases located at either end of the building. The back alley had several exit points, which allowed access back to the main street. He was now contented.

Perhaps this was the real reason for Gaggs' choice of this three-star hotel? thought Avi, who entered the bland lobby and approached the reception desk with tired eyes.

He handed his bogus passport to the breezy male receptionist, who located the picture page with nonchalant ease.

'Thank you, Herr Perl. You are booked in for tonight only. Your room is located on the first floor. If you need anything, please dial 100 for reception. I hope you will enjoy your stay.'

Avi picked up a brochure from the counter. 'Do you have a road map of Munich, please?'

'Of course, sir.' With a warm smile, he handed Avi a map from under the counter. The map was rubber-stamped *Hotel Treff.*

Avi checked the location of the fire escape exits on the landing before entering his sparsely furnished room. Taking off his overcoat, he dropped onto the single bed. The distant sound of beeping car horns seeped through the glazed window above a well-used chest of drawers.

An erect spring pressing into his left buttock from beneath the eiderdown was not a sign of a comfortable night's sleep ahead. Fortunately, sleep was not his goal. Besides, he had slept on far worse, especially in Bavaria.

He lit up another cig and opened his suitcase. Next to his bed was a small table with a lamp, a telephone, and an outdated 1955 *München Telefonbuch*. He took out his Swiss Army knife, pulled back the bed sheets, and cut along the seam of the mattress, where he eased in his spare passports and a wad of cash. With his reading glasses on, he took out a pre-threaded needle and quickly darned the seam in haste. He flipped the mattress and remade the bed with the tampered seam facedown against the wall.

Picking up the phone directory, he flicked through the pages, searching for 'S' for Spangell. There were five listings: one for A. Spangell, one for D. Spangell, and the next for F. Spangell. T. Spangell was listed a few lines below. Avi looked at his watch, exhaled cigarette smoke, and picked up the heavy black receiver. He dialled 100 and requested reception. 'An outside line, please.' He paused, then dialled.

A ringtone rang out. 'Hello. Who on earth is ringing me at this time of the evening?' came the reply with a hint of slur.

In his Austro-Bavarian accent, Avi said, 'Is that Felix Spangell. Proprietor of the Spangell Orphanage?'

'Who wants to know?'

'I have a child I want to leave in your care. I will pay you well for your services.'

'Then ring me at the orphanage tomorrow. The number is listed.'

The line went dead.

Avi hung up. He took out a pen and wrote down the private address on the front of the map, which he unfolded, then searched for the location. He put a cross next to the Feldherrnhalle and drew a route to Spangell's residence. Avi dropped the pen and clasped his hands together. He had been in the area before. Spangell could be found in the small north-western suburb of Munich called Dachau, a fifteen-kilometre drive from the city centre. It had never occurred to Avi that he might be compelled to go back there one day, even if it was just the town he was forced to visit.

He rattled his bottle and flipped out another yellow pill. Skulking into the bathroom, he shook his head in disbelief at his ironic fate.

If it has to be done, it has to be done.

Chapter 39.
The Long, Dark, Night

Avi left the hotel and stepped into the biting cold, regretting the forfeit of his overcoat and trilby hat. He weaved briskly across the bustling road as a group of tramps warmed their mitts around the orange glow of a crackling street brazier.

Once on the other side, he cut into a one-way backstreet where a few parked cars pointed in the same direction — the unlit alley reeked of rotting rubbish and stale urine. The constant chunner of the city's soundscape was broken by the shock of discarded wine bottles shattering in a distant bin. From an alcove, the giggles of a frisky young couple subsided as they finished petting and slipped away into the night, zipping and buttoning.

While wriggling his fingers into tight leather driving gloves, Avi scanned the scene, then peered into the windows of two parked BMWs. He yanked on their door handles, but to no avail.

Further up the alley, a tired-looking Volkswagen Beetle appeared more vulnerable. Using his Swiss Army knife as a jemmy, he broke into the driver's door with ease. He jumped inside, pulled the choke out halfway, and, with a fish key protruding from the knife handle, started the engine. After a quick look at the street map, he reversed out of the alley. Once the stolen Beetle was clear of the entrance, he switched on the headlights and headed for his target.

Avi drove toward *Marsstraße*, beginning his thirty-minute journey to Munich's outskirts, heading towards Dachau. Along the way, he passed through *Karlsfeld*, home of the Spangell Orphanage, where business was still active in the post-war decade. Reaching the main Dachau thoroughfare of the familiar *Sudetenlandstraße,* he turned onto a quiet road with several upscale detached houses near low-rise apartment blocks. These had been built before the War to house senior Dachau camp officers and their families.

Avi paused to examine the map more closely to find the address. He released the handbrake and drove slowly past Spangell's detached, stuccoed house. He circled the block and finally parked opposite his target on the empty street nearby. He killed the headlights. He focused entirely on his plan. His adrenaline racing, he checked the address again and then dropped the map on the passenger seat.

He climbed out of the Beetle as a German Shepherd nearby began barking fiercely. The angry dog was confined behind the tall fence of a large detached house overlooking Spangell's property.

The full moon and a sky full of twinkling stars illuminated the row of large, red-roofed houses. Heavy rain clouds closing in from the east threatened to spoil the beautiful scene.

In this bright light, Avi looked over Spangell's house for an easy entry. He knocked on the wooden fence to catch the attention of a similarly agitated guard dog. Luckily, there was no response. Meanwhile, the German Shepherd continued to bark loudly.

With his trusted knife, Avi broke into the garden shed and grabbed a sturdy flat screwdriver. He moved toward a ground-floor sash window on the side of the house and pried it open without making a sound.

The febrile dog continued to disturb the peace. Its

wizened owner opened the first-story window facing Spangell's house. He looked over the budding flowers in his window box and shouted, 'Blondi, be quiet … now!'

Did the old man catch a glimpse of a prowler entering his neighbour's house? His eyesight may have worsened with age. He wasn't sure if the window was open and hesitated over whether to call the police. With a firm grip of the banister, he began a careful descent downstairs to make the call, but then reconsidered.

The old man had never been fond of Spangell — it was mutual dislike — but the neighbourhood was vigilant. Crime had risen since the nearby camp was renovated and filled with vagrant thieves and vagabonds. The unfamiliar Volkswagen Beetle parked across the street was the deciding factor. The old man began to dial.

Once inside Spangell's house, Avi looked around the high-ceilinged study. An assortment of children's toys lay in a pile in one corner of the room. He took great care to silently release the brass door handle, cautiously edging into a carpeted corridor and toward a room where a tell-tale light shone from beneath the door.

Knowing that surprise was crucial, Avi sneaked into the hot lounge, troubled by a stale smell of sweat and Cuban cigars. A sudden burst of heavy snoring confirmed Spangell's vulnerability.

Right then, Uncle Felix, let's hear what you've got to say for yourself.

Sporting a comb-over, the obese, pig-skinned Spangell was slumped in a green, wing-backed leather armchair. His shoulders had sunk like the dying embers of his coal-fuelled fire. His pockmarked, bulbous face resembled an overgrown, last-out-of-the-sack celeriac. A generous glass of schnapps and an empty lead crystal decanter sat on a small table beside him. The smoke from his cigar slowly dissipated.

Avi hesitated at an unexpected creak from the floorboards as he drew closer. Sneaking up behind his target, he pressed the long blade of his knife to Spangell's throat. His finger stretched behind the blade for support. Spangell woke abruptly.

The knife scraped against his pink, leathery skin, causing a bead of blood to spill onto the gleaming blade. 'Good evening, Herr Spangell,' whispered Avi. 'I have some questions, and one way or another, you will answer them. Do you understand?"

Spangell gave a faint nod. With his empty hand, Avi displayed a worn picture of Helmut Lehmann receiving the Iron Cross in a Wehrmacht uniform from 1942. He thrust it into Spangell's line of sight. Once again, he whispered into Spangell's hairy ear, 'This is Helmut Lehmann. He picked up Julia Lehmann from your orphanage in 1947. You know this man. Yes?'

'No, I don't know this man,' said Spangell, his denial emphatic.

'No, you say?' cried Avi with involuntary anger.

'I'm sorry, but I have dealt with so many children that I ... I ... The picture is old, and I can't remember.'

Avi pushed the knife harder against Spangell's throat. The wound extended, becoming a bleeding scratch. He returned to his tactical whisper. 'A bad start, Herr Spangell. This is your last chance. You know this man, right?'

Spangell nodded.

'Good. Then tell me.'

'Tell you what?'

'Tell me about Lehmann of course, or I will kill you here and now, you lying, German pig!' cried Avi.

Spangell's frail resistance collapsed. 'Yes, yes. Okay. He approached me. He had a British passport but no German identity. Just army tags. It was not enough to take a child under German law. He gave me a diamond. A diamond to release her with all the necessary papers.'

'That's better,' said Avi, his tone softer. 'You did know, after all. Make it easy on yourself, Herr Spangell. Relieve your burden. Tell the truth, and it will be easy. What was Wolff's role in this?'

'*Wolff*. Yes, Wolff. He said he returned from a Siberian labour camp a year ago. He came searching for his son, but his son was never here.'

'Was Wolff former ᛋᛋ?'

No response.

Avi tightened his grip. 'Was Wolff former ᛋᛋ?'

'No, no! He was worse. He was SD, the intelligence agency of the ᛋᛋ. We blackmailed those children I passed illegally. Lehmann has diamonds. He was high on the list. I thought he was somewhere in Britain. Wolff must have tracked him down. He was very resourceful. A survivor.'

'Not resourceful enough. He's dead.'

Without warning, a child's muffled voice called from outside the room: 'Please let me go. *I need to go!*'

Avi was startled by this unexpected company. He lost his concentration and relaxed his grip. 'Why are toys in the other room?'

'My son is here.'

The young voice continued its frantic plea. '*Please, Uncle Felix!*'

Avi reached a realisation. '*He's not your son!*'

Spangell lurched from his chair and grabbed the glass

318

decanter. He turned and took a wild swing, which Avi blocked with one arm. The decanter catapulted from Spangell's gasp and shattered against the granite fireplace.

Avi punched Spangell hard with two sharp jabs to the solar plexus.

Spangell dropped to the floor with a thud. His arms hugged his chest as he gasped for breath. The young boy continued to bleat.

Avi trod on Spangell's neck. 'You are lying! Wolff wasn't working with you... *He was blackmailing you!'*

He lifted his foot, crouched, and knocked out Spangell with a punch to his double chin. Spangell's head recoiled, exposing his flimsy comb-over.

The childish shrills drew Avi to an ajar door halfway down the corridor. He pushed it cautiously, revealing a dungeon-like cellar. He descended the shallow stone staircase to the bottom, trying to understand the layout. A malnourished child lay chained to a wrought iron bed, which was bolted to a steel anchor embedded in the concrete floor.

Barely dressed in filthy underwear, the young boy cowered just out of reach of a nearby bucket. His petrified face turned away from view.

'Hello, young man. Please look at me, I'm not here to hurt you,' said Avi.

The boy stayed tightly wrapped. He turned and looked through Avi with vacant eyes.

Avi pushed the bucket closer to the boy. 'You need to use this. I understand. It will be all right.' He pointed to the wall. 'I will turn away and go to the wall over there while you go.' As he walked away, the sudden tinkling in the bucket signalled immediate relief. Avi allowed time to finish. Then he wandered back to the boy.

'What is your name?'

The grateful boy turned around. 'My n-n-name is J-Josef.'

'What is your last name, Josef?'

'H-H-Hirschfeld. Josef H-Hirschf-feld, s-sir.'

'Hello Josef. How old are you, Josef?'

'I am t-ten.'

Avi bit hard on his lip in his disgust at Spangell, but managed to retain his composure. 'We must both stay calm. I promise you that you are safe. I am going to leave the room now. Spangell will not hurt you anymore. I will call for help. Can you keep a secret, Josef?' Josef nodded.

'Are you sure?'

'Yes.'

'Good boy. I am 'The Falcon' and I have saved you. I have to go now, but I will fly back for you very soon, Josef Hirschfeld. Do you understand me? The Falcon will return, but you mustn't tell anyone who I am. It is our secret.'

Josef nodded.

Avi smiled and winked. 'Sit tight, Josef. I promise it will soon be over.'

A *Landespolizei* patrol car pulled up beside the stolen Beetle outside Spangell's house as rain started to fall. The portly *Polizeimeister* Krämer and his young subordinate Lothar Beck scrutinised the empty vehicle. The car doors were unlocked. Krämer picked up a folded map from the driver's seat, and Avi's route to Spangell's address suddenly became very interesting.

Avi marched back into the lounge. Armed with the

broken neck of the crystal decanter, Spangell jumped out from behind the wall. With the wail of a banshee, he jabbed it toward Avi's face. Catching hold of Spangell's right wrist, Avi blocked the jagged glass just a hair's breadth from his right eye. Avi held firm and then thrust the weapon back towards his attacker, throwing Spangell over his leg and onto his back. Still locked together, the momentum thrust Avi on top of the prostrate Spangell, who inadvertently pushed the vicious weapon into his own neck, severing the main carotid artery.

Spangell released the weapon. Blood seeped through his fingers as he gripped his neck while he choked in a bloody, gurgling heap.

Both officers moved toward the Spangell residence. Krämer took the front, while Beck went around to the back. A heavy knock at the front door prompted Avi to act.

Covered in Spangell's blood, Avi ran into the study and dove through the open sash window. He rushed into the glistening garden and was pelted by bouncing rain.

A locked metal gate blocked Krämer's access. He saw Avi escaping. 'Halt, halt! Beck, he's escaping out of the side window!' With his service pistol drawn, Beck rushed from the rear to the side of the house, just in time to see Avi struggling over the high perimeter fence. The inexperienced, excitable Beck fired a shot through the fence, which zipped past Avi's face. Avi sprinted up the road.

From his balcony window, the old neighbour enjoyed the spectacle with a smirk. He descended the stairs.

Beck straddled the fence in hot pursuit.

Krämer was too old and heavy to take up the chase on

foot. He trotted to the squad car, which he struggled to start.

Blondi barked and clawed at the wooden gate. The old man rushed to release his pent-up dog into the fray. The gate opened, and Blondi was off in pursuit. He saw the cat that had tormented him all night and bolted off in the opposite direction.

Krämer's engine finally roared into life. Beck was within shooting distance along the narrow street. With Avi in his sights, visible in the light from lampposts, he crouched into a shooting position. He aimed and fired.

The bullet whistled past Avi's ear and ricocheted off a nearby road sign. Beck fired a second shot that landed short and bounced away.

Avi circled the side of a house and dashed along another deserted street. He was still exposed. His initial sprint was slowing into a fast run. Another shot rang out.

Avi looked behind.

Beck was gaining ground.

Avi knew he had to shake him off. Hiding was useless. He couldn't outrun the younger, fitter man. Avi cut into a side street, vaulted over a small fence, and ran through the garden of a detached house.

Blowing furiously on his whistle, Beck kept chasing.

Hearing the approaching siren of Krämer's squad car, Avi changed direction and turned into a blind alley. The pouring rain continued to wash him clean of Spangell's blood. He glanced behind once more. He couldn't see Beck, but the sound of heavy rubber boots splashing in puddles confirmed the chase was still ongoing.

Avi knew it was only a matter of time before he was caught or shot. He was running for his life. At some point, he would have to make a stand, but he'd lost his bearings. He looked around and saw a gap in the railing. He squeezed through and then emerged onto the main road.

Tall silhouettes rose against the backdrop of sheet lightning. A large perimeter fence enclosed the place he had vowed never to return. The guard towers still stood to attention. The huts remained aloof. *Konzentrationslager Dachau* was calling its former resident back into its smouldering belly.

Avi struggled to escape his impossible situation. The wooded area northeast of the camp provided plenty of cover, but he was quickly tiring. The trees were too far to reach on foot. The buildings just beyond the front gate offered a much closer refuge. He had no other options.

Another shot rang out. The bullet whizzed past Avi's right ear and thudded into a tree trunk.

Bloody Hell. Too close for comfort.

Another glance over his shoulder. His legs were leaden. His lungs were bursting. The stitch in his side tore like he'd been stabbed with a twisting dagger. It was only a matter of time.

The repeated cracks and incessant wailing of Beck's whistle alerted the camp residents to trouble. Beck knew that the camp was now filled with rowdy ethnic Germans against whom the local police had recently been armed. Tensions were at a boiling point. Trouble was brewing in more ways than one.

Gasping for breath, Avi staggered behind the old barracks and reached the front of the *Jourhaus* entrance. Beck was not far behind. Overwhelmed by the chase, Avi stumbled into the unguarded camp. He moved around the side of the *Jourhaus* and out of sight. The heavy rain masked Avi's laboured breathing as he gripped his thighs, bent over in exhaustion.

Within a minute, Beck arrived at the *Jourhaus* gates. The young officer was desperate for Krämer's help, but Krämer had lost the scent while driving around the neighbourhood, chasing shadows.

Beck paused, pointed his gun ahead, and entered the camp through the iron gates. Unlike the old days with piercing searchlights, the pitch-black camp was illuminated in flashes of blue electrostatic discharge that raked down from the sky.

Inexperienced, Beck kept blowing hard on his whistle. Fearing that one of their own was in serious trouble with the police, many neglected people began to emerge from huts to check out the commotion.

Realising he was drawing unwanted attention, Beck stopped blowing the whistle. Instead, he shouted, 'You should come out! You know I will kill you if you keep running. Come out now! A burglary is not worth dying for.'

Avi knew that the stakes were much higher. He stood firm in the hope that Beck would come to him rather than make the better move of covering the main exit to wait for his partner. Beck also stood his ground.

Despite the rain, more people drifted out of the huts and headed for the commotion at the gates. A motley group of refugees, fresh from a late-night bout of hooch drinking in a public park, approached Beck from behind.

An irate resident shouted, 'Put that gun away, you swine.' Another spoke hoarsely: 'There has been more than enough death in this camp. This area is sacred.'

The siren of Krämer's patrol car grew louder as Beck became encircled by the mob. Flustered, he swept his gun around the rabble, which now included Avi.

'Get back or I will shoot!' shouted Beck.

It was now or never. Avi lurched forward and grabbed Beck by the arm, twisting it high up his back.

A shot cracked into the night sky.

The crowd retreated.

Restrained in an arm lock, Beck loosened his grip on the gun. Avi yanked the weapon from his grasp and pressed it against Beck's head while pulling Beck's handcuffs from his belt. Without hesitation, Avi led Beck through the crowd, pushing him toward the heavy iron gates inscribed with the phrase, WORK MAKES YOU FREE. Avi grabbed the key from Beck's waist belt. 'It will take a lot of work to make you free from this mess,' said Avi as he handcuffed Beck to the gate.

Gun in hand, Avi pushed through the crowd and ran back out of the camp as he tossed the key into the bushes.

Camp residents taunted the young police officer as Krämer finally arrived in the patrol car via what had been the Avenue of the ϟϟ. The baying horde quickly surrounded him before he could get out and aid his partner. Krämer took out his gun and radioed their location back to base, pleading for assistance.

Although drained by his exertions, Avi jogged from the camp and headed back toward the main thoroughfare. The camp and its surroundings would soon be swarming with police, especially once they discovered Spangell's dead body. Staying in the shadows, he approached the *Alte Römerstraße*.

The approaching lights of a taxi glowed in the distance.

Driving closer, a taxi driver noticed Avi flagging for attention. Sensing a potential bounty, either from the passenger or the police, the cabbie removed an illicit gun from his side holster. He trapped it between his legs as he slowed to a stop. Plucking Avi from more than just inclement weather would be a risky manoeuvre.

Avi climbed into the cab.

'You are lucky, I'm feeling charitable tonight. Money upfront.'

'Yes, yes, thank you. Much appreciated,' said the passenger as he handed him a generous 10 Deutsche Mark bill. 'Keep the change.'

'Where to?'

'Take me to the Feldherrnhalle.'

The sirens of numerous converging police cars wailed in the background as the driver kept the car stationary, its engine ticking over. He looked in his mirror and noticed Avi's driving gloves and Beck's shooter peeking out from his trouser waistband. 'Big commotion brewing. No doubt the *thieving refugees* are to blame,' said the driver, his tone ironical, but Avi took him literally.

'You should put yourself in their shoes. Those poor people are suffering a desperate plight in a desperate place.'

'I am in their shoes. They call us the *expellees*. I live there with my wife and baby. I was just on my way back in from my shift.'

'I am grateful to them. They helped me to escape from a serious misunderstanding with the police.'

With blue lights flashing and a siren wailing, a patrol car approached on the other side of the road. Avi slouched down as it passed.

'It appears you have caused major problems back there. But not to my people, I trust?'

'No, not to your people. Just the police.'

'Good. Then I will take you home, my friend.' He slipped the gun back into his side holster, put the car in gear, and steered it toward the big city.

Avi sat back and let out a deep sigh of relief, but his relaxation was short-lived as he remembered that he'd left the road map inside the Beetle he had stolen. He also recalled that the map showed his route from the Feldherrnhalle to the Spangell residence and back. But worse, it was stamped with Hotel Treff.

You bloody fool. The crass mistake of an amateur.

He bit his bottom lip in frustration. He knew he had to get back to the hotel before the police realised his error.

Without the passports and the main wad of cash, I'm right up the Suwannee.

'Put your foot down and I will double your money.'

The driver obliged, and the taxi sped off into the night.

Revolving lights from police cars and ambulances lit up a group of curious onlookers, some of whom wore unglamorous German nightwear. Within seconds, two poker-faced police officers emerged from the Spangell residence and escorted Josef Hirschfeld out of the house. The young boy was wrapped in a grey army blanket, which failed to keep him warm or stop him from shivering. A bloated body bag soon followed, balanced precariously on a stretcher carried by two police officers struggling with the dead weight.

Avi was dropped off at the Feldherrnhalle. He paid the driver his bonus, took the driver's calling card, and quickly headed to the Hotel Treff. From across the road, he saw no sign of police at the front entrance.

He played it safe and sneaked around the back, where

he climbed up onto the fire escape ladder and entered through an open window into his room. Risking a delay, he changed into a dry shirt, vest, and trousers, then packed his wet clothing into his suitcase. He put on his overcoat and trilby, retrieved his valuables from inside the mattress, and then climbed back down the fire escape.

Julius Perl's West German passport was discarded into a back-alley manhole as three police cars converged at the front of the hotel, their tyres screeching. Michael Knoller's Austrian passport was in Avi's jacket pocket, at the ready. Unchallenged, he marched a cautious route back to the Feldherrnhalle and on to the Marienplatz.

The posse of police officers charged to the front desk of the Hotel Treff, led by a sprightly old Inspector. He asked the receptionist for details about a man who fit their sketchy description, and might have recently requested a local map.

With an arch smile, the receptionist said, 'Herr Perl checked in this evening and requested a map of Munich. I didn't notice him leave the hotel, but that doesn't mean he hasn't left his room.' The police charged up to Avi's empty room.

The night traffic was in its final throes as the remaining cars scurried away like mice from a prowling owl. Avi flagged down a taxi and secured a brief ride to the reconstructed *München Hauptbahnhof.*

By the time he reached the station, it was nearing two in the morning. Despite his optimism, the ticket office was closed. The last train to Vienna had already arrived at its destination. He had checked the train times when he first arrived, but his growing paranoia prompted him to scrutinise the timetable once more. The next train was due to leave at 7.05. Too early. There would be a significant police presence at the station in the early morning, arising from his slaying of Spangell in the late hours of the previous day. The 9:05 am express was a better option. The station would be busier and should provide greater commuter cover for his departure.

Avi exited the station. He could see that the newly restored five-star Bayerischer Hof Hotel was within walking distance. He still had plenty of German cash at his disposal and decided to treat himself to a bed with better springs. Besides, the upmarket hotels tended to be more discreet and easier to maintain anonymity.

While approaching the hotel on foot via the *Promenadeplatz*, Avi declined the proposition of an upmarket, if work-weary, lady of the night. He would have enjoyed both the company and the sex, a welcome distraction and a release of pent-up tensions. But his life was too complicated to add guilt into the mix. He was vulnerable but loyal. He thought of Kathy and what she might be doing at that moment. Knowing her as he did, she would be asleep and alone. Tonight, so would he.

'Michael Knoller' checked into the luxurious hotel and requested an early morning call. His third-floor room was filled with elegance. The neat bed was soft and inviting. He removed the damp clothes from his suitcase and put on a plush towelling dressing gown.

While lying on top of the double bed smoking a tab, his wet garments began to steam on the hot radiators. Eyes wide open, Avi was wired and couldn't sleep. Beck's pistol next to his body provided some security as he reflected on the earlier events, including his brief, surreal visit to the Dachau camp …

I never could have predicted that return, especially in such circumstances. Running into the camp was reckless. I could have easily been trapped and caught ... but strangely, it was the camp that saved me. I was drawn to that Godless place as if my legs had been taken over. Was it an unscheduled but predestined visit?

Avi shook his head in confusion. His mind was too cluttered to focus on such a paradox.

Perhaps God has finally come out of hiding?

Tiredness overwhelmed him. Avi felt old — too old to be chased on foot by gun-wielding, homicidal policemen. He imagined Kathy sitting by a roaring fire with her mother, both united in disappointment and scorn. However, he was aware of the dangers of revealing his emotions.

Come on, snap out of it — one thing at a time. Stay focused. A long, relaxing bath will do you the power of good.

Steaming hot water flooding into the bath was comforting and lifted his spirits. It made him yearn to immerse his body and forget his mounting troubles, at least for the time being.

Chapter 40.
Another day, Another Deutsche Mark

After a cig and an apple for breakfast, Avi wrapped Beck's shooter in the free newspaper that was left in his hotel room. Walking to the station, he threw the gun into a public litter bin. His reasoning was clear and straightforward.

If I get caught, I get caught. I won't be shooting at the police, and I don't want to be in possession, so it's best to get rid.

To his relief, there were no headlines about Spangell's murder on the morning newspaper billboards, even though none had been expected. Despite knowing it was too late in the evening for the press to respond, he still checked with paranoid apprehension. He also scrutinised the area around the train station. No additional police cars awaited him.

So far, so good.

Avi scanned the busy station concourse.

Take a couple of tablets. No. Fly by the seat of your pants. You can do it.

Long queues formed at the four international travel windows in front of the rebuilt München Hauptbahnhof ticket office. Avi kept his head down as he joined the middle queue and moved toward the service counters. Disguised from the night before, he was clean-shaven, dressed in his overcoat, and wearing a trilby hat. His small suitcase gave him a more professional appearance. He had also switched his thin horn-rimmed distance glasses for his spare, thicker reading spectacles, which matched the photograph in his Austrian passport. The broader arms of their frame also helped conceal the tell-tale scar near his right eye. It was a noticeable blemish that the young and headstrong Officer Beck might have noticed during the previous night's events. Avi didn't know for sure, and this uncertainty added to his anxiety.

With feigned indifference, Avi bought an open return ticket to Vienna. He could have waited a few days until the heat was off, but he was keen to continue his mission. Additionally, a longer stay would pose different risks, and he wasn't eager to linger in Germany longer than necessary.

So far, so good. Remember your training. Stay calm. Stay composed.

He pocketed the ticket and headed toward the mixed crowd of commuters and tourists waiting to enter the platform.

The dormant trains hissed and heaved as excess steam drifted from their boilers. The distinct aromas of coal and oil filled the air as the mighty locomotives awaited the flags and whistles that would set them in motion from sturdy buffer stops and off to various destinations. But their carriages were beyond Avi's immediate reach.

Mingling casually within the throng, he couldn't help but notice a plainclothes police presence at the head of each platform barrier. He glanced at the large station clock. It was 8:50. He leaned against a large stanchion, trying to spot Police Officer Beck at the head of any of the queues. If he was there, Avi couldn't see him.

He then moved to a different vantage point, but the shifting movement of passengers prevented him from conducting reconnaissance. His heart missed a beat when the train announcer's monotonous voice announced the imminent departure of the 9:05 express to *Wien Westbahnhof* from Platform 6.

Suddenly, the station felt full of eyes staring at him from every angle, as if they knew he had killed Spangell, and they were waiting for the first person brave enough to identify him so they could all chant in unison: Murderer, murderer!

Come on, Avi, control yourself. You can do this. You can be Falco the Falcon.

With a copy of the Bavarian newspaper *Süddeutsche Zeitung* tucked under his arm and a fresh packet of cigarettes in his pocket, he took a deep breath and joined the queue for the 9:05 express.

Two surly-looking police officers checked the front of the line of travellers.

Avi stepped forward hesitantly. His profile loosely matched the sketchy description provided by Officer Beck.

The queue moved slowly.

A large young family was allowed straight through the barrier.

Avi was next.

He handed his Austrian passport to the taller of the two police detectives. The towering official studied the picture page carefully. He looked into Avi's eyes, then back at the picture. Then he let Avi through with a nod and a curt smile, but Avi's heart skipped a beat when the second detective extended a leather-clad arm and blocked his path. The movement gave Avi a brief, subtle glimpse of the gun resting in the shoulder holster of the blocker.

'Please follow me this way, sir,' said the officer.

Make a run for it. No, you'll definitely get caught. Come on, stay calm. You can do this.

Avi was led firmly to one side. 'I'm sorry, but may I see your ticket, please, sir?' asked the plainclothes inspector.

Avi obliged, hoping that purchasing a decoy return ticket might throw this officer off the scent.

'I trust you enjoyed your stay in Munich?'

'Not especially. Work is work.'

'When do you plan to return?'

'With luck, in a few days. It depends on how quickly I can finish my business in Vienna.'

'And what, may I ask, is your business in Vienna?'

Avi hardened his expression and directly stared at the detective. 'If you must know, following my mother's recent death, I need to handle family matters. Why do you ask?'

'I am sorry to hear that. Where did you stay last night, Herr Perl?'

'My name is Knoller.'

'Oh, yes, of course, Herr Knoller. My mistake.'

'No matter. I stayed just around the corner at the Bayerischer Hof.'

'And can you prove this?'

'Yes, of course.'

Avi pulled out his hotel receipt from his trouser pocket. The inspector examined it carefully.

'Hmm… Very good. Have a safe journey, Herr Knoller,' said the now satisfied officer.

Avi's calm expression masked his racing heart. He retrieved his passport, offered a polite smile, and stepped forward through the barrier onto the platform. He boarded the train without further hesitation.

Avi hauled his lightweight suitcase onto the overhead storage rack. The empty compartment looked almost identical to the ones where he had killed two senior ⁴⁴ officers and an innocent young boy during the War, but this older version had become tired and shabby. He sat with his back to the distant, dormant engine, which continued to build up steam before departure. From his vantage point, Avi peered above his open newspaper, keeping a watchful eye on the ticket barrier in case the police changed their mind and looked in his direction.

As luggage-laden passengers hurried past his window amid the busy platform, the station's officious train announcer declared the imminent departure of the 9.05 express train to Wien Westbahnhof. Heavy doors slammed shut along the many carriages of the snaking train, like a row of tumbling dominoes.

The sudden jolt into slow motion startled Avi, giving him an unwelcome scare. It wasn't the first time he had been forced out of Munich, and it wouldn't be the last. He had left behind something precious — something he was later compelled to retrieve.

Chapter 41.
Inner Turmoil

Despite his unprofessionalism, Avi managed to escape West Germany and appeared to get away with Felix Spangell's killing. However, rather than feel relief, he remained restless and anxious.

Fifteen minutes outside the city, in the lush Bavarian countryside, he fumbled in his pocket for something to calm his trembling hands. He took out his last two yellow pills and swallowed them. Then he took a small step toward the window and tossed the empty brown bottle onto the oil-stained train tracks, which receded into Munich.

For the first time in a while, Avi felt isolated, vulnerable, and alone. So much water had passed under the bridge since his days as an accomplished assassin. He was alarmed by the mistakes that nearly caused disaster. Times had changed, and so had Avi. He was uncertain of the man he had become, a man consumed by hatred and revenge, losing faith in his values and goals.

Once the medication took effect, Avi ceased gnawing his right index finger. He removed his hat and coat, placing them by his side, and gazed blankly out the window. Miles of open countryside streaked past, but nothing registered.

He reflected on his brutal slaying of Felix Spangell. Doubt had grown in his mind like a malignant tumour. He had never questioned the assassinations of his past, all of which had been meticulously planned. Could it be that his conscience was troubled? Only one previous victim had ever bothered that part of his mind. This was unfamiliar terrain. He tried to unravel the mystery.

Is this what I am, a cold-blooded assassin? During the War, killing Germans was necessary, but it also gave me pleasure. It was something more than vengeance. Killing was euphoric. Danger was thrilling, glorious, satisfying ... addictive. Is this what I have been missing?

But the killing of Spangell was not premeditated. I reacted to a situation. It was self-defence. Not something to be proud of, even though he abused children. Perhaps I could have tied him up and left him for the police? No. Too risky. I would have been caught in the act. Besides, he attacked me. I was defending myself. Spangell was gripping the broken glass as it plunged into his neck. I suppose that it worked out well, for me at least. He would have given them my description and a lot more besides.

Finally, he paid attention to the bucolic German countryside sliding past the window. War-torn scenes in rural Germany were tattooed in Avi's memory. But only twelve years had passed, and there were no visible scars of the War. No regiments of brazen soldiers. No lines of terrified refugees. No hordes of pitiable prisoners. No burnt-out farm buildings. No carnage of machinery. No wretched bodies. No lost children wandering in a perpetual state of shock. The wreckage had been cleared away. Only memories remained. His preconceived picture of post-war Germany bore no resemblance to reality. Instead, peace and harmony had prevailed.

The air was no longer corrupt with the smouldering stench of death and the aftermath of burning buildings; instead, it was scented with the celestial sweetness of life. Painted with God's palette, the velvet wings of gilded butterflies fluttered like kaleidoscopes in the sunlight. Clusters of wildflowers performed a ballet around the base of tall trees inhabited by carefree birds singing their melodies. The gentle breeze moved waves through fields of golden wheat, while abundant herds of cattle grazed with joyful abandon. Farmers ploughed their fertile fields with relaxed confidence, anticipating their bountiful crops and golden harvests. Life had moved forward. The destruction had faded as if it had never been there, as if it had never occurred. Memories of the War were a figment of a wild imagination.

But Avi's imagination wasn't wild. It was precise and perceptive. It was shaped by vivid experience. Some ghosts may dissolve from the physical world, but they will always remain tangible and resilient in Avi's mind. They will never leave. They will haunt and torment him until he banishes them forever... in his life or in his death.

This peace is a sham, a charade, a confidence trick manipulated by the crafty Germans. The police at the train station. What did they do during the War? Not just the Police. The media, Government Officials, and The Judiciary. The very fabric with which the new German society is tailored, stitched together with the same black thread woven into the uniforms of the ᛋᛋ death squads.

Make no mistake, the Nazis are still here. They have blended into the background. They have contaminated the hive of everyday life. Blood and soil.

Beneath the surface lie the corpses of millions of innocent Jews, conveniently tucked away from view and hidden from posterity. Absent from justice. Do not be fooled. Follow your instincts. Don't let your mind play tricks. Spangell would have hung out his arm like the rest of those fascist bastards. He tried to kill me. Remember what Gaggs said, "Keep calm. Stay focused".

Avi shook his head and took a deep breath. He held up

his treasured, comforting group photograph of his happy, smiling family standing outside his father's restaurant. He gazed at the picture, which included his beloved, angelic mother in her prime, his loving father, and his playful sisters.

I never had the chance to mourn my family or place stones on their graves — no mark of respect. The Nazis took care of Jewish cremations. It was most considerate of them.

I will find justice for my family and justice for my friend, and then I can bury the past and get on with my life, just like everybody else.

But what if Kathy was right?

Her words persisted. "What happens after you've killed him? Will your family come back? You know it will never be enough. Please stop, Avi. You have to stop".

Chapter 42.
Single File

Upon arriving in his homeland, the re-established sovereign state of Österreich, Avi stepped out of the terminus building at *Westbahnhof* station. He took a deep breath of Viennese fresh air and looked across the platform. The cityscape had changed almost beyond recognition, but he could still smell the familiar scents of *Apfelstrudel, Wiener Schnitzel,* and lingering antisemitism. The first two remained. The latter had vanished — there were no more Jews left to hate.

Avi felt like an alien in a strange land. He was no longer Austrian. He was not truly British. He had no sense of belonging, no ties to any country. His faith was shattered. His bonds to humanity were stretching thin, near breaking.

It was a short walk to a maroon taxi waiting at the front of a line of cars. Avi approached the attentive driver.

'Please take me to *Leopoldstadt*. I will tell you when we are close," he said in his native Austro-Bavarian.

After a quick journey to Vienna's 2nd District, the taxi stopped outside an ironmonger's shop. It was where Falco's Restaurant had once welcomed the gentile Viennese majority before the *Anschluss* and Nazi rule destroyed their sense of morality.

Avi hurried out of the cab, leaning toward the driver's window for a quick word.

The driver waited with the engine running as Avi headed for the shopfront, gazing at the surviving old building. A mix of emotions stirred within him. From his coat pocket, he took out an old photograph of his large family. That sunny day in 1934 was etched indelibly into his memory…

… Outside Falco's restaurant, Avi's close-knit family was laughing and joking, dressed in their best Sabbath clothing for a special snapshot. The grey-bearded photographer positioned himself beneath his folding camera's cape, which was balanced on a wooden tripod, as the eager, intimate family arranged themselves. They settled down and struck a joyful pose.

Twelve-year-old Avi stood before his tall, bespectacled mother, Meira. She looked radiant in her pristine lily-white dress and braided black hair. She smiled; her arms proudly draped over her son's shoulders. Avi's sturdy, upright father stood between his beautiful daughters, Adina and Keren, with a glint in his eye and a smile of paternal pride and satisfaction.

For now, the local people would continue to respect the honour of the Falco family. The Austrian economy was turning the corner into prosperity, but memories were short. What could possibly go wrong?

Avi wiped away a tear and got back into the taxi. 'Hotel Mozart, please.'

Having completed his usual exterior surveillance, Avi entered the hotel and headed straight for the reception desk.

A teenage female receptionist, with ROMA MOSTOVOI written on her breast badge, smiled politely and took his Austrian passport for security reasons.

'Thank you, Herr Knoller. Your room is up on the third floor.' She handed him a key labelled 309.

'Is the Soviet War Crimes Commission nearby?'

'Uh, I'm sorry, sir, I'm not sure.'

Dropping off his keys at the desk, a greying, weasel-faced man in his early-fifties interjected without raising his head. 'I know that place. It is located inside the Russian Kommandatura building. Turn right out of the hotel. It is a ten-minute walk straight up the road, on your left. Look for the shining red star. I don't know why they are still here. Those arrogant Commy bastards should have left Vienna two years ago.'

Avi frowned. 'You should be grateful, old man. Two extra years are not too much to endure. It would have been a thousand-year Reich if those arrogant Nazi bastards had prevailed.'

Avi noticed Roma's suppressed smile and the stranger's annoyed expression.

It might be enlightening to investigate this Nazi bastard's War record during my visit, but much more important matters are at hand.

After a quick walk, Avi arrived outside the imposing building labelled *KOMMANDATURA*. A yellow flag with a red hammer and sickle fluttered from a white pole protruding from the dominant, neoclassical façade. He climbed the furrowed stone steps, passing the grand monolithic colonnades freckled with indentations from bullet wounds inflicted by former enemies.

Upon reaching the top, he stubbed out his pungent Austrian Memphis cigarette on the sole of his shoe and stepped inside the vast establishment.

Impressed by the size and grandeur of the lavish marble interior of the 19th-century former local government halls of administration, he headed towards the mahogany reception desk. It was attended by a no-nonsense Siberian female linguist dressed in the smart parade uniform of the Red Army. Her gleaming brass buttons, silk medal ribbons, and red piping stitched to the steel-grey tunic added further authority to her frigid expression. Amid anonymous drones from the open vestibule, they settled on a *lingua franca*. Avi was sent in the direction of the grand staircase, towards the second floor.

With a mix of excitement and trepidation, he reached the top of the stairwell. The walk down the long corridor was illuminated by a row of Art Deco, opaline globe lights, each glowing as they hung from the tiled ceiling. His leather heels clicked sharply against the stone floor as he approached his destination.

Avi rested his clasped hands on the well-worn wooden counter labelled SOVIET WAR CRIMES COMMISSION: AUSTRIA and waited for the receptionist.

With her back to the desk, a female secretary in her late twenties crouched on the floor as she returned a shabby brown file to a cabinet drawer. As his patience waned, Avi was about to rap the polished brass bell beside her nameplate, but then the secretary rose and straightened to her impressive height. Avi's eyes widened with a ruminative stare.

Her round black glasses and oversized green peaked cap did not disturb the sculpted bone structure that defined her beautiful face. A tight, olive-green Russian military uniform hugged the curvaceous figure of the Red Army Kapral, Galina Glushenko, a Russian goddess whose pin-up poster looks would have sprained the wrist of many a lonely convict. Galena had the boys lining up like strings on a harp, and she knew how to make them dance to her tune.

With her entrancing natural beauty, the bored Galina was the first woman Avi had given a second glance to in many a long year. Like a model on a catwalk, Galina advanced toward the counter.

Functional professionalism couldn't mask his attraction. Galina was aware of her striking features, which had always attracted admiring looks. She sensed the usual signals and encroached on Avi's personal space.

Avi felt the gentle breeze of her sweet breath on his lips. He asked in a higher pitch than intended, 'Do you speak English?'

Galina smiled. Her pearly whites gleamed in the solitary light from the plain ceiling. With a tilt of her face, she replied in an alluring low voice. 'I speak a little … you want help?'

Avi put his hand to his mouth and turned away while clearing his throat. His pitch unintentionally lowered, creating a comedic effect, as he said, 'I am trying to track down a particular guard from Dachau.'

'We have only files on some camps, mostly Auschwitz, where there were over eight hundred guards, at least. You might get lucky … but luck will only get you so far.'

Avi produced his wallet and placed ten American dollars on the desk. Impressed, Galina continued, 'Many Auschwitz guards trained at Dachau, and were then re-posted. They passed on their evil practices to other camps. *Schutzstaffel* kept good files … but many were destroyed or damaged as they ran away.'

'Do you have the surviving files here?'

Galina smiled provocatively. 'Anything is possible today.'

Avi put another ten dollars on the desk. Galina continued: 'Some of the damaged files were copied with a Russian translation. My boss does not let me show them to anyone ... but my boss is out of office.'

Avi dropped another ten dollars onto the desk. Galina parted her luscious lips and issued a film star smile. 'Come with me.'

Her curled finger beckoned Avi into a large, windowless room crammed to the rafters with filing cabinets and bulging cardboard boxes. She looked around the scene and nodded. 'You are a lucky boy. These files are being packed away for a long journey to Moscow. We have orders to shut down. If you need me, just ring the bell. But not to delay. If the boss comes back, you go. We close at seventeen-hundred hours.'

The hand on the office clock hanging from the cracked plaster wall above Avi's head ticked away each precious second. Thousands of ᛋᛋ files. Thousands of ᛋᛋ murderers. Avi swapped his distance for reading glasses and got down to business.

Where to begin? How many of these Nazi bastards made it to safety on the South American ratlines through Italy and Spain? The Vatican might hold many of the answers, but now I must focus on my immediate quest.

An hour into the search, cabinet drawers were open, and Avi sat cross-legged on the floor among numerous piles of files. Each was a cardboard folder with papers stitched tightly with a knotted lace. A Nazi Eagle was stamped on each cover, along with the name and rank of the subject inside. The clock was still ticking.

Avi attempted to approach the task systematically, but the cluttered room lacked order and was deprived of natural sunlight and ventilation.

Two hours into the search and aware of the ticking clock, Avi rummaged hurriedly through each file, hoping that the buried treasure would blind him ... if it was there and if he managed to find it — *tick, tick, tick.*

With his jacket off, shirt sleeves rolled up, left arm bandaged, and tie straight, he focused more on a file with a Cyrillic word stamped in red ink on the front of the buff cardboard cover. Galina appeared at his ring of the bell. Avi pointed to the cryptic marking. 'What does this mean?'

Galina smiled, raised her eyebrows, and upturned her bottom lip. Avi handed her five more dollars. 'Deceased,' she said. The sexy conscript lifted her right leg onto a tattered tea box. She hiked up her skirt and placed the money with the other cash above her stocking top. She smiled as she caught Avi taking an irresistible glance.

Galina left as Avi returned to his files, studying and sorting them into two piles: one large and one small. 'Wrong ranks' ... 'Wrong dates' ... 'Too old' ... 'Too bald' ... 'Too short.' He broke a sweat as he pushed aside the large pile as time marched on — *tick, tick, tick.*

Three hours into the search, Avi's tie now hung loose as his desperation started to suffocate him. He checked his watch again. The sand slipped relentlessly through the hourglass as oxygen deprivation worsened the pressure headache that threatened to burst his skull — *tick, tick, tick.*

His study of the files became increasingly frantic and less detailed. Galina entered the fray once more. 'Boss soon to return. I must lock up. Not here for the rest of the week. You have twenty minutes.'

Avi nodded without looking up as Galina left. He separated a file marked ᛋᛋ - *Blockführer Gerhard Reuter.*

He moved toward another heavy pile. Reduced to looking at the front covers, he skimmed through the pile to a torn cover marked ᛋᛋ - *Blockführer Hans Brunner* 'Deceased'. 'Right rank.' Avi went to put it down next to Reuter's file. He hesitated and then opened it for a second glance. A tattered photograph caught his eye. He took it out and held it up to the light bulb. No scar above Brunner's right eye. He compared it to Lehmann's Wehrmacht picture. He took off his glasses and looked at the photo of Brunner.

The mental image of the blurred face of Lehmann at his home, and the distorted face of ᛋᛋ Brunner at Dachau combined in imagination into the present-day colour image of Helmut Lehmann. With a clenched fist, he smiled with delight.

'Der Folterknechte. At last. *Now* I have you.'

Avi let out a long sigh of relief. He straightened his appearance and then slipped the file into the black lining of his overcoat.

He stepped out of the file room to leave …

… but Galina stopped him. The gun she was holding was pointing at his head. 'Not so fast. Boss return. He not so happy if I let you leave with something you shouldn't. Turn around. Hands on head. Now!' Avi obliged. 'Now spread legs.'

He took a sideways step and then leaned his weight against the solid wall.

Galina patted him down. After a prolonged frisk of his crotch, she found the Brunner file pressing against the inside of the coat lining. 'Take off your coat.'

Avi struggled to take it off. She dragged it away from him with an outstretched shoe and then pulled out the file. 'One shout from me and you disappear quicker than

Nazi war criminal at end of War. Theft of property of Union of Soviet Socialist Republics means long stay in Gulag.'

She took a cursory glance at the file, and then a proper look inside. '*Him* again. Popular pig. German in here a while ago. Spoke good Russian. He also tried to steal file. I sold him copy of picture from file. He pay me good money.'

'Was he a tall man with black hair?' asked Avi, still propping up the wall.

'No. Skinny guy with baldy head.'

'Wolff,' said Avi.

Galina put down the file. She checked his pockets and produced his wallet and passport. 'I have more dollars,' said Avi.

'I can take all your dollars. You have no gun ... but have impressively large weapon ... like handle of Samurai Katana. What is your name?'

'Uh, Michael Knoller.'

Galina looked at the Austrian passport. 'You know Vienna well?'

'Of course. I am Viennese.'

'Well, then, Michael Knoller. You take me out on town. Show me good time. I translate file in morning. I am Galina. Apartment around corner. I need to change and put on makeup. I look much better out of uniform.' Galina smiled coyly.

Men liked Galina. Galina liked men. Avi wasn't old enough to be this girl's father, and Galina was no lady of the night looking for one last payoff after a long, hard shift.

Chapter 43.
Trial by Temptation

Galina and Avi stepped into her cosy but confined first-floor apartment. The modest dwelling had been shoe-horned into one of the new anodyne buildings that had risen within the Russian sector of the city, replacing the bomb-flattened pile of Baroque rubble bequeathed by the ruinous battle for Vienna.

Taking a key from her leather purse, Galina opened the front door. She led Avi by the hand down the narrow, dark corridor and into the small but well-kempt lounge. She turned on the tall wooden lamp placed in the corner near the solitary window. From her leather briefcase, she took the Brunner file and placed it on the coffee table, sitting in a corner of the room beside a small drinks cabinet.

Galina removed her cap and glasses. She loosened her hairpin, letting waves of blonde hair fall freely. She strutted over to Avi. After taking off his overcoat, she embraced him. With pouty red lips, she pressed a sensual kiss, a sweet aperitif to ignite his desire.

Avi was receptive, perhaps too receptive.

Galina's hand reached for his crotch. He released an involuntary groan. 'Good. I have your full attention. We have sex before we go to restaurant. Work up big appetite. Go freshen up. Bathroom down hall. Pour drinks from cabinet. I will be ready for you soon, lover boy.' She kissed Avi on the cheek, leaving a rich red strawberry print.

He could almost taste the scent of her Chanel No. 5, no doubt a present from a former lover. Avi looked at his reflection in the bathroom mirror and dabbed away the print she had planted on his face.

Galina moved into her bedroom. She slowly peeled off her uniform, revealing the full glory of her curvaceous figure.

Avi was sitting on the edge of the empty bath, pondering his next move ... *Without the file, I have no proof, no nothing. I must do this.*

Galina rolled down her fawn stockings. They slid effortlessly down her long, perfectly shaped legs.

Avi looked at his wedding finger. He rubbed the skin where the ring was missing. He had never strayed from the path of monogamy, but now he and Kathy were separated, in more ways than one. He knew the right thing to do was to leave empty-handed. He was still married ... but that was now uncertain. His dilemma was clear: at this moment, revenge felt more compelling than loyalty. He knew he would have no problem rising to the occasion.

He closed his eyes and saw Kathy. They were in bed, their faces inches apart. She opened her eyes and smiled. The smile shifted into a frown, her lips tightening and her forehead creasing with disappointment.

Galina clipped her black silk stockings to the lacy suspender belt hanging from her black lingerie.

Avi took off his glasses, rubbed his eyes, and shook his head.

Come on. This is not a David Niven movie. I don't have to sacrifice everything for Queen and country with a stiff upper lip.

He looked at his watch, the expensive Rolex Kathy and her mother had bought him, but his decision was already made. He exited the bathroom, walked along the corridor, and entered the lounge. The call of heaven from Galina's bedroom awaited. Avi's sudden view was erotic perfection...

... Galina writhed with balletic grace in a pleasure she failed to restrain as she straddled his muscular body. Her strong thighs were clamped against Avi's slim hips. The bedsprings struck notes of passion as she motioned back and forth. Her rounded breasts broke free from her silk basque, bouncing to the rhythm of Avi's pulsating thrusts. Her back arched, her blonde hair flowing through her outstretched fingers. Galina's face was contorted with the protracted joy of a good, hard shag. Avi clung to either side of her black lace suspenders as he drove the point home, releasing with pure delight the pent-up tension of his rediscovered sex drive.

The sparsely populated tram jolted to a stop. Seated on an uncomfortable bench, Avi snapped out of his daydream and wiped drool from his lips. He looked up. An overweight, wart-faced female ticket conductor loomed over him. 'Next stop, last stop. Tram terminates. Have your tickets ready,' she snarled as she tapped her right foot in expectation of proof of payment.

Bewildered, he produced a gnarled ticket from his jacket pocket and then checked that the overcoat was draped across his lap. Thankfully, it concealed both the file he had stolen from Galina's lounge and his massive erection, straining to bursting point inside his trousers.

Avi looked at the little old lady sitting opposite.

Fortunately, she can't see the images in my fantasy, or she'd also terminate at the last stop.

His imagination continued to create entertainment. He pictured Galina's anger at the discovery of his sexual snub and the theft of the file just twenty minutes earlier...

... Wearing lingerie with confidence, Galina sauntered into the lounge. Blood-red lipstick smeared her bee-stung lips. She noticed that Avi's coat and the file were gone. She hurried to the drinks cabinet and leaned over, opening the window. She saw him scurrying across the building's apron, clutching the Brunner file beneath his coat. Indignant in her sexy underwear and visible through the large sash window, Galina shouted, 'That's right, run away, just like a Nazi pig ... thieving Austrian rat that you are!'

Avi stepped off the tram, walking back to the Hotel Mozart while checking for a Russian tail. It wouldn't have been wise for Galina to inform her superiors about the missing file she let slip away, but he knew the consequences of a woman scorned. Better safe than sorry.

Perhaps a drink to celebrate or to steady the nerves?

Any excuse.

An orange sun provided a spectacular backdrop to the capital city as the last embers of daylight faded into the night. Across the road from the Hotel Mozart, a blinking neon sign caught Avi's eye as he headed back to base. With a nod and a wink, *The Long Bar* almost beckoned him to sample a shot or three.

Avi entered the saloon and climbed onto one of the

dozen vacant stools lined up along the expansive bar.

The young barman polished a shot glass while watching his solitary customer settle in and place an order. 'Cognac, double,' said Avi without looking up.

The barman was old school, knowing not to start a conversation with his customers unless they initiated it. He passed over the drink.

Avi brought the shot glass to his mouth as if he were in a drinking contest.

The barman replenished it without request.

Avi stayed lost in his own world, except for the rumbling in his stomach, which reminded him of the chaos of grey Mancunian skies and the messy case he'd left behind. His body needed food, but he was never one to eat while drinking. He lit a cig and reached for the crumpled copy of *Wiener Zeitung* newspaper resting on a nearby table. He flicked through the pages and was alerted to the article on page three, leading with the headline:

KILLER STILL AT LARGE IN MUNICH!

The article read, "The police have no clues about the whereabouts of the man suspected of the brutal murder of a local businessman, Felix Spangell, in Munich on Wednesday night. West German police have already sought the cooperation of their Austrian counterparts. It is feared that the culprit may have fled the country. However, the Joint Authorities remain hopeful of a breakthrough in their ongoing investigations."

Joint authorities means that the Austrian police are also on the lookout. No mention of the young boy in the cellar, or the fact that the murdered victim was a depraved, child-raping monster. Bastards.

A chill ran down his spine. He necked his second

double. A slight raise of an eyebrow was enough encouragement for the barman to fix him yet another shot.

As Avi held his new drink, a short, stocky man in a brown pork pie hat entered the bar. Avi's interloper was wrapped in a mohair overcoat and wore horn-rimmed glasses. He parked himself on a stool that was too close for comfort.

Avi clutched the file for reassurance. With a Russian accent, his new company ordered a vodka. Avi's heart skipped a beat. On the verge of panic, he looked beyond the bar's window and saw that a car had pulled up, containing at least three sturdy-looking silhouettes. Feigning a casual glance at the rear of the bar, he noticed a potential escape route through the back door, but it was blocked by a chain draped over the iron security bar.

The Nikita Khrushchev look-alike nailed his vodka, stood up, paid the barman, and sidled out of the bar. He got into the car, and he and his companions drove off.

Am I being paranoid, or is something else happening? Either way, it's time to go.

He gulped his last cognac, left a ten Schilling note on the bar, and hurried out onto the street.

Pay attention, Avi, this evening is far from over ...

Chapter 44.
Beauty and the Beast

Avi paced around the block. He completed two circuits before feeling confident enough to enter the Hotel Mozart, content in the knowledge that he was not being watched.

Once inside, he slipped into his room, weary from a long, challenging day. He took off his coat, steadied his arm, and looked at his watch. 10:05 pm. He pulled out the file and slumped into the light blue lounge chair, positioned between the wall and his single bed. He was eager to uncover the secrets of his nemesis, convinced that the truth was inside... well, almost. He had felt confident about his find, but the quick intake of alcohol had sown seeds of doubt.

His face twisted as uncertainty started to play tricks on him. He stood up and paced around the room. He sat down again. Fidgeting like a caged squirrel, he got up once more and went into the bathroom to wash his face.

It must be Lehmann. Why would Wolff take a copy of that picture if he wasn't Brunner? Unless Wolff was hunting down someone else as well ... No, that is preposterous. Or is it?

Avi looked in the mirror and shook his head. He moved back into the bedroom, kicked off his shoes, and lay on the pristine eiderdown. He glanced at the drawer on top of which he'd placed the file.

If only I could read Russian.

He pictured Helmut Lehmann curled up in his bed, sleeping peacefully like a baby in his large detached house, at ease with the world, no conscience to disturb his dreams.

Lehmann should enjoy his peace. When I return, he will suffer the whirlwind. But what lies in the file? I need to know that Lehmann is definitely Brunner.

Avi got up from the bed, paced across to the exit door, and then sat back in the lounge chair.

So near and yet so far. The girl at the counter at reception. She had a Russian name on her tag. Russians hate Nazis, but Russians are Russians. Corrupt, devious, untrustworthy — just like everyone else. It's too risky to involve an unvetted third party. Wait until you get the file back to England. Let Gaggs have it translated properly. Go have a bath. After the day you've had, a bit of self-relief will calm you down.

He rose from the chair and headed for the bathroom again. Taking an empty glass from the shelf above the sink, he about-turned and then paced back and forth in front of the bed. He sat back down as his paranoia took over.

What if I've got it wrong?

Frustrating indecision. Palpable agitation. Avi stood. Then he sat down again. Sweat began to trickle down his face. His right knee trembled along with his glistening hands. He clenched his fist and lightly bit the outside of his left index finger.

Another brandy or two to calm the nerves?

Avi picked up the receiver. 'Room service? Send a bottle of Cognac to my room … yes, please, as soon as possible.'

If Brunner isn't Lehmann, where will that leave me? High and dry without a hope. Confirmation is needed — and as soon as possible.

His desire to verify his revelation was intensified by alcohol, a central nervous system depressant that also hinted at the catastrophe lying ahead. The bellboy arrived at the door with a knock and a bottle. Avi paid him and added a generous tip.

'Thank you so much, sir.'

As the bellboy opened the door to leave, Avi asked, 'The girl at reception – Roma, Roma Mostovoi? Do you know if she speaks Russian?'

The bellboy frowned and looked at the bottle of cognac. 'Why do you ask me, sir? She's a very honourable young lady.'

Avi shook his head. 'Oh, I see. It is nothing seedy or sinister. I need a basic translation of a Cyrillic document. It won't take long. I will pay well for the service if she is discreet. You can stay with her if you wish.'

The bellboy touched his chin and then nodded. 'It may take a little time to arrange.'

As the bellboy left, Avi twisted the cap and poured a huge glass of cognac.

It was now 11:15 pm. His mood and intellect fluctuated inversely with his level of intoxication. His effort to keep his eyelids open was nearing failure, but a knock at the door snapped him back to awareness.

'Please come in, it is open,' said Avi with a slur.

The bellboy entered with the attractive receptionist and a second bottle of cognac. The bellboy gave a formal introduction. 'This is Roma, she speaks good Russian.'

Avi smiled and then handed the Brunner file to Roma.

'Sit down, please. Tell me about him.'

Roma sat at the end of the bed and smiled for show. She opened the file and scanned its contents. Both Roma and the bellboy noticed Avi's fragile state of sobriety as he struggled to level up his cig with his lighter. But it was not of their concern.

Letting out a chesty cough, Avi poured another Cognac and nodded in readiness.

Roma commenced a staccato recital. 'The file is of a deceased ᛋᛋ Guard Hans Brunner. He was an NCO training officer in Dachau from 1938. He rose rapidly through the ranks.'

'Including Unterscharführer?'

'Uh … yes. He held several progressively higher ranks … but then his promotions stopped. He was under investigation by the, uh, how should I say … The Public Inspector. Yes? He was accused of a series of gratuitous murders of inmates … This went nowhere. Uh … he was transferred to Auschwitz in 1941, and then he was promoted to the rank of Blockführer.'

Avi raised his hand.

Roma stopped.

'That means he would have been in there when my family was murdered.' He looked down at his shoes, rubbed the back of his neck, and slurred, 'Excuse me, Roma. Please continue.'

'I can't. The rest has been torn out.' Roma showed Avi the stubs of torn-out, missing pages at the back of the file: Wolff's blackmail evidence.

He nodded and muttered, 'Very clever. Wolff hedged his bets with Galina. Thank you, Roma, your help is much appreciated.'

The time had crept past midnight. Avi handed Roma a generous fee. She nodded in appreciation. Holding hands with her bellboy boyfriend, she began to move away. As she reached the door, Roma turned, looked Avi in the eyes, and said coldly, 'Make sure you kill him.'

Three sheets to the wind at 1:00 am, Avi was well into

his second bottle of Cognac. He returned to the room from the cramped toilet, his forehead glistening with moisture. His face remained troubled as he sank into a drunken haze. He slumped into the chair and struggled to process the chaos in his fragile mind.

His demons circled.

No Kathy for spiritual salvation.

No drugs to lift his spirits.

A flood of depression poured like water into an empty lock. His eyes were black, black like the boiling tar bubbling down his wretched road to perdition.

I should be triumphant. I have found him. I get to kill the school bully. Brunner is more than a bully. Brunner is a monster. How to kill a monster in his own backyard? It will be fine. I was a good boy. I avoided temptation. God will look after me. God? What God? When did he ever look after me?

Kathy has gone. What is she doing right now? Who is she with? Are we finished for good? No shortage of admirers back home. Bastards. Kathy. Back away, Avi. Back away. Not too close. Don't let her in. Do not let her in. Get back. You cannot come in. I cannot let you in. What if I lose you? But you have lost her!

What have I done? Her smile. Her touch. Her scent. Her company. Her love for me. Her love for us. I pushed her away, and for what? For so-called revenge? Revenge against a German monster who will die sooner or later. Tommy Green's family was destroyed, and he gained his so-called revenge, but where did that get him? How did he end up? Dead on a cold, hard slab next to a drunken fool whose head was crushed by an elephant. Kathy was right, "You will either end up dead or in a padded cell".'

Avi pressed his palms firmly against his temples. He

looked at the old picture of his family, its image flickering in and out of focus as he searched for scraps of comfort.

The lightbulb flickered while he stared at the crumpled sepia photo of his sainted mother, Meira, hugging her innocent young boy, the joy of her life. Her silky white dress and the everlasting scent of her perfume lingered on her rose-petal skin. The memory of her unconditional love broke through his defences as Avi teetered on the brink of his mental precipice.

Don't go there, you can't take the fall.

He imagined his mother's gentle, kind voice offering the reassurance only a mother could provide. He glanced at his watch and recalled Kathy on their wedding day, a perfect picture of beauty.

Where are you now, Kathy? Where are you now?

Desperate, hyper, and erratic, Avi was gasping for breath. His brain gyrated like a weathervane in a storm. He threw down his jacket and yanked off his tie. The pervasive black mood consumed his strength. It drained his feeble resistance. The faltering lightbulb flickered into extinction.

Alone in the dark, his hands were clamped to the side of his head. His grip tore clumps of hair from their roots. Fairground screams before the crash. Avi hadn't been there when the Gestapo had dragged his family away, but he pictured their Hell down to the last detail.

He could taste the pestilential stench of the cramped, squalid cattle train. Real people forced on a one-way ticket to the slaughterhouse. No food. No water. No air. No mercy. Disaster and death. Death and disaster. The blind terror of his mother and father clinging to each other. Clinging for dear life in sheer panic in the pandemonium of the gas chamber just before they perished in a toxic shower of Zyklon B: the Devil's breath. A screaming mass of frantic bodies clawing up the human pyramid for one last gasp of air before the oblivion of death.

Horror beyond all horrors …

… Then silence.

A deathly silence broken by a chanting striking up in Avi's head.

Untermensch, Untermensch, Untermensch …

An uncontrollable pulse turned into a fierce pounding, like a drum from a longship beating time. His resistance was shattered.

Avi Falco. Avi the Jew. Come here, scummy little Jew Boy. Let's play murder in the dark. Let's play murder your family in the dark. Let's play murder millions of your people in the dark. Women and children first. You can scream in hell together just before you suffocate and die foaming at the mouth with bloated green faces. You miserable Jewish swine!

Avi's senses were acute; they were hyper. His sanity teetered on the brink of collapse. He wanted to move. To run. To get away. But he was rigid, leaden, paralysed by a venom injection from the fangs of a snake. Trapped in his psychotic mind as nauseous images further invaded his sanity.

Arbeit Macht Frei was welded onto the gates of Dachau as he was shunted into the camp without remorse … Günter Kraft's shattered head after the bullet had ripped through his forehead … The Hasidic Jew lay face down, dead on the floor by the hut … The marbled pallor of Tommy Green's corpse rotting on the morgue slab … Felix Spangell lying on the floor, gurgling in a pool of his own blood … Kathy picking up her suitcase in the hotel and leaving for the last time.

Shattered marriage. Shattered Avi.

He looked down and saw blood dripping from his filthy, bare feet as he dangled from the meat hook. He screwed shut his eyes and saw the dead boy gripped by his devastated mother in the train carriage as blood seeped uncontrollably from his head.

'*I killed a child.* I killed a little child!'

His eyes opened and then rolled into white spheres. He slumped forward in the chair, dropped to the floor, and curled up into the foetal position. Whimpering like a dog. Whimpering like the Jewish dog he had become. Whimpering like the pathetic Jewish dog they had made him into.

Untermensch, Untermensch, Untermensch ...

The open suitcase was within arm's reach. He dragged it toward him.

Find a way out. Find a way out! The pills. Swallow the pills.

No pills left.

The knife. Use the knife.

Shaking violently, he grabbed the Swiss Army knife. His body was descending to the point of convulsion. He clawed desperately at the knife, splitting his frantic nails as he opened the biggest blade and thrust it to his wrist.

A nightmare within a nightmare. 'It was God's will then, and it is God's will now. One hard slash to make it go away ... one hard slash to *make them all go away!*'

Avi shaped to rip into his veins and end it all ...

... but then he was stopped.

A brilliant white light consumed the room. An effulgent light of such intensity, against which he screwed his eyelids as tightly as possible but with no discernible effect. The light was not blinding. The light was tolerable, mesmerising, hypnotic, and tranquilising. A familiar fragrance danced in the air. *Her* signature perfume.

Avi's jaw dropped, together with the knife. A deep calmness overwhelmed. His head lifted slowly. He opened his eyes. He was transfixed in awe as the shining light transformed into a scintillating abstract vision of his hallowed angel in her white dress.

A numinous apparition, Meira floated serenely before him. Her warm, loving smile toward her only son filled him with joy. Her baby boy. Her precious Avraham. She whispered as the cotton-wool clouds soothe the cool, ocean-blue pathway into heaven …

'Avi, my baby. Avi, my darling. Not now, sweet child. Not ever. You will cleanse your conscience. You will find your redemption. Be strong, my beautiful son. We will all be together soon enough.'

Looking down and frantically searching for his glasses, he found them, hooked them over his ears, and looked up.

Meira had gone.

Chapter 45.
Hans Brunner

With the help of various modes of public transport, Avi had obscured his tracks by taking a winding route from Vienna to Salzburg. Throughout his journey, his mind was busy brainstorming possible plans: one to kill the monster; the other to win Kathy back. He knew the first would be difficult at best, and the second might now be beyond his control.

Upon arrival, Avi used his false British passport, presenting himself as a well-groomed British businessman named Julian West, while successfully negotiating the single-passport counter at Salzburg Airport. He was too exhausted to feel nervous and navigated the red tape without issue.

It was a sunny day in Mozart's birthplace. Avi stepped out of the two-storey terminal building, which cast a long shadow onto its apron of hardened concrete. In the background, scaffolding wrapped around the newly built control tower as the scenic city of Salzburg — marked by its history of Nazi involvement and destructive Allied bombing — continued its recovery.

With a calming breath, he cleared smoke-dusted cobwebs from his wheezing lungs, inhaling cold, fresh air flowing down from jagged, snow-covered mountains, the same mountains that once cloaked Hitler's *Berghof* retreat on the *Obersalzberg*. That eagle had long since left the nest, but the pursuit of his subordinates remained unfinished.

Avi had been through an emotional mangle. He felt five years older than he had when he left London; his wan demeanour made it seem more like ten.

He tightened his trouser belt another notch before climbing up the steep steps to the awaiting uniform-clad air stewardess. He ignored her forced smile as he boarded the chartered flight to Croydon Airport, clutching the handle of his leather suitcase containing the Brunner file, its contents limited to only the key moments in Hans Brunner's ᛋᛋ career. Only Helmut Lehmann knew all the details of Hans Brunner's past …

Hans Brunner was born in Munich in the summer of 1919, the only son of Gregor Brunner. A proud Catholic Bavarian, Gregor had been invalided out of the First World War Imperial German Army after the Battle of the Somme. He was severely injured when the 1st Royal Bavarian Division's vesicant mustard gas attack on the British lines backfired. A sudden change in the wind caused the deadly cloud of acrid yellow-cross to swirl back toward the bedraggled attackers. Gregor's lungs were mutilated beyond repair.

He would have perished if not for the selflessness of a comrade. Max Steiger, the Jewish hero, carried his heavier sergeant to safety through enemy fire at the expense of exposing himself to the toxic fog. Steiger was posthumously awarded the highly coveted Iron Cross First Class for his bravery. It was a debt that could never be repaid.

As a result, Gregor Brunner did not join the majority of Germans who jumped onto the post-Great War bandwagon of *Judenhetze*, the anti-Semitic hatred of Jews. The Jewish scapegoat. The root cause of all German evils.

Following convalescence in the fresh air of his ageing aunt's Bavarian countryside cottage in the picturesque town of Dittenberg, Gregor returned to his native Munich. There, he found intermittent work in the building trades to survive through his country's many hardships. He was among the fortunate who had already acquired trade skills before the War; skills passed down by his father, a master builder in his own right.

Attracted by her natural blonde hair and striking cobalt-blue eyes, Gregor became infatuated with Amalie, a young shop assistant at his local tobacconist. A brief courtship led to a shotgun marriage to protect her honour, as she was three months pregnant with a baby boy. Hans was the only little monster the couple was to have.

The newlyweds made their first nest in Munich, the cauldron of violent post-war political turmoil.

Gregor Brunner was a paid-up member of the KPD, the German Communist Party, during the revolutionary days of the *Bayerische Räterepublik* just after the end of World War 1. He maintained his red allegiances into the early 1920s during the Weimar Republic. Bolshevist Brunner was at odds with Hitler and the brown-shirted paladins of the NSDAP, the Nazi Party.

Outspoken in opposition to right-wing factions, he often returned home from meetings and political rallies in bad shape, battered and bruised from rampant street and beer hall brawls. His commitment to the post-war Communist cause was strong, but his commitment to his young family was absolute.

A combination of increasingly poor health, coupled with the escalating threat of all-out civil war in Munich, meant choices had to be made. Gregor Brunner forsook his political sympathies and renounced violence. He left the Party and melted into the background until an opportunity for a safer life had presented itself.

Soon after Gregor's inheritance came into effect, the Brunners moved out of Munich, taking permanent residence in the thinly veiled utopia of Dittenberg. This was a welcoming haven where Gregor could breathe in fresh country air, which purged his lungs of further pollution, while preserving his political anonymity in the middle-class, cuckoo-clock town.

Readily accepted and respected by locals, the Brunners prospered as Gregor's dexterity was utilised to significant effect. The everyday folk of Dittenberg were taken with his reliability, along with his competitive prices.

Following innocent beginnings in kindergarten, the blonde-haired, blue-eyed Hans Brunner started his education at the local elementary school. He soon befriended Otto Lerner, a similarly attractive child with an awkward personality who got along well with the quirky little Brunner boy.

Catholic Hans and the only Jewish child in his class quickly became inseparable. They learned many things together, including the piano, but more importantly, they were taught the difference between right and wrong, good and bad. Their friendship was innocent childhood camaraderie. A friendship Hans's father was proud to defend and protect amid the disgruntled mutterings of other waiting parents at the end of each school day.

During those early days, young Hans spent many summer evenings and weekends happily helping his father with his work while building his physique and learning the building skills inherent in the family. However, he didn't see this noble trade as his future.

Hans excelled at mathematics and quickly realised the benefits of others working for him rather than the other way around. With mature foresight, his goal was to pass the Abitur, the mandatory entrance exam for university, and acquire the skills related to accounting.

Hans Brunner was a callow but muscular fourteen-year-old when Adolf Hitler was appointed Chancellor of Germany on 30th January 1933. Dachau Concentration Camp was opened less than two months later as *Der Führer* proceeded to grab Germany by the throat and choke it into totalitarian submission.

Within a year of Hitler's appointment, the pastel shades of Dittenberg's village walls were transformed into a vast harbour of flaring, blood-red swastikas which lurched high above the Führer's blindly fanatical followers. Their taut outstretched arms dangled in zealous reverence to Der Führer at every opportunity.

For the German *Jude,* the writing was on the walls, on the doors, and on the windows.

The relentless tide of fascism quickly swept over German youth. From the beginning, Hitler declared that, "He alone, who owns the youth, gains the future". Hitlerian indoctrination quickly spread through class lessons. Selected and willing Nazi teachers were used to corrupt malleable minds.

The fanatical servants of the Reich demanded and achieved total obedience in their goal to shape a domineering German youth, as Brown-shirted pupils sat at the back of classrooms, watching the process vigilantly. Pressure from the front. Pressure from behind. Send the Untermensch to the front of the class and taunt him. "Look, everybody. This is what a dirty Jew looks like".

The early days of the regime were difficult for young Hans. It was known that his father did not support the Nazis, and his son was intentionally singled out at school, given dirty jobs such as cleaning up litter during breaks.

Gregor Brunner was aware of these persecutions but hesitated to intervene. He took pride in teaching his son Christian moral values and in helping Hans develop the character to resist the pressure to conform. Gregor encouraged and supported his son's involvement in the local Roman Catholic youth league, the *Deutsche Jugendkraft*. However, like the movement itself, Hans's membership was short-lived.

Much against his father's wishes, Hans Brunner chose to join the diverse *Hitler Jugend* on his own. Once he did, the pressure at school immediately eased. As a true National Socialist, he would follow the party line and focus on the two most important subjects: German history and physical training.

Not all German youths were enamoured with the repetitive drills and conformity to the ideology of the Hitler Youth. Hans Brunner was soon in his element as yet another disciple of the *Hakenkreuz* was set in line.

He was quick to embrace obedience to the Nazi teachings: of masculine toughness, militarism, comradeship, uniformity, solidarity, patriarchy, and biological racism. He was bright enough to see his future pathway. Besides, membership of the HJ became compulsory for anyone wishing to sit the Abitur. This alone would have been enough incentive for him to join.

Hans's awakening was swift. Suddenly, he could see the future with great clarity. He was part of the first generation of the Thousand-Year Reich. The children of today would be the fighters of tomorrow, the boys who would become the men driving Hitler's New Order. The all-encompassing Nazi machine, in which the ambitious Hans foresaw he would be not just a small cog but an essential part, loomed ahead. He would discard his father's lessons of the past and reject his strict religious upbringing. *Mein Kampf* would become his new Bible.

Despite Gregor seeking and receiving help from the local priest, neither could stop Hans's new allegiance. The local Nazi leader, *Gauleiter* Ernst Völler, was ordered to increase his Hitler Youth membership. To do this for Hans and others, Völler arranged for the overnight disappearance of the protesting cleric, who had taken residence at *KZ-Gedenkstätte Dachau*.

Gregor Brunner was fortunate not to end up there. Local Nazi officials knew of his previous KPD membership and his vote against the party in the 1933 German federal election.

The persistent left-wing political statements of his father at dinner were now abhorrent to young Hans, and he soon changed beyond his father's recognition.

To complete his transformation, Hans also abandoned his infatuation with his young Jewish friend, Otto Lerner. He saw no reason to respect those outsiders branded as Enemies of the Community by the state. There was no place for the individual in the new regime. No place for the Jew Lover. No proper place in the Master Race for Hans Brunner until he turned on his former friend, inflicting and then administering a severe playground beating that pupils and teachers were reluctant to stop.

Gregor Brunner was reproached by Otto Lerner's horrified parents. Hans was confined to his room for four days, fed and watered, and forced to listen to the irony of his father's story about how the self-sacrificing bravery of the "Dirty Jew" had saved him in the First World War at the cost of his own life. Without this heroic act, Gregor would be dead, and Hans would never have been born. But any respect or appreciation was lost in a sea of teenage hatred.

Now, the Hitler Youth provided more than just Nazi idealism. Hans's violent actions had solicited the respect and attention he craved from peers. Strength, athletic prowess, and Aryan good looks helped him to blend in with other lean, muscular, and often semi-naked boys, displaying the eugenic essence of body purity.

In compulsory overnight camps, Hans excelled in highly competitive contests of boxing, wrestling, swimming, and group masturbation. Access to the promiscuous Aryan *Fräuleins* of the BDM, The Band of German Maidens, was of no consequence. Hans had no interest in the sexual pursuit of females. He disguised his homosexual fantasies and desires through competitive aggression.

Hans quickly became a favoured toy soldier among his leaders, always the main voice when singing Nazi songs around campfires. To the delight of the joyful crowds, he enjoyed his position at the front of regular khaki marches through the winding streets of Dittenburg. The locals admired the blue-eyed, blonde-haired standard-bearer deeply. However, there was one exception ...

Hans's passionate obsession with the cult youth movement led to further emancipation from his authoritarian father, worsened by regular absences from work duties. During weekends and summer holidays, Gregor relied on his son's help with the heavier jobs that were saved for such times. As cancer eroded his lungs and increasingly weakened him, Hans's support became crucial. However, he was otherwise busy with camping, hiking, and paramilitary war games, the latter in preparation for the real thing, which was only a matter of time.

Early in September 1937, Hans Brunner was appointed to lead the Dittenburg Hitler Youth Troupe at the 9th NSDAP Party Congress, a gathering his father forbade him to attend. With his regular labourer off sick, Gregor needed Hans to assist with an important and profitable job that had to be completed on time.

However, Hans had to be at the rally. He was obsessive. Fanatical. He needed to be in the Führer's view... in his line of sight... even if it was just for a millisecond... even if he was just a drop in a vast sea of anonymous fascist disciples. If he could see the Führer, the Führer could see him. And if the Führer could see him, his awakening would be blessed. He would be blessed.

Fuck father and his stupid hairy face. He can't see the glory of today or of our glory yet to come. I am the future. You are the past... you tired, pathetic old man.

Two days before Hans was scheduled to travel to Nuremberg for the Rally of Labour, the influential and all-powerful Gauleiter Völler personally visited the Brunner residence. He informed Gregor that his son had denounced him for claiming at the dinner table that Hitler was, "A funnier little comedian than his look-a-like Charlie Chaplin". Hans hoped that his father would be carted off to prison, leaving him free to attend the Nazi rally.

Ernst Völler, a former trench comrade and long-standing drinking buddy, paid lip service in front of the boy. He threatened his father with incarceration in Dachau and warned that he would act on any future accusations, keeping a close watch on him from now on. This task wasn't difficult. Gregor was three-quarters of the way through re-roofing the small but majestic Gothic *Rathaus*, the town hall building from which the Gauleiter ruled his parochial kingdom.

When Völler had left, Gregor moved to strike. It was the first time he'd ever raised a hand to Hans. Despite the heartbreak of his son's betrayal, Gregor couldn't go through with the beating he believed his son deserved. However, he remained resolute that Hans would not be going to Nuremberg …

The yellow plumage of the Alpine Citril Finch fluttered in the breeze, adding to the beauty of its silvery songs of joy. The sun poured down on the valley of the small Bavarian town. It was a glorious, sunny day — the day before Hans Brunner was scheduled to leave for his forbidden trip to the prestigious annual Nazi gathering. Bathed in the glory of an Indian summer and surrounded by red beaver-tail tiles, Gregor Brunner was working twenty metres up on the roof of the Rathaus.

Young Hans had returned from home with his mother's freshly made *Weißwurst*, a bag of pretzels, and two chilled bottles of *Weißbier*. A lunchtime treat awaited. Throughout the morning, father and son hadn't spoken beyond tiling instructions, although they had exchanged several gestures of reconciliation.

Ravenous from his hard morning's work, Gregor put down his tools, took out a clean white cotton handkerchief from his trouser pocket, and mopped his furrowed brow. The anticipation of the lunch his loving wife had prepared was now over.

Before eating with his errant young son, Gregor stood to relieve the stiffness from his creaking body, inflating his lungs to their fullest to take a deep breath of the fresh Bavarian air.

Fulfilled and reaching for the sky at the top of his stretch, the young son crept up behind his father and pushed him with all his might. Witnesses said Gregor Brunner didn't make a sound as he plummeted from high above.

It was the shattering crack of his head on the cobbles, ringing around the Town Square, that alerted everyone to the evil of the Nazi protégé Hans Brunner. With the support of Gauleiter Völler, nobody dared to question young Brunner about the incident ... except for his broken-hearted mother.

Unable to accept the idea of her son killing his father, Amalie accepted Hans's questionable explanation of an accident. The next day, as he had planned, the selfish and cold Hans Brunner left his mother to mourn alone.

With a frown on his face and pride in his heart, the young murderer led the Dittenberg Troupe at the 9th annual Nazi Rally at Zeppelin Field, their Swastika insignia overshadowed by the robotic legions of brainwashed German youth. Local townspeople believed Ernst Völler had orchestrated and approved the murder of the town's best builder. Hans Brunner and the Gauleiter knew better.

This was Hans Brunner's handiwork. Hitler liked a good little Nazi who took matters into his own hands. Survival of the fittest was an appropriate epithet. Hans Brunner saw his chance to get away with murder and seized it.

For Ernst Völler, Hans's pragmatic, cold-blooded solution to his problem was the perfect illustration of where Hans Brunner should continue his party education. In November 1937, under the auspices of his benevolent Gauleiter, Hans Brunner was accepted into the ᛋᛋ -*Junkerschule*, the ᛋᛋ Officers' Training School at Bad Tölz. Here he learnt the arts of warfare and honed his Nazi thinking with the philosophies of Martin Heidegger, Carl Schmitt, Alfred Rosenberg, and Friedrich Nietzsche.

Earlier the same year, Himmler had warned that if any homosexuals were found in the ᛋᛋ, the offender would be degraded, expelled, sent to concentration camps by the courts; and then shot while trying to escape.

During his first year, Brunner was involved in an alleged homosexual incident with a senior training officer, Reinhardt Weber. The scandal was investigated by the *Reichszentrale* under Gestapo control. Off the record, Weber was convicted of four previous counts of homosexual seduction. Brunner was never charged in a cover-up aimed at protecting the masculinity of promising young recruits from the Hitler Youth. Both were sent to Dachau KZ.

Weber was given the pink triangle of a homosexual male prisoner and was tortured to death within three weeks of his arrival. Brunner received an ᛋᛋ insignia, starting at the bottom of the ladder in 1938 as an NCO with the Grim Reaper and his Death's Head army, the ᛋᛋ -*Totenkopfverbände*.

Upon arrival at Dachau, Brunner was offered glorified stories of tyranny, related by notorious, old-school guards such as Hermann Baranowski, Hans Steinbrenner, and Johannes Kantschuster — a trio of thrill-seeking sadists who had terrorised the camp in its early days with arbitrary brutality.

Brunner was desperate to impress his superiors and banish any rumours or doubts about his character. His insouciant attitude towards cold-blooded murder soon confirmed his suitability for membership in Himmler's ⚡⚡ guards. The chief chicken farmer believed his black-shirted paladins were heroes in protecting Germany from the dregs of the new fascist society. Ironically, the disparate groups of colour-coded prisoners herded into Dachau were the oppressive state's biggest victims.

On his first weekend pass, Brunner took time to help his widowed mother move back to Munich. He also seized the opportunity to conspire with Gauleiter Völler to have his old Jewish school friend Otto Lerner transferred from Dittenberg to Dachau. Lerner was arrested on a ridiculous race-defiling charge of having an intimate relationship with an Aryan girl: the girl Völler had forced into a false testimony.

Lerner was transferred to Dachau just one week later: terrified and convinced that his imprisonment was a serious mistake. He had never paid much attention to his knowledge of Brunner's homosexual tendencies, despite consistently rejecting Hans's romantic advances when they were boys. Lerner had forgiven his attacker for his wrongdoings long before he became the target of the now-paranoid guard.

Within two days of captivity in Dachau, Hans Brunner coerced the innocent prisoner into a walk in the secluded woods outside the camp. It was a chance to reminisce about their old school days and suggest hope for an early release.

During the act of raping him against a tree at gunpoint, Otto Lerner was shot while trying to escape. Later,

Brunner regretted that he had let Lerner off too lightly. He had not yet developed the physical and psychological terror techniques he would use on tougher prisoners: driving them to suicide or madness, purely for his own entertainment.

As Germany marched inexorably towards war, the Dachau KZ was stripped of its young guards. As part of the Death's Head formations, the ᛋᛋ Guard Battalion from Dachau goose-stepped into Poland. They came under Hitler's unequivocal orders to kill without pity or mercy all men, women, and children of Polish descent or language.

Working behind the German lines, the Death's Head Battalion was used as executioners, wantonly murdering and torturing captured Polish soldiers, intelligentsia, and Jews. This exercise was an antecedent to the mass murders carried out by the death squads of the Einsatzgruppen in Russia two years later.

Brunner was caught off guard at the outset of the offensive. He was shot in the left thigh, a whisker from the femur bone, and the femoral artery. The sniper failed to follow up and finish the job. The pain was hard to bear, but the frustration was worse as he missed out on further slaughter and carnage. Young Hans had already taken great pleasure in massacring a young peasant family found harbouring two brave but terrified young Polish soldiers while behind enemy lines. He shot dead both soldiers, an old man, two women, and four children without blinking an eye.

Following a short stay in an army field hospital, with a clean injury sustained without infection, Brunner was sent back to Dachau. He quickly resumed his role as a trainer of guards once the camp had reopened and Avraham Falco had arrived.

Brunner's barbarous behaviour had become increasingly depraved. In 1940, the Dachau camp acquired the right of execution without question. There were no witnesses, and no further investigations were conducted. Guards were able to do as they pleased with total impunity.

The ruthless Unterscharführer filled his jackboots to the brim. With a free rein, he satisfied his sexual frustrations by torturing, raping, and murdering inmates. Inmates such as the young Hasidic Jew whom Avi had befriended.

Hans Brunner had also planned to murder Avi Falco, but he was reprieved when Brunner contracted typhus. He was recovering in the camp hospital when Avi's father negotiated his son's release. Signing over all his business interests and life savings to the Gestapo was a high price to pay. It was a price that Avi's father never regretted. A price that brought him hope, even in the darkest time imaginable.

Young Avi's pyrrhic liberty arrived just one week before Himmler's decree on 9th March 1940, banning all further releases of Jews. Only those Jews with valid visas who could emigrate before the end of April 1940 were freed. Avi's father made the risky arrangements in cooperation with Herbert Gaggs, his oldest and best friend, now in England. Avi escaped before Brunner could kill him.

As a talented and exemplary guard trainer, Hans Brunner was kept from participating in the invasion of Russia in 1941. The high rate of mortality of the Death's Head

Battalion would likely have led to an early death during the first year of Operation Barbarossa. Brunner was instead transferred to Auschwitz, where *Judenfrage*, the final solution to the Jewish question, had effectively begun.

Even before the green light had been given at the Wannsee Conference of senior Nazis, arrangements were in hand for the mass extermination of approximately six million Jews from an estimated total of fourteen million fellow human beings that died in the Holocaust and through Nazi persecution. Over 44,000 European camps, ghettos, and other detention sites had been set up to facilitate this despicable task.

It was a task for which Auschwitz Camp *Kommandant* Rudolf Höß recruited young men with cold hearts, iron fists, and the experience to train the new wave of subservient minions.

In 1942, after a year of his tutelage, a group of vicious recruits had inherited Hans Brunner's techniques and skills of guard training and put them into practice.

In 1943, Brunner accepted a new role. He was assigned to take up his position among the fellow ᛋᛋ officers, drivers, block leaders, and doctors who confronted new prisoners on the chaotic *Judenrampe*, the lengthy wooden boardwalk at Auschwitz-II, Birkenau. This was the infamous platform onto which prisoners were shunted from the cattle trains as the harrowing dissection of relocated loving families was formalised.

One of the new doctors at the reception was the notorious *Hauptsturmführer* Josef Mengele. A monster waiting to select subjects for his heinous and unimaginable human experiments, especially twins. Twins like Avi's older sisters, Adina and Keren. Out of

Mengele's 3,000 twins, only 180 survived. Avi's sisters were not among them.

The selection process always gratified Brunner. He took monomaniacal pleasure in playing God while deciding who should live and who should die when forcing the separation of husbands and wives, fathers and mothers, sons and daughters, brothers and sisters, relatives, and friends. Suffering souls directed to lines to the left and lines to the right. Two heaving columns of innocent people ensnared in collective terror. As the bewildered prisoners were forced away in opposing directions, Brunner spotted an opportunity. He took a keen interest in the *Kanada Kommandos* deployed to take away belongings left behind in the chaos.

In recognition of his dispassionate efficiency and the illicit sexual favours to a homosexual superior, Brunner was soon promoted to *Blockführer*. His preferred posting in charge of the *Bekleidungskammer* was no coincidence. The Clothing Chamber was a large storage area that held the clothing of inmates gathered after they had perished in the gas chambers. It was a cornucopia of rich pickings.

From the outset, Brunner ran a strict operation. He craftily allowed certain leniencies towards his *Sonderkommandos*, predominantly Jewish prisoners. These *Hilflinge* or helpers were forced to aid in the gruesome work in the gas chambers. Brunner was rewarded for keeping his promise not to execute more than the three who interfered with him on the first day. The Hilflinge were diligent in their submission of the prized jewellery, hidden within redundant personal belongings and body cavities of their captives.

Brunner was aware of the larger strategy of speculate to accumulate and submitted most of the lucrative trophies to his superiors. He consequently gained a reputation for honesty and integrity with the camp hierarchy. While outwardly claiming a fanatical ideological dedication to Nazism, Hans Brunner proved to be nothing more than an opportunist thief and a macabre nihilist. He had abandoned his boyish devotion to the Führer. Why die for Germany?

Now it was all about him and what he could become in the next life after the War. His personal philosophy was indeed "To look after himself". His plans were already underway.

Despite the *Reichsführer* of the *Schutzstaffel's* boasts that the ᛋᛋ was above taking things for personal gain, Himmler was aware of the corruption and pilfering carried out by the everyday guards in Auschwitz. Following the discovery of dental gold posted out of the camp by a medical orderly, the Nazi hierarchy clamped down. ᛋᛋ *Obersturmführer* Konrad Morgen, a former judge of the ᛋᛋ Reserve and an examining magistrate of the State Criminal Police Office was posted to the camp.

He arrived in the autumn of 1943 with a team of investigators. Morgen was assigned to root out offenders in the widespread slough of corruption, larceny, and fraud that festered in Auschwitz. Camp *Kommandant* Höß himself was also under suspicion.

To counter this serious threat, based on outstanding reports on Brunner's integrity and diligence, Höß secretly promoted Brunner to his trusted covert security officer. The move aimed to monitor Morgen's investigation team and to prevent theft from the extensive *Kanada* warehouse area, where most of the illicit bounty was sorted and processed.

To generate the fear necessary for obedience, Brunner

made an early example of a young Jewish girl he caught smuggling clothes from the sorting area, which she had acquired for multitudes of prisoners less fortunate than herself. After administering a severe beating for all to witness, Brunner escorted her to the gas chambers for a "De-lousing shower". This came after he'd made the girl's sister hack off her hair with a pair of rusty scissors. Even Konrad Morgen was impressed.

Brunner's stock with Höß rose still further in December 1943 after the Auschwitz barracks that held much of the evidence gathered by Morgen's team went up in flames. Despite investigations, the arsonist was never identified. Höß and Brunner knew better.

Although Morgen's investigations into theft and corruption continued into 1944, Brunner continued to exploit his position. He relied on intimidation and fear to ensure that Kanada workers eagerly allowed him to inspect the hidden treasure, often sewn into the linings of prisoners' clothing.

Brunner had no interest in the gold torn from the mouths of deceased prisoners, which was used to craft jewellery. Nor was he interested in the coins, pearls, dollars, or foreign currency arriving at Auschwitz from across War-torn Europe — all of which were plundered and sent to enrich the Nazi coffers in Berlin. Small and easy to conceal, Brunner was fascinated by diamonds. He systematically stole the coveted international currency in hopes of a better life after the War: a conflict that seemed lost after the tide turned at Stalingrad against the now critically wounded Nazis. The point of no return had been crossed.

Just before Christmas 1944, Rudolf Höß approved

Brunner's request for a weekend leave to visit his terminally ill mother in Munich. Before his trip to Bavaria, Germany, the entire country realised that the enemy was approaching. Brunner had applied for a transfer to combat duty to escape the retributions that would surely follow him from the camp.

Despite the ominous risk posed by increasing air raids by the RAF over the city, Brunner took the opportunity to decant stolen diamonds to Munich. His first stop was the city's Nordfriedhof Cemetery, the burial ground where several senior Nazis, including Paul Ludwig Troost (one of Hitler's favourite architects), were laid to rest. Adjacent to Troost's ostentatious shrine was the grave of a "Loving husband and father" named Archivio Stantonovic. Next to this, an unmarked headstone proved a secure place to bury his priceless treasure. The cemetery was subsequently hit when an Allied raid wrecked a large portion of it, but it left Brunner's plunder unscathed.

Hours later, in the dead of night, a knock came at his mother's house. Brunner opened the door to find two Gestapo officers armed with guns. They escorted him to the *Ernst-von-Bergmann-Kaserne* barracks without a final goodbye to his mother—a lost soul left to suffer alone on her deathbed.

Presuming he had been observed at the cemetery earlier in the day, Brunner thought his game was up. Instead, he had been assigned for transportation to the Eastern Front, with the prospect of certain death during resistance against the advancing might of Zhukov's Red Army. Brunner's approved transfer from Auschwitz was Rudolf Höß's parting gift.

Upon arrival at the barracks and reporting for duty, the

chaos of a night air raid created an opportunity. Brunner managed to jump onto the departing convoy of an alternative Waffen battalion, which was heading to support the Wehrmacht 7th Army in the Rhineland. The Germans were suffering heavy losses against the Allied advance in the West, but the prospect of being captured by the Allies was far more attractive than facing the relentless advance of the Red Army in the East.

After several months of intense fighting, Brunner quickly identified a possible escape route. He was thrown into combat alongside his doppelgänger, a Wehrmacht Unteroffizier named Helmut Lehmann. A brave and honourable soldier, Lehmann had almost completed the arduous and hazardous retreat. He had to fight his way back into Germany from the brutal destruction inflicted on the Wehrmacht during its near destruction on French soil in the fighting ground of the Falaise Pocket in Normandy. His determination to survive was driven by his unconditional love for his only child, Julia, but his courageous resolve ultimately proved futile.

In 1945, Helmut Lehmann was murdered in cold blood on the field of battle by one of his own supposed comrades — Der Folterknechte — possessed with the luck of the Devil.

Chapter 46.
A Final Ultimatum

With his hands clasped behind his back, Herbert Gaggs strutted past the French window of his penthouse office. He smiled irritably at the swirling fog that obscured his view of the early morning Fleet Street traffic as it stuttered along the thoroughfare. Horns beeped through the cloud, confirming their presence. The telephone rang. 'Hello, Gaggs speaking … Yes indeed, Sir Ross, it will be a pleasure. Usual place at 11.00?'

Like a pair of moustachioed aristocrats in bowler hats, Herbert Gaggs and old Etonian MI5 Director Sir Ross Whitfield took a late-morning stroll along the Thames' Victoria Embankment. The pea-souper was lifting slowly. The glow of bleary Victorian Yablochkov candles illuminated a sheen of velvet mist that had settled on their grey, Irish tweed overcoats.

Amid the raw smell of the recently declared "Biologically Dead" waterway, pleasantries were exchanged as choppy waves of rust-coloured river lapped against the grey stone-brick bank. A drop in the blaring fog horns from disparate flotillas of maritime and river vessels allowed the wily old MI5 sage and the elegant newspaper mogul to get down to business.

In his ethereal tones, Whitfield was first to broach the subject. 'It appears that you were right about Chief Inspector Collins. We listened in on a call he made to one of our agents. He told Collins all about your man Falco's previous association with us. By virtue of that revelation, we must assume he knows the background and history of both you and your colleague, Avraham Falco. We have dealt with our bent penny accordingly. Bernard Lewis's name was mentioned, as was Councillor Norman Simpson's. They are both involved with Collins.'

'And Collins and his henchmen are colluding with Helmut Lehmann,' said Gaggs.

'Perhaps. What have you established regarding your German *friend?*'

'We believe him to be a former ⚡⚡. We have some information, but our suspicions are yet to be confirmed. He appears to be involved in some sort of business with influential members of the local Freemasons' Lodge.'

'Nazis and Freemasons are unlikely bedfellows, Mr Gaggs. Hitler banned and persecuted the brethren in Germany before the War. No doubt you are aware that many Freemasons wore the red triangle of the political prisoner in the Nazi death camps.'

'Selective amnesia furnishes good conscience. Money and power are seducers that unite the corrupt.'

'Indeed, they are. We have also uncovered new evidence of Norman Simpson's pre-war allegiances with Oswald Mosley and his Blackshirt fascists. He helped generate support for Mosley's political rallies in Manchester in the early 1930s. Simpson leans toward the far right, despite being a Labour Councillor.'

'This is not about Mosley. He no longer poses a threat to British society. We continued monitoring him, his finances, and his political activities after his release from internment following the War.'

'As you are aware. Mr Gaggs, so did we. That's why he scurried away from these shores in '51.'

'Of course, Mr. Whitfield. Our cooperation was mutually beneficial then, and it can be again. As I said, I am sure that Lehmann and his Freemason contacts are in cahoots. They are the kind of men who seek to impose their will upon others.'

'In what way?'

'That is what Falco is finishing.'

'Mr. Gaggs, perhaps this is an opportune moment for me to remind you that this is British soil, and now is the time for us to dig deeper. MI5 will handle the matter.'

'Mr Whitfield, perhaps this is also an opportune moment for me to remind *you* that if Helmut Lehmann does indeed prove to have been an ⁌⁌ officer of some standing, it was your net through which he slipped undetected. He was able to ascend towards the higher echelons of British society unhindered on *your* watch. I might also add that one of my reporters was murdered while investigating this case. An extremely promising young man, in whom I took a keen personal interest.'

'That was indeed unfortunate.'

'Oh, it was substantially more than unfortunate, Mr Whitfield. Both Mr Falco and I suspect it was a murder commissioned from the highest level. With my hat on as a businessman, Lewis's complicity can be twisted as part of the uncovering of a murderous story of police and political corruption involving the secret service. A story which will be of great interest to my newspaper's readership and beyond.'

'Are you threatening me, Mr Gaggs?'

'However, speaking with my hat on as the Head of the Nakam's British operations, my main objective is to bring Helmut Lehmann to account for his misdemeanours against my people during the War. This, rather than any peripheral story that might be of benefit to my newspaper's sales.'

Whitfield started to interrupt, but Gaggs held on to the

talking stick. 'If MI5 wishes to work with the Nakam in the future, it is essential that *Falco* ends this. He is highly competent, and besides, I cannot stop him.'

'Well, *I* can jolly-well stop him. My people are also highly competent.'

'Maybe so, but the ensuing bloodbath will be *your* responsibility, and not mine. Besides, won't your people contract nosebleeds from having to travel so far up north, Mr Whitfield?'

'Touché, Mr Gaggs,' said Whitfield, with a wry smile. Both men paused, taking a deep breath as they stared into the dispersing Thames fog. The river's winding corridor revealed a series of blindfolded vessels. They exhaled their muted plumes into the yellow haze lingering above the murky brown waterway at the heart of London. After a brief moment to gather their thoughts, both men turned to each other.

'The fog is clearing nicely,' said Gaggs.

'Indeed, it is. The West German police contacted me just this morning. They were working with their Austrian counterparts on the apprehension of a chief murder suspect. Apparently, a lone British subject by the name of Julian West boarded a private flight at Salzburg Airport yesterday. A man — or I should say, a paedophile — was brutally murdered in Munich four days earlier. The victim was an individual by the name of Felix Spangell, the owner of an orphanage near Dachau. The same orphanage where Julia Lehmann was left in residence before Spangell signed her off to a Helmut Lehmann with all the necessary papers. She was released into his custody in 1947 after she had spent two years in care.'

'Interesting,' said Gaggs, with a coy smile.

'Interesting indeed. Particularly since it is the same

Helmut Lehmann whose credentials you had me check with German authorities several weeks ago. Not surprisingly, they now suspect that the murderer is one of my people, but we both know that is not true ... don't we, Mr Gaggs? The man who boarded the private plane in Salzburg had a distinctive Y-shaped scar on his right cheekbone. The West German Police are eager to apprehend him.'

'Eager to apprehend a paedophile killer? Perhaps they are looking to give him a medal of honour?'

'Far from it. Not only is the murder of a German citizen on German soil a very serious matter, but the killer stole a gun from a Landespolizei officer and then put it to his head while making good his escape. I seem to recall that your man, Avraham Falco, has a similarly distinctive facial feature. You wouldn't happen to know anything about this, would you, Mr Gaggs?'

'Of course not, Mr Whitfield.'

'Hmm. You have placed me in an extremely difficult position, Mr. Gaggs. As you have explained most judiciously, both MI5 and the British police are seriously compromised. However, and despite your excuse for your chief editor's involvement — if the manure does indeed collide with the propeller — I don't see your newspaper emerging from this smelling like roses.'

Gaggs smiled wryly.

Whitfield came to a halt. He rubbed his chin briefly before continuing. 'The issue of War Criminals remains a sensitive one for Her Majesty's Government. I will not allow this to escalate into a national embarrassment in any way, shape, or form. You have precisely until midnight tomorrow to discreetly remove Helmut Lehmann without a trace, or I will deploy my special agent to thoroughly clean up this mess. He is also highly capable and ruthless with it. I trust you understand my implication, Mr Gaggs.'

'I understand completely, Mr Whitfield. However, I must remind you that Mr Falco holds British citizenship.'

'I am aware of that, but sometimes sacrifices must be made for the greater good.'

'Are you now threatening me, Mr Whitfield?'

'Oh, please don't take it the wrong way, Mr Gaggs. This is not a threat; this is a promise. You have until midnight tomorrow.'

Reluctantly, Gaggs nodded as the pair shook hands on their tacit agreement.

Chapter 47.
Home Truths

A front curtain twitched as a black cab pulled up outside Avi's mother-in-law's spacious, two-storey Georgian end terrace on Brighton Road in Croydon. Avi strode up the long pathway with a purpose that masked inner trepidation. He climbed the three stone steps to the door and, seeing no knocker, rattled the letterbox flap with unintended vigour.

Kathy's mother, Eileen Cranighan, opened the door. She switched her brief blank expression into a cautious smile once she realised it was her son-in-law in front of her, wearing an expression of contrition. In her salt-of-the-earth Cockney accent, she invited him into her warm and cosy Georgian terrace home.

Avi and Eileen were sitting comfortably in the lounge, relaxed in the glow of the crackling coal fire. Its flames licked the wrought iron hearth set into the black cavern of the chimney breast. Sharing centre-stage on top of the mantelpiece, a Military Cross and a Burma Star rested in lamented glory. Both ribboned War medals were displayed proudly below the shrine of framed black and white family photographs, which peppered the gaily patterned wallpaper.

The pictures featured the tight-knit family of Eileen, her husband Derek, and their only child, Kathy. A solitary Wartime photograph of Derek Cranighan in his khaki bush hat and British Army Burma uniform caught Avi's eye. The stilted wedding picture of Avi and Kathy showed them posing outside a low-key Registrar's Office, also a smaller picture of Leonard Bracegirdle, resplendent in his ARP warden uniform.

To gain a closer look, Avi leaned towards the image of Len. A slight shake of his head expressed disbelief. The similarities in looks between Avi and Kathy's old flame were palpable. Attempting to disguise his brief discomfiture, Avi returned his gaze to the family montage and, with an admiring grin, he commented, 'These are really interesting pictures, Eileen.'

'Yeah, quite illuminatin', I should imagine. They was happy days. Shame you've never been here before, Avi. Always too busy.'

Avi could feel his face blushing with embarrassment as he pointed to a charming picture of ten-year-old Kathy embracing her father. Both framed occupants were beaming with carefree smiles on a sunny day at the beach before the War. 'That's a really nice one, Eileen. She was a pretty little girl.'

'Ooh, yeah, that's me favourite is that one. Gorgeous child, my Kathy. The apple of my Derek's eye. We had a lovely day out to Margate on the train. We was an 'appy little family. It was hard on Kathy when we lost Derek. Bourbon biscuit, Avi? Afraid they're all I got in.'

'Uh, no, thank you.'

'Did she tell you about her dad?'

'Yes, she said he was a very kind and loving father.'

'He was that, all right. Lovely fella was my Derek. Is that *all* she told you about him?'

Avi looked at Derek's medal and army picture. 'Pretty much. She also told me about his army service during the War and that he died in Singapore in 1942 when the Japanese overran the British military hospital where he was a patient.'

'Yeah, the Alexandra. He was in a really bad way,

stricken with malaria and an infected leg wound. He'd not been there long. He was in a bed down the corridor. A sitting duck when the Japanese soldiers arrived. They ran amok. Pandemonium. It was every man for themselves. One of his army pals, Alf Hillary, took the time to come and see me after the War to tell me what had happened.

'Please tell me. I am very interested to know.'

Eileen smiled and nodded. 'My Derek had saved Alf's life in a firefight with the Japs while defending the approach towards the hospital grounds. That's how Derek caught one in the leg. Alf tried to return the compliment. He managed to drag Derek from his bed, but they were both bayonetted by Jap soldiers as they were comin' down the stairwell trying to get out. Little bastards. They killed anything that moved that day. Patients, doctors, anyone they could get their dirty little hands on. They raped nurses and then stabbed them to death. They even killed a young chappie who was already out cold, lying on an operating table just before his operation. They killed Derek, and Alf was left for dead. After that, Alf spent a terrible time in Changi Prison, and then the best part of three years as a slave labourer on the Thai-Burma railway of death. After what he told me about being a Japanese POW, I think Derek might have been better off, dead as he was.'

'Not with sweethearts like you and Kathy to come home to.'

Eileen broke into a warm smile, a smile like Avi's mother's when she was smitten with his boyish charm. 'Thanks, Avi darlin'. They reckon around two hundred people were massacred in the hospital that day.'

Avi shook his head. 'Murdering swine.'

'Yeah, but that's what the *old* Japs were like.

Fanatical, ruthless, utterly barmy. Kathy was devastated. She loved her dad to bits … we both did. The War took its toll on everyone. We got my Derek's death notification telegram from the War Office on the day of Kathy's eighteenth birthday. Some present that was.'

'I didn't know,' said Avi as he looked at his shoes. 'You must really hate the Japs.'

Eileen detected the emotion in Avi's voice. 'Yeah, but hatred got me nowhere. I had to forgive and forget because there was nothing else I could do. I don't concern myself with the things in life that I can't change … or the wrongs I can't right.'

Avi finished his second cuppa. Eileen reiterated her position. 'I know you miss her, Avi darlin', and I know she doesn't want to see you right now. She's safe and sound, so don't you worry about that. Give her time to think things through. Her love is strong. But she is stubborn … a bit like her mother, really.'

Avi got up to leave. Eileen rose of her own accord and hugged him warmly. Avi pulled back and looked her in the eye. 'I can't be without her, Eileen. I love her so much. Much more than she can imagine.'

Eileen smiled. 'Yeah. I think you do, Son.'

Avi looked at his timepiece. 'I must be off now … Oh, and I forgot to say thank you so much for the watch. It is very beautiful, and I am very grateful.'

'I'm glad you like it, Avi, and you are welcome. You must take good care of life's little treasures that come your way.'

Avi smiled. As he collected his overcoat, Eileen moved to escort him to the front door.

'Please, Mrs Cranighan, I'll see myself out.'

She kissed him on the cheek. 'It's Eileen, Avi love.'

Avi smiled. She held him at arm's length by the shoulders and looked him in the eye. 'Listen to me, Avi. I know all about revenge, and so did my husband. There ain't much justice in life for the likes of you and me. Do what you have to do, Son.'

Avi stepped out of the front door. He strode up the garden path and on towards the bus stop up the road. He saw Eileen waving from the front window.

Kathy entered the lounge from the back parlour.

Chapter 48.
Stick or Twist?

Tapping the metal tip of his folded black umbrella against his leather-soled shoe, Herbert Gaggs loitered outside the Bevis Marks Synagogue.

He saw Avi approaching with slumped shoulders and a downturned expression. He offered his hand as they exchanged a Shalom. Gaggs noticed Avi's unusual insipid handshake and reddened eyes, choosing not to comment. Instead, he adopted an upbeat tone. Placing a paternal hand on Avi's shoulder, he asked, 'How was your excursion, Avi?'

'It had its moments, Sir. This is what I know. Jens Wolff was blackmailing Lehmann. Helmut Lehmann is Hans Brunner, the ᛋᛋ guard that tortured me in Dachau.'

'Are you sure?'

Avi produced Brunner's file and handed it to Gaggs. 'The loser was responsible for rewriting history, after all.'

Gaggs' eyebrows lowered, and he shook his head.

'He rewrote *his* history. He is a cozening fiend. His truth is detailed in this file,' said Avi.

'Excellent. What about Wolff?'

'Wolff was SD. He was also blackmailing Felix Spangell. Spangell was the proprietor of the orphanage in Munich where Julia Lehmann was staying. While Wolff was tracking Lehmann down, he must have come across Lehmann's picture in a local paper. Adams hadn't put it all together before he was murdered. Lehmann knew Adams was after him because of Lewis.'

'MI5 informed me that they intercepted a call between one of their agents and Collins. They know who you are.'

'It doesn't matter. I'm not going back to Manchester.

My wife has left me. I must find her.' Avi took off his trilby and scratched his head. 'You once told me that, "He who lives without a wife lives without joy and blessing, without protection and peace". It has been spinning around in my head for days. Without her, I am nothing.'

Head bowed his head and turned to leave.

'Please, Avi, slow down and listen to me for just a moment,' said Gaggs. 'Just like life, women are complicated. If she genuinely loves you, she will come back. If she has only just left you, now is not the time for the chase. Give her time to breathe … give her time to think.'

'It is not just this one thing. I'm beginning to doubt my actions. I killed a man while I was away.'

'Felix Spangell, per chance?'

'Yes. He was a bad man who abused children. Killing during wartime is morally justified, but killing during peacetime is a different matter altogether. I am not a judge, jury, or executioner. I am just an ordinary man trying to navigate the minefield of life.'

'The Lord says that, "We should maintain justice and do what is right …" '

' "… for my salvation is close at hand and my righteousness will soon be revealed …" '

' " … Blessed is the man who does this, the man who holds fast …" '

' "… who keeps the Sabbath without desecrating it and keeps his hand from doing any evil …" *Isaiah 56:1*,' added Avi.

Gaggs smiled. 'Do you think that in killing this man, you have performed an evil act, Avi? Did you have a choice but to kill him?'

'I suppose that there is always a choice. If I had spared him, I would have been caught by the German Police. Besides, it was self-defence. *He* attacked me.'

'If it was him or you, it was much better that it was him. You made your choice, and it was the right one. Besides, he was a sinner of the lowest order.'

'But I killed him at the height of my rage.'

'You know that rage can lead to mistakes that get you killed. You must control your emotions, Avi. To see this through, you need to control yourself. You are a good man, but your anger must not prevail. You must be calculated in every decision you make.'

'That is why I am doubting my actions. I am no longer confident in my judgement.'

'In our faith, we are taught that "The world rests on three things: Justice, Truth, and Peace". I believe all three are inherently connected, each leading to the other. You have already discovered the truth, Avi. The great Irish statesman Edmund Burke once said, "The only thing necessary for the triumph of evil is for good men to do nothing". Now is the time to settle your score.'

With sadness in his eyes, Avi looked at his fidgeting hands. Gaggs continued, 'I understand your concern, Avi. In consideration of your mental well-being, you are free to find your wife. However, sometimes you must prioritise your needs. If you want to settle matters with Hans Brunner, believe me, it is now or never.'

Avi took out a cig. Gaggs produced a lighter. Hesitantly, Avi accepted his light. Gaggs nodded. 'You must clear this without a trace by midnight tomorrow night or MI5 will kill you. Do you understand me, Avi? *Midnight.*'

'I understand what I have to do. Do you have the items

I requested?'

Gaggs nodded.

'Then I will finish this.'

Gaggs fished into his pocket and pulled out a bottle of pills. 'Your medication, I believe?'

Avi was taken aback. 'No, Sir. I do not need it. There are some things I can control.'

'That's the ticket. Have faith and you will achieve your goals. Speaking of which, did you manage to touch God while on your travels?'

'No… but I did see an angel.'

Gaggs put the bottle back in his pocket. 'Come with me, Avi. I have something for you that you might enjoy.' They strolled along the pathway to a gleaming, British Racing Green MGA Convertible sports car. 'This is yours.'

Avi smiled with gratitude and yet wisely hid his thoughts, *Great, another convertible in rainy Manchester.*

'I thought you might like a little more style than the rust-bucket you suffered before.'

'How did you know about that old heap?'

'There are many things to which I am privy. Things that I am sure would surprise you greatly, Avi.

'Such as your knowledge of my *private* medication prescription?'

Gaggs smiled. 'I apologise if I have intruded, Avi. You know me. I never leave anything to chance.'

Avi smiled wryly as Gaggs stretched out a welcoming arm toward the front of the synagogue, its mystical aura beckoning lost sheep back into the fold.

' "The salvation of God is like the blink of an eye",' said Gaggs. 'Look at His magnificent house. It is time to step out of the darkness and into the light. It can still shine brightly. Let Him in, Avi. Let Him into your heart, and you will see the glory that has waited for you. Come with me and pray for God's guidance.'

'There is no time for that.'

'We can always find time to pray, Avi. God is always with you, whatever you might imagine.'

Chapter 49.
Enlightenment

Carrying a fresh pot of tea brewing beneath its woollen cosy, Eileen Cranighan stepped into her sweltering lounge.

Sitting at the dinner table with her back upright and rigid, Kathy stared at her mother with an inscrutable expression.

Eileen was aware of the impending conflict. She had orchestrated it carefully. She poured the first brew into one of two bone China cups resting on matching saucers. 'Would you like me to get the biscuits, dear?'

'No, thanks. You know I don't like Bourbons.' Kathy's hands were clasped tightly. 'What I would like is an explanation when you are ready, *Mother dear*,' said Kathy with sarcasm.

'*Explanation*, dear child?' Eileen smiled as she sat at what had become a negotiating table.

'I'm a grown woman, Mother, and I'm not stupid. I was *meant* to hear your conversation with Avi, particularly your last comment.'

'What comment was that, then?'

' "I know all about revenge, and so did my husband". Did Dad murder John Winnot?'

'Ask me no questions and I'll tell you no lies.'

'Well, that's not strictly true, is it? All those years you've led me to believe that it was some sort of crazed serial killer that murdered the Winnots.'

'I've done no such thing. If you chose to believe that was true … well, that was up to you.'

'No, Mother, you said it *was* a serial killer, and I was fourteen. I believed every word you said. You told me that is that and never to mention it again ... as you know full well.'

'Come on, Kathy. You must 'ave known. You was told to lie to the police about them Winnots, so as to cover for your father.'

'Yes, you told me to lie just in case Dad was involved. You also told me the police let him go because they believed that it was a serial killer that did for the Winnots. That was all that mattered to me.'

'Well, they didn't get very far with that theory, did they? Don't be so bloody naïve, Kathy. Like you say, you're not stupid. Of course, your dad killed John Winnot. He would have killed his bitch of a wife as well if he'd ha' done the job properly.'

Kathy took a sharp intake of breath. She covered her face with her hands and shook her head. Tears welled in her eyes. At the ready, Eileen produced a crumpled hanky from inside her cardigan sleeve. Kathy waved it away. She exhaled with a heavy sigh.

'But Dad was locked up when she was murdered ... so who did kill that "bitch of a wife" of his? It was *her* murder that got Dad off the hook.'

A small mound of spent tea leaves gathered in the strainer as Eileen topped up her cuppa. She picked a sugar lump with a pair of silver tongs, plopped the cube into her cup, added some milk, and stirred in a protracted manner.

'Well?' asked Kathy with impatience while scratching at her right temple.

'I'm not exactly sure who actually killed her ...' Eileen smiled as she pulled the pin from another oral hand grenade. 'But I do know that Herbert Gaggs had something to do with it.'

'*Herbert Gaggs!*' Kathy tempered her incredulity. 'Herbert Gaggs? The same Herbert Gaggs who owns the newspaper Avi works for? Who arranged Avi's arrival in Britain from Switzerland before the War? Who sent Avi to Manchester to …'

Eileen interrupted. 'Yes, Kathy. The very same Herbert Gaggs. He was a good friend of the family after your father saved him from a gang of thugs one night. Mr Gaggs was being kicked stupid after having been slashed in the neck with a razor. He'd have died on the spot but for your dad's bravery. When your dad was nicked for John Winnot's murder, he called in the favour on offer. Mr Gaggs paid him back with knobs on.'

'So, *Herbert Gaggs* killed Winnie Winnot?'

Eileen took a nonchalant slurp of her tea as Kathy tried to process her mother's revelations — 'Not ten minutes ago I heard you telling Avi that hatred gets you nowhere.'

'I said hatred got *me* nowhere.'

Kathy shook her head. 'What happened to all that "Turn the other cheek, forgive and forget" stuff Dad taught me when I was little? I thought that meant something to him, and I thought it meant something to you.'

'It did. It meant something to your dad as well … until he was tested beyond his limit. I suppose in that regard, he was weak. He failed to do what it says in the Bible. Havin' said that, it also says an eye for an eye, a tooth for a tooth. Life is full o' contradictions, Kathy. Somewhere down the line, we're all hypocrites in one way or another.

Your dad was a man of honour. When he heard what had happened to you, he couldn't let it lie. I knew he wouldn't let it lie if he could do something about it. You were the apple of his eye. His heart and soul. When he left to go back to the army in Suffolk, I knew he was gonna take matters into his own hands. I couldn't 'ave stopped him even if I'd ha' wanted. There was more to it than just revenge. Your dad blamed himself for your evacuation. I wanted you to stay with us in Stepney, but he thought it was far too dangerous … what with all the air raids and that. He had the last word. He blamed himself for what happened to you. It was a hell of a burden for him to carry. It ate him up inside. Besides, he didn't want it to happen again to someone else's little girl.'

Kathy's eyes welled up. 'He did it for me.'

'Yeah, o' course he did it for you. He did it for us. For the family.'

'So, what happened?'

'He gave me Mr Gaggs' business card just in case there was any problems. I told him to be careful.'

'Just like you just told Avi to be careful. You gave them both your blessing to commit murder in pursuit of revenge. Avi is consumed by hate and loathing. That's why I left him. I take it you've never read *Moby Dick*, Mother?'

'Can't say as I 'ave.'

'It's a story of Captain Ahab's obsessive quest for revenge against the white whale that bit off his leg.'

'What's that got to do with anything?'

'The tale ended in catastrophe. The captain took his crew down with him, and they perished in their sea of hate. I have a feeling that Avi will meet the same fate. He's not taking me down with him. I want no part of it. From hatred comes no good. Sunday school taught me that forgiveness is more satisfying than revenge.'

'Not to your dad, it wasn't. Some things can't be forgiven without driving the victim to self-destruction. Your rape, your torture … It would have destroyed your father if he hadn't taken his revenge. Doing what he did was the only way we could get any justice. It was up to him to settle the score. Did you want them Winnots to get away with what they did to you?'

No response.

'Come on, Kathy, please tell me. Did you want the Winnots to do somethin' like that again?

Kathy remained silent.

'The police was bloody useless after you complained. To be fair to them, they was short-staffed. There was a war on. They had to take shortcuts. Just as well really or your dad might o' swung for it. He called in a favour from Mr Gaggs … and Mr Gaggs made it go away.'

'By killing Winnie Winnot?'

'Who can say, Kathy? Who can say? After that bitch was taken care of, your dad was released back into the army. Justice was served and his honour was restored. Perhaps it's a man thing, Kathy.'

'Was Dad happier after that?'

'It's hard to tell, really. He was shipped out to Southeast Asia not long after. I'd like to think he was.'

'So you don't actually know if revenge satisfied him?'

'We never had the chance to discuss it. I know that *I* was satisfied. I still am. Maybe it's just human nature, darlin'. Bastards like them Winnots didn't deserve to breathe the same air as decent people like us. Your dad and Mr Gaggs saw to it that they didn't breathe no more. I for one don't care how they did it.'

Kathy shook her head. 'You've got a right scary side to you, mum.'

'Yeah, and don't you forget it.' Eileen smiled and winked as they stopped for a slurp of their brews.

Eileen changed the subject. 'Do you ever talk to Avi, Kathy?'

'Yes, of course we talk.'

'No, I mean *properly* talk. Do you actually discuss what's on each other's minds? You clearly 'aven't told him about what happened to you durin' the War. Your dad and I talked about everythin' to each other, that's why we was so close. I always knew what he was thinkin', and I knew all about his past.'

'I used to do that with Len … but Avi's not the same.'

'You've always put Len on a pedestal. Perhaps rightly so. He was a good lad was our Len … Avi was quite open with me, Kathy.'

Eileen picked up a Bourbon biscuit and dunked it in her tea. 'Didn't you tell me there's a young girl in danger from that German bloke Avi's after … about the same age as you when you was in trouble?'

Kathy nodded and then trapped an index finger between her teeth.

Eileen continued, 'I know that Avi's not Len, Kathy, but I think he could be just as good a man *if* you give him the chance. Let him sort out his past, and then perhaps you might see what he's really capable of in the future.'

Kathy drew down her eyebrows.

'I know the dreadful worry you are going through. I have experienced it, with bells on. But your dad and Avi have one thing in common: Herbert Gaggs … and *He* will take good care of Avi. Of that I'm certain.'

Chapter 50.
Withdrawal Symptoms

Lehmann's white Mercedes glided toward the kerb in Mosley Street in Manchester city centre. He parked it outside the regal First National Bank. He reached for his silver attaché case and stepped out of the car.

An unnoticed black Riley saloon arrived from the same direction. It drove past, doubled back, and parked on the other side of the road, within a photo shot. Joe McClay was sitting at the wheel.

Lehmann's right shoe tapped impatiently as he waited in the vestibule of the ostentatious bank. Mr Freeman, a formal-looking, stiff-necked account manager, emerged from behind a frosted glass door. They shook hands.

Freeman escorted Lehmann along the well-trodden path through the main hall to a side entrance set into the thick stone wall. Once past the two heavy, iron-barred gates, Freeman led the way into the echoing vault. Each security locker had two keyholes. Freeman took out his key for box 108 and unlocked it. Lehmann reciprocated.

Freeman turned to leave as Lehmann opened the large locker door. He slid out a covered, elongated metal drawer tray, which he placed on a table draped in a purple cloth.

Glancing around the empty vault, Lehmann's face lit up as he lifted the lid off the box to reveal a large, magnificent cache of sparkling diamonds of various shapes and sizes. He carefully transferred the gemstones into a large blue velvet pouch, which he dropped into his attaché case before closing the lid.

On the table was a discreet, fixed button that

summoned assistance. Freeman re-entered the vault with a stack of cash, which he placed on the table. Lehmann began counting meticulously.

From the safe, unobstructed vantage point of his car, Joe McClay took a clear shot of Lehmann leaving the bank carrying the attaché case.

Across the road from Lehmann, tucked between a betting shop and a greengrocer's, a greasy spoon café provided a front-row view of the proceedings. From behind its grubby front window, the obsequious proprietor, Ernie Digby, watched Lehmann leaving the bank. He looked down at the photograph of Lehmann he was holding.

Lehmann glanced briefly within direct sight of his unseen spy, but he didn't notice him. Lehmann was focused on the precious treasure in his grasp.

As Lehmann got into his car, Digby picked up the phone and dialled.

'Chief Inspector Collins? It's Digby … You know, from the caf' across the road from the bank … You know, the First National on Mosley Street … You asked me to keep an eye out for a man in a flash white Mercedes … You gave me 'is picture … Yeah, that's me. Digby. He's just been in the bank and now he's driven off … Yeah, a great big shiny one, you know?'

Chapter 51.
Forward Planning

Avi enjoyed the luxury of his new sports car as he cruised along the main road connecting London to Manchester —but the novelty had worn off by the time he reached the outskirts of Luton, just about thirty miles up the road.

The journey north quickly turned into a tough, risky struggle. With only a few road lamps, he managed most of the dark trip using shining cat's eye reflectors in the middle of the winding, single-lane road. All the transport cafés along the way had closed long before midnight. Without a much-needed gallon of coffee, he almost lost the battle against his heavy eyelids on a couple of occasions. The lonely sign reading 'A6 Manchester 25 Miles' was a welcome relief, lifting his spirits.

The rising sun cast first light on dispersing squadrons of sack-laden postmen, droning milk floats, and exhausted workers trudging home from their night shifts, all of whom criss-crossed the cobbled backstreets with varying enthusiasm.

Aside from an occasional van delivering dailies to the local newsagents, the city's main roads remained deserted as Avi's convertible navigated the tangled arteries of the vast Mancunian metropolis.

Skirting behind Port Street, Avi parked at the back of a tumbledown, empty factory opposite Lehmann's depot. From the boot of his car, he retrieved an old grey army blanket, a small suitcase, a tin of red paint, and a large paintbrush. He carried this eclectic collection into the building and made his way up to room seventeen.

Joe McClay was slouched on a lonely chair beside the window, his foggy breath briefly misting the chilly glass. Forfeiting any greeting, McClay observed Avi's shattered expression and the crumpled clothes hanging from his hunched frame as if they were still on a hanger. 'Bloody hell, you look like an under-stuffed scarecrow ... 'ave you been looking after yourself, lad?'

'I drove through the night. It is freezing out there, and it's not much warmer in here,' said Avi, with a lengthy yawn.

'*Cold?* This isn't cold. You wanna change yer butcher, lad!'

Avi shook his head in bewilderment. He was too tired to respond as he placed his unlikely collection of items on an old desk.

McClay struggled to get up on stiff legs. He stretched his arms, yawned, and then handed over his newly developed monochrome photographs of Lehmann entering and leaving his bank, carrying the attaché case.

Avi examined the pictures.

'Not much to say on Lehmann,' said McClay. 'But he did go to the bank yesterday with his fancy attaché case.'

'How long was he in there?'

'A good half an hour and there were no queues. Perhaps a little something for the weekend, sir?'

'Perhaps more than a little something.'

'And perhaps for a bit longer than the weekend?'

McClay motioned to leave as Avi took out his wallet and pulled out a generous wad of crinkled notes as payment.

Noticing Avi's manoeuvre, McClay smiled. 'No thanks, pardner. This one's on the house.'

Avi nodded and returned the smile. 'Thanks, Joe. I

might be in touch soon.'

McClay stopped in his tracks as he remembered a message. 'By the way, your colleague, Peter Spencer … he tipped me the wink. He went out of his way to get in touch while you were gone. He told me to warn you that you *shouldn't* go back to the Chronicle. He said something's seriously not right. He seemed genuinely concerned, and to be fair, I believe him. He said that Lewis has been pacing around his office all week. He's as nervous as a lost sheep in a Welsh brothel. The police have been milling around the building, waiting to see if you show yer face. Spencer thinks they are onto you for something related to David Adams. He doesn't know the half of it.'

Avi nodded. 'Pete Spencer, eh? Who would have believed it?'

'Yeah. Maybe he has a pair, after all.'

Avi smiled.

'You know the drill, Avi lad. If you want Lewis, get him to come to you.'

'Don't worry about that, pardner. I will make full use of his fear.'

Avi offered a cigarette. Joe accepted, smiled, and placed it behind his ear. Avi lit his cig and looked down at the brush and the tin of red paint.

McClay winked. 'Don't forget, Avi Falco. Fly high … fly high and be *Falco the Falcon!*'

Avi shook his head and smiled knowingly as McClay closed the door behind him. He pulled out a pair of overalls from his suitcase and got down to business.

Chapter 52.
Day of Destiny

Avi was grateful for the rowdy barks from a pack of stray mongrels squabbling in the street below. His attention was drawn. Wrapped in a blanket and fighting to keep his eyes open, he squirmed in the chair beside the front window. He peered out just in time to see Lehmann's white Mercedes arrive outside the depot.

Through the hazy morning mist, the drying aphorism, *'Jedem das Seine'* was revealed, daubed on the depot wall in drippy red paint. Lehmann studied it. He looked around, unlocked the inset depot door, and then went inside.

Avi looked down at the used tin of red paint with a wry smile. Twenty minutes later, he saw Ronnie Hyland arriving in his MG Magnette Saloon.

Ah, Mr Hyland, right on cue.

Hyland stepped out of his car and couldn't help but notice the red message shining on the wall before disappearing into the inset door.

Lehmann was searching for his overalls when Hyland entered the depot office and went straight to the point. 'Jedem das Seine?'

'An old Nazi proverb meaning, *To Each What He Deserves*. This is Falco's work, and it is recent. The paint was still wet when I arrived.'

'He's not found me. Let me find him,' said Hyland.

'Falco will come to us. Collins will make a move. I know how they think.'

'*No!* I'm not leaving you alone. Falco could come here again, and Collins is the leader of a great big gang of corrupt bastards in blue uniforms.'

'You worry too much, Ronnie. You forget that I was a leader in an even bigger gang of murdering bastards in black uniforms. I don't underestimate anybody … particularly myself.' Lehmann moved over to the safe and opened the combination lock. He took out the silver attaché case. 'Trust me, Ronnie. I will deal with it. I know what I am doing.'

Lehmann handed Hyland a spare set of house keys and kissed him sensually on the lips before ordering, 'Get packed for a long journey. Go to my house with your passport. Pack me a suitcase, the large one on top of the wardrobe in my bedroom. My passport is in the middle drawer of the one with the lamp on top. Stay by the phone. I will call you when I'm ready.'

'Why can't we just leave now, together? We are home and dry. We have everything we need. If you wait, you are asking for trouble. Now is our best opportunity. Falco will not expect you to run.' As the word "Run" left his mouth, Hyland knew straightaway that he had chosen the wrong word.

'No! I never run. Besides, I have things I must finish.'

'These *things* are nothing to you. Let them go.'

'I cannot let them go, and I will not let them go. Besides, do you really think that Falco is the kind of man who will give up just because we have disappeared? He will never give up. I want him dead. Then we will leave.'

Hyland motioned to punch the wall but held back. A brief silence. Hyland shook his head. 'What about Glenda?'

'She is away for the weekend with one of her boyfriends. Julia is spending the day with a friend. She will be back home this evening. Watch her until I arrive.

This time tomorrow, we'll be at the safe house and home free.'

Lehmann handed Hyland the attaché case.

'Are you leaving anything for Glenda?' asked Hyland.

Lehmann smirked. 'Yes. A vulgar portrait of her stupid father and a lot of dirty linen for her to deal with when we're gone.' He pointed to the attaché case.

'Don't let it out of your sight ... *ever*.'

Hyland gripped it tightly.

From his secluded vantage point in the empty factory, Avi watched Hyland, carrying the attaché case, stoop into his car and drive off. He rose from the chair, stretched his arms, yawned, and then rubbed his eyes. Lying on the dusty old desk was Avi's scuffed suitcase. He snapped open the brass lock and lifted the lid. He took out a pair of horn-rimmed glasses, a pair of scissors, and a cut-throat razor, then began hacking off his thick mop of hair.

An ebullient, grey, nimbostratus ceiling engulfed the vast 19th-century Mancunian tribal burial ground of Southern Cemetery. While fine rain feathered the glass windows of the red public phone box opposite the eerie graveyard, Avi dialled Lewis's direct line.

Lewis took the call without hesitation. 'Falco! Where have you been? I've been extremely concerned.'

'We must meet urgently. Somewhere quiet.'

'My office is quiet.'

'Too dangerous. Meet me at David Adams' grave in an hour.'

The phone clicked dead. Lewis plucked out his pocket watch from his waistcoat and scratched his forehead. He pressed down on the cradle and then dialled Collins' number. 'Collins? It's Lewis … Falco's back!'

Chief Inspector Collins was sitting at his expansive desk with Brookes and Taylor in informal attention.

'I need you both to escort Mr Lewis to Southern Cemetery. He's meeting Falco. This time you finish him … understand?' said Collins.

'It will be our pleasure,' Brookes replied.

Brookes and Taylor smirked as Collins' phone rang once more. Collins answered and waved his ruthless assassins out of his office. 'Yes, Helmut, of course, it's Collins.'

'I need you to arrange an urgent meeting with Simpson and Davenport,' said Lehmann from his depot office.

'What for?'

'Today is payday. Meet me at the lodge at eight this evening.'

'I can't. We're all engaged in an official function there until eleven. We cannot be interrupted. You need to maintain a low profile. Will you meet us afterwards? It will be all over by half-past eleven.'

'Yes.'

Collins hung up.

'Yes. It will definitely be all over for you by then,' Lehmann said to himself with a menacing grin.

Chapter 53.
Grave Danger

It was yet another miserable afternoon as thunder rumbled amid moiling clouds, which released a torrent of biblical proportions. It pounded Lewis's open black umbrella to near collapse as he weaved a path between tilted moss-covered gravestones.

Arriving at David Adams's plot, the nervous Chief Editor recognised the warning of the storm. Glancing at his watch, Lewis waited outside with visible agitation. There was no sign of Avi.

Both shifting their weight from foot to foot like a dancehall comedy duo, Taylor and Brookes appeared not to be taking the situation as seriously as they should. However, after a nod from Brookes, he and his partner, Taylor, drew their guns and crept behind adjacent trees. They tentatively looked around as falling rain continued to saturate the otherwise deserted graveyard — still no sign of Avi. Brookes and Taylor continued to stalk the area.

Lewis's nerves stretched to breaking point. Once more, he checked his watch. 'Falco is a punctual beast ... but now he is eleven minutes late,' Lewis muttered to himself — still no Avi.

As muddy water began to swell in the dark, secluded pit of a freshly dug grave, Avi peered above the parapet like a U-boat periscope searching for prey. At last, he clambered up from beneath a plywood cover left by an inattentive gravedigger. The upright postures of Taylor and Brookes gave Avi a welcome glimpse of his arrogant targets.

Both corrupt coppers advanced on an erroneous path.

Neither strayed too far from Lewis, who remained rigid in the hunt.

Avi checked the silencer attached to his Webley Mark IV revolver as he trod through the tombstones and hissing trees, closing in on Collins' three stooges at a concealed angle.

Suddenly, the thunder stopped. The rain slowed. Avi was right behind his targets. He took out a handkerchief and wiped rain from his glasses. The tall Taylor was looking in the wrong direction.

'Over here, tough guy.'

Taylor turned.

Avi's shot hit him squarely between the eyes with unerring accuracy. Taylor was dead as his savage collapse flattened a loose stone cross and demolished a vase full of flowers.

The stocky Brookes emerged full-on from behind a large gravestone with his gun raised.

Too late.

Avi took his second shot, which ripped into Brookes' side and belly. He followed up with another round, which smashed into Brookes' upper right arm, straight through the bicep.

Yelping in agony, Brookes wallowed in the mud, desperately trying to reach his gun, which was only inches away.

Lewis didn't move a muscle.

Avi sidled over to his victim.

The dying Brookes saw the futility of struggling for his gun. He stopped and looked upward with dread in his eyes.

Avi's expression was emotionless as he reached into Brooke's coat and took out his handcuffs. He looked

Brookes in the eye and smiled. 'Never mind, sunshine. I could have shot you dead, just like your partner. But first, I have two small questions to ask you ... Should I piss on you first, and then kill you — or should I kill you first, and then piss on you?'

He motioned to his fly, but then ruthlessly shot Brookes dead between the eyes. Avi's face was wreathed in a wry smile as he focused on the stock-still Lewis and observed, 'He wasn't worth a piss.'

Reaching down to pick up Brookes' gun, Avi noticed an Art Deco Rolex on Brookes' wrist. He unclasped the bracelet and dropped the watch into his pocket. Turning his attention to Taylor, Avi took his handcuffs, keys, and gun.

Lewis remained motionless.

Avi grabbed Lewis's umbrella, rolled it up tightly, and used it to prod Lewis forward. 'You didn't see much action during the Wars then, Mr Lewis?' said Avi.

It took a few minutes for the prisoner and escort to navigate the path to the deceased Schlesinger family's once-ostentatious Gothic mausoleum, situated in a predominantly Jewish section of the cemetery. The unwelcoming chamber was cloaked in moss and overgrown ivy, which had engulfed most of the grey stone exterior.

Avi forced Lewis's head beneath the archway entrance and towards the heavy metal door, on which the steel padlock had already been unlocked in readiness.

Lewis recognised the prospect of involuntary incarceration in the dark, dingy tomb. Chronic claustrophobia triggered panic. 'You can't take me in there. *Please* don't take me in there.'

'Why not? Once you told me that "discretion is the better part of valour" … is this not discreet enough for you, Mr Lewis?'

Lewis dug his heels into the shale-covered ground. 'No, no, no … I won't go in there and you can't make me.'

'Get in there, *now!*' Avi kicked him up the backside and then shoved him into the fetid atmosphere of the dank, spooky cavern. He said, 'One more word out of you and you'll get the same as those two jokers … understand?'

Wide-eyed, Lewis nodded three times.

Although he stepped carefully, Avi's soles still crunched on the debris on the floor. He found his long rubber torch and then pulled the heavy door shut with a squeal. The foul odour of death reminded him of his imprisonment in Dachau. He clicked on his torch. The beam shone on greasy rats, rustling in a damp corner. Like a scene from the Nazi propaganda film *The Eternal Jew*, the squealing rodents dispersed, scurrying into hidden lairs.

Slowly and deliberately, Avi swept the beam of light onto six interned caskets resting on a rusty iron coffin rack. All were in advanced stages of decay. He uncuffed and then re-shackled Lewis to the rack. Lewis couldn't refrain from pathetic whimpering.

'No, no, no, Mr Falco … Avraham, Avi, what have I done? You are making a big mistake. Don't do this … Please don't do this to me.'

'*Be quiet and be still!* You know what you have done. Adams' murder is on your hands!'

'No, no, you've got it all wrong. You've just killed the men who murdered David Adams.'

'Yes, and you played a key role in the set-up. You were in the office that evening when Adams left to go to the cinema. You knew which route he would take because you asked him. It was you who informed those two comedians that he was on his way. His blood is on your hands. You lied to his fiancée about investigating the murder. How could you possibly do that to a young couple in love ... their whole lives ahead of them?'

Avi plucked from his pocket the Rolex he'd recovered and held it in view. 'Do you recognise this? ... *Do you*?'

Lewis took a brief look at the watch and then switched his expression of guilt to his shoes.

'Yes. I thought so. David Adams' watch, no doubt. It was you who spiked Adams' drinks at Fowler's wake, wasn't it?'

Avi wiped his brow with a handkerchief and then bound Lewis's ankles together with the second set of cuffs.

'You Freemasons are all involved. I would like to know the details of whatever scheme you are working on. This is not a lift-shaft in a busy office building, Lewis. Nobody will hear when you scream. Tell me the plan, or I'll happily leave here without you. I fed these rodents this morning. But once they get hungry, it will get nasty ... very nasty, indeed.'

'*I will tell you!* We have been buying up the slum areas on the cheap. We are forcing all the ni ...' Lewis quickly corrected himself, 'All the coloured immigrants to live there. Simpson sees to it that there is no other housing for them.'

'And so?'

'And so, we will squeeze them with extortionate rents. Iniquity is inevitable. We will control their prostitution, their drugs, and their gambling. They will depend on our loans. They should never have darkened our shores. We will bleed the bastards dry. You can join us. We'll all be rich.'

Avi yanked away Lewis's necktie and replied with a guttural roar. 'Rich like those selfish bastards who exploited the Jewish Ghettos during the War? You make me sick. You treacherous ... I ought to kill you here and now ... in fact, what is there to stop me? *Nothing!*'

He rammed the gun hard against Lewis's left temple. Lewis screwed his eyes tightly and held his breath as Avi's finger stroked the trigger. Two hearts beat in unison, but for different reasons.

Breathe Avi. Breathe. Control your anger. It would be a cold-blooded execution.

He held off and took a step backwards. 'No, Mr Lewis. I won't let you off so easily.'

Lewis's heavy panting resumed.

'How old are you, Lewis?'

No reply. Lewis was almost paralysed in fear.

'Come on, tell me. Sixty-three? Sixty-four? Come on, come on, what is it ... tell me. It is a simple question: how old are you?

'I am, uh, sixty-eight.'

'Sixty-eight years on the planet. You already hold a distinguished position and all the trappings of success. What more can you want? What more do you need? You are an educated man. You know what happened to the Jews ... you told me yourself. You know that prejudice knows no bounds ... where it can lead to ... but still you persist. You reported on the carnage of the Blitz in Manchester. You saw the devastation firsthand. You have delved into the lives of good, honest, hard-working people who lost everything. You were complicit in the murder of a War hero in Tommy Green. A soldier who went to war to fight to protect his country ... to protect freedom from tyranny ... to protect the likes of you ... while you stayed at home and feathered your nest.

You have lived through *two* World Wars. And what have they taught you? What did the Nazi's wanton slaughter of millions of people teach you? Absolutely nothing ... because profiteering from the misery of others is still your blind and selfish desire. Do you really know this man Lehmann, whom you have followed so willingly?'

Lewis shook his head.

'He was a murdering ϟϟ guard in the concentration camps. The lowest of the low. But there is no point in my elaborating on his disgusting crimes to a duplicitous, ignorant, greedy old fool. You found your way here of your own volition. Now you can stay with all the other rats, but don't get your hopes up ... I doubt that they will tolerate you any better than I. You made your choices ... now it is your turn to go to hell!'

'No, no, no, if you leave me, I will die.'

'Then you had better hope I come through this ordeal alive.'

Avi clenched his teeth as he gagged Lewis with his own necktie and then left with purposeful deliberation. The shaft that shone from the door narrowed as the light surrendered slowly to the darkness.

Muffled protests fell on deaf ears as the padlock clicked shut. Lewis listened to the crunching sound of Avi's shoes on the gravel pathway as they disappeared into the distance. His struggle was brief. The handcuffs cut into his wrists, one pain that could be avoided. There was no room to manoeuvre. With naive optimism, he stopped still and listened for the sound of Avi returning.

'Yes, yes, that's right, that's right. He is teaching me a lesson. That's it. Sit tight. Soon be over.'

No sound of returning footsteps. His panic compounded. Lewis could hear his panting breath travelling through his crusty nasal passages — a rustling in the debris. He felt the tickle of greasy rodent fur brushing against his exposed right calf. The squeal of the bold, inquisitive rat made him shudder.

Lewis's sudden movement and muffled screams alerted the rest of the rustling rat family into a frenzy of feverish shrills. An involuntary response from Lewis added to the pungent odours that lingered in the worst living nightmare he could ever have imagined.

The rain had stopped as Avi dragged Brookes' corpse across the wet grass toward the open grave. He dropped it, watching it land face down on Taylor's upturned corpse.

You have also reaped what you have sown, thought Avi as he tossed in their guns, then covered the grave with the discarded plywood cover.

He rubbed his hands together, cupped, and blew for much-needed warmth.

Inside the red telephone box across from the saturated cemetery, Avi called Joe McClay's office.

McClay answered on the first ring.

'Howdo ... Joe McClay Private Investigator, extraordinaire.'

'Joe?'

'Yes, Avi lad. Everything all right?'

'So far, I have retrieved David Adams' gold watch. You can pass it to Joan when I have finished my business with Lehmann. Please listen carefully, Joe. There is just one more thing I need you to do for me ...'

Chapter 54.
Jedem das Seine

Outside the battered F&G depot, CI Collins' gleaming two-tone Jaguar Mark 1 saloon pulled up behind Lehmann's parked white Mercedes. Collins' feet stepped onto the pavement. He closed the driver's door gently and surveyed the empty Port Street.

Dressed in low-key civilian clothes that could have been bought at a local church jumble sale, Collins opened the kerbside rear door and reached over to the back seat, tucking the Sten submachine gun under his full-length overcoat. He headed toward the F&G depot and noticed the remnants of 'Jedem das Seine' crudely obscured with dripping black paint.

The small inset door leading into the yard swung open with a hefty shove. It clattered as a large oil can was knocked to the ground. This makeshift alarm had served its purpose. Surveying the yard for signs of danger, he drew the submachine gun from beneath his coat and aimed it ahead.

In old overalls splattered with black paint, Lehmann crouched behind a metal filing cabinet with Wolff's Parabellum cocked.

Collins advanced into the yard. 'Come on out, Helmut. It's only Collins ... I know you're in here ... we need to talk.'

No reply. None expected. Collins cased the small office building. The yard wall around the property blocked any entry from the rear. The grimy windows were too small and dirty to climb through or see inside. The front door was the only way in. Collins grabbed the door lever, pulled it down, and edged into the unlit office.

He looked around. His Sten gun was primed and ready. His trigger finger was relaxed in his grip as he stepped inside.

Pointing the Parabellum, Lehmann jumped out when Collins was side on. He fired two rapid rounds. One bullet ripped into Collins' left arm, the other tore through his ribcage.

As he dropped, Collins fired a wild volley of shots. They missed his attacker and slammed through the flat bitumen roof. Sharp beams of daylight pierced the darkened room.

Lehmann kicked out a leg and trapped Collins' gun with his foot. He yanked it away from Collins' grasp. 'Be still!' Collins' heart pounded as blood flowed from two gaping wounds hidden by his punctured overcoat.

Lehmann leaned over and rifled through Collins' pockets. He pulled out his passport and a substantial wad of cash. 'Why run?'

'I can't contact my man in MI5. They're closing in. You've brought all this on us,' said Collins with a groan.

'So, you thought you'd make a break for it with my stash?'

'This is *your* fault. All those years ago, I told Fred Turner never to trust a bloody German.'

'Then you should have followed your own advice. If it is any consolation, your associates will receive the same *payment* as you. Where are your men?'

'They are lying low. They found Falco ... and killed him,' said Collins, now near-death.

'Falco is *dead?*'

'Falco is ... dead.'

Lehmann smiled. 'And you have left them to take the rap. Whatever happened to the English sense of fair play?'

Collins squinted as Lehmann pressed the Parabellum to the Chief Inspector's head and put him out of his misery.

Chapter 55.
Crescendo

As darkness enveloped the evening sky, Avi reached the back of Lehmann's spacious garden without any trouble.

Despite the net curtains being open in the bright light through patio windows, he quickly moved across the garden to the knobbly trunk of a weeping willow tree.

Through the leafy canopy, he saw Hyland pacing up and down the lounge with his gun drawn and his left hand clutching the attaché case.

Raindrops began to fall more rapidly as a heavy downpour started. Avi looked around for a better shelter. He darted around the side of the house. His faint shadow touched the brick wall as he headed toward the garden shed. Taking out his trusty Swiss Army knife, he easily broke it open.

Lehmann stepped out of the depot door, dressed in his formal three-piece suit and shielding himself with his black umbrella. He locked the depot for the last time and got into his car.

The well-rehearsed route through the city centre traffic was navigated with subconscious ease. Lehmann's mind was absorbed in the plans he wanted to carry out. He pulled up to the kerb across from the Freemasons lodge, crossed the street, and entered through the main door without hesitation.

Another glance at the watch. Avi compared the time with Adams' watch and noticed black cemetery soil wedged under the tips of his fingernails. Using the smallest blade on his army knife, he began to scrape them clean. He put away his knife and settled back to endure both the rain and Hyland's indoor vigil. It wasn't long before he nodded off…

… Avi's light snoring abated as he woke up suddenly. The flickering flame from his Zippo lighter revealed he was sitting on a deck chair, wrapped in an old canvas tent. 'Oh bugger!' he said as he looked at his watch. It was 11:20 pm.

Emerging from behind the garden shed, Avi scampered around to the back garden.

In statuesque poses, Julia Lehmann and Ronnie Hyland were exposed in light escaping through the patio windows.

Avi scurried to the back of the house. Aware of his midnight deadline, he climbed up a drainpipe onto a flat roof and then forced open a sash window.

Undetected, he slipped inside the house. Screwing the silencer back onto his gun, Avi crept toward an open door leading to Lehmann's master bedroom.

The double bed was unkempt on one side. A large brown leather suitcase stood upright, next to the wardrobe, with a convincing counterfeit British passport on top. He picked up the passport, examined Lehmann's picture, and checked the details in the name of Fitzroy Kleine. The 'exit' and 'entry' stamps inside proved the high quality of the forgery. A wry smile formed on his face as he pocketed the document and then inspected both doors in the bedroom.

One led to the main landing, while the other connected to the bathroom. Avi saw his reflection in a large mirror on the opposite bedroom wall. He entered the shared bathroom and opened another connecting door leading to Julia's bedroom.

Twitching in his doggy dream, Patch was asleep on Julia's single bed. Avi stroked the dog into calm consciousness and then looked out the window at the front of the house. Ronnie Hyland's car was parked on the street beside the house.

Downstairs in the lounge, Julia was engrossed in a school textbook while Hyland was nodding off in a chair with a glass of brandy tilting precariously on his lap. They both heard a commotion as the dog barked furiously.

Startled, Hyland spilled the brandy on his thigh. He arose from his chair. 'Stay right where you are, young lady.' Hyland pressed his index finger to his mouth, picked up the attaché case, and moved into the hallway. Seeing it was clear, he put down the case, took out his gun, and screwed on a silencer.

Still barking, Patch scurried down the stairs to find Julia. The excited dog ran past Hyland, who began his ascent while clinging to the attaché case. He arrived on the landing and tiptoed towards Julia's open bedroom door.

He entered the empty room, checked behind the door, and then crept to the connecting bathroom as Avi silently emerged from Lehmann's bedroom onto the landing.

Hyland entered the shared bathroom and moved into Lehmann's room, while Avi entered Julia's room once more, searching for the slightest sign of an enemy.

He then proceeded to the bathroom. In the reflection of the opposite mirror, Hyland caught a glimpse of Avi creeping up behind him like a cat stalking a helpless sparrow.

The phone rang.

Avi looked down at the phone, but Hyland turned

quickly and shot his target in the upper chest. Avi returned fire, hitting Hyland between the eyes. Hyland slumped onto the bed face down, trapping the attaché case as the phone continued to ring. Badly injured and coughing heavily, Avi picked up the receiver.

Lehmann stood in the darkened lodge meeting room, phone receiver in hand. In the background, Davenport and Simpson were dressed in Freemasons' regalia, both slumped over the long meeting table, their heads immersed in a pool of claret spilling onto the antique Persian rug. The clock on the wall showed 11:35 pm. Lehmann was desperate for a response.

'Ronnie? Is that you? I was delayed. Is everything all right? Ronnie … Ronnie.'

Don't give away your injury.

Avi mustered his strength. 'No, Herr Brunner, it is *not* Ronnie, and it is *not* all right. Ronnie's rigid corpse is clinging to your silver attaché case. I wonder what could be in there … *you absolute fool!'*

Brunner clenched his teeth as his face reddened with rage. 'I should have killed you in Dachau while I had the chance, you worthless, *Jewish pig!'*

'Well, you know where I am,' said Avi with calmness.

Brunner slammed down the phone. As he did so, twin ϟϟ lightning bolts slashed through the sky like white hot swords of steel.

Avi pounded onto the landing and hurried down the stairs. His blood-drenched shirt was more red than white. At the bottom of the banister, Julia was frightened and dumbfounded by the sight of a bloodied man approaching. Despite his shorn head, she quickly realised it was Avi. She overcame her fear and stood firm with her loyal dog by her side. Avi feigned a calm expression.

'Julia, it is all right.'

'Mr Falco, you are shot.'

'Yes, yes. I need you to sit down. Please sit down.'

Avi's eyes were glazed. His head spun like a clockwork ballerina.

He eased onto the couch, a nauseous wave sweeping through him. His heart pounded, and his fingers were numb. His thoughts were frantic. A mixture of adrenaline and determination kept him going.

'Is this it? Am I going to die here and now? No! It'll be all right. Come on, come on. You have a job to do. Stay out of shock. Keep talking, keep thinking. Get a grip ... get a grip!'

Struggling to stay conscious, Avi gulped in air as blood oozed from his wound and the searing pain intensified. He took a final deep breath and then focused on controlling his breathing. Soon enough, the hall stopped gyrating as he regained his composure.

Julia removed her cardigan and gave it to Avi.

He tried to smile. He pressed it inside his jacket, firmly against the wound. His face was marked with pain. 'What did you hear on the telephone?'

'My father called you a *Jewish Pig*. He said that he should have killed you in Dachau. Why would he say that?'

'Because he's not your father.'

'Then please tell me who he is.'

Avi mustered his strength once more. 'He is Hans Brunner. He was an ᛋᛋ guard in the Dachau concentration camp. I know because I was there. He killed many people. He tortured me and many more. He was transferred to Auschwitz where millions of prisoners were ...'

'Gassed?'

'Yes. In 1945, Brunner came to Britain as a prisoner of war who had stolen diamonds from Auschwitz victims. He somehow managed to smuggle them out of the camp and hide them in Munich. He must have retrieved them when he came to get you from the orphanage. You were his cover.'

'His cover?'

'He needed an excuse to go to Munich, pretending to be a family man. You provided both opportunities.

'But how do you know he isn't my father?'

'In April '45, Hans Brunner fought alongside your real father against the Allies advancing from the West. Brunner was found dead in Mannheim, the place where the final remnants of the German 7th Army made their last stand. But it wasn't Brunner. It was your father. Brunner took his life, his identity ... and then you, his daughter.'

From the dry side of his jacket, Avi handed Julia the picture of the *Blockführer*.

'This is Hans Brunner.' Then he handed Gaggs' copy of the Helmut Lehmann photograph in the Wehrmacht. 'This is your real father. It was Hans Brunner's identity tag that was retrieved. Brunner killed your father because, as you can see, they looked the same. He even cut his own eye to copy the scar.'

'But why go to such trouble?'

'He knew that the British and the Americans would hunt the ᛋᛋ, especially those from Auschwitz. He was then sent to England as a prisoner of war. He was lucky to be moved up North. He worked on Turner's farm. You know the rest.'

'Are you going to kill him?'

'He's coming to kill me.'

Avi noticed Julia's black eye and gently cupped her cheek. He frowned and then whispered, 'I'm so sorry, Julia.'

'You weren't there when I called.'

'I know. I won't ever let you down again.'

Julia gazed down at Patch, then back up to Avi. She nodded.

Avi struggled to keep his eyes open, knowing he had to stay awake and alert. Brunner wouldn't hesitate to kill Julia. In fact, it would bring him great pleasure.

Avi's survival was her only chance.

He rubbed his face as hard as his declining strength would permit. He gulped down watery saliva and strained to his feet. When he reached the front door, he asked, 'What will happen if I let the dog out?'

'It's all right. He'll run off. He'll come back when he's ready.'

Avi opened the door, and the dog bolted off into the night.

Crazy dog. thought Avi. 'Did you ever play hide and seek in this house?'

'Yes, why?'

'Did you have a special hiding place that nobody ever knew?'

Julia held Avi's hand and led him into the lounge. They entered the room illuminated by a solitary lamp. A speeding car screeched in the distance.

'Whatever happens, you must be silent until you hear my voice and *only* my voice. It is essential. Do you understand me?' said Avi.

'Yes, I understand.'

Julia ducked into the large fireplace and climbed up the chimney without disturbing the soot. Avi turned out the lamp and left the room.

Julia couldn't see car headlights flashing through the curtains, but she could hear Brunner's white Mercedes skidding into the drive. The rain started to fall.

Avi was nearly at the top of the stairs in his effort to retrieve the attaché case.

Holding Collins' Sten gun, Brunner climbed out of the car. Wolff's Parabellum was visible in his side holster.

Lowering the attaché case onto the flat roof with a slight drop, Avi crawled out of the sash window at the back of the house. Taking out his handkerchief, he wiped the blood off the frame, then lowered it shut.

He tossed the blood-stained cardigan out of view and sat beneath the window, taking a deep breath that filled his lungs with cold, moist air and helped clear his mind again.

That's it. Take a rest. Take a rest. Gather your thoughts. Come on, you have survived Dachau ... twice. You are still here. There is nothing to fear. Remember what Mother said: "Once it is over, we will all be together soon enough".'

He looked up at the sky. The tempest rumbled as lightning flashed from dark, black clouds. He opened his mouth to drink in the refreshing rain and quench his thirst.

Gripping Collins' Sten gun with murderous intent, Brunner approached the front door. He pushed it open with the tip of the gun and stepped into the empty hallway. He looked down at the trail of blood leading towards the stairs. Further splashes of spilt claret pointed towards the lounge door. He stopped and considered both directions, then decided to investigate the lounge, where Julia was hiding.

Brunner stepped into the room as intermittent lightning flickered through the gaps in the curtains. Unaware of her presence, Julia's heavy breathing was masked by thunder.

Brunner paced to the far end of the room. He looked behind the bookcase. He examined the floor — no blood. He circled around and then moved toward the fireplace. He stopped just inches from the hearth. The thunder subsided as if someone had flicked a switch. The wall's breadth separated hunter from hunted. Brunner could almost touch his prey.

With her eyes screwed tightly, Julia's fingers clutched the chimney breast. Sensing danger, she held her breath. A ricochet of thunder shook the room, and then silence ...

... Brunner was statuesque for what seemed like an eternity to Julia. Suddenly, he turned to walk out of the lounge.

A small stream of soot fell from the chimney.

Brunner stopped in his tracks.

He walked back to the fireplace, where frantic lightning unveiled the Hieronymus Bosch painting of Hell with the grotesque faces of damned sinners, which matched Brunner's vile expression. He recognised the portent. His eyes narrowed as he lost focus through fear, forgetting about the distraction.

He left the room and entered the hallway. The grandfather clock read 11:50 pm. He examined the blood trail and moved toward the stairs.

A Triumph TR3 sports car pulled up and parked across from Brunner's house. The headlights were killed.

Following the blood trail, Brunner moved carefully up the stairs.

A thunderclap masked the sound of the attaché case dropping onto a bush outside. Avi tried to climb back down the drainpipe, but lost his grip and fell onto the lawn with a heavy thud.

His gun landed on the wet grass, followed by his glasses. Desperately trying to suppress groans, he fumbled in the dirt. With more luck than judgment, he found the frames and hooked them on. The gleaming shape of his gun beckoned, and he crawled over to retrieve it. Using the cast-iron drainpipe for support, he hauled himself to his feet and then grabbed the attaché case.

Brunner reached the top of the landing. He moved to examine the sash window, but was distracted by the creaking of the bedroom door.

The storm intensified as febrile lightning illuminated the sky like fireworks on Guy Fawkes night.

Avi took out the Swiss Army knife and entered the lounge through the patio door. Soaked to the bone, he faltered into the lounge. With trembling hands, he took off his glasses and struggled to wipe them dry. His head pounded. His heart pounded. He managed to stand upright and then hobble toward the chimney.

'Julia, it's Avi. Are you all right?' he whispered.

Julia was standing on the ledge, still holding onto a protruding brick. 'I'm very tired.'

'Hang on tightly, Julia. It will soon be over … I promise.'

Brunner entered the master bedroom. Hyland's stiffening corpse was lying on the bed. He gripped a pallid hand, studied the blood patterns, and realised that Avi had been shot. 'Well done, Ronnie … and now I am going to kill that bastard for both of us.' The red mist descended as Brunner turned and exited through the door.

The clock on the wall behind Avi read 11:55 pm.

Avi placed the attaché case on top of the piano. He lifted the lid and then struck the piano keys with a sudden surge of strength. Striding like a mad professor, he threw open the patio doors and invited the howling storm into the room.

The doors fought desperately to stay on their hinges. The net curtains flailed like rampant ghosts, straining to be unleashed into the chaos.

Avi ducked low behind the bookcase.

Furiously out of control, Brunner marched along the landing and then stomped down the stairs two at a time. He heard the shattering of windowpanes as the patio doors continued their struggle for freedom. Brunner burst into the lounge, illuminated by dazzling electric blue lightning.

After a thunderous boom, his itchy trigger finger pulled back forcefully. A storm of bullets flooded the walls, perforating the hangings and the piano while striking the attaché case, its lid flying open in the chaos. A wild concerto played as cash notes fluttered around the room like a swarm of demented bats.

Firing frantically until the magazine finally ran out, Brunner threw the smoking Sten gun to the floor with disdain. He slapped his hands together and then wiped them on his trousers. Panting heavily, he took out the Parabellum and moved toward the open attaché case.

The blue velvet pouch lay unblemished on the floor. Brunner smiled as he retrieved it.

Avi emerged with his gun pointed at his smiling target.

Brunner looked up, and his smile faded.

Avi closed one eye. He aimed, but his arm started to waver as Brunner raised his gun.

Avi managed to fire a shot that hit Brunner in the right shoulder. The impact knocked him backward as he fell onto the hearth.

His gun fell just out of reach as Julia crashed down from the chimney in a disoriented state.

Barely able to hold his gun, Avi dropped to his knees with his head bowed.

Grounded, Brunner shuffled to his gun and grabbed Julia by the hair. She squealed as he pulled her up in front of him, using her as a rigid shield. He transferred the Parabellum into his left hand and pressed it hard against Julia's head.

Avi's focus was blurred. His legs were weak. The heavy gun hung like a lead weight dangling from a flimsy fishing rod.

Seeing Avi teetering on the brink of death, Brunner played for time. 'Your revenge is obsessive, but you won't risk killing a child. You value your place in heaven too much! Drop your gun … *now!*'

Avi's gun dipped further still.

'Give it up. Make the noble gesture. Sacrifice yourself for her. I don't need to kill her.'

'That's right … that is right,' said Avi. 'I should expect no more. The coward hides behind the innocent. The coward will hide no more.'

The words were lost on Brunner.

'Come on, drop it. This is her only chance to live. *Drop it, I tell you!*'

Lehmann tightened his grip around Julia's neck. Her face reddened as she struggled to breathe. The grip tightened still further. Her eyes swelled as if straining to escape from their sockets as tears leaked down her cheeks.

Cold sweat dripped from Avi's furrowed brow. His sunken eyes rolled to their whites and then back again. Their lids lowered like drooped canopies. He was on the verge of collapse at the moment of truth. The moment of truth that had overwhelmed him long before he settled in the northern city. Before him lay Lucifer, cloaked in black. The red swastika on his arm glowed as a Devil's insignia. Cudgel in hand, Luger at the ready. Prepared to extinguish another innocent victim.

Above the fireplace, the tilted painting of Hell flashed like a beacon.

Another crash of thunder as a heavy gush of rain rushed into the room and hit Avi full in the face. He blinked back into reality and focused on the eyes of the leviathan.

Brunner stared back, desperately searching for weakness, but Avi's eyes were blackened, crazed, and lifeless, like an executioner just before the swing of the axe.

Another surge of inner strength rose within Avi, a

moment of clarity before he took his last breath.

Through the open patio door, Patch the mongrel charged into the room. He barked fiercely as he confronted Brunner, stopping at point-blank range.

Julia's eyes rolled, and then blinked shut. Her head dropped.

The snarling dog moved closer to Brunner, who fought to stay hidden behind Julia's limp body. He kept her head against his wounded shoulder.

The dog was primed like a rabid beast, with his side teeth exposed as he snarled and lunged.

Brunner failed to keep one eye on the dog and the other on Avi.

As Brunner shot the dog dead, he was fleetingly exposed.

Avi raised his gun. 'It is time for you to go to Hell.'

Brunner's expression betrayed his bravado as fear revealed the panic behind the demon's mask a second before Avi's bullet tore through his left eye. Brunner was already dead when Avi fired another shot through his neck for good measure.

The Devil's poisoned claret spewed over Julia's limp body as Avi's lifeless frame collapsed to the floor.

The grandfather clock in the hallway struck midnight.

A handsome male MI5 agent in his mid-twenties was sitting across the street from the Brunner residence in his Triumph sports car. Dressed sharply in a black shawl-collar evening suit, he glanced at his watch. It had just passed midnight. He had heard the commotion. Now it was time for him to act — time to clean up the mess without leaving a trace of evidence. Time to erase Avraham Falco from the face of the earth.

He reached into the glove compartment and pulled out a Beretta 418. He put on a pair of tight leather gloves and stepped out of the car. He slipped on his cream trench coat and raised the collar. Gun at his side, the agent strutted across the road. He opened the gate, looked around, and then sidled up the garden path.

His light carriage softened the crunch of the gravel as he aimed his gun at the slightly open front door.

As he moved closer, a figure in a black balaclava with three holes suddenly emerged from the shadows. With a quick, smooth motion, the commando had his Browning pistol pressed against the agent's head. The agent was at his mercy.

'Drop it now, sonny,' said the gruff voice.

The agent dropped his Beretta and was instantly struck on the head with the bottom of the Browning's handle. He fell to the floor unconscious, his fall cushioned by his attacker. The dark figure took out a cigarette and lit it with his Browning gun lighter. He inhaled, exhaled heavily... and then shook his head.

'Kids today ... no bloody idea.'

The commando lifted his balaclava. With blacked-up eyes and a cigarette hanging from the corner of his mouth, Joe McClay looked like a satisfied panda.

He flicked away the cig with casual disdain, picked up the agent's gun, and slipped cautiously into the house.

Epilogue
Part I.

Suddenly, his eyes opened. He was stiff and lying flat, tightly wrapped in yellowing, mummified bandages and trapped in a hot, silent, pitch-black tomb. He quickly realised that he wasn't wearing his glasses. He tried to move but was paralyzed by panic. He made another attempt, but the pain from his adjustment made him stop. Now he knew not to struggle. Avi's brain shifted into gear. His mind began to race ...

Am I trapped in a straitjacket in an asylum dungeon? No, no. You are far from that place. Ah, yes. Yes! The shootout with Brunner. Brunner! Oh my God, Julia. Did I keep her safe? Is she alive? Have I caused the death of another child? No, not again! What happened? Come on, think man, think!

His heart picked up a rapid beat as sweat moistened his brow.

That's it, I was shot. Shot in the chest. Did he kill me? Am I dead? Is this place Gehinnom? Is this my purgatory? Have I awakened in the next life? Am I wedged between heaven and hell? Is this the waiting room? The queue for expired individuals lingering before the Final Judgment of their ultimate destinies. Is this my time? Is this my Judgment Day? Two dead children on my account? If so, I will be damned for all eternity!

As his blurry eyes adjusted to the dark, Avi gradually focused on the hot cuppa steaming on the wooden drawers beside his bed. It helped him regain his mental clarity. It was unlikely that the angels of heaven would serve him a brew before such a judgment of his destiny. The homely aroma of slices of hot, buttered toast on the plate beside the white mug and the empty chair next to his bed were enough earthly details to ease his initial concern.

The nurse, away from her vigil to reassure Avi in such a potential scenario, had just stepped out for a bathroom break. Her supper, however, had already done the job. Baguley Hospital was definitely an unfamiliar place, but it certainly wasn't a bridge between heaven and hell.

At last, Avi managed to relax. He turned his head slightly and took a breath with some ease. The returning nurse was quick to tell him that the surgery to remove the bullet from the upper left side of his chest had been difficult but successful.

Over the next three days, Avi's bedbound solitude gave him time to reflect on the past few months and to evaluate where the pieces had fallen on his table. It was a perfect time to recover, relax, and clarify the many remaining questions.

A wry smile crept onto his face as he remembered the terror in Brunner's eyes when he sent him into eternal darkness, or perhaps an endless hell. Avi preferred the latter. He believed his actions were right and justified. He was at peace with what had happened, but the details of what came next remained confusing.

No matter how hard he tried to recall, the answer stayed just out of reach. He remembered Julia Lehmann's eyes closing and her body relaxing into a deathly surrender. He longed for confirmation of her well-being, but who could he turn to? For now, he would have to wait and stay silent. The cards had been dealt. He would play them soon.

Avi was unexpectedly happy to have survived his ordeal. A new glow of optimism appeared in him, along with a confidence that he would eventually find Kathy again and fix their marriage. That was something he was determined to do.

His calm reflections inspired him to adopt a more positive outlook. It became clear to him that there was no future in the cemetery. There had always been a narrow margin between Avi's life and Avi's death. He had cheated the Grim Reaper many times, but he was no longer willing to keep doing so. He had won again, but every gambler's winning streak must end. He had seen enough death for one lifetime.

Life was a gift to be fully experienced and cherished. Avi was born a human, blessed with time on earth to be positive, fulfilled, and to do good and selfless things that would benefit and promote well-being. If this life was the only one, why end it prematurely without necessity?

God had given him another chance, a chance to live differently. He owed that much to his family, especially to those who had perished at the hands of the Nazis. He also owed it to his estranged wife and to his unborn children. If there was a life beyond this mortal coil, he would have plenty to do in preparation for his Final Judgment from God.

Regarding what would happen next in life — with Brunner banished to oblivion — Avi believed he now had greater control over his destiny. The heavy burden he once carried felt like a floating balloon. He had always been cautious of change and of his own limitations. But many of those limitations he had imposed on himself. Now he was unshackled. Free to experience life from a new perspective.

He had come to realise that the overwhelming guilt he

carried originated from being a good man. Because of this, he had allowed the guilt of the boy on the train to consume him. Avi shared the anguish of the distressed mother. He took on her pain as his own to help carry the burden. It was an illogical, selfless penance that he felt he had no choice but to pay. A ridiculous price that eventually pushed him over the edge, four months before he met Kathy. The ultimate sin of harming a child was something he couldn't imagine reconciling, but maybe he could at least now try to make amends?

Finally, he understood that this tragedy was an accident. The boy who was killed was collateral damage in a noble effort to eliminate two high-ranking and despicable Nazis during a total war started and fuelled by the worst people in human history.

Avi did not mean to hurt an innocent child, but Hans Brunner caused the opposite. Avi had seen Brunner's murderous, sadistic behaviour firsthand at Dachau. The tyrant was also a guard at Auschwitz, where Avi's loving family was slaughtered — one of many death factories that liquidated millions of children and innocent people. Brunner showed no regret or remorse. His actions proved the opposite.

Here was a man without conscience, mercy, or empathy. A man lacking basic humanity, a psychopath who continued such behaviour, arrogant in his belief that others were there to serve him alone. He did not believe in God. He thought he was his own wicked god, a god who never questioned his actions — a god who did as he pleased.

But Hans Brunner was *not* a god. He was a *man*. A greedy, yellow, cowardly man who didn't possess the decency to crawl under a stone and live out his life in a passive manner after he escaped from the horrors he had perpetrated during the War. He had, instead, continued to abuse the ill-gotten gains that had fuelled his power and wealth. A convenient disciple of Hitler, but only because it suited him to hide behind the swastika. After the War, he saw himself as a worthy eagle, soaring above the fundamental laws of humanity and the common laws of society. He was wicked, and as he had observed, "There will always be good, but there will always be bad. It is a constant struggle of one against the other". It was a struggle, and he had finally succumbed.

Brunner's relentless desire to prey on others had been extinguished by Avraham Falco, for the good of humankind. It was both confusing and comforting to see Brunner's terror in that last moment. Maybe he realised he would have more than Avi to answer to? The space remaining on Bosch's eternal hellscape for Brunner to occupy had now been filled in.

Avi also reflected on his Wartime experiences. Could he have been appointed as an SOE agent by a higher power to help ensure the triumph of good and righteousness? Perhaps his father had spoken to that higher power in heaven, where Avi's parents resided? After the War, was it possible that he continued as a chosen soldier of God, fighting against evil?

In Avi's clear mind, everything was beginning to make sense.

He wondered with awe how all those falling roof tiles failed to kill him in the builders' yard. It was an absolute miracle that he survived with only a few bruises and no injuries from above. Not a single tile struck him after the cascade. Looking back, he believed the burly site foreman planned to finish him off with his claw hammer, but was momentarily stunned into reverence by the miracle he saw. So much so, he hesitated and let Avi go free with a confused whimper. The quick arrival of that bricklayer no doubt helped Avi, but now he saw it as part of a sacred intervention.

It was also miraculous that Avi saw the vision of his mother during his darkest moment, just as he was about to end his life in utter torment and despair. The paranormal experience of his mother's visitation was deeply impactful and set him on the road to recovery. Maybe she was an angel of God? Or perhaps, deep down, he didn't want to die before his time despite all his previous failed attempts? It could also have been the result of the copious amounts of drugs and alcohol he had consumed in recent months, causing a temporary hallucination. Avi preferred to believe the first explanation.

He had finally realised that he did have a future and that he had many gifts to give to others. Now he would start planning how to do it… with a little help from the Lord above.

Part II.

Herbert Gaggs breezed into the private single room of the surgical ward at Baguley Hospital in South Manchester, the only one of its kind in the infirmary. He had paid generously for a converted Matron's office to help Avi's recovery.

A large window offered a clear view of a distant railway. His chest was heavily bandaged as Avi lay in bed with his eyes shut.

'There you are, my wounded soldier!' said Gaggs triumphantly.

Avi's eyes opened instantly. Gaggs was a blur until he reached the locker beside him and fumbled for his glasses. He wiped them clean on his hospital-issued flannel pyjama top.

'The doctors tell me you will be fine in just a few more weeks,' added Gaggs as he placed a folded copy of the Manchester Chronicle next to Avi.

Avi opened the newspaper to the front-page headline of LET THE GOOD TIMES ROCK N ROLL by Peter Spencer.

'You were right about Spencer,' said Gaggs with a smile. 'He has demonstrated both loyalty and talent. There are new senior vacancies to fill at the Chronicle. Speaking of which, I was surprised to learn that you informed Mr. McClay of your entombment of Mr Lewis. He was screaming blue murder when they found him.' From the open window, a passing steam train was heard pulling a procession of rattling cattle trucks. 'He knows nothing of the vivid horrors a confined space can provide. Years locked away in a mental asylum will help broaden his knowledge.'

449

'Indeed, they will,' said Avi. 'But what about Julia Lehmann? Is she okay? Is she alive?'

Gaggs smiled at the concern in Avi's voice. 'Do not worry yourself, Avi. She is alive, well, and in very safe hands.'

With a beaming smile and a grunt, Avi pulled himself up on the bed for a better position.

'The British Establishment has closed ranks,' said Gaggs. 'If we can all keep a lid on this, MI5 will look the other way from your indiscretions … and the three stitches in the head their special agent suffered. I have paid Mr McClay handsomely.'

Avi scratched his forehead in total bewilderment. 'Joe McClay is worth his weight in gold, but …'

'Mr McClay gave me a message for you. I must apologise, but my northern accent requires further refinement. I do hope this means something to you. His exact words were: "A message from The Commando to The Falcon. Joan says ta for sortin' the Rolex".'

Avi laughed, and then winced with pain.

Gaggs allowed him to settle before continuing. 'MI5 want you to work for them, but I want you to come back to the Nakam. We have many Nazis to find. Josef Mengele is still on the loose.' Gaggs took out Wolff's Parabellum and offered it to Avi.

'Thank you, Sir, but no. It is one thing to kill during wartime, but we are now at peace … and *I* am at peace. While I have been in here, I've had more time to think … to contemplate. Killing Brunner was the way it was for Tommy Green.'

'How do you mean?'

'Revenge was satisfying, but only temporary. Tommy Green was not content, and I am not content either. We

450

were both consumed by hatred and guilt. In the end, Tommy let it destroy him. That will not happen to me. I must move forward. I will move forward. My days of killing are over.'

Gaggs nodded. 'Some things we must learn for ourselves.' He noticed that Avi was wearing his wedding ring and put the gun away.

'If God will forgive me for my sins, perhaps I can forgive myself. I will try to make amends.' He looked at his treasured watch. 'But first I must find Kathy.'

'I understand and I will help. Do you know what day it is today?'

Avi looked down at the newspaper. 'Uh, Friday.'

'Yes, but it is also *Yom Kippur*, the Sabbath of Sabbaths — our day of repentance. Today is the day that God teaches us that we can still attain ritual atonement through acts of loving kindness. This is the day we seek forgiveness from God for our wrongdoings to Him and to other human beings.'

Gaggs produced the blue velvet pouch and spilled a large number of diamonds onto the eiderdown. 'Your family were good people. See these as your inheritance from heaven, Avraham Falco. What you do with them is your business. Maybe they will help you find peace of mind. Maybe they will help you find your salvation. Perhaps you recall our concept of Tzedakah — our religious obligation to do what is right and just.'

Avi nodded. 'I do indeed. I will put them to good use. Thank you so much.'

'Oh, please don't thank me. Remember, Avi, God is always with you, whatever you might imagine. Shalom, my friend.' Gaggs smiled, tapped Avi's right hand, and left the room.

Avi looked at the diamonds clasped in his bony fingers. Bony fingers cleansed of nicotine stains.

Gaggs entered the main corridor where Kathy was sitting in a chair, awaiting her turn. He caught her eye and smiled. 'Avi is determined to find you and has asked after the young girl.'

Returning his smile, Kathy stood up. 'Thank you, Mr Gaggs. Thank you for *all* you have done. You are a special friend to our family.'

Gaggs offered his hand, but instead, Kathy stepped forward, gave him a brief hug and kissed him gently on the cheek.

'*Now* he is all yours, Kathy.' He doffed his homburg hat and strode out of the door with his head held high.

Kathy took out her compact. She checked her face, rose to her feet, and paced gently towards the door.

Avi was standing by the bedside locker with his back to the door. The diamonds had been removed from the bed. Sensing her presence, he turned around.

A broad smile greeted Kathy as she opened the door and stepped into the room. He held out his hands and gently pulled her toward him for a warm embrace.

'*Ow, ow* ... not too tightly.'

'Oh, sorry, *sorry*.'

'I have been praying that you would come back to me.'

'Well, I couldn't miss your fortieth birthday, could I?' Kathy stepped back. They looked at each other and smiled.

'I love you, Kathy, my beautiful wife.'

'And I love you too.'

'We need to talk.'

Part III.

The sharp rattle of the front door knocker sent Bruno the dog into a barking frenzy; his claws tap-danced on the linoleum kitchen floor as he jumped up and down as if riding an invisible pogo stick.

Despite the sunny weather, Millie Green was wrapped in a thick woolly cardigan. She put down her steaming cuppa, struggled to her feet, and trudged wearily to the front door. She opened it to a friendly, toothless smile.

'Hello, Mrs Green. Special delivery, I need you to put yer X on this,' said the postman, tapping the visor on his cap.

'Sorry, love, I can't sign anything without me specs.'

'Sorry, Mrs Green. Rules is rules. Besides, yer glasses are dangling around yer neck.'

Millie shook her head. 'Who the bloody hell would send me anything valuable?'

She signed and then took the lightweight package inside.

She entered the neat and tidy, but perishing, front room, shuffled across to her dining table, and sat down. Grabbing a butter knife, she opened the package. It contained a box and a calligraphic note:

Go to Rathman's Jewellers in St Anne's Square. Mr Rathman will give you a very good price if you tell him Avi Falco sent you. Be comfortable, Mrs Green. X

Millie opened the box. Inside, perched on sky-blue cotton wool, a large, sparkling diamond dazzled her eyes. She removed her glasses and wiped away a tear. She looked at the ceiling and muttered with a smile, 'We'll be all right now, Tommy.'

Bruno danced at her feet, wagging his tail.

Part IV.

His rapid eye movement flickered like a failing light bulb. His Garden of Eden bathed in a hypnotic haze of beguiling sunshine. A vibrant flutter of restless butterflies tangoed with gay abandon as they hovered above the vivid rainbow of fragrant flowers that swayed in God's gentle breath. Joyful Kathy came to the fore as she played on the lush green grass with their precious twin daughters. A mother radiant in the sensuous white of silken attire. Children's laughter. Beaming smiles. Happy hearts.

Avi awakened with a contented smile. Sitting beside a dowdy, aged Jewish couple, he stared out of the aeroplane window and basked in the expansive freedom of a blue sky lacquered with the sun's hue.

Snapping out of his trance, he reached into his jacket pocket and pulled out a medium-sized manila envelope. It contained a monochrome photograph of a young, happy couple on their wedding day. An inscription was written on the back:

All our love, Doreen and Peter Spencer.

'Chuffed to little mint balls,' said Avi with a satisfied grin.

The El Al plane landed roughly on the Lod Airport runway in Tel Aviv. Warm sunshine welcomed its arrival.

Avi Falco walked into the arrivals lounge with his wife, Kathy. She looked glamorous, radiant, and recently pregnant. Avi's hair had grown back, and he had gained weight. He appeared calm and composed in his elegant cream suit and a *kippah*.

The couple entered and queued at passport control, with two children and Kathy's mother, Eileen, following behind. The group handed over their pristine Israeli passports to the smiling security guard. Josef Hirschfeld's passport was stamped. Julia Lehmann's passport was stamped.

The party arrived in the terminal's sparsely populated lounge. No one paid attention to an impeccably dressed man relaxing in a plush leather chair, obscured by an expansive, broadsheet Israeli newspaper.

To mutual relief and joy, Avi's party was greeted by Avi's ageing Uncle Max and Aunt Trudy. It was the first time Avi had met his father's brother since he and his wife fled Nazi Germany early in 1939.

Avi hugged and kissed his aunt with affection, then embraced his uncle.

Max looked Avi in the eye, kissed him on both cheeks, and smiled. 'Come, Avraham. Let us go home to *Yerushalayim*. We shall celebrate God's union with a *L'Chaim*.'

The new family trooped down the airport corridor, with Avi at the front whistling a wonky version of *Blue Velvet* while holding Kathy's hand in a loving caress.

Back in the arrivals lounge, the Israeli broadsheet newspaper was lowered to reveal the debonair Herbert Gaggs. Stylish in a linen suit, hazel-brown brogues, and a rich cream Panama hat, he removed his dark green sunglasses, rubbed his eyes, and looked at the terminal apron.

Out of the blue, droplets of light rain descended,

sparkling the sky like glitter from a comet's tail. A shimmering rainbow seemed like a sign of approval from heaven.

Gaggs smiled. From the leather satchel by his feet, he retrieved a pen and his notebook filled with amateur poetry. On the first page was written The Falling Rain. He crossed it out and rewrote his old poem with enthusiasm.

The Fallen Reign

The curtain falls, the pain has passed,
A calmness that is set to last.
With hands to help, with eyes that see,
His torture gone; his mind set free.

Looking forward, not looking back,
The recovered patient is back on track.
A steady joy with moods that sing,
His pledge to savour everything.

Upon the precipice no more,
A chance to open up the door.
A family new, with all to gain,
And grow beyond … the fallen reign.

Herbert Gaggs – 1958

The End.

Acknowledgements

Writing any book is a labour of love with no guarantees. The chances of securing a publisher — particularly for a first-time novelist — are fairly remote. However, I got there in the end, and my sincere gratitude goes to *Blossom Spring Publishing* for giving this book a chance to fly. In addition, thanks and appreciation to my following friends and acquaintances for their time, expertise, and encouragement from the outset, which seems like years ago (probably because it was).

Colin Muir, Michelle Tilling, Lyn Weinrich, Noel Bayley, Andy Conway, Gary Fry, Claire Voet, Laura Cosby, Jeff Spencer, Sam Gilsenan, John Eaton, April Lockyer, Richard Kalervo Leatherdale, David Frohlich, Mike Jenkinson, Tor Soensteby, Daniel O' Keefe, Steinar Sel, Per Arne Rennestraum, Terry Hyland, 'Sir' Paul Ramsey, Peter Evans, Pat Loftus, Shaun Roberts, Cliff Doyle, Morag Roberts, Eileen Moxon, John Tomlinson, Ros Fielding, Julie & Joanne Worthington, Graeme Duncan, Gary Tipper, Mark 'Bibby' Bowden, Julie Freeman, Aiden Ball, Phil Bennison, Jeanne Davies, Elliot Boylan, John Scott, Paul Templeton, Mike Relph, Richard Ellor, Dave Wallace, Jo Fogg, Peter Fogg, John Duggan, John Billingham, Richard Ellor, John Sweeney, Steven Sands, Ole Morten Egadal, Francis Ayscough, Alister Turner, Jim Grant, Lyndon Greenlees, Chris Hulme, Arch Stanton, and The Scandinavian Branch of the Manchester City Supporters club.

RIP the legend that is Tommy Muir, Manchester City's greatest ever supporter.

In memory of my mum and dad, Kathy and Derek; Jane's mum and dad, Stephen and Joan; and of Paul Gilsenan. All gone, but never forgotten.

Dedicated to Sergeant Stanley Moore, CSM Augustus Jennings, and Captain Lynn-Allen for their selfless, heroic bravery in the barn at *La Plaine au Bois*; and to the many courageous German people blessed with the noble human spirit of *The White Rose* during perilous times in Nazi Germany.

This is a work of fiction and as such, I apologise for any inadvertent insult to Freemasons or the Manchester Police Force during the period in which the book is set. There is good and bad in all of us.

Thanks for reading my novel. I hope that you enjoyed it.

Front Cover Picture: Courtesy of Linz Franciz.
Cover design: Paul Harker.

Worthy Independent Mega Productions (WIMP) in association with Leon Yelyab Productions.

About The Author

I began writing for a football Fanzine in the late 1980s, adopting a tongue-in-cheek style that seemed popular with its readers. As my writing further developed, I wrote my autobiography, *Once in a Blue Moon: Life, Love, and Manchester City* — the story of a downtrodden, everyday working-class football fan brought up on a council estate in Wythenshawe in the 1960s and 1970s. This became a best seller for its publisher in 2010 and was reprinted on three separate occasions. Fifteen years later, it remains available to purchase on Amazon.

With this modest success and having achieved my goal of being published, I hadn't planned on writing anything further. However, having suffered an unexpected redundancy when serving as a Local Government Officer, I used the opportunity to adopt a different approach. I pursued a Master's Degree in Scriptwriting for Television and Radio at Salford University, developing my creative writing skills that may become fruitful in the future.

'The Falling Rain' was the final project for my MA and was originally written as a movie script, of which I soon found out became nigh impossible to attract suitable attention. Subsequently, I decided to develop the script into a novel in the hope of moving the project forward. This was an entirely different form of writing, which certainly had its challenges, but I am extremely proud of the outcome.

The post-war 1950s period in Britain is largely unexplored in contemporary literature, and proved to be a fascinating period to research. Throwing a former Nazi soldier into a working-class Manchester housing estate certainly gave my imagination room to run riot.

I have been married for 33 years and have two wonderful daughters. I retain a passion for Indie music, Laurel and Hardy, and remain a devoted supporter of Manchester City, the mighty Blues.

www.blossomspringpublishing.com